WILDE ABANDON

A Dark Horse Dive Bar Novel

JENNIFER RYAN

Cover design by Angela Haddon – www.angelahaddon.com

Edited by Susan Barnes – www.susanbarnesediting.com

Copyeditor – Melissa Frain – www.melissafrain.com

For you, the ones who leap, who chase dreams and love with wild abandon.

PROLOGUE

Second Grade—Fox's Birthday

Fox Bridges waited by the tree he and Melody met at each morning after they were dropped at school. He spotted her mom's car as they parked in the lot, confused that she didn't just drop Melody up front like all the other parents did. Melody's mom climbed out, then helped Melody out of the back. She held a gift bag with colorful balloons all over it.

His heart beat faster in his chest. She remembered. It surprised him, though it shouldn't. Melody, Dee to him, was the only person who really cared about him.

His mom had dropped him off in a huff this morning without so much as a goodbye. Not even a *Have a great day*. Certainly not *Happy birthday!* Not when she was mad about him waking her up. He didn't want to be late again. She didn't want the principal hounding her about it.

"Happy birthday, Fox! You're seven now!" Melody called as she rushed toward him, her pigtails curled into spirals on either side of her head.

Mrs. Wilde rushed to catch up to Melody, but she stopped short a few steps away, her gaze narrowing. "Goodness, Fox, what happened to your lip?"

Fox froze. He didn't know what to say.

Melody turned to her mom. "Yesterday we played catch during recess. I accidentally hit him in the face with my fastball."

Mrs. Wilde's eyes filled with concern. "Oh, Melody, you have to be careful."

"I know. I said sorry."

"I'm okay," Fox assured Mrs. Wilde as he took Melody's hand. "I know she didn't mean it. She'd never hurt me on purpose. We're best friends."

Which was why Melody had lied about what really happened. She didn't want him to get into trouble.

She was keeping his secret.

Mrs. Wilde stared at his lip. "You should ask the nurse at lunchtime to give you some ice to put on that."

"I will," he promised. The sooner it healed, the sooner everyone would stop asking about it and looking at him funny.

Melody held out the gift bag. "Open it. Open it. I picked it all out just for you. I used my allowance."

He set the bag at his feet, pulled out the dark blue tissue paper, then found the red Hot Wheels Mustang Mach 1. "I love it. Thanks."

"There's more."

He pulled out a Batman Pez dispenser with a whole thing of assorted candy flavors and a coloring book with a box of colored pencils. It would give him something to do when he was alone at home in his room.

He looked at Melody. "Thank you." He hugged her tight, letting her know he appreciated it. He had no idea if his parents had anything planned for him later when he got home. His mom hadn't said anything to him when she shoved him out the door this morning.

Melody gave him one of her big smiles. "You're welcome."

Mrs. Wilde held out the plastic container to Melody, who took it, popped the lid, then pulled out a ginormous chocolate cupcake with vanilla frosting. Mrs. Wilde pushed a blue candle into the center and lit it with a lighter.

Melody held it out, presenting it to him. "You gotta make a wish."

To his utter astonishment, Melody and Mrs. Wilde sang him "Happy Birthday" right there in the front of the school with everyone watching. A lot of the kids and the crossing guard sang along with them. His cheeks felt like they were on fire.

"Make a wish and blow it out," Melody coaxed.

There was only one thing he wanted. *I wish that Melody and I stay best friends forever.*

Later that afternoon at recess, he sat with Melody, coloring in the book she got him. Some of the boys from their class walked by. Brian turned and asked, "What are you doing with her?" He gave Dee a dirty look. "Don't you want to play soccer?"

Fox shook his head. "Not today." He liked hanging out with Dee a lot more.

Brian shook his head, then grinned. "Fox and Melody, sitting in a tree..." The others joined in. "K-I-S-S-I-N-G!" They all pointed, like they thought he'd actually kiss her.

He liked her. But gross.

Melody rolled her eyes. "Go away." She waved them away and went back to coloring.

The boys left.

Melody looked at him. "If you want to go play with them, it's okay." She tried to hide a frown and her disappointment that maybe he'd rather be with them.

He liked being with her. "I want to color with you."

Her bright smile made his tummy light and a warm feeling come over him. She made him feel this way a lot. If he could, he'd spend all his time with her.

Third Grade—December—Drop-Off

Melody Wilde had a secret. It made her tummy hurt. That pain made her mouth taste sour as she scanned the front of the school and didn't see her best friend. Yes, Fox was a boy. But he was nice, and she liked him a lot. It made her feel good when she shared her lunch with him because he didn't have one.

He didn't want anyone to know that.

But that wasn't *the* secret.

Though she suspected her mom knew about the lunch thing, because she'd packed Melody two of everything every day since she caught Melody sneaking extra stuff from the pantry a long time ago. Like first grade when Fox was in her class, too. And second grade. And now third.

But today he wasn't waiting by the tree where they always met.

She twisted to look out the back of her dad's truck, but she still couldn't find him.

The truck stopped and her dad turned to her. "What's wrong, Mel?"

"He's not here. I can't find Fox. I have to find him. He has to be all right."

Three days ago, he hadn't been all right. He had been hurt. Bad. She didn't know exactly what happened, but she thought he might have a broken arm. She tried to get him to go to the office to see the nurse, but he didn't want to go. He got mad. He begged her not to tell.

It wasn't the first time she'd kept a secret for him. It felt like he was always hurt and asking her not to tell. She didn't like it that he was hurt. It made him not smile. It made him sad.

And when Fox was sad, so was she.

But three days ago he was really mad, too. He said he hoped his dad would just die and his mom would go away.

It seemed really bad to say something like that about his mom and dad even if the few times she'd seen them they did seem mean. They yelled at Fox a lot. And she was pretty sure the bruises Fox tried to hide and the hurts he didn't want to talk about...those came from them.

"Daddy..." Her bottom lip trembled and her eyes filled with tears.

"What is it, sweetheart? Are you sick? Do you want to go home?" He put his hand on her forehead, feeling if she was hot.

She took his hand and squeezed. "I think something bad happened." Her stomach churned more and her chest hurt.

"What, honey? What happened?"

She stared at her lap. "I'm not supposed to tell. I promised to keep the secret."

"If you think something bad happened, then you need to tell. It's okay to break a promise if you think someone is hurt or something bad could happen."

She looked up at her dad and the tears slid down her cheeks. "He's my friend. I promised. But I'm scared."

Her dad undid his seat belt and hers and pulled her into his chest, hugging her close. She felt safe and whispered, "He's not here. I think they hurt him again."

"Fox?"

She looked up at him. "Yes. You have to go see. You have to find him. His arm hurt real bad. I think it's broken but he wouldn't go see the nurse. I tried to make him go, but he made me promise not to say anything. What if it's worse?"

Her dad put his finger under her chin and made her look right at him. "Is he hurt a lot?"

"All the time, Daddy. But he always comes to school. He doesn't like to be home. Please, you have to go see. Make them stop. He can stay with us. I'll share my room. We won't hurt him. You and Mama are nice. I'll take care of him. I will. I promise." She'd do anything for Fox.

Her dad gave her a sad face and brushed his hand over her hair. "You are taking care of him right now, sweetheart, by telling me he needs help. I'll take care of it. I promise. But I need you to go to class now. I'll pick you up later."

"You'll bring him to school, right? He doesn't want to be at home."

"I will make sure he's all right." He kissed her on the head. "Go. I'll drive out to his place right now."

She scrambled out of the truck and pulled her backpack on. Before she shut the door, her dad was on the phone and saying, "I need a wellness check immediately on Fox Bridges."

Melody closed the door, her tummy not so tight. Her daddy would help Fox. He'd be okay, and they'd be friends forever.

Fox heard the sirens in the distance and a truck driving close. He lay curled up on the dirt. He'd been there all night listening to the sounds of the critters scurrying and the wind blowing through the cracks in the barn. The pain...it wouldn't let him sleep. He was so tired.

When sunlight glinted on his face, he knew he was supposed to wake his mom, avoid his dad at all costs, and go to school. He liked school. It was safe there. No one yelled at him. No one hit him. He always got something to eat, thanks to Melody. They had lunch together every day.

Last night he'd wished she was here with him. She'd tell him stories. She'd probably have tried to keep him warm.

He didn't feel the cold anymore.

It hurt to move, so he just didn't move at all, though breathing hurt, too. He couldn't stop doing that, so every second he felt that pain in his chest and tried not to breathe too deep.

But his heart started racing as he heard those loud sirens.

They'd wake his dad and mom. They'd be so mad. It seemed like they were always mad. His mom was sad a lot. She wasn't always nice either.

Dad liked to hit her, too. But she got her licks in sometimes. She hardly ever stopped Dad from hitting him anymore.

Better him than her, he guessed she probably thought, angry all over again. They were making him like them.

He hadn't done anything last night. He'd been quiet. He stayed in his room. Didn't matter. It never mattered if he did something or not.

The cars didn't make any noise now.

His eyes were drifting shut. So tired.

He hoped the cops were here to take his dad in for another DUI, whatever that was. It had something to do with him being drunk all the time. That's what Mom said.

Fox liked it better when his dad went away, though being with his mom wasn't much fun—just not as bad as being with his dad.

There was a lot of yelling all of a sudden.

They woke up my parents. Not good.

Then his dad was yelling, "You can't come in. You can't search without a warrant."

Fox didn't know what that was, or what they were looking for. He didn't care. His eyes were closed. He felt like he was drifting away. That pain in his belly hurt worse now.

He didn't want to hurt anymore.

The barn door slid open and the light blinded him. He squinted his eyes closed tight and didn't move, hoping his father wouldn't find him, even though he'd barely made it inside the door.

"Fox."

He didn't recognize the man's voice. It sounded shocked and sad at the same time.

A hand brushed over his head. He flinched. Not from the pain, but because he expected another blow.

"I won't hurt you, son. I'm here to help. Melody sent me."

Anger, betrayal, and fear washed through him, making his aching muscles tense even more. How could she do this to him?

This would be so bad. His dad would kill him. "T-told her n-not t-to t-tell." Anger filled his voice and he grimaced as a wave of pain—physical and emotional—hit hard.

Something warm was draped over him. Until he felt the heat, he hadn't realized how cold he was.

"This will never happen to you again."

Fox didn't believe him as he drifted in and out.

My dad's going to kill me. Maybe he already did.

A little while later, there were lots more voices around him, people talking about him, how cold he was, how many injuries he had. A blast of pain went through him when they gently moved him, and Fox thought, *Doesn't matter what Dee did. I'm never going to survive to see her again.*

It should have been a relief when she walked into his hospital room the next day. But all it did was ignite the fear that at any moment his dad would walk in the door in a rage, looking to punish Fox for everything. For nothing. He didn't really need a reason.

Pain, sharp and aching, radiated through him as he lay in the hospital bed. Fox could barely move without something hurting, but seeing Melody's eyes filled with sadness and pity...he lost it.

"This is your fault. You told them. You promised you wouldn't tell. He's going to kill me. Get out! I hate you!"

Alarms started going off. He couldn't catch his breath. He felt blood on his stomach. He'd pulled the stitches from his surgery. He didn't even know why he'd needed surgery. The cast on his arm made sense. His dad had broken his wrist several days ago. Again.

Melody's lips trembled. Tears poured down her cheeks. "I'm sorry."

"Get out!" He didn't want her to see him like this. He didn't want anyone to know.

Mr. Wilde held up a hand. "Son, you need to calm down. She only wanted to help." His voice was so familiar.

The man who'd found him curled up in the barn. Melody's dad.

Mr. Wilde took her hand and pulled her toward the door as a nurse rushed in, ordering them out.

The last he saw of Melody, tears were running down her face, and she was saying over and over again, "I'm sorry. I'm sorry. I'm so, so sorry."

He didn't care in that moment. But he would later, when he discovered his parents were in jail, he was never going back to them, and he was safe. Because she saved his life.

And all he wanted was to find a way back to her, so he could make things right.

CHAPTER ONE

"*I'm sorry. I'm sorry. I'm so, so sorry,*" *Melody wailed.*

Fox woke up in a rush, his hand reaching out and catching nothing but air as he shouted, "Come back." The words he should have said all those years ago. Because when she left, all the joy she'd brought into his world went with her.

A hand clamped onto his shoulder. "Man, you've got to stop falling asleep at your desk." Dean set a cup of steaming black coffee in front of him.

Fox dug the heels of his hands into his tired, scratchy eyes. "What time is it?"

"Time to put an end to this shit and get the fuck out of here. This place is messing with your head."

Fox had been back in Blackrock Falls for several weeks and the memories—nightmares, really—made him feel like that lost and broken boy all over again. He didn't like the feeling. In fact, he'd worked damn hard to make something of himself under some really tough circumstances. Six different foster homes, two group homes, several school transfers, aging out of the system, and feeling abandoned and inconsequential yet again.

But he'd done one thing right. The only thing he had control over in his life. He took his education seriously. It was the one piece of advice he'd received that made sense to him. *The smarter you are, the better you'll do in life. Do well in school, you'll get a better job. You'll make more money.*

He didn't rely on anyone. After all, he'd just been passing through those foster homes. Always a guest. Never family.

He didn't have one of those. Not anymore.

Even if he was back in this town to take care of his sick mother.

Well, that was his excuse to come.

Tanya hadn't changed much from what he remembered. She was still sad, lonely, angry, bitter, and now dying of cancer. She didn't have much time left. She used that to guilt him into coming.

He got no apologies from her. Barely a kind word. Though she did seem happy to hear that he'd made something of himself and he was doing okay.

Well, better than okay.

Dad had died years ago in a bar fight after getting out of prison early. Overcrowding. He'd picked on someone smaller and someone bigger came along and stopped him. Shocker. Nope.

Not even a tiny bit surprising given what Fox remembered about his nightmarish childhood.

Once he was away, he had feared they would come for him. Best day of his life, the day the social worker showed up to tell him his dad was dead. First day he could remember taking a deep breath and feeling like a weight had been lifted. He had actually slept the whole night through and woke up feeling like everything was different. Better.

He'd woken up that morning thinking maybe he could finally go back and see Melody again. It was safe now. He was safe. And so was she. But he had been fourteen and living in another part of the state. He didn't have any way to get to her. Running away from his foster home would only get him into trouble. And he'd learned, the less trouble he got into the better things went for him.

Instead of going to her, he had reminded himself twenty times a day about the promise he intended to keep. *Melody is out there. You'll see her again. You'll make things right.*

Now that he was back in town, he'd snuck into the bar where she worked to catch glimpses of her, but he hadn't approached her and made things right. Not yet. But soon.

"You're doing it again." Dean shook his head and studied the security camera feeds he'd installed yesterday outside of the building.

A building Fox bought two months ago when he moved back to town after a social worker at the hospital where his mother was being treated tracked him down to tell him about Tanya.

He never called her Mom anymore. She didn't deserve that title.

That social worker hadn't done him any favors by finding him. In fact, she'd been so enthusiastic about her success, she'd told his mom everything about his new life.

He'd had some good luck and learned the hard way that not every good thing was a blessing. It could also be a curse. He tried to keep his good fortune a secret because he'd learned everyone wanted something from him.

Like his mom. She thought his success was her ticket to easy street. What was his, should be shared with her. Family. Why? Because she gave birth to him, then treated him like a burden and turned her back on him time and time again when he needed her the most.

Anger, old and new, roiled in his gut.

"Dude! Get out of your head." Dean picked up the coffee mug and held it inches from Fox's face. "Drink. Wake up. We have shit to do."

Fox took the mug and downed a quarter of it, then tried to focus on the screen in front of him and the lesson plans he was putting together for the computer class he was teaching later that day.

"You should not have come back here. This place...it makes you sad."

This place and the memories it held made him angry. And, okay, sad. The kid who left here still lived inside him, and he hated it here.

But he remembered something—someone—good.

That little brat inside him had lashed out and been mean to her. He'd made her cry. He told her he hated her. And then he'd never seen her again.

Fox relived that nightmare night after night.

His biggest regret.

The thing he wished he could take back and couldn't.

Maybe she didn't remember. He did. And he hated himself for saying it and pushing her away like that when she was the only one who ever really cared about him.

Well, he had Dean and Max now. When Fox's life changed in an instant and he needed help, he called them, the best friends he'd made in foster care. They didn't even blink or take a breath. Max already worked with him at his software startup, Fox Solutions, back in Boston. But Dean, he quit his last job in security to be by Fox's side. And for the last two years, it had been the three of them figuring out what mattered most.

For them, it was about helping kids who aged out of the system like them. The ones with no family, no support, no means. The forgotten. Because that's what happened. You turned eighteen and your support disappeared. You were left to figure your life out on your own.

He'd had help. And Fox owed that person so much, because he didn't have to go out of his way to help Fox. But he had. And Fox knew why, and owed him a huge, long overdue, in-person thank you.

Fox drank more coffee and checked his phone. No new messages. "Fuck."

"I take it she hasn't responded." Dean shook his head, an I-told-you-so look on his face because Dean had said over and over again that Fox's plan to be back in Melody's life sucked.

Fox had been following Melody on social media for years, but he'd never contacted her. He didn't know what to say. What happened between them needed to be cleared up face-to-face. He wanted a chance to say his piece, apologize, and beg her forgiveness without her shutting him down and blocking his ass. He spent far too many hours scrolling through her pictures and posts, learning everything he could about her life.

Stalker vibes—totally.

Which was why he did it using a fake name and profile.

That didn't really help eliminate him being a stalker, but what was he supposed to do? Send her a text? *Thanks for being the best thing to ever happen to me. Sorry I said I hate you and haven't spoken to you in years. I missed you every single day, but I had to save my ass and stay away, because I was too afraid to run into my dad because I knew if he laid a hand on me again, I'd kill him.*

Not exactly a Hallmark card for that kind of sentiment either.

When he got to town, he'd walked into the Dark Horse Dive Bar she owned and worked at, stood right next to her, and though she'd definitely checked him out, undressing him with her eyes, she hadn't recognized him at all. It disappointed him. He didn't blame her because after those few short seconds, she'd been pulled back into work.

Damn, but Melody had grown up into a beautiful woman. One every guy stared at and wanted. And he'd realized he didn't want her to remember the boy. He wanted her to see the man.

One who was keeping secrets, even as he tried to connect with her by sending her all those private messages over the last couple of months.

It started so simply, with asking basic questions about everyday things they liked. Favorite food, color, movies, music, that sort of thing. And then they dove deeper. He scrolled back through the many messages on his phone.

@LOST_GEEK_FOUND: What are you passionate about?

@WILDE_BAR_GIRL: Family, friends, work. Being myself. Creating a fun environment for my customers to enjoy themselves, so they can let loose. Being creative with my jewelry designs.

@WILDE_BAR_GIRL: What about you?

@LOST_GEEK_FOUND: Coding. Solving problems for my clients. Being the best at something. Standing on my own. Being a good friend. Taking care of the people who always have my back.

@LOST_GEEK_FOUND: What do you want most out of life?

@WILDE_BAR_GIRL: Love. Laughter. To be surrounded by the people who matter most. To feel fulfilled and that I have purpose.

@LOST_GEEK_FOUND: Same. And to know that the people I care about are safe.

Because he hadn't always felt that way growing up. Certainly not with his parents, and not always in foster care.

Things often got flirty, too.

@LOST_GEEK_FOUND: Best compliment you ever received after sex?

@WILDE_BAR_GIRL: Aside from—That was awesome! Your pussy wrecked me.

@LOST_GEEK_FOUND: Fuck that's hot!

@LOST_GEEK_FOUND: Mine was—Your dick is magical. I saw stars.

@LOST_GEEK_FOUND: It is impressive. I can't wait to show it to you.

@WILDE_BAR_GIRL: No dick pics. I want it live and in person. Which means you'll have to come out to play.

That last one killed him, because he'd like nothing more. But he'd been playing a long game, giving them both time to get to know each other without the baggage of their past.

In those messages, they opened up to each other about so many things. They were honest with each other, even though he'd held back the one thing she really wanted to know. His true identity.

Not a great way to start. But now he knew that she was as amazing as she was when they were young. He hoped she could forgive him for...everything.

"You're thinking about her again." Dean smirked. "You get this dopey look on your face. For god's sake, just go up to her, tell her who you are, apologize, and ask her out. If you don't do it soon, I will. Because that girl is smokin' hot."

Fox glared at his best friend. "Not happening, asshole. Stay away from her."

"Why? Because she's yours? Buddy, she doesn't even know you're here. She thinks she's talking to some guy who is such a chump he won't even meet her in person."

Okay, yes, his strategy sucked. It had backfired, actually. He'd wanted a chance for them to get to know each other again without their history getting in the way.

But after weeks of messaging each other since he'd come back, sharing stories about their lives, and really getting to know each other, last night she'd laid down an ultimatum.

He stared at her last message.

@WILDE_BAR_GIRL: Either meet me in person and tell me your name, or this is over.

His gut clenched at the thought of losing her again.

The boy in him wanted her to know he regretted what he'd said the moment she'd walked out of his hospital room. He never forgot her. He owed her.

The man...he wanted her back in a way that had nothing to do with simply being her friend again. His whole body heated with just the thought of kissing her, touching her, holding her in his arms as he sank into her.

The girl stole his heart. The woman starred in all his fantasies.

Dean leaned back against the desk. "Stop stalling. Stop thinking about what could happen and *make* something happen. You keep this up, you're going to lose her all over again."

Voices sounded out in the main part of the building. They needed to get started on today's lessons.

Amy, their resident chef for the next three months, poked her head into his office. "It's egg day. Let's make some omelets." Her gaze never strayed from him. It landed on him every time they were in the same room.

Fox didn't acknowledge her hungry gaze. He'd hired her to teach the students at the New Adult Education Center he recently opened here in Blackrock Falls, Wyoming how to cook, not to flirt with him. "On our way."

Her head tilted to the side. "You look tired. You feeling okay?"

"He slept on his desk again last night." Dean's disapproval matched the look in Amy's eyes.

"I had a lot of work to catch up on after the lessons ran long yesterday."

Amy frowned. "You work too hard. You need to take care of yourself." She bit her bottom lip. "Or let someone take care of you." She waved her hand for him to come along. "I'll make you the best omelet you've ever had, and you'll be feeling better in no time." Amy backed out of his office.

Dean said under his breath, "I'll just bet she has other ideas about how she'd like to take care of you."

Fox stood, stretched his aching back, raised his arms to loosen up his stiff shoulders, and *accidentally* smacked his friend. "Shut up. She works for us."

"She'd like to *work* on you."

"Not interested." Even if he hadn't been hung up on Melody, he wouldn't have been interested. It seemed like a recipe for disaster. Amy continually said that food was her love language, and she was always trying to feed him. He made sure to take her cooking lessons seriously, because it was a skill he needed to learn to do better, but otherwise tried to keep his distance.

"Then go after the girl you are interested in and lock that down before you miss your chance and someone else steals her away from you."

"What if she doesn't want me?"

"I catch you smiling at your phone while you two are sending messages back and forth. She makes you happy. And if she's frustrated with you because she wants more than you're giving her, doesn't that tell you something?"

He desperately wanted to believe that they'd see each other again, she'd forgive him, and everything would be as easy as it used to be with her. Nothing in his life had ever been that easy.

Except with her.

"I'll talk to her tonight." A swarm of butterflies took flight in his belly.

"Finally." Dean stared him down. "If she still makes you happy, hold on to her. Do whatever you have to do to make her forgive you, then be everything she is to you. Put a smile on her face. One that isn't just for show for the customers tipping her."

Dean had seen what Fox picked up on every time they were in the bar and saw Melody competently doing her job, serving customers, fending off drunken cowboys making passes at her because they wanted in her pants, not necessarily in her heart. She grinned and bore it, used snappy comebacks for indecent requests, sloppy compliments, and pick-up lines, and expertly dodged grabby hands as she did her job. Only when she was with her sisters or brother did she smile like she meant it.

He hated to think that the conversations they shared had turned into something she didn't think was authentic or real, just some online troll using her as a distraction. He needed to set her straight. He needed to make this right.

Because Dean was right, he needed to hold on to her, because she was one of the few things he truly cared about losing in a life where he'd lost so much, or never had to begin with.

Tonight, he'd reclaim the place he'd had in her life in the past and hope she didn't kick him out of her future, because he was tired of living without her and eager to show her the man knew how to be a good friend—and a whole lot more if she'd let him.

CHAPTER TWO

M elody sidled up to the bar and shouted over the crowd, "Two chardonnays, six shots of tequila, one cosmo, four Bud Lights."

Her dad was behind the bar covering for Jax tonight because her brother was home with his fiancée, Layla, who had the flu. It was sweet he wanted to take care of her. They were so happy together.

Lyric had Mason, who worked for the FBI.

Aria was still flirting with Mason's brother and boss Nick.

Melody had her online geek...sort of.

They'd spent many weeks doing the get-to-know-you thing. Now she wanted to spend some time in person, to see if the spark she felt was an attraction they could build on.

She knew he came into the bar sometimes. She'd never figured out who he might be. In the packed space, it would be easy for him to disappear into the crowd. He loved to send her cheeky messages telling her how sexy she looked that night. But he always remained hidden in the shadows. She'd asked to meet him in person more than once. He kept putting it off.

For all she knew, he was some creep just stringing her along.

Though she did enjoy their conversations. The questions he asked, the things they revealed to each other, it all felt real and deep. She could be herself with him because online she could take her time, find the right words, and be brave in the privacy provided by distance.

But she wanted more than conversation. She wanted connection in the real world. She wanted to see his face when he spoke, the look in his eyes, and hear the way he said things. She wanted to believe that what had started online could exist in the reality of their day to day lives.

Her dad nodded that he'd heard her order and started pulling beer bottles out of the fridge and filling her tray.

Her phone vibrated in her back pocket. She pulled it out of the tight black denim skirt she'd worn tonight and tried not to get her hopes up. Her heart raced as she stared at the message from @lost_geek_found. She pressed her hand to her fluttering belly, took a steadying breath, bracing herself for possible rejection, then tapped the message.

@LOST_GEEK_FOUND: I'll be there in ten minutes.

@LOST_GEEK_FOUND: I lost you once. I can't do it again. Just remember, I'm the guy you've gotten to know again all these weeks.

@LOST_GEEK_FOUND: Please just give me a chance.

"Here you go, honey. All set."

She lifted her gaze from her phone to her dad.

His eyes narrowed with concern. "Everything all right?"

"You know that guy I've been chatting with?"

"Yeah." The grumble said he wasn't so sure about a guy who didn't ask his daughter out on a proper date like a gentleman.

"He's coming to see me tonight."

"About time. I can't believe it took him this long."

"Maybe he's shy." That's the excuse she'd used to console herself when he refused to meet her until now.

"Glad he found his confidence for you." Wade Wilde didn't suffer fools or men who didn't treat his daughters right.

She glanced at her phone again. "The message he sent doesn't make sense though."

"Why not?"

"He said he lost me once and can't do it again." She frowned at her dad. "Again?"

Some kind of knowing flashed in her dad's eyes. "I guess you'll find out soon."

She lifted the heavy tray of drinks. "I'll deliver these, then take my break when he gets here." She went to turn away, but her dad's words made her turn back to him.

"Sometimes the people we think we lost in the past come back to us."

She thought about her mysterious chatter's online name. Could it be that someone she'd lost touch with in the past had found her again?

She didn't have time to think about the possibilities. He'd be here soon.

And with the noise in the bar, it was hard to think about anything besides her aching feet, the tables that she needed to service, and whether or not the tips would be worth the handsy and mouthy customers.

Not that she didn't love this place and her job. She just wanted something more. Something that was hers.

She delivered the beers to the firefighters who were here to blow off steam. They gave her big grins and hot looks, but she didn't take any of them up on the implied offers and sauntered to the next table of cow punchers, who greedily reached for the shots, before a couple of them turned to the table one over and the ladies there, who'd ordered the wine and cosmo.

One of the women leaned around the table crashers, and her eyes went wide. "Oh my God, I want the one on the right."

"Only if I get the one on the left," the strawberry blonde announced, practically drooling.

Their third wheel didn't look the least disappointed that there were only two and said, "I'll take both of them."

Melody laughed with the trio, and turning to head back to the bar, had to agree with the first woman. She'd take the guy on the right, too.

Tall, lean, dark hair cut short around the back, longer on top with just enough wave to make her want to sink her fingers into the thick mass. Dressed in jeans that hugged his perfect ass and a simple untucked black dress shirt with the sleeves rolled up, he wasn't a cowboy, but something more polished.

His friend was cute. Blond hair cut neat and short. Black military boots, jeans, and a dark gray thermal. His blue eyes were sharp as they landed on her right before he tapped his buddy's shoulder to get his attention, then pointed right at her.

Turning, the guy's green gaze met hers and something shifted inside her chest, making her breath catch. His jaw hardened for a second before a smile broke out on his face that was so lethal it could have had every woman in the room dropping their panties for him.

She forgot how to walk as she halted and just stared at the perfection that was this man she'd never seen but wanted with everything inside her.

Was this how Lyric felt when she laid eyes on Mason, and how Jax felt when he saw Layla for the first time?

Was this even real?

Was he?

Time seemed to slow as they just stared at each other, then it suddenly sped up as her dad rushed to the guy and threw his arms around him, giving him a smack on the back and hugging him close.

Stunned, she found her feet and walked toward all of them.

Wade held the man by the shoulders. "Why didn't you tell me you were in town? It's been too long since I've seen you. You should have called or come by the ranch." Her dad didn't work the bar very often, only when they needed extra help.

The man looked from her dad to her and back again. "I needed a little time to get settled in town with Dean and deal with my mom."

"Hey, I'm Dean." The blond held his hand out to her.

She took it and shook, not really looking at him, still staring at the other one.

Her dad let the man loose and met her gaze. "Aren't you going to say hello, honey?"

His green gaze met hers again. For some reason, tears gathered in her eyes.

"It's been a long time," he said, his deep voice soft, like he didn't want to spook her.

Her heart beat so fast she could barely breathe. "Fox?" A tear slid down her cheek.

"Yes." Fox's eyes narrowed and the muscle in his jaw ticked.

The past came back to her in a slideshow of them as kids and the nightmare of how it all ended with him yelling at her that he hated her.

She couldn't stop the tears now; they ran down her cheeks one after another as her heart broke all over again. "I'm sorry. I'm so, so sorry. I never meant to hurt you." She couldn't breathe. She couldn't stand there and look at him, knowing what she'd done and that he hated her. "I'm sorry." She dropped the tray she'd been holding and ran through the kitchen. Lyric called out to her, asking what was wrong, but Melody didn't stop until she shot out the back door and ran across the wide patio area. She bent over and tried to catch her breath and wipe away the tears, but they just wouldn't stop.

Strong hands settled on her shoulders and pulled her upright. "Hey now. You need to stop that because I seriously have no idea what to do and it's killing me to see you so sad. Please, Dee, give me a chance to explain."

She caught her breath when she saw the guilty look in his eyes and she put the pieces together. "You're him."

"Yes. It's me. Fox."

She shook her head. "No. You're *him*. The guy who's been DMing me online."

Even in the dim light she could see the flush of red hit his cheeks. Embarrassment and guilt lit his eyes. "I know it was stupid to try to slip back into your life that way. I should have just talked to you. But there are so many people in the bar and every guy has his eyes on you and I didn't want to just show up and tell you I'm sorry and dump all our past on you in the middle of your shift with everyone watching." The words came out in a rushed plea.

She raised a brow. "How did that work out for you?"

A pained look came into his eyes. "I made you cry. I'm sorry." He ran his hand through his gorgeous hair. "I blew it just like I thought I would. That's why I tried to talk to you online. I thought if I took the time to get to know you again and you got to know me without everything else from the past, then when I did finally talk to you in person we'd be friends again."

Both brows shot up this time. "You deceived me, so we could be friends?"

"Yes?"

Why was that a question?

His hand raked through his hair again. "I am so not good at this."

"What?" She really didn't understand any of it.

"Talking to people. In foster care, you keep your head down, mouth shut, and just get through another shit day."

Tears welled in her eyes again. "It's all my fault. I'm sorry."

He rushed forward, cupped her face, and brushed his thumbs across her cheeks, wiping away her tears. "Okay, you need to stop doing that. I can't take it. Nothing is your fault. You don't owe me an apology. You aren't to blame for anything. You are everything good and happy that I ever had in my life.

"Because of you, I'm alive. I survived. I'm the one who needs to tell you I'm sorry. I lashed out at you, but I didn't mean it. You know I could never hate you."

His eyes burned bright with need for her to understand. "You were my everything." His mouth crashed into hers in a kiss that stole her breath and commanded all her attention.

She hooked her fingers around his wrists as his hands held her face much more gently than he kissed her. She felt the need and punch behind the kiss that told her he meant what he said.

Just when her body was about to combust from the heat in that kiss, his lips broke from hers and he took one huge step back and released her.

Her hands fell empty at her sides. Her lips felt abandoned and desperate to be claimed again. Her heart thrashed in her chest but it also cried out for that feeling she couldn't identify to return. Her body vibrated as she held back from leaping back into his arms.

He stuffed his hands in his pockets. "I'm sorry. I shouldn't have done that."

All the heat inside her went cold. "Are you sorry? Because that kiss..." She touched her fingertips to her swollen lips.

Something new sparked in his eyes. Hope? "I came here to apologize and beg your forgiveness for my careless words. If you knew how much I missed you, how many nights I thought about you—then and now—maybe you'd believe me when I say you're the most important person I ever had in my life." He took a step back toward her. "I'm sorry I left you. I'm sorry it took me so long to come back to you." Another step closer. "And whatever it takes, I'll do anything to be your friend again." The last step brought the toes of his work boots right up to her. "And more. If you'll let me. Please. Because I think we had a good thing going. I always knew there was no one like you. I just can't *not* see you anymore." He huffed out a breath. "See. I can't speak coherently or think clearly with tears on your face and knowing you thought all this time I actually hated you."

She did. She had. But now... "I betrayed you. You trusted me with your secret and I told my dad."

He put his hands on the outside of her shoulders. "You saved my life. If your dad and the police hadn't found me..." His eyes turned stormy and the fear and pain came back that she'd seen so many times when they were little.

She hadn't liked seeing the nightmare in his eyes in the boy and she liked it even less in the man. "I just wanted to help you, but you never let me, not in a way that would make things better for you."

He squeezed her shoulders. "You helped me, Melody, in so many big and small ways. Knowing I'd get to see you at school was sometimes the only thing that made me not want to curl up and just die most days. When I was with you, I could breathe. I had fun. I laughed. I smiled. I had someone who listened and held my hand. I had someone who cared. Dean is not just a friend, he's like a brother. But you are and will always be the one I trust the most." He released her and slid his fingers through his hair, and pleaded with his eyes and words. "Please, Melody. I want you back."

She launched herself into his chest and wrapped her arms around his neck, hugging him with everything she had. She didn't want to let him go again. Not if it meant more days and years wondering if he was okay, if he was even alive. Because a world without Fox was just not a world she wanted to live in.

He held her just as fiercely. "Is this a yes? Because if you're still mad about me slipping into your DMs and not telling you who I really am, then I'm prepared to bribe and beg as often and as much as you want."

She leaned back against the hold he had around her waist. "Is that who you think I am now? That I need you to buy me off?"

His eyes rolled and he let out a heavy sigh. "Dean is right. I should stick to coding and stop trying to talk to people." He pressed his forehead to hers and looked deeply into her eyes. "But I want to be in your life. I want us to hang out, go out, and learn everything there is to know about who we are now. I want to be able to pick up the phone and call you just so I can hear your voice. I want to hear you laugh and make you smile the way you did for me all those years ago. Maybe you'll do that for me again. Maybe this time I won't be the one who leans on you all the time and I can be the one you know will never let you down." He seemed to stall out, but he looked so cute, all frustrated and anxious. "Seriously, this is the most I've spoken to anyone outside of teaching a class in I don't know how long, so put me out of my misery and say yes."

"Yes."

It didn't seem to ease him. "Yes to which part?"

"Yes to finding our way back to being best friends."

"And about the more part? Because that kiss, as tame as it was, was the best kiss I've ever had, and I'm hoping you felt the explosion of sparks too."

She liked his honesty, so she gave it back to him. "You mean the wildfire you set inside me?"

He gave her one of those killer smiles. "I'm happy to do it again. And again. And again. We'll make it an infinite loop."

She got the hint. "Is that a coding thing?"

"Yes. But it's also a *you* thing, because I—"

"Melody!"

She leaned sideways, keeping her hold on Fox's impressive biceps, so she could see her dad behind him at the back door of the bar. "What?"

"I know what you're doing is long overdue, but it's Friday and the bar is packed. We need you."

Fox held her with one hand and used the other to brush his fingers over the side of her hair. It was the second time he'd done it to her, like it was becoming part of the habit he did to his own hair. "My timing sucks."

"I'm on my way," she called to her dad, then refocused on Fox. "Come inside. I'll buy you a beer and get you something to eat. Maybe we can chat more later?"

"I'd like that. Feels like old times, you feeding me." That smile made her stomach quake every time he used it.

"This feels different from when we were kids, Fox."

"It feels even more important now that we get this right because it feels like if I lose you again, I'll be missing a part of me forever."

The words touched her so deeply, that melty heart thing happened in her chest and she just wanted to wrap him in her arms and never let go. "And you think you suck at talking to people."

He took her hand and squeezed it. "I'm trying extra hard with you."

She brought the back of his hand to her heart. "It's just me, Fox. All you need to do is be you. That's good enough for me. Always was. Always will be."

He traced his fingertips lightly across her forehead and down the side of her face. "There is no one else like you."

She stepped back, caught the disappointment in his eyes when they were more than mere inches apart, and walked back into the bar with him, the music and noise blasting at them as they came through the door.

Lyric's eyes went wide when she saw Melody holding hands with Fox, then turned to an I-want-all-the-details-later look. Melody had a hard time believing some woman hadn't snatched up the gorgeous man beside her, but over the last few weeks, they'd covered the whole thing about neither of them being in a relationship. They'd even talked about exes and how they hadn't found the one yet.

All those conversations they had took on a whole new meaning now that she knew she'd been talking to Fox.

As they entered the main part of the bar, she asked him, "Why did you ask me all those questions about my favorite things when you already knew most of them?"

"I know what eight-year-old Melody liked, not what smokin' hot Melody likes. People change. You have in some ways, but at the heart, you're still the girl I knew. The one who likes peanut butter cups, riding horses, quiet time by the river, being with your family, and me."

She did like him. Then and now. Because the adult Fox had charmed her over the last few weeks and made her want things that she'd never wanted with anyone else.

But they weren't quite done putting the past to rest and moving on. "I'd like to get to know more about what happened to you back then, over the years, and who you are now."

He pulled her hand up to his lips and kissed the back of it, their fingers still entwined. "We have all the time in the world. I'm not going anywhere."

She quirked a brow. "You're staying in town?"

"I have a place downtown. I'm doing some work at the New Adult Education Center."

"I've seen that place. The building was completely renovated over the last couple months. What do you do there? I thought you worked at a big software company."

He hesitated for a moment. "I do work for a big company, but I also run the center and teach an intensive computer programming course for certification in certain programming languages for young adults who age out of foster care and need to learn skills quickly to get work and be independent."

"Wow. That's amazing. You're giving back to others like you."

"I had help to get to where I am. I'm just paying it forward."

"Who helped you?"

He paused. "Your dad."

The news shocked her.

Fox glanced over at Wade. "He looked out for me ever since I went into foster care. Didn't matter how many times I moved, he found me."

Joy and pride lit her heart because her dad had kept watch over Fox, but anger twisted her gut because he'd kept it from her. "I had no idea."

"I asked about you every time we spoke."

A shrill whistle went up from the bar. Her dad. "I need to get back to work."

Fox pointed to a booth to the right of them. "Dean's waiting for me. We'll hang for a little while, but then I have to head home and finish some work. Can we meet up for lunch tomorrow?"

She desperately wanted to see him again. If for no other reason than to believe this was real. It seemed so surreal. "How about the diner at two? I know that's kind of late, but I don't get out of here until at least three in the morning, and I sleep until noon most days."

He brushed his hand up and down her arm. "I'll meet you anytime you want."

She turned to head to the bar, but spun back around and threw her arms around his neck again. She hugged him close and whispered, "Don't disappear on me again."

He kept one hand at the small of her back and the other fisted her hair. "Never. You want me, I'm here."

She wanted to hold on to him, but let him go and rushed away to get his beer and food, so he'd stay a while. She brought enough for Dean, too, then started working her way from table to table taking orders, filling them, and collecting her tips. Time, like most nights, slipped by quickly and before she knew it, Fox and Dean were standing in front of her as she held a tray full of drinks. "Thanks for stopping by. Sorry I couldn't talk more."

"Tomorrow. The diner downtown." Fox made it sound like an order but one filled with anticipation.

She nodded. "Lunch is on me if you promise to fill in the gap between third grade and now."

"Like always, I'll tell you all my secrets."

She was still spinning about her dad being in touch with him all these years and not saying anything to her. She intended to have a talk with him about that very soon.

Maybe he thought she'd moved on and forgotten Fox over the years, but she never had. She never would. Not after he'd broken her heart in so many ways years ago. That was too much history, even for a child, to let go of the person who touched her heart and changed her forever.

She watched him walk out of the bar with Dean, knowing this wasn't the end of their reunion but a new beginning.

She just hoped this time around it didn't end in tragedy.

Which made her think of his mother. Melody had heard she was sick.

Maybe that was why he'd come back to town.

Did he know his mother hadn't changed over the years? She was still the manipulative, mean woman she'd been when Melody was a kid. Once, she'd cornered Melody in the grocery store and told her that it was Melody's fault the state had taken her son. Melody ran back to her mother crying and made an excuse because she'd been too scared to tell her mom what the mean woman said. As an adult, she knew better, but Melody had believed it was true back then.

And that meant if Fox was helping his mother, someone needed to watch his back. Melody wouldn't let anyone, especially his mother, ever hurt him again.

CHAPTER THREE

Melody woke up early and headed to the Wilde Wind Ranch to get answers to the questions that nagged at her through the end of her shift last night and into her dreams. It was the first thing she'd thought about when her eyes opened this morning.

Why didn't Dad tell me he'd kept in touch with Fox?

What really happened the day my father found him?

She knew Fox had been seriously injured, but her father had been vague with the details because he didn't want to scare her even more than she had been for her friend.

Thoughts about whether he was hurt or hungry, sad or lonely, afraid and hiding used to tie her in knots all the time, especially after he left. Now, she wanted to know everything that happened from the last time she'd seen him until now. But she didn't want to ask him about that traumatic event that changed everything for him. She didn't want to make him relive it.

Someone else knew what happened that day. And her father wasn't going to give her a watered-down version again. She wanted the truth. Everything, including what Fox meant about her father keeping in touch with him all these years.

She parked at the house and walked in the front door. Her mom and dad were in the kitchen, standing close together. Mom loved music. It was always playing in the house and car, usually to her mom singing along. Today, it was old-school Bill Withers' "Lovely Day."

Neither of her parents was singing. Their stares were filled with guilt and trepidation, so she dove right in.

"Why didn't you tell me you knew where Fox was all this time and that you kept in touch with him?"

Her dad leaned on his forearms on the counter and met her gaze straight on. "I owe you an apology."

"I don't want an *I'm sorry*. I want an answer."

"You were devastated when Fox left town."

"Of course I was." She'd stayed in her room for days, wouldn't speak to anyone, cried a river of tears, barely ate, and didn't participate in school until her teacher told her if she didn't, they'd hold her back for another year. "Fox hated me for what I did. I didn't get to apologize. I didn't know what happened to him. I never saw him again."

"We tried to protect you." Her mom's eyes filled with the apology Melody didn't want. "You were so young. We thought it best not to tell you all the terrible things that happened to him, but focus on the fact that he was going to live somewhere better. After he left, you grieved, but you didn't ask any more questions."

"Because I thought you didn't know anything more once he left. Every day I wondered if he was okay."

Her father rubbed at the back of his neck. "We should have told you everything long before now. We just didn't want you to hurt for him."

"Hurt for him? Since the moment I knew he was being hurt to this very day, I ached for him. It never stops. It is a part of me. That boy…he was mine." The pain throbbed anew. "You always told us it was our responsibility to take care of those who can't take care of themselves."

One side of her dad's mouth kicked back in a half grin. "I was mostly talking about the horses and cattle on the ranch when I was trying to get you kids to do your chores, but your heart is so big you knew I meant to take care of those who are vulnerable."

"He was my best friend. He needed me. And I didn't help. Not in the way he needed me to."

"You couldn't stop what his mother and father were doing to him. You needed help. And when it mattered most, you did the right thing," her father praised.

"You never told me what happened when you got to his house. All you'd ever say was that Fox had been taken to the hospital. You never said why. I heard the gossip around town, but could never be sure what was true, assumed, or flat-out false." Her parents had only placated her with benign statements that he was going to be okay and that he was going to be placed with someone who would take care of him. Not exactly a lot of specifics in those inadequate assurances. "I want to know everything now."

Her mom frowned. "He told your father not to tell you. Maybe it's best if you ask Fox."

She shook her head. "I won't make him relive that." She turned her gaze to her dad. "Please. I'm not a little girl anymore. I don't need you to protect me from this hard truth. I want to know, so I can be the friend Fox needs me to be."

Her dad let out a heavy breath. "I found him in the barn. He'd been there for hours. Probably all night. He was nearly frozen to death, barely conscious. He was so terrified his father would kill him."

"Fox told me last night that I saved his life. Is that true?"

Her mom and dad shared a look that spoke volumes between them.

Her dad met her gaze and gave it to her straight. "If I hadn't gone there to find him, and his parents left him out there even an hour longer, he'd be dead. He had major organ damage from the beating he'd taken. A lacerated spleen and liver."

"He was bleeding internally?"

"Yes. Along with several broken ribs, a broken wrist, a black eye, contusions all over his back and legs from being kicked, and..." Her dad couldn't seem to finish.

"And?"

"Bruises around his neck from where his father had choked him."

She tried to breathe, but it was so hard when it felt like she was suffocating on the immense sympathy she felt for Fox and the fury she wanted to unleash on his parents. "Was it all his father? Or did his mother hurt him, too?"

Wade rubbed his big hand over the back of his neck. He'd never raised that hand in anger to any of his kids.

She'd known his disappointment. She'd been punished plenty with extra chores and lost privileges. Never, not once, had her parents ever put their hands on her in violence.

Her dad sighed. "His mother broke his ribs when she literally kicked him again and again to get him out of the house."

"Did Fox tell you all this?"

"He asked me to stay with him while the police and social worker interviewed him. He said he felt safe with me because I was Melody's dad and you swore to him that I would never hurt you or him or anyone. He trusted me, because he believed in you, sweetheart. Because of that trust and how incredibly proud I was of you, I looked after Fox the best I could over the years. I made sure that if he was ever in another bad situation, I got him moved someplace better. I made sure he knew that the person you sent to help him would help him no matter what, whenever he needed it."

"Why didn't you just bring him here to live with us? He could have had a real family who loved him."

A pained look came over her mom's face. "We wanted to, but the system is complicated and his parents fought the charges against them. His father swore he'd get Fox back to his mother."

"I don't know why when they treated him like they didn't want him at all."

"He was theirs," her father said simply, though it made no real sense. "The threat to Fox was real. Your mom, me, the police, the social workers, everyone knew the best thing for him was to get him as far away from his parents as possible if he was going to have a chance at finding a normal life. If he was too close and his father found him..." Her dad let her fill in the nightmare that would have been. "Unfortunately, foster care isn't perfect. He had a couple of good homes, but he got moved a lot for different reasons. I checked in with him once a month. If something seemed off, or he revealed he was unhappy and not being treated right, I contacted his case worker and made sure he got moved somewhere else. I hoped it would be better. It wasn't always." He shared another of those looks with her mom. Melody recognized it now. Their shared pain and regret.

They'd had four kids of their own to raise.

"I'm so grateful for what you did for my friend."

Her dad didn't look at all relieved to hear her say that. "We wish we could have done more for him, but it just wasn't safe for him here."

Her father had to think of the safety of his family, too, because she knew Fox's father didn't spend as much time in prison as he deserved. There'd been a deal struck and Fox could have very well paid the price if his father got his hands on Fox again.

She wondered if it was safe for him to be here now. Did he come back to face his abusive mother and his past? Was he hoping for a reconciliation and an apology or something from his mom? Because Melody didn't see that happening.

After what his mother did to him, why had he come back to help her?

"Is that all?" she asked them.

Her father took a deep breath as if bracing himself to say the next words. "Nearly seventy bone fractures by the time he was eight. Several of those bones, like his wrist, were broken multiple times."

"They didn't just hurt him. They tortured him." It made her stomach tight and sour. She tried not to throw up.

The quiet only amplified their resounding unspoken *yes*.

She put her hands on the island and hung her head, trying to breathe and think about everything she'd learned and reminding herself he got out. He was safe. He survived.

"Melody? Are you okay?" Her mom's hand was gentle and warm on hers.

She stood to her full height and wrapped her mom in a big hug. "Thank you for being my mom. You've loved me so well it never occurred to me that a mom could hurt her child that way. I know that's naïve and stupid, but that's the safe space I got to live in my whole life because of you."

Her mom had tears in her eyes when she squeezed her hard, then let her go, so Melody could wrap her arms around her dad. "You are safe and strong and confident and encouraging and never treated any of us girls like we were weaker than the men on this ranch in any way. You always make me feel like I can do anything."

"Because you can. And when you do, it's with that big heart of yours. You act like nothing bothers you, but we know you feel things deep."

Most people thought she was the life of the party. And she was a lot of the time. She liked to have fun.

Some guys thought because of that they could use her and walk away and it didn't hurt.

She'd gotten tired of that and stopped dating because flings were fun in the moment, until you were back to being alone. She wanted something real. Something deep. A connection that could stand up to the good and bad and everything in between.

Two people who had that were standing right in front of her. Her parents' marriage wasn't perfect. They argued. They had issues. But they worked through them. Year after year. Change after change in their lives. Because nothing stayed the same.

Not even Melody.

She'd changed a lot since she and Fox were grade school friends.

Now she wanted to find out if that little boy and girl could be what they were—and more—now.

Because the other thought that had crept into her mind last night had come when she reflected on why none of the guys she dated ever lasted. What about them hadn't worked for her?

The answer had stunned her.

They weren't Fox, the boy who had always treated her like she mattered, like she was not just important, but necessary in his life.

No one had ever come close to making her feel that way again.

Her dad brushed his hand over her head. "I didn't tell you about Fox because you seemed to have moved on after he lashed out at you. I thought about taking you back to see him, but Fox was just not in a good place. I made a mistake. I should have given you both a chance to talk and say goodbye before Fox went into foster care. I didn't know you were still carrying the guilt and pain of losing him until I saw the devastated look on your face when you saw him last night."

"Remember I told you about the guy I've been talking to online?"

Her mom gasped. "It was Fox?"

"He wanted to get to know me again. Now that we have over these last many weeks, he wants us to be together again."

Her mom proceeded with caution. "You were really interested in him. Are you still, now that you know it's Fox?"

She thought about the sexy as hell kiss she and Fox shared last night. She'd kissed a lot of other men. None of those kisses were as scorching hot as the one Fox laid on her. "Yes. When I talked to the mystery guy online, there was something so familiar about him. Now I know why. It was always so easy to be me with him. I felt that when we talked now. It's why I waited so long to give him an ultimatum about meeting in person. I really didn't want to lose what we had online, even though I wanted more." She pulled her phone out of her back pocket and checked the time. "I have to go. I'm meeting him for lunch."

"Tell him I'd love a chance to catch up with him. He's welcome at the ranch whenever he has the time." Her dad tugged her hair.

This time she didn't want to keep things fun and flirty and casual. She wanted Fox to be her Mason, her Layla, the ones her sister Lyric and brother Jax couldn't live without. Melody wanted to be the one Fox couldn't leave. Not this time.

CHAPTER FOUR

F ox finished the programming job he'd been working on the last couple
of weeks for his company. He sent the final product to his client and
a note to his assistant at his Boston office, asking her to mark the job
complete and have billing send the client the final bill. He shut down his
computer with plenty of time to make it to the diner. Anticipation jacked
his heart rate as he checked his pockets to make sure he had his keys and
phone. He got distracted when he got lost in the code and wanted to be
sure he had everything he needed for his meeting with Melody. His date?

He didn't want to presume anything. He'd tried to tell her what he
wanted last night, but most of what happened was a blur in his mind
because he'd been desperate to get her to listen to him and agree to see him
again.

Desperation is not a good look. Which reminded him he should check
himself in the mirror before he left and make sure his hair wasn't standing
on end and he didn't have anything on his face, clothes, or in his teeth.

"What?"

He jumped at the sound of Amy's voice. "What?" he asked back, feeling
like he'd missed something. He often did because he was usually in his head
and not paying attention to the actual people around him.

Amy raised a brow. "Did you say I look desperate?"

"No." He felt a flush rise on his cheeks. "Why would you think that?"

"I heard you say something about being desperate when I walked in."

I said that out loud? Fuck. "I was talking about me."

"Oh well, then you obviously weren't talking about being desperate for
someone."

"Why not?" He was really having a hard time following this conversation.

"Because you're you. Brilliant. Nice. R...ridiculously handsome."

He didn't think that was what she was really going to say. Rich was probably the word she was going to use, and it gave him pause. "Um...thanks. I need to go. Did you need something?"

She stood perfectly still. A look came into her eyes that said she did in fact want something as her gaze swept over him again. Since he didn't want to hurt her feelings by not reciprocating her feelings, he ignored it.

He often missed social cues and meaningful looks like that because he was preoccupied with other things on his mind. Like Melody. He couldn't stop thinking about her. But he quickly gave himself a mental kick in the ass to pay attention to why Amy had come looking for him in his office.

"You."

Uh oh!

She took a step closer. "You didn't come down for lunch today. I know you get caught up in your work, but you always make it to lunch with the others to check in on their progress."

Oh. Okay. That was easy. He'd deviated from his normal behavior. And she'd noticed. Hmm. "Yeah. Not today. I have a date."

Her brilliant blue eyes went wide. "You what?"

"I have a date. I don't want to be late." He patted his pockets again, found his keys and phone, then touched his ass. "No wallet. Going to need that." He pulled it out of his top desk drawer. When you sat as many hours as he did each day, a thick wallet could be a real pain in the ass. Literally.

"With who?" Amy sounded dumbfounded.

"An old friend." Someone he'd spent nearly every waking moment thinking about since he got to town. Not that she was ever far from his mind on any given day for the past seventeen years.

"Really? Here?"

"I lived here a long time ago. Melody was my best friend until—"

One golden eyebrow rose on Amy's face when he didn't finish his sentence. "What happened?"

"Too much to talk about now. Being late is a dick move, especially on a first date." He tried to rush past her, but she grabbed his arm and pulled him to a stop.

"You can tell me anything, you know."

He only shared his past with a very select few. And he and Amy didn't know each other that well. But he didn't want to hurt her feelings either. "Thanks for being a good friend."

The hand not holding his arm landed on his chest, her palm over his heart. "I'd like to be more."

He stepped back and tried to let her down gently. "Listen, technically, you work for me. I don't want to cross any boundaries."

She gave him a seductive look. "I don't have many of those."

Wow. Okay. He wasn't expecting that overshare. "Unfortunately, this is a business. I need to maintain a professional distance." He started out the door again, hoping she dropped it.

Most of the time, he worked in his office alone for long hours. Now there were students, teachers, a chef, and a financial advisor at the center, all wanting to connect with him because he headed it all.

Don't even get him started on how many people worked at his company in Boston. Thankfully most of them were like him and stuck to email and text messages.

He missed his administrative assistant gatekeeping his office door.

All he wanted right now was to be with the one person he'd been waiting to see forever.

"Fox," Amy called out to him before he got to the stairs that would take him down to the first floor and out to the street.

He reluctantly turned back, wondering what she'd say next.

"You should be careful. You're a great guy. Don't let anyone take advantage. Everyone wants something. And you have *a lot* to give."

He thought the comment strange, especially the way she emphasized *a lot*. What did she mean? Maybe he didn't want to know.

Melody didn't want anything but his companionship. He hoped it stayed that way. Because he'd been disappointed in the past by other women and didn't want to count Melody among the people who only saw him for what he was worth, not who he was.

CHAPTER FIVE

Fox walked into the diner expecting to have to wait for the next ten minutes, in which he'd tie himself in knots wondering if she'd show and what she thought about the kiss they shared last night.

Had the initial shock worn off that he was the guy DMing her?

Now that she'd had time to think about it, did she just want to be friends?

Did she have any idea how much he wanted her?

Yes, his mind was spinning.

"Fox."

Her voice sent a wave of heat through his system. God, the way she said his name. It rolled through him in a wave of desire and longing.

His gaze went from the counter in front of the open kitchen to the booths lining the front windows. She sat three down with a cup of coffee in front of her.

She was early.

He hoped that was a good sign, that she was as anxious to see him again as he was to see her.

He walked up to the table and stared down at her, wondering if he should kiss her hello like he wanted to or just take his seat.

She cocked a perfect arched dark brow and her gorgeous blue eyes held him enthralled. "What's wrong?"

"Nothing." His insides quaked and felt funny as happiness bubbled inside him. He liked it because he rarely felt this way.

"It's something. So just spit it out, because it's just me, and you can tell me anything."

He'd never had trouble spilling his guts to her. He wasn't about to start now. Not when he wanted to be close again like they used to be. "I really want to be the guy who gets to kiss you hello, goodbye, and for no reason other than we both want it."

A fork clattered onto a plate. The woman at the table next to them let out a surprised gasp. He felt her gaze on them, but didn't take his eyes off the gorgeous woman in front of him.

Melody stared up at him, her eyes bright with mischief and challenge. "You are the only one in my life who gets to do that. So by all means, kiss me. Because I want you to."

He didn't need to be told twice. He slipped into the booth right beside her as she scooted back just enough to give him room. He cupped the side of her face, brushed his thumb over her amazingly soft skin, looked her in the eye, and said something else he wanted her to know. "I am so tired of missing you." He swallowed her little gasp as his lips claimed hers and he sank his tongue deep, tasting her. Coffee, mint, her, it all mixed into the need they shared.

Before he dived in for more and pulled her closer, he remembered their rapt audience and gentled the kiss to just a simple brush of his lips that had enough spark in it to set him on fire again—she was that potent to him. "Good morning."

She licked her plump lips. "It's the afternoon."

"Yes, but it's the morning for you."

Someone cleared their throat behind him.

He looked around, saw all the stares, then focused on the waitress, Bea, staring at him. He hit the diner often since it was just down the street from the center, so he understood this was gossip central for the town. People were going to be talking about him and Melody.

"Hey, honey, that was one hell of a show. Can I get you some ice water to cool down?" The amusement in her grin and eyes infected everyone in the room watching him. They all went back to their meals and conversations. "Are you ready to order? I know you don't have a lot of time."

Melody looked up at Bea. "The usual."

"You, too?" Bea asked him.

"Yes. Thank you." Finally alone with Melody, he stared at her, trying to decide what to talk about first. "I'm sorry we didn't do this instead of me taking the roundabout way of contacting you."

She shook her head. "No more apologies. Let's just agree that we both enjoyed our online chats and that maybe it was better to take some time to reacquaint ourselves with each other without the past wedged be-tween us."

He let out a sigh of relief. "You don't know how grateful I am to hear you say that."

"I spoke to my mom and dad this morning. They'd love it if you stopped by the ranch to see them soon. They told me about that day and how they kept track of you all these years." Her hand settled over his on the table. "We don't have to talk about it. You don't need to say anything. I just want you to know, I'm here if you need someone to listen."

He appreciated that she gave him an out from dredging up his nightmares. "Thank you."

"I also want you to know, I'm concerned about your mother."

"The new drugs they've got her on seem to be working. She's not getting any better, but she's also not getting worse." He didn't have any wishful thinking when it came to Tanya's diagnosis and prognosis.

"That's good news. But that's not what I'm talking about. Are you sure being here, helping her, is healthy for you after what they put you through?"

He pulled her close and kissed the top of her head. "You never stop, do you?"

Those big blue eyes held a world of concern. "Stop what?"

"Caring about me."

She pulled back and stared at him. "Never. I never forgot you. I never stopped wondering about you. I never let myself forget that I hurt you, even if I was helping you. Because of what I did, I lost you. But if I hadn't done it, I'd have lost you forever."

He leaned in close. "Nothing is going to pull us apart again. It's time for both of us to leave what happened in the past where it belongs."

"Are you sure about me? Because you've been in town long enough to hear the rumors about me. It's not just my name. I've been called the wild Wilde child since middle school."

"I don't get what that has to do with me and you. From everything I've heard, yes, you like to have a good time. You're the life of the party and the bar is a party every night. I've seen the way guys look at you. I've seen them put their hands on you."

"And how did that make you feel?"

She was going to judge whatever he said, so he went with the truth. "Like I wanted to kick every one of their asses." He twirled a long strand of her dark hair around his finger. "But I didn't do anything because I paid more attention to you than them and realized, none of them held your interest in the slightest. You blew them all off. Politely. With a smile. With a few playful words. Because you're not mean. You know what you want. And it's not them, because we had our online thing going. Right?"

She nodded.

Good. "You're loyal. You like a good time. You like to have fun. I've seen you join in dancing with everyone and singing along to your favorite songs. I don't see anything wrong with what you do, or the way you let yourself enjoy the moments. I wish I was more like you. I spend far too much time alone. And mostly I'm okay with that. I'm not comfortable dancing or partying just for the hell of it."

"You could have anyone you want. I got no less than a dozen requests for introductions once the women in the bar saw me with you."

Nerves fluttered in his belly. "And what did you tell them?"

"That they could have at Dean all they wanted, but you were off-limits."

He liked that she'd staked a claim and gave her a cocky grin. "I like that. And this. You and me having a conversation, spending time together. But I also love to watch you move when you dance at the bar, too."

Her gaze turned sultry. "Yeah?"

He raked his gaze over her. "Oh, yeah."

She sucked in a steadying breath. "I don't know how you stayed under the radar at the bar and I never saw you."

"Simple. I never sat in your section. Dean and I stuck to the back where it's the darkest in the bar. There's always a crowd, so anytime you got close, I simply looked away. You saw me, you just didn't know it was me."

Her gaze dropped down, then swept up him. "You grew into a very good-looking man, Fox. I am not the only woman to notice. You must have been fending off advances in the bar left and right."

He shrugged. "Like you, I dismissed them with a little charm and a simple, 'I'm taken.'"

A lopsided grin tilted her lips. "You were that sure of yourself."

"Based on the chats we shared and how you flirted with me, I hoped." A lot. "You insisted we meet in person, letting me know you wanted more than just us hiding behind our computers where it was safe to say whatever we wanted without looking at each other. So, yeah, I knew you wanted more than just a friendship."

She studied him, probably saw his nerves. "At first, you needed that distance."

He nodded. "It helped break the ice. I'm not great with new people."

"I'm not new to you."

"No. You're more important than anyone."

She glanced away, then back at him. "Fox. I don't know what to say to that."

"It's just the truth. You don't have to say anything. I know you have a whole life with lots of people in it and a ton of happy memories growing up with your family at the ranch. You had a really good life. And I'm happy for you that you had that."

She frowned. "But your life was nothing like that and it made you cautious and wary of others."

"Yes. And there are other reasons for that, too. But you and I shared a connection. Most eight-year-old boys don't want anything to do with girls."

"Boys are yucky," she teased, then leaned in and kissed him softly. Her gaze flared with need. "Men can be a lot of fun." She put her hand on his chest. "But there was this one boy I found fascinating."

He touched his forehead to hers.

She rubbed her hands up and down on his chest. "You liked me. You made sure the other boys never pulled my hair or teased me. You used to hold my hand all the time. I loved it. You always made me feel special. I was the youngest at home. I thought my big sisters got to do everything and I was left behind a lot because I was so much younger and smaller than them. But when I was with you, we did everything together."

"You knew I needed you. Someone who was always kind. Someone who didn't make me flinch or feel scared."

"When did that finally go away?"

"When I met Dean. He was a tough kid. Way more aggressive than me. No one messed with him. Well, not the other kids. He liked me because I was quiet. He got yelled at a lot. I liked him because he could glare at someone and make them go away."

"How old were you when you two met?"

"Fourteen. Seventeen when Max joined our group. You'll meet him later. He's in Boston still taking care of some business for me."

"What kind of business?"

Most of the time when someone asked about him, he either avoided the question or gave a vague answer. Not with Melody. He wanted her to know he'd made something of himself. "I started my own software company in college. It was just me and Max at first. Simple projects we could do in a short amount of time while we were finishing our classes. Max and I were a good team. We had a lot in common. We were both in the system and trying to be something more than the throwaway kids we'd been for so long."

She squeezed his hand. "You are not a throwaway anything."

He turned his hand and linked his fingers with hers. "You were the only one who made me feel like I was worth something."

"Fox. You defied the odds. You're strong and smart. An amazing friend. You built your own company. You're worth knowing."

"You make me feel that way." He thought about his agonizing past. "When all you know is pain, kindness is precious. It's everything, even when you feel like you don't deserve it, or that it comes with a price attached. With you, I knew you meant it and you didn't want anything from me. That is so rare in my world, Mel."

She scooted a bit closer. "Then you'll just have to keep me in your world so you'll always have it."

So I'll always have you.

God, he wanted that to be true so badly.

"I guess that won't be easy when you go back to Boston." Sadness filled her eyes.

Hell no. He didn't want Melody to ever be sad. "I'm not going back anytime soon. I'll stay here until Tanya..." He never called her Mom. He couldn't say the word. Maybe he didn't like her. Maybe he even hated her. But she was his mom and she needed him.

He cleared his throat. "I've set up an office here. I've got great people, like Max and Dean, working for me. I can fly back if I'm needed, otherwise I can code and do business from here, no problem."

"What's Dean's role in the company?"

"Security."

She cocked her head. "Then shouldn't he be in Boston keeping watch over the company?"

He didn't want to lie to her so he gave her part of the truth. "We're working on something together here."

Dean was watching his back, like he always did, even though Fox doubted anything would happen in small-town Blackrock Falls, Wyoming. But you could never be too careful.

CHAPTER SIX

Melody smiled at Bea when she set down their plates.

Fox stared from his plate to hers, then grinned at Melody.

Bea gave them a knowing look. "I couldn't wait to see your faces when you figured out you both have the same *usual*."

Grilled cheese, fries (extra crispy), mixed fruit, and a chocolate shake. *Yum.* Melody had been getting that at the diner forever. She worked hard, was on her feet for hours every night at the bar, and could afford to indulge in the extra calories for her favorite comfort foods.

Fox held up his shake, a big, silly grin on his face, and a look in his eyes that said this little thing meant something to him. "It's like we're back in the school cafeteria, but with shakes instead of chocolate milk."

She clinked her glass to his, put the straw in her mouth, and sucked up some of the thick, decadent shake. "My sisters always tell me I eat like a toddler."

"You like what you like." He took a huge bite of his grilled cheese and hummed with satisfaction. "I have a chef working at the center. She teaches cooking classes, because that's not something a lot of foster kids learn, and when they're out on their own their diets aren't that nutritious. Health and well-being aren't always a priority for foster families. Once on their own, they eat a lot of cheap, prepackaged junk. I want the people who come to us to learn the things that will keep them healthy and safe and allow them to rise above whatever circumstance they're in."

"You're not just giving them career skills, but life skills."

He turned and stared her right in the eye. "Because that's what your father did for me. When he called, he focused on things that would make my life better. School was the priority. Every job I took as a kid and teen and now, he told me to learn every skill I could, then use that skill to apply it to better jobs that paid more money."

"I still can't wrap my head around the fact that he stayed in touch with you."

"He was the dad I never had in a lot of ways. I owe him so much. At first, I didn't really listen to him. But then, he started making a lot of sense. Especially after one particular incident."

"What happened?"

"The lady I was living with locked up the food. We could only eat when she said, and the meals were small, basic stuff like sandwiches and canned soup. The free school lunch was better than what she gave us. I was ten. Your dad called to check in. He asked a lot of questions. Most of the time I told him everything was fine. I figured if something wasn't bleeding or broken, everything was better than what I'd had back home."

She put her hand on his arm and squeezed. "Fox. That's just not true and not good enough."

"Your father felt the same way. He didn't let me get away with a 'fine.' He asked specific questions about school, the place I was staying, if I felt safe, and what they were feeding me."

Melody adored her dad. He didn't ever take things at face value. He looked deeper. She swore she could arrive home from school and in two minutes he knew what kind of day she'd had.

"So you confessed that you hated the food."

"I told him I was starving and the ache in my belly wouldn't stop." He took a long pull on the chocolate shake. "At that point, I was so tired of feeling like crap all the time."

"What did my dad do?"

"He contacted my case worker and told her what was happening. Me and the others staying there were moved to new foster families. And when I arrived at mine, there was a lawn mower waiting for me with a note from your dad."

"Let me guess, it said something about you using that mower to earn your own money so you would never be hungry."

"Yes. With detailed instructions on how to approach the neighbors and get clients. How to work the lawn mower, get gas for it, and to save some money for emergencies. That foster family was actually pretty cool. The guy worked a lot, but the woman, she went over your dad's instructions, then helped me step by step to turn it on, mow the grass, empty it. She even took me to the gas station and taught me how to fill up the little can, and then fill the lawn mower tank. She made me go to each house on the block and ask about doing their lawn. At first, only one family said yes. I did that lawn every week. I guess I did a good enough job, a couple of the neighbors asked if I'd do their lawns, too. I didn't need the money for food at that place. But I only got to stay there for six months before I went somewhere else. I took my lawn mower with me and started my business back up again."

"Wow, that was really nice of your case worker to make sure you got to take the mower."

"She didn't. The lady at that house asked her husband to drive it over for me in his truck. He smacked me on the back and said, 'Good luck. Keep up the good work.'"

She raised a brow. "Why didn't they keep you?"

"Because she found out she was pregnant right after I arrived. When she was about to deliver their second child, they decided they needed the space and five kids was too much. They already had two fosters that had been with them a long time. A sister and brother. They wanted to be sure they could keep those two kids together. She wanted to focus on her baby for a while."

"I'm sorry. They sound like they were a nice family."

"They were. They helped me for as long as they were able."

She read something in his face. "You wanted to stay there."

"They were a close family, the five of them, going on six. I didn't fit in."

Her heart ached for him. "You do with me. Always."

He kissed her on the side of the head. "Enough of the bad stuff. Let me tell you about all the kickass stuff that happened to me, because I don't want you to see me as some poor, left-behind kid. Your dad was right. School was my ticket to success."

She grinned and listened as he told her about the science competitions he won in high school and college. The scholarships and grants he'd received because her dad pushed him to get a degree. He graduated top of his class with a bunch of job offers but decided to take his business and expand it.

She'd never really thought about self-made people. The term sounded like they'd worked hard, took risks and opportunities, and believed in themselves. But of course they didn't do it on their own. They had family, friends, colleagues, and mentors along the way.

Yes, Fox had help, but he'd been the driving force to get from nothing to a business with nearly a hundred employees that was profitable and thriving. So much so that Fox had been able to open the center there in Blackrock Falls.

"Why did you open it here and not in Boston?"

"There is one in Boston. It seemed fitting to open one here in Wyoming for kids who won't find the opportunity I'm offering them anywhere here. I work with social services to identify those in need. There are a lot of them here. Everywhere."

"Is that what you hope to do? Open one in every state?"

"Wouldn't that be amazing? There are other foundations that do what we do in some way. There are career counseling centers, and stuff like that. But we train people to do specific jobs that will get them working fast and earn them a good salary, so they can provide for themselves, and then hopefully take those skills and build on them."

"It's amazing and necessary." And she felt like she wasn't doing enough for her community. Sure, they fed those who couldn't afford a meal. But that was mostly Lyric's endeavor.

"Tell me about you. It must be a lot of work to run the bar."

"What do you mean?" Most people believed she was just a waitress. Though everyone knew she and her sisters and brother owned the bar together. They just thought Aria and Jax ran the bar while Lyric ran the kitchen and catering. Melody was just there.

"You manage all the waitstaff. You're in charge of setup and cleanup at the bar. You take care of most of the bar's marketing and social media. Not to mention your side gig."

Her eyes went wide. "How do you know about that?"

"Your dad. You only talked about waitressing at the bar in our online chats, but you do so much more than just sling drinks."

"I don't like that you and he have this whole relationship that I never knew about."

"I asked him not to tell you. I didn't want you to worry about me. I didn't have a lot of good stuff to tell you over the years." He clenched his hand into a fist. "Every time your dad called, I thought maybe it would be the last time anyway. He didn't have to do what he did for me. I thought...eventually he'd stop calling and checking up on me."

"You thought he'd stop caring. You thought I did."

"I pushed you away. But I knew one day I'd find you again and explain. Until then, you had everything I wanted and I knew you'd be okay."

She squeezed his arm again. "Except I didn't have you and that was *not* okay."

"Your dad is so proud of the business you started. Why do you hide it?"

"I don't. No one really cares about anything I do. They think I'm just a waitress."

"You are so much more. The job doesn't matter. Who you are does. And you have a lot to offer. I'd love it if you came to the center and taught a class on how to set up an Etsy shop and how you run it. I know you could give the students some valuable insight into owning, operating, and marketing a business."

"What?" She couldn't believe he wanted her help.

"What?" he asked back, confused.

"Why would you want me? You've done all those things with your business."

"My business is very specific. Yours is creative and caters to a specific clientele, but can be applied to any sort of creative product." He turned his body toward hers. "How did you get into making custom bridles?"

"My grandfather taught me. I liked hanging out with him in his shop. He'd give me a piece of leather, some tools and stamps, and let me make whatever I wanted. But I liked making the bridles and imagining them on the pretty horses I adored."

"And now you sell them for top dollar." He looked so impressed with her.

"I know my dad didn't tell you about my other side gig, because he doesn't know about it. Did you find out about it some other way?"

"What kind of computer guy would I be if I didn't do some online digging to find everything I could about you?"

Annoyance pinched her full lips tight. "The kind who should have simply asked me what he wanted to know?"

He chuckled. "You're not going to let me off the hook anytime soon, are you?"

"I understand why you wanted to get to know me again without the past getting in the way. I just wish—well, I can't have what I wish. But you're here now, and that makes me happy."

His gaze narrowed. "What do you wish?"

She leaned in and brushed her lips to his. "That there had never been a reason that you had to leave me in the first place."

He brushed his fingertips down the side of her face. "What if I promise to never leave you again?"

The words melted her heart. She leaned into his touch. "I hope you keep that promise."

"I will as long as you let me." He kissed her this time. It was slow and thorough and toe curling, making her body lean in closer to his and her mind start daydreaming about what it would be like to be alone and naked with him. He ended the sultry kiss with a hum as he pulled away, then said, "You're not getting out of admitting you also run a thriving jewelry shop."

Busted. She made custom leather bracelets for men and women. "I design everything myself and stamp it all by hand. I've even created some of my own stamps. I have a guy who makes them for me."

"I want you to make me something. I'll pay whatever it costs. I just want it to be something you made just for me."

She'd already thought about making him a gift. "Okay. But I want to spend more time with you, so I can come up with something that matches who you are now."

His phone alarm went off. He swore, then checked the time. "I'm sorry. I didn't know we'd been here so long. You do that to me. I think about you, I'm with you, and I lose track of time."

She pulled a fifty-dollar bill out of her bag and placed it on the table.

He snatched it up and tried to hand it back to her. "I'll pay for lunch."

She grabbed the bill and set it on the table again. "I told you it was on me. Just like last night when I told you the beers and food were on me, too. But you left me that tip, so I'm paying it forward. It's more than enough to cover our lunch and give Bea a big tip. So you kind of are paying for lunch."

He obviously made more money than her as a computer programmer, but that didn't mean she couldn't hold up her end when she invited him to lunch.

He shook his head, cupped her face, and kissed her again. "You surprise me."

"I don't know how. It seems like you know a hell of a lot more about me than I do about you."

"And that annoys you." An apology lit his eyes.

"I just want to know you the way you know me." She didn't like the sad look on his face. "And that's what we're doing, right? Spending time together so we know each other again."

"There are so many things I want to know about you. How you take your coffee in the afternoon when you wake up. What you sleep in. Hopefully, that's in my bed very soon. How you taste."

Since he'd kissed her many times now, she quickly realized he had a whole other place on her he'd like to taste, and the heat level in the diner went up a million degrees, it seemed.

"Fox?"

"Yeah?"

She put her hand on his chest, right over his thumping heart. "You and I think a lot alike."

He leaned in to take her mouth again, but froze when a second phone alarm went off. "Shit. I have to go."

"Where's the fire?"

He probably had some big important meeting.

"I visit my mom every afternoon and make sure she's got everything she needs and is taking her meds. I have a night nurse who watches her, but she's alone during the day, so…"

He wanted to check on her. Such a good son. Too bad his mother didn't deserve it.

"Why do you do it?" She wanted to understand.

"When the social worker contacted me about her health, I thought, 'Good. She deserves it.' She never did a damn thing for me my whole life. Why should I do anything to help her now? And then I thought this was my chance to tell her how I feel and what my life has been like because of her.

"But if she cared, she'd have reached out. She never did. Not a birthday card, a Christmas gift, not even an attaboy for graduating top of my class. I realized the only person I was trying to make proud was myself. And your dad," he tacked on. "Because he was the only one who believed in me."

"That's not true. I thought about you all the time. I wondered what you were doing, and what you'd be like in every grade I started. As I grew up and changed, I wondered how tall you'd be now, if your face had changed, if the shadows in your eyes were gone, if you were lanky, pudgy, or built. Did you still have this soft, silky hair?" She brushed her fingers through the side of it like she used to do when they were kids and she wanted to soothe him the way her mom had done for her when she was sick.

His gaze sharpened. "How'd I turn out in your eyes?"

"Smart and gorgeous. I think that's really hot."

"You're creative and stunning, with a whole lot of curves you didn't have last I saw you." Wicked delight lit his eyes now.

"You're not the same boy. I'm not a girl anymore."

He leaned in. "No, you're the woman I want. Desperately."

She grinned. "That's a mutual thing." She pumped the brakes. "But we're still doing the catch-up thing."

He nodded. Letting her know they'd go at her pace. "About Tanya...I couldn't live with myself if I let her die alone and didn't at least attempt to understand her, what happened, why, and whether any of that meant I could find a way to forgive her."

"What she did to you...it's a lot to carry."

"It's hard to forget. At least the nightmares are gone. Or were."

She understood exactly what he meant. "Until you came back here."

"Everything I'd locked down so I could survive got stirred up. That's partially why I wanted to see you so badly. You always made me feel better. You still do. I thought you'd be different now in some way, but deep down you're still my Melody. The girl who loved me is still you." He seemed to catch himself and what he said. "I didn't mean—"

She pressed her fingertips to his lips. "I know what you meant." And it was true. She did love that boy. Her tiny heart had ached for him. She'd missed him desperately.

The man had her full attention and her heart. But was what she was feeling the kind of love that Lyric and Mason and Jax and Layla shared? She wanted a bond like her sister and brother had with their partners. It was palpable. When they looked at the ones they loved, you could see it in their eyes and feel it surrounding them.

Right now, she was feeling a whole lot of attraction and gratitude to have Fox back in her life. But was it the forever kind of love her sister and brother had found?

Maybe not yet. But she wanted it to be.

He winced. "I really have to go."

"I'll come with you."

He went still. "Why?"

"Because I want to see if the woman I've seen and interacted with around town is who she's showing you, or if she's trying to manipulate you."

He narrowed his gaze. "What do you mean? Has she said something to you?"

She gave him the cold, hard truth. "Only every time we meet. And it's not pretty. She blames me for them taking you away from her."

Anger filled his eyes. "That's not true. It's her fault. She could have taken me away from him. She could have been a hell of a lot better of a mother than she was. She could have tried to get me back. She refused to do any of the counseling or parenting classes she was ordered to take to get visitation."

She put her hand on his cheek. "And you were better off for it, because she doesn't know how to love. Not even her own son."

"I couldn't tell."

"What?" she asked, not understanding his meaning.

"Whether she's still the same or different. I'm bigger now. She can't push me around. And she needs my help. So is she careful about what she says and does around me now? She doesn't want to talk about the past. She says it's done."

"Maybe for her. Not for you, because you still have questions."

"I'm probably better off not knowing the truth."

"That's up to you. But I get that turning your back on her, the way she did to you, just isn't who you are. So let's go visit dear ol' Tanya."

He frowned. "You really don't like her."

She didn't hide it. "She hurt you. I will never forgive her for that."

Fox kissed her softly, then touched his forehead to hers. "So fierce."

"Always. Especially when it comes to you."

"How did I fucking get so lucky?" He hugged her close and so hard it almost hurt, but then he rubbed his big hand over her back and eased up.

"Sorry. I still can't quite believe this is real. You're here. With me. After all this time. Finally."

She smiled up at him. "It's real. And just the beginning. Right?"

"Absolutely. Do you want to have dinner with me?"

She laughed under her breath at his earnest request. "I'm working tonight. Another time."

He slid out of the booth and held his hand out to her. She slipped across the seat and took it. His fingers locked with hers. Perfect. Strong. Warm. A little rough. That crackling charge that always happened when they touched shot up her arm.

He looked down at her, need in his eyes.

"I feel it, too," she answered his unspoken question.

"When are we going to do something about it?"

The guy who thought he wasn't good at talking to people could sure say what he wanted to her.

"When the time is right." Because right now wasn't it. They were just getting to know each other again.

She didn't want to go too fast and mess things up. This was too important. *He* was too important to her.

Now, if they could just get through this visit with Tanyar without Melody going ballistic on the abusive bitch.

CHAPTER SEVEN

Fox stared up at the old house and felt the same rush of anxiety he always felt when he came back here. Memories flooded his mind, along with the dread, fear, and desperation he'd always felt when he was trapped in this house.

Melody put her hand over his on the steering wheel. "You're safe. I won't let anything happen to you."

He turned and stared at her, knowing she meant those words. Because she had saved him from this place. From the torment.

She would never hurt him.

So why am I keeping a secret from her?

Because he didn't want her to turn out to be like so many others who'd changed when they found out.

He wanted Melody to always be the girl he remembered, the woman she was right now in this car. The one who only cared about him.

She didn't want anything from him. She just wanted to be with him.

Even for this trip back to the past, and the present that still sucked, but at least he wasn't going to get a beating. Not today. Never again.

Because if his mother ever laid a hand on him again, he'd be out the door for good. And he knew she didn't want that. Not now. Not when she needed him the most.

"Some days are good," he explained. "Some are bad. She can be...cranky."

"I've seen her be a royal bitch. She doesn't scare me. I don't care what she says, so long as she doesn't hurt you."

Fuck. This woman, she got to him so deep he didn't know if he'd ever be able to take losing her again. "The one thing I can tell is that she's trying to be on her best behavior when I'm here. We're strangers who share a bloody past, and still don't know how to talk to each other."

"It must be really hard to want her to be the person you imagine she could be in your head if only she tried. Or cared to do it. It must be incredibly disappointing and frustrating that she won't. You can't change someone who doesn't want to change."

No one had ever come close to understanding his complicated feelings about his mother and what it was like to be her son. "How do you understand that so clearly?"

"She taught me that lesson, same as you. When you're ready, you'll see her for who and what she really is and you'll know it's time to cut this anchor dragging you down."

I'm not there yet.

"She's dying. I can't turn my back on her. It's just not who I want to be."

She put her hand on his thigh. "You're a good man. If nothing else, you'll know in your head and heart that you did everything you could to make this relationship work. It's not you. It's most definitely her."

He laughed.

She eyed him. "You aren't the problem, Fox. She is. There is nothing wrong with you, and everything is wrong about her. She should have loved and protected you. She didn't. She only cared about herself."

"He beat her, too, sometimes."

Her lips pressed tight and anger filled her eyes. "The answer to that is not joining in when he beat you."

Those words hit him right in the chest. He hooked his hand at the back of her neck and pulled her into another of the amazing kisses they shared. "So fucking fierce."

"She is the abuser. You are the survivor. You should be smug when you walk in that door because you are a million times better than she will ever be. You have a life she could only dream of having because she's done nothing but wallow in self-pity and rail at the world that she deserved more and everyone should give it to her for no fucking reason at all."

Maybe it made him a little off, but he loved seeing her riled up on his behalf. She cared. For him, that mattered more than anything.

So fucking tell her the truth.

Still, he kept his secret. "Let's go." The sooner they got through this, the better. Plus, Melody had to be at work soon. That gave him an excuse to leave earlier than Tanya would expect.

She always tried to get him to stay as long as possible. She always complained about him living in town and not at her place. He simply couldn't stand to be in that house. The memories overtook him. Especially the more she tried to get him to do what she wanted with that tone that came into her voice sometimes. He remembered it well from the past.

Tanya and this place were best taken in small doses.

He met Melody at the front of his car and halted before going to the porch steps. "You didn't say anything about the car."

"It's awesome. What's not to like about a cherry-red Mustang Mach 1?"

He grinned. So easy to do with her. "Do you remember the car?"

She raised a brow. "Should I?"

"You gave me one for my seventh birthday in second grade."

She turned and stared at the car. "Seriously? You bought a life-size one because I gave you a *Hot Wheels*?"

He grinned. "Yes."

One side of her mouth drew back in a half grin. "You still have the toy, don't you?"

His most prized possession. "Yes. You don't give up the few gifts, or toys, you ever got. And they came from you. I kept all the memories and pieces of you I could."

She turned into him. "Fox. I don't know what to say to that. It's sweet and sad and you're so sentimental and adorable." She kissed his cheek.

"All of my memories of you are good ones. When I drive that car, when I look at it, I think about you."

She rose up on her toes, put her arms around him, and kissed him. The tenderness in it made his heart ache. Her soft lips, the feel of her body pressed along his, the way she made him feel alive and desired and special could send him to his knees. "Let's make a lot more happy memories together."

Those words held a world of promise, and he wanted to believe they had a future together more than anything.

He hadn't only come back here to help his mom. He'd come back for Melody.

"What the hell do you think you're doing bringing *that* girl here?"

Those words, that disgusted tone, the snap of anger in her words, made Fox's back teeth grind and a million memories come to life inside his head of her taunting and ridiculing him in that tone.

He glanced over at Tanya and barked, "Watch it."

Her eyes went wide for a second, then narrowed.

In that split second he realized she'd backed off for the first time ever. Why? Because he stood up to her? More likely because she wanted something from him.

That resourceful social worker had found more information on him than just where he worked and his contact information.

I hate that she knows my secret.

Tanya's eyes didn't soften, even if her voice did. "Why would you bring her here? She's the reason they took you from us."

"Really? Is that why Child Protective Services declared you unfit?" Melody glared daggers at Tanya.

Maybe this was a mistake.

He regretfully let Melody loose and turned to his mom. "Are you ready to talk about the past in a real way, or do you want to just keep living in an alternate universe where you're the only victim?"

Tanya jolted as if she caught herself before saying something, then let out a breath. She kept her chin high, eyes on him. "What's past is past. It can't be changed. Your father, God rest his soul, isn't here to defend himself."

He had no idea how she could speak of his father that way.

There was no excuse for what he did. What they did.

"She's putting it all on your dad," Melody whispered.

Tanya always did. She wanted him to absolve her of her complicity and treat her only as a victim. She wanted his sympathy and compassion. He'd lost any hint of those things for her when she'd hit him, too.

He didn't want to fight. It was pointless. She wouldn't apologize or find a drop of remorse for what she'd done. So he changed the subject as he walked toward her. "Did you take your meds?"

"The morning ones. Still need to take the afternoon ones. That pill thing you got me helps."

Yeah, he spent his Monday visits sorting her pills into three weekly containers so she knew what she'd taken in the morning, afternoon, and at night each day. Before, she'd had to figure out which ones to take once a day, twice, and three times. She got confused sometimes and couldn't remember if she'd taken something with all the bottles lined up in front of her, so she'd accidentally take one more than once. Luckily, she didn't have an adverse reaction, though he suspected there were times she took more pain meds than she was allowed each day. He couldn't blame her. After the hysterectomy and having part of her bowel removed, she'd been in a lot of pain, barely able to get out of bed.

Now, though, she was mobile and doing better, though the cancer had spread to her liver and lungs.

The drugs and chemo were only extending her life expectancy at this point, turning months into maybe more than a year if she was lucky. Though she had also gotten into a clinical trial a few months ago. Time would tell on that front. Ask her, she'd never been lucky in her life.

Bitter. Annoyed at the world and everyone around her. One of those people who just sucks the energy out of a room and you.

"You should have taken the midday ones with lunch."

"I was going to, but the pizza burned and set the toaster oven on fire."

"How bad is it?" He rushed past her and into the house and to the back kitchen.

She followed at a much slower pace.

He shook his head at the blackened toaster oven. A tall glass sat beside it.

"I tossed a glass of water on it. No harm done. But I do need a new toaster oven. Maybe one of those air fryer things I've seen on TV."

"I'll get you one tomorrow. I'll bring it with the groceries. Do you have a list for me?"

She pulled it off the fridge.

Melody stood behind them, watching everything.

He took the appliance and headed for the back door. "I'll put this in the trash and move the cans out to the road."

Melody knew the second the back door closed behind Fox, Tanya would pounce.

"You better stay away from my boy this time around. I won't have you filling his head with things."

As threats went, that one didn't even trip a warning bell inside her. "What things are you afraid I'll say to him? That you're not worth his time and energy after what you did to him? Because I already told him that's what I think. Hell, it's what everyone thinks. But Fox, despite what you did to him, is a good man. He believes in doing the right thing." She took a step toward Tanya and issued a warning the woman better believe was real. "So if you hurt him, if you make him regret helping you, you better watch your back, because I'll be coming for you."

"Don't you go thinking you're better than me when you're standing in my house."

"You know I'm better than you. So do us both a favor and treat him with every ounce of respect you can muster from your black soul, then I won't have to come after you, and you'll get to benefit from your son's good heart."

"What do you think you can do to me, little girl?"

Melody narrowed her gaze. "You've already done it for me. He sees right through you. You're never going to change. You'll never be sorry for what you did. It's just a matter of time before he's fed up with you and leaves."

Tanya glared daggers. "Fuck you."

So not a worthy opponent.

Melody didn't back down. "He's helping you even though he sees you're just using him. How long before you revert to your old ways and push him away?"

The woman's face turned deep red with rage.

"Careful. You should think about your health and what little time you have left." Melody sucked in a calming breath and tried to do something for Fox. "Find a way to make amends to him. You owe him that much."

"I'm his mother. I brought him into this world. Now he's a big shot with his own company. I don't owe him anything."

"And that's why you'll lose him again. He doesn't need you. He doesn't need this."

"So you know, too."

That got her attention. "Know what?"

Tanya studied her, looked her right in the eye like she expected to see something, then let out a laugh. "You don't know. He didn't tell you." She laughed again. "Maybe he doesn't care about you the way you think."

"We've just gotten started catching up. He's told me plenty about his past and how he grew up. How my dad helped him all these years."

Tanya's gaze went wide.

Smug satisfaction shot through her. "You didn't know that, did you?"

"No. All you Wildes are interfering assholes."

"We're so terrible for protecting an abused child. Oh, the shame we feel." She rolled her eyes. "If not for us, Fox might be dead."

"It wasn't that bad." Tanya snapped out her indignation.

"I'm sure you told yourself that over and over again those eight years Fox lived here with you and your bastard of a husband."

Tanya pointed a finger at her. "You don't know nothing about nothing."

"I know what Fox sounds like when it hurts for him to breathe because his ribs are bruised, cracked, or broken. I know the anguish I felt every time I looked into his eyes and saw nothing but pain and desperation and resignation that nothing would change. You two would never stop. I know he sometimes hoped that it would end and that he knew that end would be his death. I know the look of hunger in his eyes because he didn't get anything to eat all weekend and the desperation when he saw me Monday morning at school knowing I'd brought him food. I know what it's like to feel his arms wrap around me and shudder with the relief and longing he felt to be held with love. I know that you never gave him that. I know you don't deserve—"

"Melody, stop." Fox stood in the doorway, his gaze locked on her. "Just stop."

Tanya stepped closer to Fox. "The only thing I want is to spend time with my son. I need help. And he's offered it. Without him, I don't know what will happen to me. I need him."

She was using him. Worse, she was playing on his sympathy with that soft, pleading voice she used to spout those words.

Melody wanted to grab Fox and haul him out of there as fast as possible. But Melody caught the slight shake of Fox's head, telling her to leave it alone. She pressed her lips tight and kept her mouth shut.

"How about I make you something to eat, Tanya, before I have to get Melody to work."

For Fox, Melody held her tongue, went to the fridge, and stared at the contents. "I can whip together a ham and cheese omelet if you'd like." She turned and stared at Tanya's narrowed gaze. "Or if you have some canned tomatoes or even spaghetti sauce, I could make you some bagel pizzas with the cheese in here and the ham."

Fox's gaze went from her to Tanya and back again.

"Why would you do that?" Suspicion lit Tanya's eyes.

"Because I'd do anything for Fox. My mother taught me to cook. Me and all my siblings." She didn't miss the sharpening of Tanya's glare that she'd mentioned her mother had seen to it that her kids knew some basic skills and the only thing she'd taught Fox was pain and hurt. "So what'll it be?"

"The omelet I guess since I don't have the toaster oven."

"I can make the pizza bagel and pop it under the broiler."

"Oven doesn't work. Like a lot of things around here."

Fox folded his arms over his chest. "I'll get the toaster oven. You've got a new microwave. You said you didn't want me to get a new oven because you don't cook a lot."

Tanya gave Fox a wan smile. "I was just letting her know it doesn't work. That's all. You've been so generous, I didn't want to ask for too much, son."

Fox flinched at the reminder that he was home with a mother who'd hurt him.

It wasn't lost on her that he stood across the room from Tanya, his back to the door. The easiest and quickest exit.

He still saw his mom as a threat. Good. Maybe it would save him more heartache.

Chapter Eight

S ome strange sense that something was off made Melody take the long way around to work that evening. It took twice as long, but took her right past Tanya's place again. Sure enough, she spotted a very familiar beat-up orange Chevy truck in the drive, shotgun in the back window rack with a pot leaf bumper sticker. Like that wasn't an advertisement for Brian's business.

It didn't surprise her that a cancer patient wanted to buy some weed to help with the side effects from her treatment, though marijuana was still illegal in Wyoming. You could buy edibles, just not smoke a joint.

Whatever. None of her business.

She drove on, thinking about how she and Fox had parted after the visit with Tanya. He'd been quiet in the car. He'd felt a million miles away, not just a couple feet away. When he dropped her at her car, he thanked her for making Tanya lunch and doing all the dishes in the sink while Fox and Tanya chatted in the other room with a *Big Bang Theory* rerun playing in the background.

Tanya complained that she'd had to add an extra blanket to her bed because the heater in the house didn't work as well as it used to. Fox told her he'd get her a new oven and have someone come out to check the furnace. His business must be doing really well if he could afford to fix up Tanya's place without batting an eye.

He was trying to be a good son.

Tanya kept things cordial, but always seemed to work in a complaint about something that would cost Fox money.

She'd tried to bring it up with him in the car, but Fox simply put his hand on her knee, squeezed, and said, "I know what I'm doing. Don't worry about it."

But she did worry. About him. What this was costing him, both financially and emotionally. And what his mom was up to.

She pulled into the Dark Horse Dive Bar parking lot and left her old Bronco in her spot. The one she claimed every day anyway.

She used her keys to enter the big building and found Aria behind the bar and Lyric working in the kitchen.

"So, how did your first date with Fox go?" Aria's excitement made her grin even bigger.

The time they'd shared at the diner was... "Amazing. We caught up on the past, talked about moving forward."

Lyric walked out of the kitchen. "So it's serious? Up until now, you weren't sure if he was just stringing you along."

"Keeping things focused on now during our online chats was his way of getting to know me again, so I could get to know the grownup him, too. He apologized for not telling me it was him."

"But you got his point, didn't you?" Lyric asked, concern still in her gaze.

"Yes. I liked the online guy enough that I wanted to meet him in person and see if the connection we shared was real and could be what I'm looking for."

"And is it?" Aria asked.

"Now that I know it's him...it's a million times better. The way he looks at me...I can't describe it. It's like I feel it everywhere, all the way deep inside me." She turned to Lyric. "I thought the way Mason looked at you was special."

"It is," Lyric confirmed. "Everything he feels about me is in his eyes."

"I've dated lots of other guys." No need to sugarcoat it. She liked men. She liked a good time. She didn't apologize for trying to find someone who saw all of her, not just the outside, but everything inside she had to give. "Fox is different. Maybe because we have a history. We were such good friends. He never treated me differently because I was a girl. If he wanted to play baseball, we played baseball. If I wanted to stay in the classroom and draw, we did that." She thought about their talk today. "He wants me to come and teach a class at the New Adult Education Center in town. He thinks people could learn something from me about running my own business here at the bar and the Etsy shop I run."

"You'd be brilliant at that," Aria encouraged.

Lyric nodded her agreement. "Absolutely." Her head tilted. "You don't talk much about your business. At least not to us."

"It's mine." She didn't know what else to say. "We have this." She waved her hand to encompass the bar. She managed the waitstaff. Lyric the kitchen. Jax managed the bartenders. And Aria oversaw the bar as a whole, including ordering supplies and payroll. "I love it here, but I also needed something more creative."

"You don't really get to express that here. Except in the marketing and social media stuff you do with me." Lyric's insight eased Melody. She didn't want them to think she didn't love working at the bar. She did. And sometimes it just felt like too much work and no fun.

"Of course you'd need an outlet for that side of you. That's why Lyric sings and writes her amazing songs." Aria didn't have a second job or hobby. She'd had a boyfriend who she thought she was going to marry and start a family with until he cheated on her. Aria wanted a family. She wanted to be a mother. She wanted stability and someone she could trust.

Nick, Lyric's brother-in-law, sure seemed interested, but work kept him away too much.

"How are things with Nick?"

Aria leaned against her forearms on the bar. "Stalled out. We're both too busy to make the long-distance thing work."

"So it's over?" Lyric asked, concerned.

"No." Pain and confusion darkened Aria's blue eyes. "At least I don't think so. We still talk and text, but it's sporadic. It's not that I don't like him, I just want more than a day here and there when our schedules finally line up." Aria held Melody's gaze because that's how she'd felt about her relationship with Fox until he finally met her IRL. In real life was way better than online messaging. Mostly because there was kissing. But also, when they talked and she could look him in the eye and see the emotion there, she didn't second-guess whether it was real. She saw it plain on his face and heard it in every word.

What she had with Fox was special.

This time, nothing would tear them apart.

She and her sisters got back to work. Hours later, the bar was packed, the music was loud, the drinks were flowing, and she spotted Fox and Dean headed right for her. Luckily, she had an empty tray in her hand or she'd have spilled a lot of drinks when Fox wrapped his arms around her waist, hauled her close, and kissed her like he'd never get to do it again.

The passion flared and she lost herself in the press of his lips, the sweep of his tongue gliding over hers, and the heat that swept through her, making her press closer to all those lean, hard muscles. His rain-on-the-wind-with-a-hint-of-lime scent wrapped around her.

He squeezed her tight, then slowly ended the kiss and looked down at her. "Missed you."

"I'm not sure you convinced me yet. Kiss me again."

He flashed a grin, then swooped in for another kiss.

Several whistles sounded and one, "Get a room."

She didn't care about their audience.

He wasn't putting on a show. He was as lost to the magic happening between them as she was.

"I need a beer," Dean announced. "And a woman." She felt the brush of his hand on her shoulder as he walked by. "Hi, Melody. Good to see you, Melody. Nice job keeping my boy happy." The last words were nearly swallowed by the noise of the music and crowd.

She couldn't answer because she was too focused on the man blowing her mind and making her panties wet with just a kiss. It took some effort and came with a lot of regret, but she pulled back, tried to catch her breath, and smiled up at Fox. "I believe you now."

"Happy to keep on proving it to you." He glanced around them. "Somewhere private. Where I have you all to myself for many, many hours. Days."

Her wild heart and a huge case of lust made her blurt out, "I could come to your place when I get off shift." She hadn't been thinking about sleeping with him tonight. Soon, yes. But this thing between them was just getting stronger and it felt like she'd been waiting for him forever. More than that. She hadn't just been waiting for Fox to come back into her life; she'd been waiting for someone who made her feel more than sparks but passion based in friendship and connection and trust.

Fox's gaze went wide, then heated with desire. "I'd love that, but are you sure? I don't want to go too fast and fuck this up. It means too much to me to rush when we have as much time as you need."

She'd said at the diner that they should go slow. But... "I know what I want, Fox. It's you. It's us."

He cupped her face, his fingers brushing her skin as he leaned down, put his forehead to hers, and looked deep into her eyes like no one was watching and they weren't in a crowd. "I am so fucking lucky."

You're going to get lucky later.

She wished she could take the rest of the night off and just leave with him.

Someone bumped into her from behind and she crashed into Fox.

He held her close and glared at the person behind her. "Watch it."

"Sorry. My bad."

Melody knew that voice and turned to Brian with a raised brow. He'd been kicked out of the bar so many times, she was surprised to see him back again.

Brian held up his hands in surrender. "I'm just here playing pool with some friends." His gaze swept down her, then back up. "Damn, Mel, but you get hotter every time I see you."

While she liked bad boys, this one was nothing but trouble. A mistake waiting to happen for any woman who got involved with him. She'd never been that dumb.

Brian was only out for himself. He didn't care who got hurt because of him. He'd put the blame on others and sell out his mother if it kept him out of jail.

"You get a little rougher around the edges every time I see you. You've been keeping some interesting company lately."

"You know me, Mel, I have lots of friends I like to visit."

"Uh-huh. Just make sure you keep your business off my property and out of my bar."

Brian held his arms out wide. "I'm just here for a good time, like everyone else." His hands dropped and his gaze shot to Fox, who still had his hands on her waist. "Who's your new friend?"

She didn't buy his bullshit. "You know Fox. We went to grade school together." She glanced up at Fox. "Do you remember Brian from second grade?"

His gaze narrowed, a vague sense of recognition in his eyes. "I think I remember you."

Brian held out his hand. "It's been a long time."

Fox reached around her to shake. "You were a really good baseball player. Pitcher, right?"

Brian seemed stunned for a moment. "Yeah. Then I tore a bunch of stuff in my shoulder and all those big league dreams went out the window." So did his college scholarship, and then pain killers became an addiction that derailed his life and took him down a dark path until he was selling drugs instead of hitting home runs.

She felt sorry for high school Brian, but not the man standing before her. He'd had a long time to change his ways and make a better life for himself. He used what happened to him as an excuse for why his life was so shitty, instead of working for a better future.

Some people just didn't know how to cut the anchor of the past and move on.

Yeah, that went for her and Fox, too.

Maybe they were all just doing the best they could in the moment and she needed to ease up on herself and others.

Brian pointed behind him. "Me and some friends are shooting pool. Join us. I'll buy you a beer and you can tell me what happened after Melody got you taken away from your parents."

"Subtle," she snapped at Brian, knowing he was just poking at her because she'd never given him the time of day.

Fox took a step in front of her. "Melody saved my life. She's not to blame for what happened to me. Anyone who says she is, is wrong."

Brian did that whole surrender thing, holding up his hands like he was harmless. *Hardly.* "My bad, man. I didn't mean any disrespect to her or you. It's just...that shit was a big deal back in the day. Everyone wondered what happened to you."

"I lived," Fox said, so matter-of-fact, but with an end-of-story point to it. He wasn't about to open up old wounds to satisfy anyone's curiosity.

Brian tilted his head. "Why didn't I hear you were back in town? I'd think everyone would be talking about it."

Fox shrugged. "I like to keep a low profile and focus on work."

Melody bet he'd anticipated the town gossip and used Dean or others at the center to help get things set up and done for him.

"Come on, man. Hang with us." Brian grabbed Fox's shoulder and pushed him toward the back. "Bring us a round, hot stuff. On me."

Fox glanced back at her with an I've-got-this glint in his eyes.

She rolled hers, headed to the bar to get them a pitcher of beer, and met Dean on his way back to catch up with Fox. She stopped right in front of him. "Keep an eye on Fox with Brian back there. The tall blond, who looks like he's been stoned his whole life."

Dean raised a brow and his gaze narrowed in on the group at the pool table. "What's his deal?"

"Using people. Manipulating them. Taking everything he can get from them." He'd left a trail of unhappy girls in high school as he used them and discarded them for the next conquest. As a high school jock, it hadn't been hard to find willing girls desperate to be with the most popular boy in school. But with his downfall came an even darker side to Brian. He'd blackmailed some of the very people he sold drugs to and punished others for not being able to pay up.

The golden boy's crown had turned as black as his heart.

She didn't know how someone could be so callous about other people's lives. He kept pushing his poison, and they kept buying. He preyed on the weak and benefited from their pain.

After what he'd been through, she thought he'd be more sympathetic. As far as she could tell, he didn't seem to care.

Dean's gaze swung back to her. "On it." And he walked away with an even more determined stride than usual.

She sidled up to the bar and placed her tray down on the counter. "I need a pitcher for four." She turned and watched Fox break at the pool table.

Fox looked serious. Competitive. And sank two balls.

Admiration and surprise lit Brian's gaze as he stared at Fox.

Dean sat on a stool watching the byplay like this was nothing new.

And there was Josh right behind Brian. She'd never understood their unlikely friendship. The jock and the quiet kid in class. After high school, Josh had gone to a nearby junior college for a couple of years. Now, he worked in town at his father's tire store.

He seemed to know she was looking his way and held her gaze. Something in it always seemed desperate.

They'd dated briefly a couple of years ago. Three dates in, he had showed up at the bar, said he didn't like her short skirt and low-cut tee, every guy in the bar was staring at her tits and ass, and she should go home and change. Yeah. No. That didn't fly. They got in an argument. He apologized for being a dick. She gave him a second chance. Two dates later, they ran into one of her exes in a restaurant. When Tom slid his hand across her waist and pulled her close to kiss her on the cheek in greeting because they'd remained friendly, Josh shoved him away and they nearly got into a fight. She ended things right then and there.

She liked a protective guy, not a possessive, controlling one.

Fox knew how to make her feel like she belonged to him without making her feel like she was a possession or trophy.

"Melody, you going to stand there all day staring at that hot piece of ass or are you going to make some money?" Aria groused behind her.

Her gaze shifted to Fox. She could look at him all day and night and never get tired of the view. "I like him more than money." *I like him more than anything.*

She took the tray and weaved her way through the tables to the back of the bar.

One of the other waitresses stepped in front of her. "I thought Brian was banned."

"Keep an eye on him. You catch him dealing in here, you tell John to bounce him hard and fast." Melody continued on, set the tray on Josh's table, and set the pitcher and glasses down.

Brian came up behind her, real close, too close for comfort, and dropped a wad of fives and ones on her tray. "Thanks, baby."

She grabbed the tray and pulled it toward her, elbowing Brian in the gut in the process to get him to back off. "Not your baby." She glanced up at him. "Behave."

His gaze narrowed. "I'm not a toddler."

Before she could snap, *Then don't act like one,* Josh grabbed her arm. "It's been too long, Mel. We should go out."

She glanced at his hand on her, then met Josh's gaze. "I'm—"

"Seeing me," Fox said, coming up beside her and crowding Josh as he glared daggers. "So hands off."

Josh slowly took his hand away and backed up a step. "Didn't you just get to town?"

Fox hooked his arm around her shoulders. "Been here a couple months on and off." He kissed Melody on the side of the head. "Should I know him, too?"

"Josh wasn't in our classes but went to the same school. You probably saw him around back then."

Fox turned to Josh. "Sorry. Don't remember. It's been a long time."

Josh glanced from her to Fox, his expression tense. "And now you're back and she's with you."

Brian poured a beer and handed the glass to Fox. "Some guys have all the luck."

Melody didn't know how to respond to the compliment.

Fox held her tighter. "I didn't want to let a good thing go." He kissed her forehead.

She didn't want to be let go, but she had a lot of tables to catch up on. But first... "I need a word." She cocked her head for Fox to follow her away from Josh and Brian. When they were out of earshot, she put her hand on his shoulder, went up on tiptoe, and whispered in his ear, "Brian is the local drug dealer. It's the worst-kept secret in town. You don't want to be associated with him, especially when you're trying to help so many at the center you just opened. Now laugh like I said something funny."

Fox did as she asked and brushed his fingers along her cheek. "Always looking out for me, aren't you?"

"Always. Now have one beer, kick his ass at pool, then get the hell away from him." She brushed a quick kiss on his lips, then turned to get back to work. She felt Fox's eyes on her and turned back to catch the grin on his face and desire in his eyes. She swung her hips just a bit more for his enjoyment.

She couldn't wait to see him again later tonight at his place.

Chapter Nine

Melody parked outside the apartment complex she'd watched change as construction crews refurbished the old building. Rumor was someone from out of town bought the building, renovated, then never advertised for renters, though judging by the cars, there were plenty of folks living here.

Now she guessed that Fox must be the out-of-town owner.

Fox had given her the code to enter the building and she admired the clean and spacious lobby area with mailboxes on the right next to a door that had a PACKAGES sign and a lock that required you type in a code. A security camera surveilled the area.

She hit the button on the elevator and the doors immediately opened. She stepped in and hit number 4. She exited on the top floor, turned to the left, and found Fox standing in an open door down the hall in nothing but a pair of low-slung jeans, showing off lots of abs, his wide chest and shoulders, strong arms, and sleepy grin.

"Hey," he called out softly.

She raised a brow. "How'd you know I was here?" She'd texted him before she left the bar, wondering if he was still up for her coming over tonight, or if he'd fallen asleep and she should just go back to her place. He'd texted back immediately saying, *I can't wait to see you.*

"I can monitor the camera feed downstairs from my phone or laptop."

Of course her tech dude could do that.

She glanced at the door across from his. "Dean's place."

"How'd you know?"

"Good guess you'd keep your brother close."

He hooked his arm around her neck and pulled her close. "How do you do that?"

Her cheek pressed to his bare chest and his heart pounded beneath her ear. Such a reassuring and strong sound. "What did I do?"

"You understand."

She looked up at him. "I try, because you matter. And I want to know the you that you are now."

He pulled her into his place, backing up and pushing the door closed.

She glanced around the open living room and kitchen area. "Wow. This place is not what I expected."

He let her loose and glanced around the place. "You don't like it?" He punched in a code on the alarm keypad by the door.

"I love it. I wish I had a place like this." It was spacious and clean and completely updated with white cabinets, black countertops, an island that sat four. Stainless steel appliances and brushed nickel fixtures. Recessed lighting and black pendent lights over the bar. In the living space sat a long black leather sofa, wood coffee and end tables, a black entertainment center with a huge flat-screen TV. On the right she spotted a doorway that led to what looked like an office. On the left a bathroom. And behind her, past the huge pantry cupboards, was a door to his bedroom. "How big is this place?"

"About eighteen hundred square feet. When I renovated the building, I expanded some of the units. Most on this floor for me, Dean, and Max. There's one smaller unit at the other end we can use for guests, though we haven't had any. The first three floors are for the teachers and employees for the center. There's another apartment building a block up where the students stay. Those units are much smaller."

She tilted her head and studied him. "I know the tech world is lucrative, but...you own all this?"

His lips pressed tight. "Yes."

She shook her head, then smiled at him. "It's really impressive what you've done to give back."

His eyes went wide. "Thank you."

"You're welcome." She pressed her hand to his cheek and brushed her thumb under his eye. "What were you doing before I got here? Because you look tired."

"I was working in the office."

"I guess your company doesn't run itself."

"No. And I've been away for a while now. I can do a lot remotely, but I've got to head back soon for a couple of days."

"Really?"

"Yeah." He grinned. "Want to come with me?"

"Um. Maybe." She could probably take a couple of days off. Her siblings would cover for her if she asked, which she hardly ever did. She was usually the one who covered for everybody else.

She brushed a kiss against his lips and trailed her fingers over his amazing abs. Seriously, how did a guy who spent his days coding get abs like that? "But first, you should take me to bed?"

Fox took her by the hips and pulled her close. "I have wanted you for so long. Not sure how long I'm going to last the first time. But I'll make it up to you the second and third and fourth. Promise." He took her mouth in a ravenous kiss that heated her blood and made her grab onto his sides so tight her nails bit into his skin.

He didn't seem to mind. In fact, he picked her up and held her close, so he could change the angle of the kiss, his tongue sweeping deep into her mouth, sliding along her tongue. He tasted like chocolate and peanut butter.

"What were you eating?" she asked against his lips.

"Protein bar." He carried her into the bedroom. Light spilled in from the attached bathroom. "Need it to spend the night making you feel nothing but pleasure." With that declaration, he leaned over, pulled back the bedcovers, then laid her out on the bed.

She wanted to keep kissing him and holding him, but he slipped from her arms, stood by the bed, grabbed her foot, unzipped her boot, and pulled it and her sock off. He used both hands to massage her foot and she moaned like it was the best thing ever, because damn his hands were magic on her sore foot. She'd been hustling around the bar from table to table for hours. He did the same with her other foot and she lost track of time, closing her eyes and enjoying every second of what he was doing to her.

It wasn't lost on her that he was taking care of her. She needed it. She often put herself last and pushed herself too hard. It felt nice to let someone do something nice for her for a change. He had her willing and desperate for sex, but he didn't dive on top of her and take. No. Not Fox. He wanted to make her feel good. He cared.

Tears gathered in her closed eyes and a tear slid free and into her hair on both sides of her face.

Fox's hands stilled, then he gently set her foot on the bed, and crawled over her, his hips settling between her thighs, and his thumb brushed away the tear on one side of her face. She didn't open her eyes, she just leaned into the sweet touch.

"What's wrong?"

She didn't want him to think he'd done something to upset her. She opened her eyes and found him staring down at her, concern clouding his blue eyes. "You...make me feel so much."

"Oh, Mel, all I want to do is make you feel how much I want you. More than just as a friend. I want you to be mine."

She got that by the way he'd let Brian and Josh know tonight that they were together. She liked that he didn't want any other guy trying to get with her. Because she only wanted to be with him.

He kissed her again and rocked his hips to hers, his hard length brushing against her sensitive folds.

Not enough though. There were too many barriers between them.

She wrapped her arms around his back and held him close as he laid a trail of kisses down her neck, his hand skimming over her chest and covering her breast. He molded it to his palm and brushed his thumb over her aching nipple. She arched her back, pressing into his warm palm. "Fox." His name came out as a greedy plea.

He slipped his hand under her shirt and pulled it up and over her head. He stared down at her full breasts encased in a fuchsia-colored bra. "Damn." He kissed the swell of her breast and slid his hand to her back to unhook it, then pulled the barrier away and tossed it off the bed. His gaze blazed down at her.

She wrapped her legs around his hips and rubbed herself against him.

"Fuck that feels good." He lowered his head and took her nipple in his mouth, sucking and laving as he gripped her hip in one hand and pressed his hard cock to her clit.

Their clothes needed to go. She needed him. Desperately.

"Fox."

He kissed a trail from one breast to the other and licked her other nipple, then sucked it gently and blew some air over the tightened bud, making her groan.

"Oh, I like that sound." The deep rumble of his voice sounded like a purr.

"Stop teasing."

He answered that by licking her nipple again, then taking it into his warm mouth.

Suddenly he was tugging the button free on her jeans and unzipping them. He left her breast to pull her jeans and panties down her legs. They went the way of her bra.

Then he was just staring at her laid out on the bed, naked, wanting him. "I need you." She ached for him. She wanted to be filled with him. She wanted to make him hers.

Instead of ditching his clothes, he leaned over and kissed her knee, then her thigh, then her hips. His hands settled over her breasts and squeezed as he placed another openmouthed kiss on her belly, then sank lower and licked her pussy from bottom to top, the tip of his tongue flicking against her clit. She rolled her hips and her sex up to his mouth and his tongue sank into her.

"You fucking taste like heaven." Fox had a dirty mouth during sex.

She liked it. She liked everything he was doing to her. Especially when he sank one finger deep inside her and stroked her.

His gaze shot up to hers. "You are so fucking gorgeous." He thrust two fingers into her and sucked her clit.

Her eyes rolled back as she moaned his name.

He kept working his fingers in and out of her as his tongue did wicked things to her clit and the tension coiled and she could feel her orgasm building.

"Give it to me." That guttural order sent her over the edge as wave upon wave of pleasure washed through her. Fox kissed her inner thigh and slowly withdrew his fingers, setting off a round of aftershocks.

He finally ditched his clothes.

The man was glorious naked. Abs and rippling muscles for days. Wide shoulders, lean hips. His big, thick cock stood proud.

Her mouth watered. With her eyes glued to him, she reached up.

"One sec." He pulled a condom from the nightstand drawer beside her and rolled it on, then settled back between her legs and kissed her like a hungry man. It was all tongue and desperation as the head of his cock nudged her wet, slippery entrance.

She wrapped her legs around his waist and pulled him in as he plunged deep. He filled her, stretching her sensitive walls, and she let out a sigh and rocked into him, taking him just a bit deeper.

He swore, pulled out, then plunged back in, his breath coming out a sultry groan. "You feel so fucking fantastic, Mel." He took her mouth again and kept up a slow but steady rhythm as his dick moved in and out of her, his length gliding against her clit each time he sank into her.

She had one arm around his back, her other hand on one ass cheek. He had a really firm ass. Her nails raked his back as he increased the tempo and slammed into her, setting off another orgasm. Her tight core clenched at him as he continued to rock in and out, setting off more aftershocks as he slammed into her one last time, his body tense as his cock pulsed inside her.

She pulled Fox into her arms and he collapsed on top of her, his face in her neck. He pressed his lips to her pounding pulse point, then licked the spot. She held him close and never wanted to let him go.

The quiet settled around them. She didn't feel the need to fill the silence. Not with him. She heard everything he didn't say in the way he held her. His body covered hers. His fingers played with her hair. His breathing evened out with a soft moan of pleasure as she stroked his back with her fingertips.

"Will you stay?"

"Someone made promises about doing this two, three, and four times. I intend to collect."

He raised himself up on his forearms and looked down at her. "No. I mean, will you stay with me?" His parents had hurt him and abandoned him to the system. He had no siblings. His closest friends had become his brothers. God knew how many families had taken him in, then let him go.

As kids, they'd been torn apart, too young to do anything about it.

They weren't those kids anymore. This time, they'd made the choice to come back together and build a better relationship.

She understood his need to know that she would never walk away.

She cupped his face and looked him in the eye. "I'm not going any-where."

He kissed her, the passion banked by a tenderness that melted her heart. "I'll be right back." He slipped from the bed and walked naked into the bathroom.

With the light on in there, she got a perfect glimpse of him in all his glory before he disappeared from view to ditch the condom. But he turned off the light and came right back as promised and slid in beside her, pulling her back to his chest and into his arms, then he rolled onto his back with her lying on top of him, one hand over her breast, the other on her belly.

"What are you doing?"

"This," he whispered in her ear and slid his hand down her stomach and over her mound, where his fingers slid through her soft, wet folds. He stroked her slowly, tenderly, making her legs fall apart and a moan pass her lips. The hand on her breast molded her flesh to his palm as he squeezed her nipple between two fingers.

She rocked her sex against his fingers. He sank one, then two deep, keeping up a slow and steady pull and plunge as his thumb stroked her clit. Pleasure pooled low in her belly. Her clit was so sensitive after the last two orgasms that it only took a few masterful strokes to have her panting and writhing on top of him before she let go and the pleasure pulsed through her.

Fox hugged her close and held her as she relaxed into him, the sense of utter bliss filling her. "You are so beautiful in every way." He turned to his side so she was lying beside him. He settled in, his face pressed to her hair. He probably thought they'd get some sleep.

She had other ideas for the swelling cock nestled against her ass. This time, she reached for the condom, then turned to him. She nudged him back onto his back and straddled his thighs.

"Baby, I thought you might be tired after your shift." He was so sweet.

"I'm not done with you quite yet." She stroked his long, thick length in her fist.

He hissed, then sucked in a ragged breath.

"You like that."

"I like everything you do to me."

That got her even hotter. "Good. Because I want you." She rolled the condom on him, then moved up, brushing her sex along his hard length before she reached between them, placed his dick at her entrance, and sank down on him.

He groaned and clamped his hands on her hips. "Nothing has ever felt like you." He rocked his hips into her deeper, harder as she rose and plunged back down on him. He pulled her down for a kiss, then left her mouth to suck her nipples as she rocked and rolled her hips over his hard length, the pleasure building in both of them.

Melody rode him fast and hard.

Fox slid his fingers to where they were joined and stroked her clit. She went off like a rocket and his hands clamped onto her hips and held her down on him as his orgasm slammed into him. The pleasure was so intense and pleasurable she let out a soft giggle as she fell on top of him.

He kissed her on the head and wrapped his arms around her. "You fucking blow my mind."

"Sex has almost always been fun. A release. A moment to feel connected. But with you..."

"What?"

"It's a whole other level. It's not good. It's not great. It's amazing. Everything I hoped it could be with the right person."

He was still inside her. She could feel his heart beating against hers. His breathing matched hers. They were in perfect sync. At least, that's how it felt.

And she'd never felt like this. Like even the thought of losing this, him, would break her heart.

"Melody, look at me."

She lifted her head and stared at him in the quiet darkness.

"You were my everything when we were kids." He cupped her face and kissed her softly. "You still are, my sweet Dee."

He hadn't called her Dee since they were kids. It brought back so many good memories. Especially when they were in preschool and he could barely say Melody. It always sounded like "Eldy." After a while, he had just gone with Dee.

She loved having a nickname.

She loved that he gave it to her and was the only one who used it.

"You remember," he said.

"I never forgot anything about you."

He kissed her softly, then pulled her back down on him and into his arms. She listened to his breathing even out along with hers as they fell asleep and into sweet dreams for both of them, she hoped, because he was back and they were just getting started on making new happy memories.

CHAPTER TEN

Fox turned off the light in the bathroom before he opened the door and stepped out. He didn't want to wake Melody. He'd woken her an hour ago for a third round of the most amazing sex he'd ever had in his life. Now, she lay in his bed on her stomach, her head turned toward him, one arm stretched out to where he'd been beside her until he dragged his ass out of bed for work. Since she was on her stomach, the swell of her breast rounded at her ribcage. The honey-sweet taste of her seemed to bloom on his tongue even now. The sheet barely covered her heart-shaped ass and gorgeous legs. He could still feel how they wrapped around him.

"Is that her?" Awe filled Max's voice.

Fox's head snapped to the doorway and Max, standing there staring into the dark room at his...Melody.

"Get the fuck out!" He whisper-barked the order, then turned back to make sure they hadn't woken a naked Melody.

Max's shit-eating grin infuriated Fox. "Who could take their eyes off that sexy scene?"

Wearing nothing but a towel wrapped around his hips, he shoved Max out of the room and closed the door behind him. "Hands and eyes off."

Max just laughed it away.

Fox raked his fingers through his damp hair. "What are you doing here?"

"I came to get you up to speed on the call we have this morning with CrossTec. I didn't know she was here." Max kept his voice down, but his eyes went to the closed door. The fucker was probably imagining Melody lying naked between the sheets in his bed.

"When did you even get here?" Fox thought Max was still back at the company headquarters in Boston.

"Late last night. I was tired, so I crashed and thought we'd meet up this morning. Is Dean up?"

As if Dean had heard his name, he came walking in the front door.

Fox regretted giving them both a key. Of course he had their keys, too. And they'd always had an open-door policy for each other.

What if she'd walked out here naked to get a glass of water or something and they walked in?

He'd have to warn her, because he didn't want Dean and Max to think he chose her over them. She already understood his brothers were important to him.

Dean's gaze narrowed on him. "You're not dressed."

"I got a late start."

Max grinned. "Because of the naked woman in your bed."

"Yes," he snapped. "Because of her." *And I'd like to still be in that bed with her.*

"Melody's here?" Dean eyed the closed door. "Damn. Nice. Congrats, man. You got her back. Like for real, you two are together now."

"What have I missed?" Max asked.

"Our boy here finally made his move on his dream girl." Dean and Max shared an approving look. "Oh, I forgot to tell you last night. Your girl warned me about those two locals. Brian and Josh. I did some digging. Brian has a record. Mostly possession and a couple minor intent to sell. Dude knows his business and how not to get caught is all that tells me. Josh is nearly squeaky clean. He's got a parking ticket he hasn't paid, a speeding ticket, and one assault incident where he was hit first, but the guy who hit him claimed Josh was assaulting a woman in the parking lot. He wasn't charged because the woman said she was drunk, he hit on her, things got handsy in the parking lot, she changed her mind and pushed him away, but he didn't stop before the other guy came to her rescue."

"That is fucked up," Fox said, raking his hand through his still-damp hair.

Dean nodded. "Yeah. So he's not our kind of people."

They'd seen a lot of shit happen growing up in foster care and they steered clear of people who liked to hurt others and take what wasn't offered. They'd all been victims of it themselves in some way, shape, or form.

"I don't think Melody liked them at all, though she put up with them. I noticed the waitresses working the back of the bar kept an eye on Brian." Fox had kept his eye on Melody most of the night, though she handled herself well with the drunk and flirty customers. For the most part, no one took advantage of her. They'd probably learned a lesson a time or two trying.

She didn't take any shit.

She stood up for herself and those who worked for her.

He liked that about her.

Fox was tired of standing around practically naked with his buddies. "They're off our radar. We've got other business to handle. I'll meet you guys downstairs in ten."

"Is it everything you hoped it would be?" Max asked, because Fox only confided his most personal feelings with them.

"No." Before he could say more, a soft gasp sounded behind him.

They all turned toward her, standing in the open bedroom door, her in one of his T-shirts. She looked adorably rumpled and awesome in his shirt as it draped over her curves and hit her mid-thigh.

But he did not like the devastated look on her face. "It's a billion times better than what I hoped it would be."

She leaned her shoulder against the doorframe, stared at him, and a huge smile lit up her whole face. "Is that right?"

"The dreams I had of you don't even come fucking close to the outstanding reality that is you."

Her grin widened. "Such a filthy mouth on a guy built like a god."

Now he grinned. She'd surprised him. And just looking at her made him hard. Which was why he kept his back to his friends. "I'll meet you both downstairs."

"We have a meeting in less than half an hour," Max reminded him.

"I'll be there. But first..." He walked toward Melody, who couldn't possibly miss his intention with the way he'd tented the towel at his waist.

The only thing that signaled his buddies had left was the closing of his front door.

Melody looked up at him as he stopped in front of her. "You didn't introduce me to your friend."

"I'm not doing introductions when you're naked."

She looked down at the shirt she'd put on. "I hope you don't mind my borrowing this."

"You can have anything of mine you want. And it's better than him seeing you naked again."

Her eyebrow shot up. "Again?"

He scrunched his lips. "Full disclosure. They both have keys to this place. We come and go from each other's apartments all the time. So don't be surprised if you're here and they just walk in."

"Um. Okay."

"And as much as I love you naked, maybe keep that in our bedroom. Just so I don't have to beat the shit out of my brothers."

"Wouldn't it be my fault for walking around naked if they saw me?"

"Don't care. You can do whatever you want. They don't get to see it. You're all mine."

She went up on tiptoe and brushed a kiss against his lips. "That's sweet. But I only got up because I thought something was wrong when I heard all the voices."

He took her by the hips and walked her backward toward the bed. "Everything is fine. Max just wanted to go over some stuff before our call."

"Shouldn't you get dressed for work then?"

"After."

"After what?" She gave him a teasing grin.

"I promised you a fourth time. I was going to let you sleep and make it up to you later, but…"

"I don't want to make you late." The back of her legs hit the bed. She sat and scooted back, then lay down, tempting him with those legs and the barely there hint of her sex as the shirt rode up.

He pulled the towel off and dropped it on the floor. "I'm still learning all the things you like. All the things that make you fucking moan and gasp and get me so fucking hot I think I'll explode."

"That mouth."

"Where do you want it?"

"We don't seem to have a lot of time."

"I'll make time for you." He'd do anything for her.

She bent her knees and spread her thighs wide as she pulled off the T-shirt and tossed it. "Then I want you to make me come with that dirty mouth, then fuck me hard and fast so you can make your meeting."

"You're so fucking perfect." He practically dove onto the bed, hooking his arms around her thighs as he licked her pretty pink flesh, circling her clit with his tongue. She was already turned on and wet, but he wanted her writhing on the bed. So he lapped at her and thrust his tongue into her. She rocked her hips to his rhythm and moaned. She was getting there, but he wanted her wild, so he slipped one finger into her and sucked on her clit as he thrust his finger in and out of her. He could feel her body tighten with tension and slid another finger inside her, stretching her delicate walls.

"Fox. Oh god. Yes. Keep doing that."

He lapped at her clit with the tip of his tongue then pressed on it, his tongue flat and soft against her.

She exploded, her sweet release like honey in his mouth.

He left her long enough to grab a condom from the drawer and roll it on. She stared up at him, her legs splayed apart, her chest rising and falling with her fast breaths. She looked incredible.

He took her by the hips, rolled her over, then pulled her up on her knees.

She raised herself up on her hands and glanced back at him over her shoulder. "Start slow, so I can find a good position. You're much taller than me. Then you can let go."

He loved that she gave him some direction. He never wanted to hurt her. And she was right. Their height difference mattered in this case. So he spread his knees a bit wider on the bed so he was lower and in line with her hips. He nudged the head of his cock against her wet folds, slowly sinking in to the hilt. "You good?"

She rocked back into him, sighed, and said, "Oh, yes."

He pulled out slowly and slammed back in. With his hands on her hips, he controlled how far she could move.

"I said let go."

He gave her what they both wanted, but he built the tempo, getting into it as she moved with him, making sure she was feeling every inch of him with pleasure. It washed over him with each pounding thrust. His lower back tingled and his balls drew up; his release was imminent but... "I want you with me. Touch yourself." He needed to keep his grip on her.

She lowered her chest and head to the bed.

He loved the view and the new angle.

Her hand and arm disappeared beneath her and he felt the brush of her fingertip touching herself and him as he drove into her.

She moaned.

That sweet sound made him want to come right then, but he held out, sensing she was close as her inner muscles tightened around his cock. And then her panting turned into a series of moans as her release hit, triggering his. He pulled her hips tight to his and held her there as his release surged through him. He'd never felt anything this intense.

She lifted up. He released her hips, and she fell forward onto the mattress with a bounce just before she rolled over and stared up at him. He fell beside her and kissed the side of her breast because it was right there.

She gasped, then let out a pleasure-filled hum. "That was..."

"Amazing. Again."

She rolled toward him so they were lying face-to-face. "That was a really great way to start the day."

He glanced at the clock on the nightstand and winced. "I'm sorry we woke you up so early. You can stay as long as you like and get some more sleep."

"I should probably go home, since you're going to work."

"You can stay. I like you here."

"Is that what you say to all the women you bring home?" she teased.

But there was a serious question in there. And he had no trouble answering it. "I don't bring women home."

She raised a brow.

"I mean, don't get me wrong. I've dated. Like I told you before, I'm not great at talking to people. It takes me a while to get comfortable."

"So you went to their place because you weren't comfortable with them in your space?"

"Yes. And..."

"What?"

"You fit here. You fit me. You're sweet and kind and independent and feisty and you have such a huge heart. No one ever compared to you. No one is in your league. I didn't want them in *my* bed. I didn't let them into my heart. Because I was always coming back to you."

She placed her hand on his cheek and kissed him softly. "What took you so long?"

"I was afraid that what we had back then wouldn't be what we had now. I didn't want those memories tainted if the reality of us now didn't live up to my memories of you."

"You thought that maybe I changed so much that I wouldn't love you like I loved you then."

He knew she was talking about the kind of love you had for a dear friend. He wanted more. But he'd take that for now. "Yes. After I said that I hated you, I thought you'd hate me back and forget all about me."

"That is just not possible. I will never forget you, no matter what happens next between us."

He kissed her, then looked into her beautiful blue eyes. "I hoped we'd have this and so much more, but I never let myself really believe it would come true."

"I'm here, Fox. I'm not going anywhere. You make me happy. In case the many orgasms didn't convince you." She grinned. "But we have more than just great sex. All those weeks we chatted online...I haven't felt that close to someone since...well, you."

His phone buzzed with an incoming call on the nightstand. "Crap. I'm late." He reached for the phone the second he jumped out of bed, then frowned at the caller ID. "Tanya. Is everything okay?"

"No. This place is falling apart around me."

"What's wrong?"

"The pipe under the kitchen sink cracked. There's water everywhere. And my ride to the doctor fell through."

Fox raked his hand over his head. "Okay. I'll, um, be there soon."

"Thank you. You're such a good son."

He rolled his eyes and hung up.

Melody was on the other side of the bed, pulling on her jeans over her sexy panties. She already had her bra on and pulled her shirt over her head. "Do you know where I left my bag?"

"It's on the kitchen island."

"Okay. What does Tanya need?"

"A plumber and a ride," he called from the bathroom as he ditched the condom and cleaned up.

She tucked in the shirt and finger combed her hair in the mirror from behind him. "Okay. You better get dressed or you'll miss your meeting."

He turned and stared at her. "I can't go to the meeting now. I'll have to reschedule."

"You go do your thing. I've got Tanya covered."

He stared at her, still not believing what was happening. "What?"

"Dean and Max are waiting for you. Hurry up."

"Melody, you don't have to..."

"I know. I volunteered. I'm up. I've got a few hours before I need to be at work."

"I'm sure you have other things to do today before work."

She planted her hands on her hips. "Fox. Say thank you."

He sighed. "Thank you."

"Awesome. Now get dressed before I drool all over the place." She grinned and ran her hand over his chest before turning and walking out of the room.

He chuckled, then rushed into the walk-in closet and pulled on a pair of jeans and a lightweight sweater. He grabbed his socks and a pair of shoes, sat on the bed, and put them on, wondering if Melody had left before he actually said goodbye to her.

"Hurry up," she shouted.

He found her in the kitchen. She turned with two travel mugs in hand. "Do you want anything in yours?"

"No. Black is good. What do you put in yours?"

"Milk, but you're out, so I'll just go stripped down and dirty like we did earlier."

God, this woman. She kept on surprising him.

"I'll return the mug later. Okay?" She shooed him toward the door.

He went because she was following him. "No problem." She could keep the damn thing for all he cared. "Will you come back tonight after your shift?" He opened the front door for her.

"Do you want me to?" she asked, walking out and heading to the elevator.

He set the alarm, locked up, then rushed to push the elevator button for her. "Yes." He wanted her to spend every night with him.

She looked up at him. "It'll be late again."

"I don't care what time it is." He brushed his hand down her long, tousled hair.

"You will when I keep disturbing your sleep and keeping you up."

He pulled her into his arms. "Please do."

"You say that now, but it's been a problem in the past and I don't want it to be one for us."

"It won't be. I often get lost in work late into the night. And if I sleep through the night, you can be sure I'll make it up to you in the morning."

She leaned into him and smiled. "I look forward to it."

They stepped onto the elevator. She hit the button for the first floor.

He kissed her, long and deep. He lost himself in her.

"Hey, I told the client we'll be ten minutes late, but if we don't hurry, we'll be later than that," Max grumbled.

Fox kept kissing Melody because that seemed infinitely more important than whatever Max was saying.

"Come on, man. I get you. She's your real-life fantasy, but we have to go." Max's exasperation finally penetrated.

Fox broke the kiss and stared down at Melody's cheeks, which were blush-kissed thanks to Max's comment. "See you tonight."

She patted his chest. "Yes."

He took her hand and walked through the lobby with her. Outside, he pulled out his wallet. "Let me give you my credit card, so you can call the plumber for Tanya."

She held up her hand. "No worries. I've got this."

"I'm not letting you pay for her plumber."

She shook her head. "I'm actually a decent plumber. I fix the sinks and bathroom fixtures all the time at the bar."

"Seriously?" Dean asked.

"One of my many hidden talents, boys." She went up on tiptoe and kissed Fox quick. "Have a nice day, dear." With that, she walked toward the parking lot, her hips swaying, his heart somehow tethered to hers.

"I'll call you later."

She raised her hand and waved at him, but didn't turn around.

"You are so gone for her." Max slapped his hand on Fox's shoulder. "Can we focus on work now that the hot brunette with the killer walk is gone?"

Fox turned and faced Max eye to eye. "Don't look at her that way."

"Dude. I get it. She's yours."

"Damn straight. And this time I'm not letting anything or anyone mess it up."

"Good," Dean said. "So I guess that means you'll be telling her *everything*."

He hesitated, even though he shouldn't, because it was her. "Eventually."

Max, ever cautious, especially when it came to money, nodded his agreement. "You should wait."

Fox waffled. "I know everything I need to know about her to trust her."

Dean stared him down. "And yet, you're keeping something huge from her."

He thought about why he hadn't said anything yet. "She doesn't need to know it to be with me."

Dean shook his head. "You're scared she'll be more interested in—"

"She's not like that. She cares about me. So much that she's headed over to deal with Tanya's drama so I can go to work."

"Did you tell her you were making a multimillion-dollar deal?" Max asked.

Fox sighed. "Does that even matter?"

Dean started walking and they followed. The center was only a few blocks away. "It might matter to her that you'd rather take her to bed than be on time for a deal worth that much."

"It's not like we'll lose the deal. This call is just a formality for them to accept the terms and hire us to do a job that no other firm can do as well as we do it."

"You mean *you*. *You're* delivering this project," Max pointed out. "This one is all you. And maybe she would like to know what a fucking genius boyfriend she has."

He rolled his eyes. "You guys just don't get it. Maybe that will impress her, but what she really cares about is me. I asked her to come back tonight. Instead of agreeing right away, she was concerned about me getting enough sleep."

"Guess she doesn't know that's the one thing you don't do well," Dean pointed out.

They reached the New Adult Education Center and entered the building using Dean's key card.

"Can't you guys just be happy for me?"

Max nodded. "I am happy for you."

"Me, too," Dean added. "I just don't think you should hide parts of yourself from her. It's like lying. And it will come back to bite you in the ass."

Fox never dismissed a warning from his friends. But he wanted to get to know Melody better, and for her to get to know him, without her being influenced by his success and what that meant in his life.

CHAPTER ELEVEN

Melody's day started off right with Fox. The man knew how to keep his promises. She appreciated that he thought one more time with her was more important than any business call he had scheduled. Maybe it wouldn't always be like that, but with things between them so new...it made her feel special.

That's what she'd been looking for all this time.

And she wanted to show him that he meant everything to her, too. So she'd stopped at the donut shop on her way out to Tanya's place. A peace offering of sorts. No matter how Tanya felt about her, Melody intended to make things easier for Fox by not giving in to temptation and spewing all the hateful things she wanted to say.

At least, she'd try. For him.

And a chocolate glazed donut or two never hurt.

She pulled into the drive, grabbed the box of donuts and her coffee mug, and headed up to the porch.

Tanya opened the door with a frown and anger in her eyes. She looked about to blow her top. "What are you doing here?"

"Fox had an important meeting. I volunteered to fix your plumbing problem."

Tanya's dismissive gaze raked over her. "You?"

"I'm actually quite handy." She held up the box. "And I brought donuts."

Tanya's gaze narrowed with suspicion, but she held the door wide for Melody to walk in. "Is he coming at all?"

"I'm not sure. He didn't tell me his schedule for today. He's with Dean and Max. Seemed like the call they had was important." She looked around the living room, noting the dust on the tables and shelves, the dirty dishes on the coffee table, and the basket of laundry sitting on the floor of the bedroom down the hall. "So, where is the leak?"

"Kitchen sink. A pipe broke. And the faucet leaks."

Melody headed to the kitchen, noting how slow Tanya was to follow. At first she thought maybe it was because Tanya was mad about her being here. But the second Tanya got close to the little table by the window, she nearly fell into the seat.

"You okay?"

"The treatment wears me out. I wake up tired. Every little thing feels like a chore some days." Tanya rubbed at her forehead with her index finger and thumb.

"I'm sorry to hear that. Do they think the treatment is working?" Melody wasn't clear on what type of cancer Tanya battled, but by the pallor of her face and dark circles under her eyes, it was taking a toll on her.

"At this point, the treatment is just prolonging my life. Though it's not much of one, if you ask me. I'm stuck in this house just like I've always been."

"Maybe you can visit Fox in Boston."

She rolled her eyes. "I think Fox wants to keep me as far away from his new life as he can."

Can you blame him? She kept that to herself.

Tanya's irritated tone said she knew all too well Fox remained leery of Tanya's intentions.

Melody noticed the toolbox on the counter, then squatted in front of the open cabinet under the sink. Several bottles of household cleaner and dish soap had been taken out of the cabinet and placed on the floor. The pipes were fairly simple. One came out of the garbage disposal and went into the wall. Two pipes went to the hot and cold water up to the sink knobs. The sink trap was loose, the pipe cracked. Water and sludge coated the bottom of the cabinet.

She looked around the kitchen and spotted the roll of paper towels. She grabbed a half dozen and laid them over the mess. She eyed the toolbox with the hammer right on top and frowned.

"How'd this happen?"

"Sink got clogged. I tried to undo the pipe and made things worse." At least she owned up to that part.

Melody had a suspicion the hammer had something to do with the cracked pipe. "Any chance you've got some spare pipe and pipe glue around here?" It was a simple fix with the right parts. She didn't want to have to go all the way to town to get them and come back.

"Check the storage room in the barn. Lots of odds and ends in there."

Melody stood as Tanya started working on a chocolate glazed donut.

She spotted the half pot of coffee on the counter and a mug next to it. She poured a cup and held it up to Tanya. "Cream or sugar?"

Tanya's eyes went wide, then she shook her head. "Why are you being nice?"

"Because I care about Fox. And apparently he cares about you enough to upend his life and come here to help you."

Tanya sneered. "Like you're not telling him to steer clear of me every chance you get."

"I did tell him that's what you deserve. But the man has a good heart despite all the shit that's been done to him. He could be bitter and angry and take that out on others. Instead, he's kind. Maybe because he's known so much hurt. He knows what that feels like and doesn't want to inflict that on others."

"I wasn't a bad mother."

"No one believes that. Not even you. You hurt him. And you need to own that."

"Like you own what you did."

"Saving him from you is the best thing I ever did, even if it meant I lost him for a while."

Tanya's gaze narrowed. "You were with him this morning when I called."

"You think I was fiercely protective of him when I was eight? That is nothing compared to how I feel about keeping him safe and happy now."

"You love him."

"I always have. I always will."

Tanya nodded. "Good."

Surprise burst in her chest. "What?" She never expected that response.

"Does it stun you to think I want my son to be happy?"

"As far as I can tell, you only care about yourself."

Tanya shook her head, lips tight with condescension. "You don't know me. You think you do, but that's from a child's perspective. You don't know how trapped I felt. There was no escaping his father. Sometimes you have to play the hand you're dealt."

"That's bullshit. When your husband went to jail, you could have divorced him. You would have been free. Instead, you welcomed the viper back into your home the second he was released. Why?"

"I don't have to explain myself to you," she snapped. "Some things aren't always what they seem."

Melody didn't know what to make of that. She wouldn't have made the choices Tanya had made. But she also hadn't been in Tanya's shoes, so who knew what choices she'd have made to keep a roof over her head and food on the table. Tanya had chosen to work for a local house-cleaning service and as cashier at the tire store on the weekends.

Huh. Josh worked there for his father. That's probably how she found Brian and whatever drugs she was using to dull the pain now.

Since Tanya had been expecting Fox to show up, she'd probably stashed her stash.

None of that mattered.

"Some people never change." Melody held Tanya's gaze. "I hope you have. For Fox's sake."

"He's a little too big to let me get away with knocking him around."

Melody fumed. "There are a lot of ways to hurt someone." She headed for the back door. "Enjoy the donuts." She walked to the barn, thinking about how her father had found Fox out there nearly frozen and dead the day she'd begged him to check on Fox.

No, she'd never forgive Tanya for what she'd done. She'd never forget.

And if Tanya tried to use and abuse Fox now, she'd protect Fox at all costs, even if that meant pushing him to go back to Boston to keep him away from Tanya.

CHAPTER TWELVE

Fox knocked on Melody's door, hoping it wasn't too early. She was supposed to come by his place last night. He'd tried to wait up, but fell asleep sometime around one a.m. She'd left him two text messages. The first telling him she'd knocked and to answer the door. The second saying she wasn't going to wake the whole building pounding on his door and she was going home and to call her later.

He hated that he'd missed her after he was the one who practically begged her to come to his place again. He wanted more of what they had the night before. And he blew it.

They'd barely gotten any sleep that night, he'd worked all day on multiple projects, then he had spent dinner and most of the evening catching up on work from the office with Max. Working remotely meant he had to rely on others at the office to take up the slack his absence created, but the company was his, and he was responsible for everything, so he needed to look over all the major projects, expenses, and income still.

The door opened and everything inside him lit up with warmth and happiness. Melody stood there in a pair of flannel boxers, a black tank top, her hair a wild mass of waves, and her eyes squinting against the bright afternoon light. "Hey." She yawned and pressed the back of her hand to her gaping mouth.

Then her eyes went wide on the to-go cup and bakery bag in his hand. She snatched both. "Please tell me these are for me."

He chuckled. "All yours, sweetheart."

She took a sip of the caramel macchiato and sighed. "Delish." She opened the bag and groaned. The smell of cinnamon filled the air around them. "That is the biggest cinnamon roll I've ever seen."

"I made sure it was the biggest one."

She finally really looked at him, then narrowed her gaze. "You're too nice to me."

"Not possible. And I owe you an apology."

She pulled out the cinnamon roll and took a huge bite. "Why?"

He barely understood the word, her mouth was so full, and a dollop of icing clung to the corner of her lip, distracting him. He wanted to lick it off. So he gave in to that compulsion, leaned in, and brushed the tip of his tongue over the sweetness that was her and the icing mixed together.

Her breath hitched. She set the coffee on the entry table beside her, where she'd also tossed the bakery bag, grabbed him by the front of his thermal, and pulled him inside, kicking the door shut. "How do you make me feel this way?"

"I hope it's the same way you make me feel." He brushed his fingertips along her soft skin, tracing the side of her beautiful face. "I'm sorry I fell asleep last night and missed you knocking on my door."

"Sounds like you should apologize to yourself for that, too, because we both missed out."

"When I woke up this morning and it was light out...I wanted to kick my own ass."

She took another bite of the pastry. "I'm not upset. You had a really long day. You were tired. It's no big deal." She raised a brow. "Wait. Aren't you supposed to be at work?"

"I needed to see you. I waited as long as I could, then I rushed over here to catch you before you left for work."

He finally took a minute to look around her place. Pictures of family and friends and a large mirror hung on the wall above the entry table. He caught his breath when he found one of them. A close-up. Her lips were tinted blue raspberry from the Popsicle in her hand. His orange. They were both smiling, big toothy grins. She was missing a canine. Adorable.

He looked happy. At ease. The way he always felt around her.

"I love that one. It was a good day."

Fox nodded. "I was with you on a field trip to some museum. Your mom chaperoned. She bought us the pops from an ice cream truck out front. She took our picture." He turned away from the pretty little girl to face the gorgeous woman she'd become. "You kept this all this time."

"To keep you with me." She waved for him to take a seat in her living room.

She retrieved her coffee and they both plopped down on the couch.

The living room had a wood entertainment center with a flat-screen TV. Several lush green plants sat atop it, catching the light from the windows on either side of it. In addition to the black leather sofa and reclining chair, there was a coffee table and two end tables with wrought iron lamps.

Just past the living room at the back of her apartment was a small galley kitchen and dining room table and chairs. On the right, past the open bathroom door, a short hallway led to her bedroom, he presumed.

She caught him checking out her place as she finished off the cinnamon roll. "Yeah. You could fit my whole place in your master bedroom."

"This place is so you. I love the blown-up pictures on the walls."

"They're my favorite places on the ranch."

"The one of the apple orchard in bloom is amazing. And the alleyway down the barn with all the horses peeking out of their stalls... How did you get them to do that?"

"Treats."

"You brought home to your place here."

"I love the ranch. I just needed my own space to grow into who I want to be."

He bumped his shoulder to hers. "I think you're amazing."

She tilted her head and grinned. "I think you're biased."

He shook his head. "I still can't believe what you did yesterday for my mom."

She shrugged one shoulder. "I did it for you." She'd not only fixed the kitchen sink, she'd cleaned the whole house, then gone to work yesterday afternoon until midnight.

"I planned to hire a cleaning service to go out there and take care of the place."

"Now you don't have to, and she doesn't have to contend with all that dust, making her allergies worse. But I do think you need to check in with her doctor about her meds. I think she's in pain and the meds aren't working as well as they should for her."

"Did she say something?"

"No. I just saw her take the pain meds a couple hours apart while I was there. They should last longer than that."

"Okay. I think she has an appointment day after next. She prefers to do it alone, but I'll try to coax her into letting me go with her, so I can see what's what."

Melody pressed her lips tight, but didn't say anything.

"What is it?"

"It's nothing."

"Dee..."

"She's trying to get your attention."

"She has it. I'm here."

Melody shook her head. "She broke the sink and pipes herself to get you to come fix it."

He raised a brow. "That seems..." Now that he thought about it, he had suspicions. "Seriously? You think so?"

She raised a brow back. "Yes."

Every time he went over there, something needed to be replaced or fixed. Everything was old and worn out, so he hadn't really thought anything about it. But was Tanya actually breaking things on purpose to get his attention?

"While I was cleaning up the living room, I found a stack of cruise brochures."

He narrowed his gaze.

"When I asked her about them, she said she wants to go on a cruise with you. Bonding. A vacation you never got to have together."

He rolled his eyes. "Because I was in foster care and she didn't give a shit." He ran his hand through his hair. "She chose to take my father back, knowing there was no way family services would let me return to them. So a cruise...trying to make up for lost time...fuck no."

She shifted on the couch so she was facing him. "Then what are you doing here, Fox?"

"I came back for you."

"You could have done that without ever seeing Tanya. Admit it. You came back because you hoped her illness changed her. It didn't. She won't change. Not even for you." She slid over his lap, straddled him, hugged him, and whispered in his ear, "You deserve better."

He wrapped his arms around her and held her, maybe a little too tight, but she didn't resist. She melted into him.

"I got the best thing to ever happen to me back."

She pressed a kiss to his neck. "Still...I'm sorry about your mom."

"If you dislike her this much, why did you do all of that for her?"

She leaned back with her hands braced on his shoulders. "Because she's sick. It needed to be done. And I wanted to see if she was hiding something."

"Like what?"

"I don't know. I just feel like she has an agenda. Maybe it's as simple as she wants to use you for your money. She's never really had anything but bad luck, abuse, and back-breaking work. That's a hard life. Her son is amazingly talented and successful. She wants a taste of the life you've created for yourself. You're nice enough to give her what she wants. My problem with her is that she thinks because you're her son, you owe it to her. I don't like that."

"I don't mind helping out. I have the money."

She nodded. "Okay."

His brow went up again. "That's it?"

"I've said my piece. And it's nothing you probably haven't already thought yourself."

"Tanya is..." He didn't know quite what to say. "I know who and what she is. I gave up my hopes and dreams of having a close relationship with her when I had this chance to reconnect with her and it didn't go the way I hoped. Two minutes into being at her place and speaking to her...I knew I was never going to get what I wanted. But I couldn't walk away. Not when she's sick and needs help." He rubbed both hands over the back of his neck, then dropped his hands onto Melody's silky bare thighs. "I know she's going to get worse. I've planned for that. There's a nearby hospice where she'll be taken care of round the clock. I know I don't have to do it, but it's what my conscience needs so I don't have to live with turning my back on her when she needed me like she did to me all those years ago."

She brushed her thumbs over his cheeks and held his face. "Okay. I won't bring it up again. We'll take care of her."

He shook his head. "It's not for you to do."

Her gaze narrowed. "Are *we* an *us*? Or not?"

He gripped her hips. "We are definitely an *us*." And he loved it that she was his.

"Then we do it together." She leaned in and kissed him. It was soft and way too short.

He stood with her straddling his waist and his hands clamped on her ass. "I want to see your bedroom."

She kissed his neck and whispered in his ear as he walked to the hallway. "I think you really just want to see me naked."

"I do. Always. Every second of the day. You're all I think about." The room was dark. He could barely see any of the details in the room, but he found the rumpled bed and laid her out beneath him on it, kissing his way down her neck, following the V of her tank to her cleavage. He kissed a trail from one rounded breast across to the other, then ran his tongue from that side back to the other.

She moaned.

He tugged her tank up and over her head. Her tight pink nipples tempted him to lick then suck one into his mouth. She tasted so sweet.

Her fingers slid through his hair and held him close as he licked and laved one nipple, then the other. He brushed his fingers over her rib cage. She arched up, only giving him a better mouthful of her soft breast, the hard tip pressed to his tongue.

He skated his fingers down her body as he dipped them underneath her flannel shorts and found her bare to his fingers. He slid them over her soft folds, finding her wet and rocking against his touch. He sank one finger deep, then two.

"Fox. I need you."

He licked her nipple, making her moan. "I'm right here." Where he always wanted to be. With her.

She pulled his shirt up and over his head. "Too many clothes. I want skin." She pulled up her legs so he could slide the shorts right off her bare feet. "I want you. Now." She twisted and fumbled with the bedside drawer, while he got rid of the rest of his clothes.

He turned back and found her sitting up, a condom in hand. Since he was on his knees on the mattress, she took hold of his hard shaft, stroked him once, twice. He bit his lip, trying to hold on and not end this with her hand on him, giving him so much pleasure. She stopped the exquisite torture, rolled the condom down his length, then fell back on the bed.

The most beautiful woman laid out before him.

Mine.

He covered her body with his and kissed her. Softly at first, then with a ravenous stroke of his tongue along hers. Her hips rolled up to his and the head of his cock sank into her welcoming heat. Then she pushed up and took him in all the way.

He lost all finesse and rhythm and pulled out and slammed back into her again and again to her soft pants and moans, her nails biting into his back and hip. She wrapped her legs around his waist and he thrust deep, pulling out and making sure his dick glided against her clit.

He felt the storm building in her. In him. And then she cracked like lightning, the pleasure coursing through her and him as it rolled like thunder.

He collapsed on top of her, trying to keep most of his weight on his forearms as he kissed her neck and rubbed his head into her palm as her fingers slid through his hair.

"You can wake me up every day if we get to do this." Humor laced her words, but also truth and something more. Something he hoped she felt as deeply as he did.

Because that special thing they had between them...it filled him up.

He raised his head and stared down at her. "Any time, any way you want it, I'm your man."

"I like the sound of that."

"Get used to us spending a lot of time together."

Something came and went in her eyes.

He settled next to her on the bed on his side and hooked his arm around her waist, and pulled her over so she was facing him. Barely a few inches separated them. "What is it?"

She brushed her thumb over his bottom lip. "You're so...amazing. And I don't want to lose you. But you have a home, a business, a life in Boston that I know very little about."

He sobered. "And you live here." That complication weighed on him.

"Yes. My life is tied to the ranch, the bar, my family. Mason moved here to be with Lyric. Layla decided to stay to be with Jax. I can't ask you to do that." Her gaze dropped to his chest. "Maybe it's too soon to even talk about this, but..."

"You're thinking of a future with me." That's what mattered. That she wanted it. Him.

"Yes. And if you feel like it's too much, too soon, I'll table this until you're thinking—"

He kissed her to stop the rest of that statement from falling from her lips because he didn't want her to think for even a moment they weren't on the same page.

She fell into the kiss immediately.

He loved that she didn't hold anything back.

The kiss broke as both of them took a breath.

"I've been thinking about a future with you for months. All those online conversations we had... All I wanted was more with you. Now we have it. I've tried not to get ahead of you because I knew who you were during those conversation and you didn't know it was me. I'm a shit for doing it that way. I could have had you this whole time." He brushed her hair back over her shoulder. "I wasn't honest about who I was, but I never lied to you in our conversations."

She nodded her agreement.

"So be honest with me now. Do you see yourself leaving Wyoming and coming to Boston with me? Is that something you'd be willing to do? Do you think you could be happy there with me?"

She bit her lip and stared at him for a moment, then admitted, "I don't know. This is my home. I've barely been out of the state. I got my bachelor's degree in business online through the university because I wanted to help my siblings when we took over the bar. I've never lived anywhere but here."

"Then come to Boston with me when I have to go back for some meetings. See my place there. Come to the office. We can do some sightseeing. You can get a feel for the place and my life there."

She rubbed her hand over his chest and stared at his throat, not his eyes. "What if I hate it?"

He used his finger to tip her chin up, so she'd look at him. "What if you love it?"

She looked a little scared. Because she might like it and that meant a huge change and telling her family she was leaving? Or because she didn't think she would? "What would I even do there?"

He couldn't answer that for her, though he had some ideas. She was good at a lot of things. "What would you do if you were free to leave the bar and your family?"

"I don't know. I love working at the bar. Though I think I'd rather run it than keep waitressing. It's hard on my feet and back."

"You have your Etsy businesses. You could focus on those."

"I like doing that, but I still feel like I'd miss the bar. I love the atmosphere, the music, talking to all the people who come in. A lot of them I know really well. I feel like I'm a part of their lives." She went quiet for a moment.

He gave her space to think and dream about the future.

"You know, maybe I've never let myself think about what I'd do if I didn't have the bar."

"We have time to figure things out. I don't have to go back right away. Yes, for some meetings and things, but those will only be for a day or two each time. Everyone knows I'm here for Tanya as long as she needs me."

She ran her fingertips up his arm. "Have you thought about taking her back to Boston so you can be at your company?"

"I want to be here with you more than anything."

"But that's not exactly something you can do forever. You can't run your business from a couple thousand miles away."

He rubbed his nose against hers. "Let me worry about that."

She shook her head. "We're in this together."

"We'll figure it out. But it doesn't have to be today." He kissed her again, hoping to ease her mind, letting her know she had time to think about what she wanted. "I have to get back to the center. I have some coding to do and a conference call later." He rolled out of bed and headed to the bathroom to take care of the condom. He found her in the bedroom, still naked but standing by the bed. She'd picked up all his discarded clothes and laid them on the mattress. "You make it hard to leave." His gaze roamed over her naked body and he hungered for more. He wanted to touch her and taste her all over again.

"Isn't everyone wondering where you are at this time of day?"

"Dean and Max know I'm with you."

A pretty blush brightened her cheeks. "And what do they think you're doing with me?"

"Exactly what we did the other morning and a few minutes ago." He didn't care who knew he was having sex and spending time with Melody. He wanted everyone to know they were together. "Don't worry about them. They're happy for us." He pulled on his boxer briefs and grabbed his jeans, tugging them on.

"I would like to get to know them better. They are your brothers."

"They want to get to know you, too." He pulled his shirt over his head and sat on the end of the bed to put on his socks and shoes.

Melody waited for him to finish, then stepped between his legs.

He put his hands on her bare hips and looked up at her. "This is really not helping." He was hard again. He leaned forward and nuzzled his nose and mouth against her breast.

She brushed her fingers into his hair, trying to straighten it out for him. She tipped his head back so she could look him in the eye. "Maybe I don't know what I want to do in the future, but I know whatever it is, I want to do it with you by my side."

He wrapped her up in his arms and held her close, his head on her chest. The sound of her steady heart eased him. "I want that, my sweet, sweet Dee. More than I can say."

"I need some time to think about it."

He looked up at her again. "I'm not asking you to leave. I'm only asking what you want and need to be happy. If it's staying here, we'll figure it out." He had money. He'd buy a damn plane if that's what it took and he'd fly back and forth. No matter what, he'd be with her.

But would that really work? It would be time consuming. They'd spend so much time apart. Eventually, would it fray their relationship until it tore them apart?

She gave him a nod.

He stood, nudging her to step back. "I have to go."

"Thank you for the coffee and breakfast."

He brushed her hair back over her shoulders and stared down at her. "You're welcome." He kissed her softly. "Can we try the whole *you come to my place after work tonight* thing again?"

"Yes."

"Good. Because as you can see, I can't go a whole day without seeing you."

Her smile brightened her eyes. "I was actually going to stop by the center on my way to work to see you."

"Yeah?" His whole chest lit up with joy. "Will you do that anyway so I can give you something?"

"What?"

"You'll see. Promise you'll come by."

"I'll be there in a little while. I just need to shower and dress and pack up some orders that I need to drop at the post office for some customers."

"Is that what is all over the dining room table?"

"Yeah. I usually just eat in front of the TV and use the table for work stuff."

"But you make the bracelets and bridles at the ranch?"

"Yeah. I usually spend Sunday there working on that stuff because we have Sunday dinner as a family."

"Okay."

"Do you want to come to dinner on Sunday? You could catch up with my dad and mom. They can't wait to see you."

He hesitated. "It's a family thing."

"My dad has been looking out for you since you were eight. I'm looking out for you now, too. Sounds like you're family to me."

He didn't know what to do with the burst of emotion her words let loose inside him. He'd given up on ever having a family like hers.

She put her hand on his chest. "Breathe." Of course she understood how overwhelmed he felt by her statement.

He sucked in a breath. Then another.

"I'll see you at Wilde Wind on Sunday. Six o'clock."

"Are you sure?" Because this felt like another step deeper into their relationship. Was she ready for that?

"I wouldn't have invited you if I didn't want you there. You belong with us, Fox. There's no changing that now."

He pulled her close and practically crushed her to his chest.

She wrapped her arms around his back and held on just as tight.

He needed to get a grip and tried to lighten the mood. "Can we have all our talks like this with you naked?"

"As long as we're alone, I don't see why not."

He chuckled because he knew she meant that and because she was obviously comfortable in her skin. She had every reason to be confident about herself and her body. He loved everything about her.

He didn't let his heart follow his mind down that path. He knew how he felt about her. But did she care enough about him to change her whole life?

CHAPTER THIRTEEN

Melody couldn't stop thinking about her conversation with Fox. One day soon, he'd have to return to his home and company. It wasn't like he could move his entire business. Not just to be with her. That was absurd. And she couldn't expect him to work remotely. Maybe that was okay for a limited time because of his sick mother, but long-term, that wasn't a viable option.

And after living in the city, rural life probably wasn't exciting for him. If he'd wanted that, he'd have opened his business somewhere less bustling than Boston.

She pressed the buzzer on the center's door and waited.

A woman's voice came over the speaker. "Can I help you?"

"I'm here to see Fox."

"Do you have an appointment?" The upbeat voice had turned hesitant.

Do I need one? "Uh, I'm a friend of his."

"Only staff and students are allowed on the premises," the clipped voice stated emphatically.

"He asked me to stop by."

"I believe he's in a meeting."

Seriously? "He's expecting me," she grumbled and pulled out her phone to text Fox because this was getting ridiculous. All she wanted to do was see him. And she didn't have a lot of time before she needed to be at the bar.

The door opened before she sent the text and a woman about her age with blonde hair, blue eyes, and sporting a chef's hat poked her head out. "The receptionist just came back. Fox told her you were coming, so I guess you can come in."

She walked in behind the blonde and looked around the reception area. Mostly it was a huge set of stairs that went up to the second level on one side and the reception desk and seating area on the other. There was a door on both sides with electronic locks.

"I'm Amy. I'm the resident chef." Amy looked Melody up and down, then asked, "Who are you?"

Melody had on a pair of super-comfy biker-style boots, a black jean skirt that hit her mid-thigh, and a Dark Horse Dive Bar T-shirt with the bar name and logo over her left breast. Her hair was down for now. She loved the look.

Amy seemed to disapprove. Not that Melody cared.

They were obviously very different.

Amy tall and slim with soft curves.

Melody a little shorter with a whole lot more in the curves department.

"I'm Melody." Should she say she was Fox's girlfriend? She kept it to herself, unsure if Fox wanted everyone to know about them, and went with something relevant that explained her presence here today. "I'll be teaching a class on setting up an Etsy store and running your own online business."

"Oh wow. That's great." Amy's eyes went bright. "I've thought about setting up my own little cookie company."

"Well, I guess you can join the class and I can give you all the tips and tricks I've learned running my two businesses."

The chef quickly glanced at Melody's chest. "Don't you work at the bar?"

"I own it." With her siblings Aria, Lyric, and Jax. "But I also make custom leather belts and bracelets in one shop and custom horse bridles in another."

Amy started up the stairs and Melody followed.

"Wow. That's cool." Amy used a badge to get through the door on the right side of the stairs.

"Thanks." They passed several rooms with glass-fronted doors. One was empty. Two had students and an instructor in them.

Amy led her past an office marked SECURITY, another marked DIRECTOR, and finally to one with no description, where Fox sat behind a desk with three monitors as he typed like a hundred words a minute, staring at the screens. "Fox, you have a visitor."

It took Fox a second to look up as he finished whatever he was typing. "Huh. What?"

Amy stepped out of the way so Fox could see Melody.

"Hey." She grinned at him, loving the way his glazed eyes went bright when he saw her.

His whole face lit up and a big smile bloomed on his face. All for her. He'd just seen her not even two hours ago. And he was this happy to see her? "Hello, gorgeous."

She tried not to blush and failed miserably because he'd surprised her by saying something so sweet in front of someone else, even though he'd told her several times that he thought she was beautiful.

Fox rose and came around his desk. "Come in."

Oddly, Amy stepped in first, instead of leaving them alone.

Fox stopped and stared at Amy.

She put her hand on his arm. "You didn't tell me your friend was coming on board to teach a class."

Fox took a small step away from Amy, putting some distance between them, so Amy's hand dropped away.

Melody looked from Amy to Fox and back again, wondering if she'd missed something. Why would Fox tell her about Melody teaching the class?

"We have several students who want to start their own businesses and be their own bosses," Fox explained now.

"Like you," Amy chimed in. "You did it all on your own."

"I had help. Dean and Max backed me up."

"But you were the one with the coding experience. You built your reputation and the company's." Amy gushed over Fox.

He looked a bit uncomfortable. "Anyway, Melody agreed to teach the class."

Amy stepped closer to him. "I'd like to take it. I've been wanting to start my own thing too."

Melody wondered if what she wanted to start was something with Fox.

He took a step away from Amy and closer to Melody. "As long as it doesn't interfere with your job here, no problem. Some of the other staff have sat in on classes just to learn something new, too."

"Great." Amy threw her arms around Fox and hugged him. "Thank you so much." She released Fox and headed for the door, but turned back before she disappeared. "I'll see you soon." The desire in her eyes couldn't be missed.

If Fox saw it, he ignored it.

Melody tried to excuse it. Maybe the comment was for her, not Fox, and she raised a brow at him when they were finally alone. "Is there, or was there ever, something between you two?"

Fox caught himself from taking a step back. "No. Not now. Not ever. She works for me."

"Apparently I will, too, when I teach this class."

He held up his hands. "Not the same. Amy and I met casually at a business meeting and then a charity event several years ago. Since then, I've used the company she works for to cater business events, meetings, and a few things I've hosted at my place. I always request her because we're...not really friends. We don't hang out, outside of those things, but we are friendly acquaintances. She knows what I like and understands what I want."

Melody raised a brow at that comment.

He huffed. "Not like that. Nothing like that. No. Clients appreciate a little wining and dining. It's part of doing business. She's a great chef. I can tell her what the event is, if there's a theme, and she puts the menu together. That's all. She's personable and usually professional. So when I was looking for a chef to teach here, I hired her. While she is...interested, there's nothing going on between us." His hands dropped to his sides. "And I can't believe you'd think that when we've been seeing each other for months." The hurt in his eyes pinched her heart.

"Our online relationship wasn't the same as what we have now."

He took a step closer and cupped her face. "Now I have everything I ever wanted. And it's not Amy. Never was." He pressed his forehead to hers. "All I think about, all I see, is you."

Well, wasn't that just the most amazing thing anyone had ever said to her?

She hooked her hands on his wrists. "I'm sorry."

He kissed her softly. "Don't be. You're jealous. That means you care." And apparently it didn't bother him that she was, in fact, jealous as hell.

"You know I do."

He grinned, amusement in his eyes. "Yeah, but it does my ego good to know even you get jealous."

She cocked her head. "What does that mean? Even me?"

"No other woman holds a candle to you, yet Amy's friendliness—"

"Came off as you two having a close relationship."

"Why would you think that?" He still didn't get it.

"Why would she think you'd tell her about me teaching a class here?"

He brushed his thumb over her cheek. "I don't know."

"Why was she touching you like—"

"I won't let it happen again." He brushed his hand over her hair, soothing her. "It bothers you, so I won't let her or any other woman touch me."

She let her head drop back and rolled her eyes at the ceiling. "I'm being ridiculous."

He pulled her head forward so they were eye to eye. "No, you're not. Because if some guy put his hands on you, I'd make him stop."

She had a feeling the guy would lose his hands based on the look on Fox's face. And she felt the same way. In the moment, she'd wanted to rip Amy's hands away from Fox.

And hadn't he made it clear to Josh at the bar the other night to keep his hands off her? Yeah, she remembered that now.

Fox's gaze turned thoughtful. "I don't like it when she or others are so touchy-feely."

"Why?"

"Because when you grow up with little to no affection, it's weird when someone so casually touches you, because you're always looking for a threat or their angle."

Her shoulders sagged. "Fox. I hope you don't feel that way when I touch you."

He pulled her into a hug. "I can't get enough of you touching me, or me touching you. It's different. It's...I trust you."

She hugged him hard, not letting go, letting his words and what they meant sink in. She leaned her head back and looked up at him. "I could never hurt you."

"I know. You hurt for me, because you care so deeply."

"I do. And I know that's how you feel about me."

"I'd do anything to keep you safe." The vehemence in his voice was tempered by something she couldn't name. It felt like he was holding something back.

He took her hand and tugged her toward the door. "Come on. I'll show you the classroom and you can tell me what you need to do your class."

"A badge to get into the building. Amy almost didn't let me in, even after I told her I was your friend and you'd asked me to meet you here."

Fox kept walking, but glanced at her and raised a brow. "Friend?"

"Do you prefer something else?" She didn't want to be presumptuous.

"We're more than friends."

"BFFs," she suggested, teasing him.

He walked into an empty classroom that had a whiteboard at one end, cupboards at the back, chairs and desks in the center for at least twenty students, and a table and chair in front of the whiteboard with a laptop and projector.

As soon as the door closed behind them, he tugged her around so she ended up in his arms. He captured her mouth in a blazing kiss that had an eruption of heat and passion as his tongue licked into her mouth, tasting, tempting, destroying every thought except one. More.

She wrapped her arms around his neck and fell into the fire with him, pressing her body to his. Her breasts ached against his chest. She went up on tiptoe and rolled her hips into his, feeling his hard length against her. The mind-blowing sex they'd had earlier had satiated the sharp edge of her desire when he'd walked in her door with breakfast. But this ignited it all over again.

She bet that table, or even one of the desks, would support her as he stripped her bare and took her right here, right now. To let him know she was on board with that, she slipped her hands up under his shirt and over his rock-hard abs and up to his sculpted pecs.

The growly sound he made turned her on even more.

Someone pounded on the door. "We can see you through the window."

Fox came up for air. "Fuck." He stared down at her, his eyes blazing with sexual frustration. "I'm sorry."

"I'm not." She slid her hands down those washboard abs she loved and over his hard length.

He groaned.

"All that and this is for me. Never be sorry about that."

He crushed her to him and looked over his shoulder at his buddy Dean. "Make her an all-access badge." Fox turned back to her and, reluctantly by the look in his eyes and the groan of disappointment he let out, gently set her away from him. "Boyfriend."

"Huh?" She tilted her head, making her long hair fall back over her shoulder.

"After the other night, this morning, what we feel for each other, you're mine. So I believe the proper term for that, though I feel it's wholly inadequate because I want to be more to you, is boyfriend."

The smile she gave him made her cheeks hurt. "So now I'm your girlfriend? You used to think girls were yucky."

"Yeah. But never you. You were always sweet Dee, the girl who made me smile and laugh and think that maybe life wasn't so bad."

She'd hated when he'd get those dark looks in his eyes when they were young. She didn't understand exactly what they meant back then, but they scared her. They made her hold on to him all the more. "Can you believe we ended up here?"

He brushed his thumb over her kiss-swollen bottom lip. "We're still just getting started." Then he pulled something out of his pocket, took her hand, and set the hidden thing into her palm.

She held up the key. "What's this for?"

"I can't stand it that you came all the way to my place last night and I slept through you knocking on my door. I woke up missing you. I don't want to do that anymore. So now you can come and go as you please. And I hope that means you'll come by tonight, every night, and slip into bed with me."

She gripped the key tight and grinned, loving that he trusted her with access to his place. She'd have to get a copy of her key made for him. "Don't get grumpy with me when I wake you up."

He hooked his hand at the back of her neck and pulled her close. "I'm begging you to wake me up." He kissed her again, this time with heat but restraint since they'd already gotten caught lost in each other.

Good thing, too, because another knock sounded on the door. This time, Dean popped his head in. "Here's your badge." Dean tossed it to her.

She turned it over. "Where'd you get the picture?"

"Fox texted it to me after you sent it to him, so I could see what you looked like."

She'd sent the picture of herself during one of their many online chats. Her wavy hair was a bit wild in the pic, but she looked cute in a pink blouse. Fox had not reciprocated. He'd still been pretending to be shy.

She glanced at the name below the picture and burst out laughing. "Seriously?" She held up the badge so Fox could read it.

"Fox's Sexy Lady. Perfect." Fox's smile was amused and sultry before he turned to Dean. "Thanks, man."

"No problem. Just part of the security job you pay me for."

Which begged the question... "Why do you need so much security here? Isn't Dean needed back at your company headquarters?"

Fox and Dean shared a look that told her nothing.

"I needed a break from Boston," Dean answered. "And I wanted to see Fox get his girl back."

"But you've been here for months. Right?"

"Off and on. I like it here." Dean glanced at Fox. "I've got a call about that firewall attack."

"Let me know what you find out," Fox said before Dean left them, closing the door for their privacy again.

"Did someone try to hack into your system?"

"Yeah, but they didn't get through. Dean's on it. Nothing for you to worry about."

"I worry about you. If they get through, that could be catastrophic for your company."

"That's why I have Dean and a team of highly skilled IT people taking care of it."

She raised a brow. "Are you sure you're not needed in Boston?"

He took her hand and squeezed it. "I'll let you know if I am. Until then, I'm here with you. So tell me what you think of the classroom and what you'll need for your class."

"The room is great. I'm not sure how many people you think will want to attend my class, but this seems adequate."

"I put up the class on our site last night. Twenty-three of the forty students we have right now want to attend."

"Seriously?" She couldn't believe it. She'd hoped at least a handful of people would come. But that many? Wow.

"It's a great way for people with limited means to start their own business. Some of them probably don't have a clear idea of what their shop would be, but knowing how to do it is a first step into actually dreaming they could do it. Sometimes, that's the hardest part working with people who have never been given a chance to dream because they're too busy surviving."

She'd always had the space and encouragement to dream. No one had told her she had to work at the bar. She'd wanted that because it meant working with the siblings she loved, carrying on the business her grand-mother loved and left them. "My dad gave you that chance, didn't he?"

"He made me think about the future and what steps I needed to take to get there. Every call, after I'd update him about my life, he'd ask the same question. 'What's next?'"

"He wanted you to succeed."

"He encouraged me to rise above my circumstances."

"And you did that with Dean and Max, didn't you?"

"We were a team. Brothers. We helped each other. Now I want you to help my students so they can be like you. Independent. Successful, doing something they love."

"Then I better put together a step-by-step presentation on how to do that."

"Do it fast. The class starts in two weeks. I've set it up for a week, but let me know if you need more time. It'll be two hours a day, starting at eleven in the morning. I know that means you'll have to get up early."

She put her hand on his chest. "It's fine. I don't mind."

"If, as you go, you think you need more time, just let me know and I'll adjust the schedule. Every student will have their own laptop, so they can follow along with whatever you do."

"Do you expect them to set up a shop as we go along?"

"If they want to, and so long as they don't fall behind what you're teaching, but mostly they can take notes and create a folder of ideas and inspiration from what you teach them."

That was actually incredibly helpful. She needed to think about not just setting up the shop, but also how to take pictures of products so they stood out and caught shoppers' attention. Marketing. Advertising. How to use social media to draw people to the shop.

Before, she'd had a vague idea about what she could teach others, but now the ideas were flowing.

Fox brushed his fingers through her hair. "I see your wheels spinning."

She grinned. "This was a good idea. The internet can walk anyone through setting up a store, but now I know what I need to tell the students about competing with others in the market and how to stand out."

"That's why I hired you."

"Have you though?" She cocked her head.

"The paperwork is on my desk. Wait here. I'll get it." Fox left her, and she pulled out her phone, tapped on her notes app, and started jotting down her ideas while they were flowing.

"Oh. You're still here." Amy stood just inside the doorway. She glanced at Melody's hand. "What's that?"

Melody held up the badge. "It's official. I work here."

"And the key? Are you moving into one of the apartments?"

She shook her head. "No. It's to Fox's place."

Amy's brows shot up. "I guess you two really are friends."

"We have been since preschool."

Amy's lips pressed tight. "I had no idea he grew up here. He never mentioned it in any of our many talks."

Fox walked in behind Amy and headed for Melody, keeping a wide distance between himself and Amy. He handed Melody the paperwork. "Sign all that and give it back to me. Then you'll be officially on the payroll."

She didn't bother to ask about the salary. Whatever it was, it was fine with her. She'd do this as a favor to him no matter what. She liked helping people. And it was only a couple hours a day for a week.

Fox took her hand. "I'll walk you out."

Amy watched them with open curiosity. "I can't wait to take your class."

Melody gave her a nod, thinking she probably wanted to take Fox instead of a class.

CHAPTER FOURTEEN

Melody had a tray full of drinks up on one hand as she scooted between two cowboys and headed for the pool tables, where a pack of rowdy customers were having their own little Friday-night tournament. Brian and Josh were taking on two cowboys. The insults were flying. The girls with them were cheering on their men as each of the guys tried to impress their respective dates.

She skirted a few more customers, her mind drifting to Fox. It drifted to him a lot. But the last few days had been amazing. They'd fallen into a routine. She worked her shift and landed at his place every night, using her key to get in and slip into his bed, waking him with a kiss. Every night, he found her naked beside him. Sex got better and better. He made her feel like he missed her every second she was away.

He left her sleeping in his bed each morning when he went to for work. Every morning she found a fresh pot of coffee waiting for her. And since she woke up at most people's lunchtime, she either made them lunch at the apartment or they went out to a restaurant. Afterward, she'd sprint home to shower and change clothes, take care of stuff, including working on the class she was nearly ready to present, then headed into work at the bar.

Their opposite schedules didn't seem to bother Fox. Though, like her, he voiced the desire to spend more time together.

Unfortunately, it was Friday night at the bar, and they didn't close until two a.m. Which meant she wouldn't get to Fox's place until well after three.

He wasn't here tonight. Fox, Dean, and Max planned to stay in and play some video game. Max was headed back to Boston on Sunday, so they wanted some bro time.

She loved that they were so close.

She'd made it a point to get to know Dean and Max better. Dean was—

Lost in thought, she miscalculated the distance between a customer and the pool table—specifically Josh with the stick, about to take a shot—and got jabbed in the ribs. The dude next to her tried to grab her as she stumbled, but all he did was upend the tray she was carrying. The whole thing fell from her hand, crashing to the polished cement floor. Her feet got tangled up together and she went down, catching the side of her head on a wood stool.

Pain blasted through her skull.

She saw the next disaster coming but couldn't stop her momentum as she slipped in the spilled beer and landed in the pile of broken glass and booze. Glass punctured her calf and thigh as she landed on her hip. She instinctively put her hand out to catch herself. Her palm and finger got sliced too.

"Fuck!" Josh spun and dropped the stick and lunged for her before her head hit the floor. He grabbed her hand and pulled her up to sitting.

Blood poured down her hand and dribbled down her leg. Mostly because there were two huge chunks of glass from the broken beer mugs embedded in her skin.

The crowd gathered around her. A chorus of "Are you all right?" came from multiple people.

Josh squatted in front of her. "I'm sorry. I didn't see you there."

"Not your fault. Totally mine."

"I should have checked behind me before I went for the shot." He ran his hand over the back of his neck, his eyes filled with remorse as he swore again.

She met his concerned eyes. "It was an accident on both our parts."

He scrunched his lips and grabbed the napkins someone held out to her. He pressed them to the side of her head, making her wholly aware of the cut and goose egg swelling just inside her hairline.

His thumb brushed along her cheek.

She flinched back from the intimate touch.

He frowned, his eyes narrowing. "You're going to need some serious stitches for all this."

Jax and Lyric pushed their way through the crowd around her.

Lyric held several clean towels. "Melody! Oh God!" She nudged Josh out of the way and bent close, replacing the soaked, bloody napkins at her head with one of the towels.

Melody winced, then looked at Jax. "I dropped something," she teased, trying to erase the look of horror from his face.

"Damnit, Mel, this is bad."

"It's just some cuts."

"There's two chunks of glass sticking out of you."

It had been a long time since she'd broken anything. Hazard of the job, especially with a packed crowd. Still, this was on her. She should have been paying better attention.

She looked up at her flustered sister. At nearly nine at night, the kitchen would be closing soon. "Can you drive me to the ER?"

"I'll take you," Josh cut in. "This was my fault. Lyric's working. I'll take you."

Melody held Lyric's gaze. "I want you." She barely glanced at Josh before saying, "She's family," hoping that explained things to Josh without her having to say she didn't want him taking care of her.

Lyric pulled the cloth away, winced, then pressed it back over the wound. "Of course I'll take you. Can you stand?"

She wasn't really sure, so she held her hands out to Jax. He immediately took one of the towels and wrapped it around her cut and bloody hand, then took her wrists and pulled her up. The glass in her leg pulled and stabbed at the movement, but she made it up with a wince.

Josh put his hand at her lower back. "I'm really sorry."

"I'll be okay."

She caught Brian staring from his table against the back wall. His gaze shot to Josh and then to her again. She glanced at Josh as he shrugged at Brian, some kind of silent communication between them.

She turned to Jax. "Get one of the others to replace table twenty-three's order and clean this up."

Jax brushed her hair away from the wound. "I'll take care of the bar. You let Lyric take care of you."

Melody let Lyric lead her out of the bar. John, their bouncer, held the door open for them and had already pulled Lyric's car up, leaving the driver's side and passenger doors open. Lyric helped her in, then got behind the wheel.

"What happened?" she asked.

"I wasn't paying attention and got knocked in the ribs by a pool cue. It was my fault." She pulled her phone out of the back pocket of her skirt, wishing she'd worn jeans tonight because maybe they'd have given her some protection. Lyric had tied a towel around her leg in both places, helping to catch the blood below each piece of glass. They knew if they yanked them out, she'd probably bleed more and that was best done in the ER. Just in case.

Lyric pulled out onto the main road and headed for the hospital. "Are you calling Fox?"

"Yes."

She glanced over. "You two are getting really close, huh?"

She'd always been able to open up the most with Lyric. "I think I've totally and irrevocably fallen for him."

Lyric sensed something in her words. "What's wrong, then?"

"Nothing. Really," she assured her older sister. "It's just so easy. He's so perfect."

Lyric raised a brow. "And that scares you?"

"I'm not scared. Just…"

A soft smile tugged at her sister's lips. "It feels so right you don't know what to do with it."

"Yes."

Lyric stopped at a light a few blocks from the hospital and turned to her. "You deserve it, Melody."

She'd wished for a relationship like the one Lyric shared with Mason for a long time. She didn't like being alone. But alone was better than being with the wrong person. That's why she'd tried so many times to find the right one. And all along, she'd already known who was right for her. It just took a while for him to come back.

She hit the speed dial for Fox and waited for him to answer. Instead, she got his voicemail.

"Hey, it's me. I had a little accident at work and am at the ER. Nothing major. Just need a few stitches. Call me."

"He's not answering?" Lyric raised a brow.

"He's with his buddies. They're having a boys' night. Beer, pizza, and gaming. It's apparently a thing they do. Bragging rights are on the line.

Or so it seemed, so he probably can't stop until his character is safe, or whatever."

Lyric helped her check in at reception and settle into a cubicle while they waited for a doctor to arrive. The nurse came in and checked her injuries, hissing when she saw the glass in her leg and that her hand was still bleeding. "Back in a sec, hon."

Just to be sure Fox got her message, she texted him.

MELODY: Waiting on ER doc for stitches. I guess I'll be home early tonight.

She didn't send the message right away. It hit her when she typed *home* that she meant it. But maybe it was too soon to be calling his place hers. She backtracked that last statement, rewriting it.

MELODY: Waiting on ER doc for stitches. I guess I'll be at your place early tonight.

She sent the message this time.

"Why'd you do that?" Of course Lyric was watching everything she did.

"It feels like we went from online chatting to being in a really deep relationship."

"Because you guys have a history. You knew each other already. You just needed some time to catch up with the in-between stuff."

"True." Those chats had only proven the friendship they shared as kids was deeper and stronger now. "I spend every night with him now." Though it hadn't been that long. And wasn't the beginning of the relationship the best part? That time when you just couldn't keep your hands off each other and you wanted to be with that person every second.

"That's promising."

"It's amazing. Better than I've ever had with anyone else. And I'm not just talking about the sex."

"He's the one." Lyric always had this way of cutting to the core of things.

"Yes. We've even talked about the future. But I have a key to his place, the code to his alarm"—which he'd given her when he kissed her goodbye the day she met him at the center—"but he hasn't said I can leave anything at his place or that he wants me to move in. It's too soon for any of that anyway."

"Why?"

She stiffened her spine. "Why? Because it is."

Lyric held her gaze, hers open and inquisitive. "Who said? Fox? You? Is that how *you* feel?"

"I feel like a pincushion." As diversions from a conversation went, that one wasn't bad.

Her sister wasn't deterred. "Answer the question."

"I feel like when he's not with me, something is missing," she blurted out. Like right now. She desperately wanted him to be with her. He'd hold her hand, comfort her, and everything would be all right.

Lyric grinned. "There you go."

She raised her uninjured hand and let it drop. "I don't even know what you mean by that."

"Yes, you do. You're just scared to admit that you love him."

"I know I do. It's just... How did this happen?"

Lyric put her hand on Melody's knee. "I think what you really mean is, how do you hold on to it?"

She didn't get a chance to figure that out.

The drape pulled back and a young doctor in dark gray scrubs walked in. "I'm Dr. Torres. Heard you took a dive at the bar and..." He glanced at the glass shards sticking out of her leg. "Ouch."

She stared at her throbbing leg. "You could say that."

He scrunched his nose. "You smell like a brewery."

She pointed to the glass. "Beer mug."

"Okay. I'll numb you up, then we'll wait for it to take effect. Once that's done, I'll start with your hand." He gently put his hand under hers and unwrapped the blood-soaked towel from her palm and fingers. "A few stitches in each of these should do it. You'll want to take a couple days off work to give yourself time to heal, so you don't just pull the stitches out."

Melody glanced at Lyric.

"Jax has probably already covered your Saturday shift. You don't need to be back to work until Wednesday. Unless you need more time. In which case, we'll cover for you. The weekday crowds aren't as packed."

She resigned herself to a few days off at the bar. She wasn't great at doing nothing. Hence the two side gigs. But maybe she and Fox could spend that time together.

The doctor got to work, poking her with a needle in a couple different places around the glass in her leg, her finger, and palm to numb her. He cleaned out the wounds on her hand, then put in three stitches in her finger and five in her palm. She flinched when they took the glass out of her leg. She was shocked to see that one piece had gone at least two inches deep. The other only about an inch. But she had to turn away when the doctor dug into her thigh, opening the wound to be sure there were no tiny shards left behind.

She'd been sitting up while he worked and didn't realize her head was still bleeding.

But the doc did when blood dripped from her hair onto her shirt. "You've got another wound?"

She pressed her hand to the knot on her head. "I hit it on a wood stool as I fell."

"Any dizziness or blurry vision?" He checked her pupils with a small flashlight.

"No. It just stings a lot."

The doctor stood and gently probed the tender, swollen skin. "Bonus stitches. Only a couple though. Head wounds bleed a lot." He grabbed another syringe and numbed her head. "We'll give that a few minutes to kick in while I pull the shard from your calf and finish that one."

It took another fifteen minutes to sew up her calf, shave a small patch of skin on her head, and put in four more stitches.

The doc wasn't finished with her though. He flashed a light in her eyes, checking her pupils again, and asked her several basic questions to make sure her cognitive skills were intact. "I don't think you have a concussion."

"I've had one before from a fall from a horse. This is nothing."

"Okay. I'll get you a prescription for some pain meds."

She shook her head. "I'm good with over-the-counter ibuprofen."

The doc nodded. "Okay. But I am going to prescribe antibiotics to stave off infection. I'll have the nurse bring you some sterile dressings for your wounds. Keep them dry and clean. If you notice any discharge from the wounds, see a doctor immediately for infection. Contact your doctor and have them check the stitches in ten days. Any questions?"

"No. I think I'm good."

"I'll get your discharge papers and the nurse should be back in a few minutes." Dr. Torres left them alone.

Melody checked her phone. No calls or texts. Fox must be really into his game.

"You okay?" Lyric asked.

"Fine. Everything's still numb. But I'm sure in an hour or so it's all going to be throbbing again."

"Yeah, that's what happened when I cut my wrist in the kitchen on that plate shard."

She held up her hand. "Who knew working at a bar was so dangerous?"

Lyric grimaced. "It could have been worse."

The nurse popped back in with a bag of supplies and her paperwork. "You're all set. Prescription for your antibiotics was called in to the pharmacy. You can pick them up in the morning. Change the bandages twice a day for the next two days. They need to remain dry and clean. Pat them dry after you shower. No baths until they are completely healed and the stitches are removed. Any questions?"

"No. Thank you for everything."

"You're welcome. You're free to go."

Lyric helped her up and they walked out to the parking lot together and got in the car. "Where to?"

"Fox's place."

"I figured that. Point me in the right direction."

"Take a right out of the lot."

The drive only took ten minutes and by then Melody felt done for the day. She wanted to crawl in bed and sleep for a week after the anxiety rush from the fall and hospital visit. Lyric pulled up in front of the building and parked.

Melody stayed Lyric from opening the door by putting her hand on Lyric's forearm. "I've got this. You don't need to walk me up."

She raised a brow, eyes filled with concern. "Are you sure?"

"Yes. Jax probably needs you at the bar."

"We texted while you were getting stitches. He's got everything covered."

She grabbed her bag of medical supplies off the floorboard. "Then go home to Mason. I'll be fine."

"Call me tomorrow."

"I will." She opened the door and realized she'd left her purse as well as her car at the bar. "Shit."

"What?"

"Nothing. I'll get all my stuff from the bar tomorrow."

"I can ask Jax to drop it off to you."

"No. It's out of the way. It's fine." She squeezed her sister's hand. "Thank you."

"You're welcome. Get some rest."

Melody climbed out of the car, closed the door, and headed up to Fox's place. She entered her code in the front door, took the elevator up to the fourth floor, then dragged herself down the hall to Fox's door. She could hear the guys talking and making noise as something happened in the game, and one of them cheered while the other shouted, "No!"

She knocked and waited, hoping they heard her.

Dean opened the door. "Why didn't you—Fuck." His eyes went wide as his gaze roamed over her. "What the hell happened?"

"Can I come in?"

He was standing in her way.

"Who is it?" Fox called.

"You need to see this," Dean called back as he stepped aside and she walked in.

Fox dropped a controller on the table, stood, then turned to her. "Hey, sweet..." Shock filled his eyes as he took her in, then leaped over the couch and rushed to her. He gently brushed her head with his fingertips by the bandage covering her stitches. "What happened? Why didn't you call me?"

"I did. You didn't answer." She waved that off when guilt filled his eyes. "I had an accident at work. It's fine."

"Fine? Your hand, head, and leg are bandaged. What happened?"

She wrapped her arms around his neck and leaned into him. "I had a bad night. I was distracted and got knocked in the ribs with a pool cue. I stumbled, dropped an entire tray of drinks, and hit my head on a barstool as I fell." She pointed to the bandage covering a small portion of her hair. "Then I landed on my thigh and hip in the broken glass." She pointed to her leg. "Then tried to catch myself, only to cut up my palm and hand." She held it up. "The doctor had to pull two wicked sharp pieces of glass out of my thigh and calf."

"Damn," Dean said.

"Does it hurt?" Max asked.

"A little bit. The numbing stuff is starting to wear off." For the first time, she noticed Amy sitting in the chair next to the sofa. "Looks like boys' night, plus one."

Fox's gaze shot to Amy, then back to her. "She caught the pizza delivery out front and brought it up to us. She stayed for a slice and to watch us play. But forget about all that."

Dean and Max winced, like even they couldn't forget that Amy crashed their party and they knew why.

Fox gently rubbed her back. "How many stitches?"

"Twenty-one total in my leg, seven in my hand, and four in my scalp."

Fox cupped her face and made her tilt her head back. "I'm sorry I didn't answer the phone. I didn't even hear it go off."

"It fell under the coffee table." Amy held it up, then set it on the table.

Melody wondered if someone had helped it disappear from Fox's sight. He usually kept it close. "It's fine. Lyric took me to the hospital and dropped me off here. You guys can finish your game thing. I'm going to bed. Well, first, I'm going to wash off the beer stink, then crawl into bed." She gently pressed the heel of her hand to her head, barely touching the swollen part and wincing.

"Do you have a concussion?" Fox asked.

"No. Just a little headache. Probably more from the stress than the head wound." She pressed her hands to his chest. "I'm fine. Really. I just need some sleep."

"Okay. Come on. Game night's over. I'll help you get cleaned up and put you in bed."

She shook her head. "No. I don't want to ruin your night. Max is leaving soon. Spend time with him."

He shook his head all through that. "No. I'm taking care of you."

Dean headed for the coffee table covered in wrappers, beer bottles, and food. "We'll clean this up and get out of here."

Max took a step closer to her. "Sorry I didn't get to spend more time getting to know you. But I'll be seeing you both soon." Max's gaze landed on Fox. "I'll call you from the office on Monday." He turned back to her. "Take care. And don't let Fox obsess about letting you down. None of us heard his phone. He's not going to let that happen again."

She shook her head. "It's not a big deal. I'm fine."

"It's a big deal to me," Fox said, his words tight with anger.

Max nodded. "We protect each other. You're included in that now."

She stepped away from Fox and hugged Max. "Thank you. Have a safe trip back."

Fox took her hand and tugged her away from Max. "Come on. I've got you." He led her toward their bedroom.

She looked over her shoulder at Dean holding the door open for Amy to exit and Max bringing up the rear. "Goodnight."

"Night," the guys called out. Amy glanced back, frowning like Melody had ruined her night.

Tough shit. She wasn't supposed to be here anyway.

Fox escorted her to the bathroom. He flipped on the light and said, "Sit on the toilet so I can get your boots off and clean you up."

She took a seat.

"Why did you let Amy crash your boys' night?"

"It felt rude to make her leave. And anyway, we were too busy playing to really interact with her. I'm surprised she didn't just get up and leave."

"I'm not."

Fox stared down at her, his face a mask of sorrow and guilt. "Fuck, Mel. Look at you."

She dropped the Amy bullshit and took his hand. "I'm okay. I'm not mad, not even a little bit, that you didn't get my message."

"I should have been there."

"It's just a few stitches."

He brushed his hand over her head on the opposite side of her wound. "I'm sorry."

"Nothing to be sorry about. Just help me with my boots and maybe give me a warm washcloth to clean myself up for now. I'll shower in the morning before I change the bandages."

Fox pressed a soft kiss to her forehead, then dropped to his knees in front of her and pulled off her boots and wet socks.

"The beer and blood soaked into them."

"I'll toss all your clothes in the washer and dryer so they'll be clean for you in the morning and you'll have something to wear." He cocked his head. "Why don't you have anything here to wear?"

She met his gaze. "Because you never said I could keep anything here."

His eyes went wide. "Fuck. I didn't think about it. I just thought you would..."

"What?"

"Make yourself at home because this is *our* place."

She shook her head. "This is your place, Fox. I'm your girlfriend, but we haven't talked about whether it's okay for me to...make myself at home."

He scrubbed both hands over his face. "I've never done this before."

"What?"

"Had a serious relationship with someone. Not like this. I want you here. All the time. I want you to feel like this is your place, too. That's why I gave you the key."

"You gave me the key so you didn't sleep through me knocking on your door in the middle of the night so we can have sex."

He leaned away from her. "Is that what you think? That this is just sex?"

"No. But I also didn't want to assume that you want me all up in your space and taking up your closet when you haven't said that's okay."

He leaned in and took her by the shoulders. "How is this? Take up all the space you need and want. Here, in my Boston place, in my car, wherever the hell you want, because I want to share everything with you."

He blew her away.

"Really?"

He touched his forehead to hers. "Yes."

"Okay. But I don't want to hear you complain when you realize there is no space for your stuff in my apartment closet. Like at all. It's dinky."

"This place is big enough for all your stuff and mine."

She hadn't expected that and it must have shown on her face.

Fox brushed his hand up and down her arm. "Too fast? We'll get there. Just know, it's on the table whenever you want to, you know, move in. And stay. I'd really like that. But take some time. Think about all that. Get back to me whenever you're ready. Because I am. Actually, it feels like I've been waiting for this...you...for too damn long. I promise, I'll try to be patient. And I'll be a better boyfriend. I'll keep my phone on me so I'll know if you call. I just thought you were at work and I wouldn't hear from you until later tonight, if at all before you showed up here, so I left my phone on the table."

She hooked her hand around the back of his neck and pulled him in for a kiss to stop his rambling.

He immediately took her by the hips and held on as the heat between them exploded and he took the kiss deeper. Their tongues tangled and a moan escaped her lips as he changed the angle and dove in for more.

Suddenly, he pulled away. "Hey." He brushed his thumb over her bottom lip. "Sorry. I got carried away."

"Yay for me!"

He chuckled. "You're in no shape for what I'd like to do to you."

She sighed. "As much as I want you, you're probably right." She felt drained and the pain in her leg and hand was starting to get worse.

He slipped his hands beneath her shirt. "Let's get this off."

She cocked a brow. "You're just trying to get me naked."

He grinned. "I'm going to take care of you in a different way."

"Oh? Do tell. I'm very interested in whatever fantasies you have."

He stared at her for a long moment. "We'll save that for another day." The look on his face said he had a few ideas rolling around his head.

"Or you could tell me now and I can surprise you later."

He pulled her shirt off, making sure not to hit her head wound or her hand as he pulled it free. "Uh-uh. I start talking and I'll want to touch. And right now the only touching I'm doing is to get the stench of stale beer off you and getting you into bed."

"Where you'll?" she prompted, still flirting with him.

He clamped his hands on her hips again. "You drive me wild, sometimes."

She undid the button on her skirt and unzipped it. "Happy to oblige." She stood and he tugged the denim down her legs as he leaned in and kissed her belly. Heat pooled between her thighs. "You're making it very hard to be good."

"You're just making me hard."

"I can take care of that." She was tired, but not too tired for him.

"Not tonight, sweetheart. Tonight, I get to repay you for all the times you took care of me as a kid."

She sat on the toilet again and leaned in so they were just an inch apart. "You don't owe me anything."

"I want to do this for you."

She gave him a tilted smile. "Well, okay then."

"Stay put." He pulled a washcloth out of the cupboard by the door, then left for a moment and returned with one of his T-shirts. He turned on the faucet and dampened the washcloth with warm water, then turned off the tap and used the cloth to wipe down one arm, then the other, then her hands, and fingers, working around the bandages. He rinsed the cloth, then ran it over her right leg, avoiding the bandages, before cleaning her calf and foot. He did the rinse-and-repeat thing on her other leg.

Chilled a bit as the warm water on her skin cooled then started to evaporate, she shivered as he pulled the shirt over her head and helped her get her arms in the holes, then he pulled it down her torso.

"Do you want me to wash your face?"

She didn't want to sleep in her makeup. "If you don't mind, though we're going to need some soap for that. Probably best if I lean over the sink. I can probably do it with one hand."

"I want to help."

She went to the sink.

Fox pulled her hair back and tucked it into the back of the shirt to keep it from falling forward.

She leaned over the sink. He cupped his big hand under the warm water and splashed it over her face. She helped, using her good hand. Then he rubbed the soap over her hand and she massaged it over her eyes and face, cleaning her skin. Fox helped her splash more water over her face, then gently dabbed a towel over her skin, drying her off.

"Feel a little better?"

She leaned into his chest. "Actually, yes. But I could use some ibuprofen before I crash for the night."

He opened the medicine cabinet and pulled out a bottle, uncapping it. "How many?"

"The throbbing pain is ratcheting up. Let's go with three."

He handed them over, then filled the glass he kept by the sink with water.

She took the pills and hoped they worked soon.

He brushed his hands up and down her arms. "Need anything else?"

She shook her head.

He took her hand and led her to the bed. He'd already turned down the covers.

She crawled in and settled in her spot as Fox covered her with the blankets. "Thank you."

"I'll be right back." He kissed her on the forehead and left their room, probably to put her clothes in the washer and turn out all the lights.

She was slowly drifting into sleep when he slipped into bed behind her and hooked his arm over her waist, pulling her into his warm body. "I like this."

"This is where you belong. With me." He kissed the back of her head. "Sleep, baby. I'm right here with you."

It felt like she'd just closed her eyes and let go of everything except that one lovely statement and the feel of Fox wrapped around her when someone pounded on the door and wouldn't stop.

CHAPTER FIFTEEN

The pounding on the door stopped as she reached for the handle. Barely awake at this godawful hour of the morning, she had a surly "Fuck off" ready to leave her tongue when the offensive person on the other side of the door yelled, "Melody. Open up."

She took a step back and glared at the peep hole. She knew that voice. And *he* shouldn't be here.

How did he even get in the building?

She heard the shower go off in the other room and opened the door to her unwelcome guest. "What the hell are you doing here?"

Josh tried to come in.

She stood her ground, holding on to the door, creating just enough space for herself, but not for him to look inside Fox's place.

The alarm started beeping beside her. She huffed and quickly punched in the code to disarm it.

Josh had somehow inched closer. "I came to see if you're okay."

"Why?" For the life of her, she didn't understand why he'd show up a few minutes after eight a.m. at her boyfriend's place. "How did you even know I was here?" That really stumped her.

"Jax and Aria were talking about you last night and mentioned that Lyric dropped you off here."

Aggravated, she raised a brow and narrowed her gaze. "You eavesdropped on their conversation, then thought it a good idea to show up here?"

Josh held out his hands, then let them drop and smack the sides of his thighs. "I know the last time we were together things got...tense. But last night was an accident," he emphasized. "You wouldn't let me apologize the last time when I got a little overzealous."

A little! He'd shoved her up against his truck and groped her in a parking lot.

He eyed her up and down. "Can you blame me?"

Yes! She did. That's why she'd ended things. Boundaries mattered. Consent mattered.

His gaze dipped to her bare legs.

She'd thought it was Dean at the door, so she'd only put on Fox's T-shirt to cover up. Then again, if she hadn't been woken out of a dead sleep, she would have realized that Dean had his own key and didn't need to pound on the door.

She needed coffee. Stat.

His gaze met hers again. "But last night, you were seriously hurt. And I'm sorry. I'm a good guy. So I came to check on you."

"As you can see, I'm fine."

He shifted closer, his eyes going soft on her. "Can I come in, so we're not talking in the hallway?"

Fox suddenly grabbed the door and swung it wider, so he was standing partially in front of her and glaring at Josh in bare feet, faded jeans, no shirt, rippling muscles on display, his hair wet and tousled. "What are you doing here?"

She'd heard him coming and appreciated the whole protective vibe coming off him, even if she could take care of herself.

Josh tried to look nonchalant, but a flash of apprehension and nerves lit his eyes. "I came to check on my girl, Mel."

She couldn't believe that shocking statement came out of Josh's mouth. Not after their last date years ago.

Fox took a step forward. "She's not *your* anything. Melody is *my* girlfriend. I take care of her."

Josh glanced at her, then into the apartment. "I can see why she likes spending time here. Nice place. Classy." He made it sound like Melody was seeing Fox for the swanky apartment and his money.

She didn't like that at all. Offended to her core, she glared at him again. "Goodbye, Josh." She took Fox's hand and pulled him back with her.

"Wait." Josh stepped forward, blocking the door. He scanned her again, his gaze concerned. "Are you really okay?"

"I'm fine. Just a bunch of stitches and a few days off to let the cuts heal. I appreciate your concern, but coming here was not necessary."

Something like remorse crossed his eyes, there and gone before she could be sure, but for some odd reason she felt uneasy.

That's how he always made her feel.

"We're done here." Fox pushed the door closed in Josh's face and locked it. He turned to her and crossed his arms over his chest. "What the hell was that?"

She put her hands up in an I-don't-know pose, then dropped them. "He's just feeling guilty or something about what happened last night."

The suspicion in Fox's eyes deepened. "He's the one who hit you last night."

She put her hand on his forearm. "It was an accident. You know how packed the place can get, people bumping into each other all the time."

Fox's arms went limp at his sides and her hand fell away from him. "Okay. And the 'my girl, Mel' bit?"

It dawned on her. He was jealous.

"We went on a few dates years ago that went nowhere because he's a jerk. I'm not and never was *his* anything." She stepped closer to him and looked him straight in the eye. "I'm *yours*."

He cupped her cheek and brushed his thumb over her bottom lip. "That makes me the luckiest man alive."

"And I'm the luckiest woman. Now can I have some coffee? Because it is too damn early to be awake." She tried to turn and head for the kitchen.

He took her hand and gently tugged her to a stop. "Tell me how you're really doing?"

She glanced at him. "First, I'm really loving the view this morning." She lusted after those rippling abs, his wide shoulders, and gorgeous face.

He shook his head, undeterred by her attempt to change the subject. "Uh-uh. What's wrong?"

She let loose the tension riding her and let her shoulders sag. "Everything hurts. All the cuts. But especially my head." She squinted, the light bothering her eyes. "I'm a little worried about it."

"Get back in bed. I'll get you some coffee and ibuprofen. We'll see if that helps. If not, I'm taking you to the doctor to get checked out again."

She pressed her hand to her growling belly. "Do you have anything to eat?"

"Go. I'll make you breakfast. Probably best to eat something if you're going to take another high dose of ibuprofen anyway."

Grateful that he really was taking care of her, she brushed a kiss to his lips, and walked back into the bedroom. His wet towel was on the floor. He'd obviously heard her at the door and hastily pulled on a pair of jeans, and rushed out to see what was going on. She'd let him pick it up.

She propped up her pillow, crawled back under the covers, and closed her eyes.

Fox brushed his hand over her hair. "Hey, sweet Dee, here's the meds and some water."

She opened her eyes and stared up at him. "Thank you." She took the glass and the meds, then downed the pills and a gulp of water.

He took the glass back. "I'll bring you some coffee and have breakfast ready in a few minutes."

She sat up. "You know what? I think I'll come out and curl up on the couch. We can eat together."

He grinned. "I'd love that, if you're sure you're up for it."

"That's about all I'm up for at the moment. I'll shower later and maybe you can help me re-bandage my wounds."

He leaned in and kissed her forehead. "I'd love to play doctor with you." He brushed his lips over hers, then winked. "Whatever you need."

She took him up on it. "Some clothes from my place would be nice."

"I just put your clothes in the dryer. You can wear them, or something of mine, back to your place, where I hope you'll pack a bag to bring back, so you'll have stuff here."

She held his gaze. "You really mean it."

He tilted his head. "That comment Josh made about the apartment...me..."

"What about it?"

He'd never looked more serious. "I don't think you're after my money."

She shook her head. "Not even a little bit."

"But I've been burned by others, so I'm cautious. It's a hard habit to break when you grow up like I did."

"As you should be. But know this. I care about *you*. What we feel for each other, what we have together, it's special."

He leaned down and kissed her again. "You're special. I knew that when we were kids. I see it even more now." He took her hand and helped her out of bed. "I have a spare blanket in the closet. I'll grab it for you and meet you at the couch."

She walked out to the living room and curled into the corner of the leather sofa.

Fox came out and draped the super-soft blanket over her, then kissed her on the head and went to the kitchen.

She rested against the pillows and closed her eyes, hoping the meds kicked in and the throb in her head and body ceased. Before she knew it, she smelled pancakes, and Fox was sitting next to her, holding out a plate.

"While I get by in the kitchen, I'm confessing right now, the pancakes are the frozen kind, but I scrambled the eggs." He held up a bottle of syrup. "I want to say you like powdered sugar and butter on yours. Is that right?"

She grinned. "Yes."

He smiled back. "That was a deep memory. And sorry, but I've only got butter and syrup."

"Butter is fine, unless you've got strawberry syrup."

"We need to do a grocery run so the place is stocked with everything you like, too."

"If I'm feeling better this afternoon, let's do it."

He stared at her for a good twenty seconds, then said, "Okay. Let's do it."

Look at them making plans. She took her plate and the fork he held out to her and dug in.

He did the same.

She thought about their earlier conversation and decided a Saturday-morning heart-to-heart was a good idea for both of them. "What do you see for us in the next year? The next five?"

"I see you and me," he said without hesitation, handing her the mug of coffee he'd placed on the table in front of them. "Take that timeline out as far as you want and that's what I see."

She pressed her lips tight and blinked away tears. That's what she wanted to hear. But... "What does that look like? You and me and what? Are we living here? Boston? Both?"

He chewed and swallowed his bite of eggs and never stopped looking at her. "With the way things are with my mom right now, I'm needed here. But you know my company is in Boston. While I could move it somewhere else, Wyoming is not the place where I'd have the talent pool to choose from for a lot of the high-tech expertise I need."

"I've been thinking about living in Boston with you and what it would be like. I want to be with you. A new place seems like an adventure. But I'm not sure if I'll like it because I've never lived in a big city. I mean, where would I keep my horse?" The last she said with humor, hoping to wipe the anxiety from his eyes.

Fox chuckled, like she hoped. "I'll find you a barn in the city, someplace you can ride any time you want."

She actually hadn't thought about that, but it could work. She loved to ride. And having that piece of her life in Boston might help her feel more at home. "So, I'd move into your apartment?"

"Yes. But if you don't like it, we could get something else. A house."

"Just like that. Just buy a house?" It blew her mind that he was ready to do something so huge to make her happy.

His gaze narrowed. "Are you asking if I have the money to do that?"

"I don't," she confessed, because she wanted it to be clear she didn't make the kind of money he made. He had to know that already, but she needed to say it.

He simply grinned at her. "I do, sweet Dee. I can give you anything you want."

She wanted to be his partner. "I have some money saved up."

"Okay. What did you plan to do with it? Go back to school? Open another business? Get a house?"

She tilted her head and studied him. "Would it bother you to introduce me to your friends and clients and say that I'm just a waitress?"

"No. Because I know you're a hell of lot more than just that."

"It doesn't bother you that I have no idea what you do on the computer? All that code stuff means nothing to me."

"If you're interested, I'll teach you what it means. If you're not, it's no big deal." He shrugged it away.

She thought it was important. "But it's your life's work."

"So? It's what I love doing. You understand that it's important to me. That's enough. You don't need to understand code to support me. I have no idea how to run a bar. I don't need to, to know that you love that place. We can have a conversation about my projects and your night at the bar and still connect about that without knowing all the bytes and how many shots you can get out of a whiskey bottle."

"In a fifth of whiskey, about sixteen shots."

Fox grinned. "Well, there you go. I learned something."

"Shots will only make the world turn you upside down on your ass. You actually create things that are useful and necessary."

"Everyone who comes into that bar is looking to feel useful and necessary to someone. You give them a place to let loose, relax, and have fun. That's important to the soul."

She wanted him to understand. "I want to be useful in *our* life together. I guess I'm just not sure what my place will be in a place I've never been and a life I never thought I'd live."

He put his hand on her thigh and squeezed. "We have time to figure it out. And if what you want is to bring some of Wyoming to Boston, we can figure out how to do that, too."

"I don't even know what you mean by that."

"I'm not real sure either, but if what you're looking for there is what is familiar to you here, let's figure out what that is and make it happen."

That actually kind of made sense to her. "Huh."

"I hope that means you're going to let that ruminate in your mind until you know what it is you need there to feel like it's home."

She would. But she already knew what made her feel safe and appreciated and necessary. "First and foremost...you."

He leaned in and kissed her softly. "You always felt like home to me, too." He lifted his chin toward her plate. "Finish up."

The food was delicious and made her feel better. But so did their talk. She saw her future with Fox, but the details had been fuzzy. That scared her. It seemed the most obvious that she'd have to make the sacrifice and leave this place. But what if it wasn't a sacrifice so much as an opportunity to reinvent herself? She liked the idea of bringing some of what she loved into their new life as she found a place in his.

She didn't want to lose him because she didn't compromise.

Her ties to Wyoming were about family.

He had an entire company built and operating in Boston with dozens upon dozens of employees depending on him.

Her family could visit anytime they wanted. She could come home and see them.

Fox couldn't move his business. Not here.

So if she wanted him and the relationship she imagined in her mind where they lived together and made a life filled with happy memories, then she needed to move to Boston to be with him.

Mind made up about that, all she had to do was imagine what her life looked like in the big city. A new job. A new place. A chance to grow into a new version of herself.

CHAPTER SIXTEEN

F ox opened the apartment door and found the last person he expected to see on the other side. "Hey."

"Hey yourself." Amy's gaze swept over him and she licked her lower lip when her gaze met his again. "You look amazing."

"Uh, thanks." He and Melody had been lazing on the couch all day. She was feeling better, so he'd offered to take her out to dinner tonight since she had the night off because of her injuries. He'd put on a pair of black jeans and a blue dress shirt with the sleeves rolled up.

Melody was still getting dressed.

The way Amy was looking at him, he guessed Melody would like that he'd made an effort for her.

Amy held up a plate of cupcakes. "I made your favorite. Chocolate chip, chocolate cake with vanilla frosting."

They looked amazing.

She took a tiny step closer, a sultry look in her eyes. "Can I come in?"

"Uh." Just like he didn't want Josh in his place, he didn't want Amy there either. Not when Melody already sensed Amy's interest in him.

She tilted her head. "What? These are your favorite, right? Because that's what you said when I made them the other day for the class."

He shifted his weight from one foot to the other. "No. I mean, yes. They were really good."

She beamed at him. "Great." She stepped even closer.

He didn't move. He wasn't exactly sure how to handle this situation. "Listen, I was just heading out to dinner."

She knew he had a girlfriend.

Shouldn't that make her stop being so flirty?

"Really? I haven't eaten either. Except for a few licks of the icing." She bit her lip. "It was just too tempting." She gave him another sultry once-over. "Anyway, let's go together. I've been dying to try that new place downtown. There's not a lot of choices beside the diner and pizza place, unless you go to the bar, and I just hate eating alone in public."

Yeah, that was not happening. "Um. I actually have a date."

"With *her*?"

He didn't have to guess who she was referring to, since she'd met Melody.

Amy pressed her lips tight and shook her head. "I thought you were just friends."

"We're best friends. And now we're more." Why was he explaining himself? "But I appreciate that you made the cupcakes for me." He grabbed onto the plate.

She didn't release it. "You know she's never going to fit into your world back in Boston. She's not...sophisticated enough." Her gaze shot past him.

He didn't need to glance over his shoulder to know Melody was standing behind him. He felt her like a warm caress against his soul. "Melody is everything I ever wanted. She fits *me*. And I think anyone who gets to know her would find that she's smart, creative, generous, and kind. And if that doesn't fit with someone, then they don't deserve to know her, and I don't want to be around them."

Amy leaned in like she was telling a secret. "The elite in Boston will always treat her like an outsider. I've catered enough of their parties to know how to handle myself around them. How to dress. How to speak. Who the right people are and the ones to avoid. They'll tear her apart." She made it sound like she was trying to save him and his reputation.

He didn't like the implication that Amy felt that Melody wasn't good enough for him. She was better than he deserved. But that didn't mean he wouldn't try to be worthy of her every day for the rest of his life. "Melody can handle them and anyone else who comes at her." Melody had seen right through Amy and her interest in him.

Amy let go of the plate they'd both been holding. "You haven't told her anything about your life back there, have you?" This time her voice carried. "Maybe it's better you keep your secrets. Then again..." One shoulder rose and fell. "Enjoy the cupcakes."

He closed the door as she walked away, then turned to find Melody studying him. "What was that about?"

"Nothing."

She eyed him. "She mentioned something about secrets."

"I don't know what's gotten into her lately. She never used to act like this."

"She doesn't like that you're with me."

He held up the plate. "She brought us cupcakes."

One eyebrow shot up. "*Us*? I don't think so." Her hair cascaded past her shoulders in waves. She wore black jeans and a flowing red top. The bandage that she'd had on her head was gone, since she'd just showered, but she'd wrapped her finger and hand. He bet her thigh and calf were also wrapped beneath the jeans.

"You're so beautiful." They'd made a quick trip over to her place a little while ago to pick up some clothes and toiletries for her to leave here. He'd like to pack up her whole place and move it. But he was trying to be patient.

Amy's words still rang in his head.

Would Melody like Boston? The people in his life? Would she feel accepted and at home there with him?

Melody moved closer. "You're gorgeous. And I'm starving. Are you ready to go? Or would you prefer to be with Amy tonight?" She looked dead serious about that question.

"No." He shook his head and set the plate of cupcakes on the counter before turning back to her, his anger rising. "Hell no. And you should know that the only woman I want, the only one I think about, dream about, obsess over, is you. I'm not blind. I see that she's got a thing for me. But I haven't encouraged it. I don't even pay that much attention to it. Because I am only ever thinking about you. You are the only woman I see."

Her shoulders sagged, and her face fell into remorse. "I'm being a bitch. I'm sorry."

"Don't say that. You have every right to be upset that another woman showed up at my door with a gift."

She eyed him. "A gift you accepted."

Fuck. He had. "I'm sorry. I thought it was just a nice gesture until she started talking about you."

Everything about her tensed. "What about me?"

"She thinks that you won't fit in with the elite in Boston."

Her head tilted to the side. "Do you think that?"

"I don't give a fuck what anyone thinks but you. I think you're perfect."

"Hardly."

"For me, to me, you are perfect. So forget about Amy and let's go to dinner." He glanced toward the bedroom, her in those tight jeans, her breasts swelling at the V in her blouse. "Or I can take you to bed and spend the rest of the night worshipping you until you truly understand how much I want you."

One hand went to her thigh, the other she raised and slid her fingers along the hem of her blouse from her shoulder down to her sexy cleavage. "Can we do both?"

Double fuck. He got hard just looking at her posed like that. "I'll give you anything you want."

She smiled, looking at him from beneath her lashes, all sultry and sexy. "You. Always you."

He closed the distance between them, cupped her beautiful face, and kissed her soft, lush lips. She smelled like raspberries. Her scent drew him in and wrapped around him.

She put her hand on his chest and nudged him back, breaking the kiss. "First dinner. Then you can have me. I'm starving."

That was a good sign she was truly feeling better.

He took her hand and led her to the door. "Still up for that American bistro that just opened up?"

"Yes. I've been wanting to try it for weeks. I just never have the time. And they're open and closed the same time as the bar, so I'm glad I got tonight off to spend it with you and try someplace new."

Fox set the alarm, locked the door, and walked with her to the elevator. "I checked out the menu online. They've got a lot of varied choices. The chicken pot pie sounded delicious, but so did the beef stew." They entered the elevator car and he hit the button to take them down to the first floor.

"I was thinking of the chicken and dumplings. Or maybe the pot roast sandwich."

"It all sounds good." They exited the elevator hand in hand and walked out of the building, and turned right to head down the street. The bistro was down four blocks. The fall evening air was crisp but not cold enough to need a jacket.

"Are you sure the walk isn't too much for your leg? I don't want you tearing your stitches."

"It's fine. They're a little tender still, but it's only a few blocks. Plus, it's a beautiful night for a walk."

He hooked his arm around her shoulders, drew her close, and enjoyed the hell out of being with her as they passed the center, the diner, several downtown shops, a hole-in-the-wall liquor store, the bakery, and a florist.

He should get her some flowers. They weren't open now. He'd put it on the list of things he wanted to do for her.

"You're quiet."

He kissed the side of her head. "Just enjoying the walk and being with you. It's quieter here. In Boston, walking down the street, it's noisy. Traffic, a ton of people out, and music and sounds pouring out of bars and restaurants." He glanced up at the night sky. "There's so much light pollution you can't really see the stars. Not like here."

"At the ranch they're even brighter. You can see so many more than in town."

"If you move there with me, it doesn't mean we won't come back here. We can come back as often as you like."

"I know." She squeezed his side. "I don't want to talk about that tonight. I just want to enjoy our date."

"I wish we could do this more often."

She leaned into him. "I've been busy. You're busy. We live on different schedules."

"Yeah. I'm trying to figure out a way to fix that because I want us to spend more time together."

They arrived at the bistro.

"Table for two. We have a reservation under Fox."

The hostess smiled. "Of course. Right this way, Mr. Fox."

"It's just Fox." He let Melody go ahead of him as they followed the waitress to a table by the windows. He held out the chair for Melody to sit, then took the seat across from her. They both sat near the window, leaving the two empty seats next to them at the table set for four.

"The specials for tonight are listed on the front of the menu. Shari will be by in a moment to take your order. Enjoy your meal."

Fox scanned the drink list first and slid his hand across the table to rest it over Melody's.

She glanced around the restaurant. "I love this place. It's small and quaint, but cozy."

The restaurant only had about thirty tables and a low bar with about fifteen seats for diners that spanned the area that opened to the kitchen space. You could watch the staff preparing the meals. All of the wood tables were topped with a wide candle with three wicks on a wood base with a glass cylinder around it, silverware, green linen napkins, and unexpected salt and pepper shakers in all kinds of pairings. Their table had a horse and apple cart. The horse was the salt. The cart the pepper. On the table beside theirs…Mickey and Minnie. On another table, a dog chef and cat waitress.

"It smells amazing in here." His stomach rumbled.

The couple next to them had just gotten their plates. They'd both gone for the pot roast sandwich with a mountain of fried potatoes.

Melody groaned. "That looks amazing."

"It does. We're going to have to come back here to try everything."

She grinned at him. "Deal. But it's probably going to have to be lunch."

Yes. Their schedule issue. "Deal."

A woman in black pants, a white tee with the bistro logo and name on it, and a green apron stopped at their table. "Hi. I'm Shari. Can I get you both something to drink?"

Melody ordered the Moscato. He got a hazy IPA.

"Is that your favorite wine?" he asked.

"Layla got me hooked on it. It's sweet and light. But maybe I should have ordered something stronger. Like a shot."

He lifted a brow. "Why?"

"Because we're not alone."

"Oh my God. I can't believe we ended up at the same place." Amy stood by their table and looked around the restaurant.

Melody gaped at her.

Fox tried to hold in his what-the-fuck expletive.

"I've been dying to try this place. The food smells amazing." She turned back to him and frowned. "Unfortunately the place is packed."

Which was why he'd made a reservation earlier today when he asked Melody if she'd be up for going out. "I'm sure a seat at the bar will open up soon." He hoped she took the hint.

"There's a bunch of people waiting in line. But I saw you through the window and knew you wouldn't mind if I joined you."

Fuck me!

She looked at Melody. "We can chat about the course you're going to teach. I'd love to know more about your shop and what you do."

Melody stared at him, her face completely devoid of any emotion, and his heart sank. He should shut this down immediately, but he wasn't sure how without creating a scene. Who knew what Amy would say or do if he told her to leave.

Shari arrived with their drinks. "Moscato for the lady. Hazy for you." She focused on Amy. "Will you be joining them?"

Amy held Fox's gaze.

Fox opened his mouth to object, but Amy fell into the chair beside him.

"I knew you wouldn't mind."

Shari looked expectantly at their uninvited guest. "What can I get you?"

What the fuck! Now he'd look like a total dick if he asked her to leave.

Amy snagged his beer. "Mind if I try this?"

"Hey!"

She took a sip, ignoring his outburst, and scrunched her lips. "Too bitter."

He sank into his seat, feeling run over.

Melody picked up her wine and took a big gulp.

Amy set his glass back in front of him. "I think I'll stick to my favorite. Cabernet."

Shari nodded. "I'll be back to take your orders."

Amy snagged his menu, leaned in like she was sharing it with him, and stared at it. "What are you having, Fox? I've heard the prime rib is amazing."

"I'm so glad I got the night off," Melody said, eyeing him.

Amy looked at Melody for the first time. "Right. Must be hard to have a personal life when you work until all hours of the night." Amy caught her breath. "What happened to your hand?"

"Cut it on a broken beer mug."

"Bar fight?" Amy shook her head and pressed her lips tight like that kind of thing seemed inevitable. "I'm not surprised. That place you work at is rough."

Melody raised both brows. "You've been there?"

"Sure. A couple of times with Fox and Dean. They're always talking about how pretty the women are there."

Anger made him tighten his fist around his beer glass. But he never took his gaze off Melody. "There's only one woman I'm looking at, at the bar. The same one who's in front of me right now."

Amy seemed to catch herself. "Oh. Right. Yeah. Of course. Sorry." She winced like she'd given away a secret. "I think I'll get the prime rib. I hope they haven't run out. I hear they don't always have it."

Fox squeezed Melody's hand. "Did you decide?"

"What are you getting?"

This time Fox answered. "The pot roast sandwich."

"Will you share some with me if I get the chicken and dumplings? I'll share with you."

He grinned, liking this way more than it merited. "Sounds perfect. I was torn between the two."

Shari arrived with Amy's wine and took their order.

Frustration filled Fox. He'd wanted this night to be special. He'd wanted to sit across from Melody and enjoy some good food and conversation. He'd wanted to talk about some of the places they could go in Boston and tempt her to take a trip there with him sometime in the next couple of weeks.

Amy bumped her shoulder to his. "How's it been trying to run your company remotely? I hear you on the phone constantly or typing a mile a minute on your computer."

"It's a challenge, but it's working out so far."

She eyed him. "You must miss the city though."

"Not really."

"Oh, come on. I do. I can't wait to get back. And you...you've been spotted at all the hot spots in town. Don't tell me you don't miss that."

Actually, it got old fast. "Clients expect a certain amount of wining and dining when they're paying top dollar for my services."

"And the women you've been photographed with?" Amy raised a brow. "A man could get a reputation for all the different women in your life."

Fox took exception and shifted sideways to face the woman who at every turn was trying to ruin this night for him. "The women in those photographs work for me. They're smart and talented. I make sure to hire women because they're often overlooked in the male-dominated industry. That doesn't make me the player you seem to think I am."

"Oh. Right. Yeah. My bad." Amy winced but didn't seem the least contrite or apologetic. "I just kind of got lost in all the press you and your company have received over the years. The pictures look one way, but I'm sure it's more accurate that those women only worked for you."

Fox clamped his jaw shut before he said something he'd regret.

"How is Tanya doing?" Melody asked, sipping her wine as she changed the subject.

"Fine. She wants me to stop by tomorrow."

"Who's Tanya?" Amy glanced from him to Melody and back.

None of your business, he wanted to say. "My mother."

"Oh. You have family in town."

"Not really. I'm closer to Melody and her family than I am with Tanya." Amy leaned in closer to him. "Oh. Why?"

He glanced at Melody. "Because I didn't grow up with her."

"Oh. Right. You were a foster kid."

He gave her an I-don't-want-to-talk-about-it look and sipped his beer, hoping she dropped it.

Amy put her hand on his shoulder. "I'm really sorry. That must have been really...hard."

He shook off her hand and didn't care that she frowned at his rejection of her unwanted touch.

Melody slid her hand up his arm and squeezed. "I'll go with you tomorrow if you'd like."

"I'd love that." He pulled his arm back, so he could take her hand. "And we're having dinner with your folks, right?"

She nodded. "The whole gang actually, so be prepared for us to be the center of attention." The gleam in her eyes said he should be prepared for a lot of questions about his intention toward her.

Not a problem to assure her family he cared deeply for his Melody.

"I get it," Amy said. Her obliviousness to the undercurrents had to be an act. "Families are complicated. My parents left me to my own devices most of the time, too busy with their own stuff to pay much attention to what I was doing. It sucked. All they want for me is to find a good guy and settle down."

"Is that what you want?" Melody asked her.

"Yes. I want someone to take care of me."

Melody frowned. "What's your dream guy like?"

Amy's gaze shifted to Fox, then back to Melody. "Handsome. Smart. Hardworking. A guy who goes after what he wants. Someone who's his own boss. A guy who's sexy and charming. Stable. And makes a better than good living. I'm tired of scraping by."

Melody nodded. "Sounds like you and I like the same kind of man. Except for that last part about the money. I can make my own. I don't need someone else's."

"Says someone who's obviously never missed their rent or couldn't afford anything more than ramen noodles at more than one time in their life."

"Nope. Not me. I bust my ass to make sure I have what I need. The things I want...sometimes those things have to wait until I can afford them."

"But don't you want nice things?"

"I have nice things. My family's support. Good friends who always have my back and love to hang out. A boyfriend who treats me like I matter more than anything."

"You do." And Fox was loving hearing her say that what mattered most to her was the people in her life. Not a bunch of stuff.

She squeezed his hand. "I'll add Dean and Max to that list of friends."

"They both love you." They loved seeing Fox happy with her.

Melody glanced at Amy. "I'm surprised, based on what you're looking for in a guy, you haven't made a move on Dean."

Like Dean would go for Amy. But Fox understood Melody pointing out that Dean was single, while he was taken, so it made more sense for her to hit on him.

Amy shrugged. "He's nice and all, but he seems a little hard to get to know."

"Once you do, he's a great guy," Melody encouraged.

Fox didn't think Dean was interested in Amy at all. She was too in-your-face. Plus, like him, Dean didn't date people who worked for them. Just not a good move. Things could get complicated.

Like right now.

How did he end up having dinner with his employee and his girlfriend?

Shari finally arrived with their food.

"Oh my God, this looks delicious." Amy cut into the prime rib, dipped a piece in the au jus, then slid the fork in and out of her mouth. She chewed and moaned. "So good."

Fox cut off a slice of his sandwich and slid it onto Melody's plate. "Try that, sweet Dee."

She used her knife and fork to cut off a thick piece. She grinned at him as she chewed and swallowed. "That's good." She picked up her bowl and handed it to him. "Put some on your plate."

Instead, he took a big bite from the bowl and handed it back. "That's amazing."

"My mom used to make this when we were little. I'll have to get her recipe, so I can make it for us."

He stared at her, knowing she'd know how much it meant to him that they'd be cooking and sharing meals together in their future. "I'd love that."

"Do you cook?" Amy asked.

Melody swallowed a bite, wiped her mouth with her napkin, then answered. "My sister Lyric is the chef at the bar. She's a whiz in the kitchen. But I'm pretty good, too. My mom and grandma taught us all how to cook."

"I didn't have a lot of options after high school. I needed to get a job quickly, so I went to culinary school. The program was ten months long. I had to get a student loan, but at least I got to eat at school."

Melody's gaze softened. "Your parents didn't help?"

Amy shook her head. "They had their own struggles. Alcohol mostly. And trying to keep a job. I pretty much raised myself."

Melody stopped with her fork in the air. "I'm sorry to hear that. It must have been really rough."

Amy glanced at him, then back to Melody. "Sounds like maybe Fox knows something about that based on the fact he didn't grow up with his parents."

Fox didn't comment. He didn't want to give Amy any room to feel like they connected in some way, even if they did. He focused on Melody. "Did you say you were going to work at the ranch tomorrow before dinner?" He knew that's what she said, he just needed to change the subject.

"I've got some orders to fill. I have a design idea for something new, too. I'll head out there after we see Tanya in the morning."

"I've got a bunch of coding to do on a project, plus I have to go over some financial stuff Max left me."

"I could come by your place with lunch if you'd like," Amy suggested.

Melody eyed him.

He quickly shut that down. "No, thank you. I've got some leftovers in the fridge."

Melody scraped her bowl with her spoon. "I could eat a whole other bowl of that if I wasn't already stuffed. It was so good."

Fox had demolished everything on his plate. "Mine was really good, too. I love it when the beef falls apart like that. And the gravy...so good."

"Those fried potatoes were delicious, too." Melody had stolen one, or ten, from his plate.

He didn't mind.

Amy finished off the last of the prime rib and roasted garlic mashed potatoes on her plate. She left the asparagus behind. "Who's having dessert?"

"We have cupcakes back at our place," Melody chimed in.

Amy scrunched her lips. "I thought I saw cheesecake on the menu with fresh strawberries. Maybe I'll get it to go."

Shari arrived at the table a moment later. "I thought I heard you'd like some dessert."

"Not for us," Fox said.

"I'll take the cheesecake to go." Amy's cheeks flushed. "I just can't pass it up, even if it will go straight to my hips."

Shari rushed off to fill the order and bring back the check.

Amy nudged Fox's arm. "Not like I need to worry about a few extra calories. Right, Fox?"

Now she was fishing for compliments. "Everyone loves a good treat," he said instead of falling into that trap, and kept his eyes on Melody.

Shari arrived with Amy's boxed dessert and the check.

"Are we splitting it three ways?" Amy asked.

Fox couldn't let Melody pay for her meal when he'd invited her out. And he couldn't pay for both of them and not Amy and look like an asshole. At least in his mind. "It's on me."

Fox dropped his credit card on the bill.

Shari scooped it up. "Back in a moment."

A server arrived to clear their dishes.

Melody smiled at him. "Thank you for the wonderful meal."

"You're welcome, sweetheart."

"Yes, Fox, it was very generous of you."

Fox didn't miss that one of the qualities Amy wanted in a guy was generosity. He thought what she meant was a guy who had the money to take care of her by buying her expensive meals and whatever else she wanted. "You're welcome. Just keep it quiet. It's not like I take the other employees out to eat."

Amy beamed. "Oh, I know. This was a special thing."

Fuck. He did not want her thinking she was special, but had no way of getting out of this without saying something very blunt and embarrassing her. Then again she was doing a good job of it all on her own, though she seemed oblivious to it. Or she just didn't care.

Maybe he should be flattered she liked him that much.

If she hadn't crashed his date, maybe he would be. Right now, all she did was make him angry. Because this could have been a really romantic evening.

Shari arrived with the check. He pocketed his credit card, filled out the tip and total, and signed his name.

Fox looked across at Melody. "Ready?"

"Definitely."

Fox had to wait for Amy to vacate her seat so he could get out. Then she seemed to wait by the table as he inched out and took Melody's hand. "Let's go," he said, hoping she'd take the hint and move.

Amy turned, went up on tiptoe, and before he knew her intent, brushed a kiss on his cheek. He stepped back and knocked into Melody.

"Thank you again for dinner."

Melody's hand went tight around his.

Amy turned and headed out of the restaurant.

Melody stepped past him and rushed after her, pulling Fox along. "Amy. Wait."

Amy turned on the sidewalk. "Yes?"

"Don't ever do that again. I put up with you bringing my boyfriend cupcakes, hoping you'd score some points with him. I didn't say a word when you rudely interrupted what was obviously a date."

"I—"

"Don't." Melody shook her head. "I've spent too many years watching women flirt with good guys who were with someone else in the bar. He's your boss. That's all. So keep your hands to yourself and never kiss him again."

Her lips fell into a pout. "I was just saying thank you."

"Do it without touching him. Fox has boundaries and you crossed his without consent. End of story."

Amy glanced past her at Fox. "You know how much I appreciate you. I'll see you later." She crossed the street and started walking back toward the apartment complex.

Melody fumed next to him.

He cupped her cheek and turned her head toward his, then he took her mouth in a searing kiss that was all heat and tongues and passion. They got lost in the kiss and each other for a long moment. "You're amazing. So fucking fierce."

"What?"

"To put up with all that, then put her in her place with grace, and claim me. Damn. That was fucking hot." He kissed her again.

Someone nearby whistled at them.

They lost track of time and where they were and got lost in the kiss and each other again.

"Baby, I can't wait to get you home and show you how much I appreciate you." Fox took her hand and started walking down the street like a man on a mission.

CHAPTER SEVENTEEN

Fox walked into the apartment building lobby and headed for the elevator with Melody.

Dean rushed in behind them. "Hey, wait up."

Fox held the elevator so Dean could join them.

Melody smiled at Dean. "Did you go out to eat, too?"

"Sort of." Dean eyed Fox. "Something came up. I need to talk to you privately for a few minutes."

Fox caught the intense vibe. "Sure. Okay. Can it wait until tomorrow?"

Dean shook his head. "I think we need to discuss it now."

The elevator doors opened and they all walked down the hall to their apartments.

Fox opened the door for Melody and turned off the alarm. "Sorry, sweetheart. Sometimes business stuff can't wait. I'll be back in a few minutes."

Dean was standing just inside his place with the door open, indicating he didn't want Melody to hear whatever he had to say.

"I'll just get ready for bed."

He hoped that meant he'd find her naked in bed.

She smiled at Dean. "Goodnight."

"Night, Melody." Dean waved him over the second Melody turned for their room.

Fox closed his apartment door and walked across the hall into Dean's place. The second Dean closed the door behind him, he asked, "What's wrong? Why did you follow me tonight?"

"I caught the whole scene with Josh and Melody this morning. I let it go when he left, thinking he'd just been there to check on her. You handled it. Done. But then I watched to make sure he left the building and it dawned on me. How did he get in the building?"

"Someone let him in." Fox didn't like that. He made it clear to every tenant not to let others in without asking the person they were there to see if it was okay.

"Guess who?"

Since Dean had followed them tonight, he had a very good guess. "Amy."

"He met her outside the building when she returned from a run. They spoke for about five minutes outside, then she let him in."

"She knows Josh?" Fox wondered how they'd met.

"I don't think so. It's clear in the video that she tried to brush him off at first. She puts her hand up, like she's telling him she can't let him in. Then he says something that gets her attention. They speak back and forth for another couple minutes and she lets him in."

"Okay. What prompted you to follow me and Melody tonight?"

"I got a weird vibe about that scene with Josh at your place. The same one I got when I saw Amy on surveillance when she showed up to deliver you cupcakes." Dean gave him a look. "I didn't get any cupcakes. Guess I'm not as special as you."

"Shut the fuck up." Fox did not want to be goaded, not after the dinner disaster with Amy.

"Can't. Because I have to tell you that Amy was waiting downstairs for you and Melody to leave the building. She hid behind the potted plant at the back corner until you two came off the elevator and walked out. You were so engrossed with Melody, you didn't see her."

"Shit. She followed us. You're sure?" The stupid question got him an eye roll from Dean. "Right. Why else hide?"

"I think she might be stalking you."

"She's definitely interested, but...stalking." He shook his head, not wanting to believe it.

"She knows you have a girlfriend and is actively trying to mess that up, so she can have you."

"I'm not interested. Not even if Melody wasn't in the picture."

"I get it. You only see her. But Amy is, at best, a nuisance. At worst, she's dangerous."

He didn't want to hear this. But... "She mentioned something at the restaurant about me keeping my secrets. And it was all a part of a conversation where she said she wants a guy who can take care of her and basically give her financial security."

Dean's eyes went wide. "How the hell did that even come up?"

"Melody asked her what kind of guy she was looking for. She listed all her qualities and Melody said they had the same taste in men. Except for the part about a guy providing financial security, because Melody said she could make her own money and take care of herself in that way."

Dean grinned. "God, I like her for you."

"Me, too. Except Amy basically hinted that she knows my secret."

"How?"

"She lives in Boston. There are rumors..."

Dean shook his head. "This isn't good. If she's targeted you—"

"That's ridiculous. If anything, she's overzealous about how much she likes me."

Dean raised a brow. "She busted in on your date without a shred of remorse and lacking any kind of logic that you'd welcome her there with your girlfriend present."

"It crossed a line," Fox admitted annoyed.

"You're in love with Melody. I don't want to see that get messed up because of Amy. You need to nip this in the bud now."

Amy had to know her behavior tonight wouldn't go over well with Melody or him. So why do it? Amy's behavior puzzled him.

Which led him back to Josh and her having a long—considering they didn't know each other—conversation.

"Amy purposely tried to make it seem like I'm dating a lot of women back in Boston."

Dean gave him a WTF look. "You date. But it's not like you have a new woman every week or something."

"You think they're working together to break me and Melody up so they can have the one they want." It sounded stupid and juvenile to his own ears.

"Maybe." Dean planted his hands on his hips and stared at him. "But it's plain to see you're completely gone over Melody and she's all about you. They can't think this could possibly work in their favor. It's too...obvious."

"So what are we missing then?"

"Josh is a dick. Amy, a stalker. Melody is possibly in danger."

Fuck. "I do not want to hear that."

"Security risks are my thing. I'm telling you, I don't like what's happening here."

"What are we supposed to do about it?"

Dean had never looked more serious. "Protect Melody at all costs."

Fox swore again. "How am I supposed to explain this to Melody?"

"If this is just an infatuation for Amy, maybe it will wane once she sees you and Melody together more. If it's something else...then we have to tell Melody, so she's not taken off guard. Or used against you."

"Fuck! This is the last thing I wanted."

"I know. But maybe if you just come clean with Melody about just how much your life has changed, then maybe she'll be willing to come to Boston now versus later."

"Is she any safer in Boston?"

Dean hung his head, knowing that she wasn't.

"Is this what it's going to be like? Am I going to be constantly worried about her?"

"Yes. But it will be worth it if you two are happy together." Dean took a step closer. "She's smart and tough and independent. She knows her own mind. She's made it clear, you're the one she wants to be with. Have you talked to her about moving to Boston?"

"Yes. She's interested. She understands that I need to be there. But this thing with us is new."

"I get that. But it's also years in the making. I know you want to be here for your mom, but maybe you take both of them back to Boston."

"I'm not living with Tanya, I don't care how big my place is. It won't be big enough."

Dean shook his head. "You could put her in an assisted living place close by. She'd have round the clock care and maybe make some friends."

It would make things easier. But... "Tanya wants to stay at her place as long as possible. It's the only home she's known."

"Except she also keeps telling you she wants to travel."

Fox shivered. "Yeah, I'm not up for that kind of togetherness."

Dean frowned. "You can't stay here and run the business the way you normally do."

"I know." Things were starting to get away from him. Since he wasn't in the office and everything had to go through email, his assistant, or by phone, it seemed to not be handled as expeditiously as when he was actually in the office.

He had an idea. "Melody is off work for a couple of days because of her injuries. Perfect time to take a short trip to Boston."

"Do you think she'll go?"

"Yes."

"Do you think she'll suspect you're trying to get away from Amy and possibly Josh for a few days?"

"No. And I don't want to tell her about those suspicions yet. When we get back, we'll see how things stand."

"You know she's going to have questions when she sees your place in Boston and the company."

"I know. And maybe that will be the perfect way to tell her everything."

"What do you want me to do about Amy?"

Fox wasn't sure there was anything he could do, except stay away from her. If she was looking for a payday, firing her would only play right into her hands because she performed her job well. She only had two months left on her contract. After that, he'd send her home. "Keep a close watch on her. I don't want any more surprises or dates ruined."

"Should I have stepped in tonight?" Dean looked torn because his job was to protect Fox and the company.

"No. That was awkward as hell enough without you coming to my rescue. And I should have stopped it before it went so far."

"You're a nice guy, Fox. Don't let her take advantage of that again. Tonight, in her eyes, you wanted her there because you let her stay. You bought her a meal, shared conversation with her. It was almost a date. Except you had to go and have your girlfriend there." Dean was teasing, but not. "She wants you enough that she's making herself a nuisance and trying to annoy Melody enough to get her to dump you. I don't like that."

"You and me both." Fox ran his hand over his head. "I have to go. Melody is probably wondering what's taking me so long."

"She's cool. She'll wait for you."

"I can't mess this up. It's the most important thing in my life."

Dean smacked him on the shoulder. "You won't. Go. Let me worry about Amy tonight."

"Is she in her apartment?"

Dean could monitor the hallway on her floor. "Yes. And if she leaves it, I'll know." He seemed to have a thought pop into his head. "Maybe we need to reprogram the elevator and put in a security code for the fourth floor, so only we can get up here."

"Why didn't we think of that before we moved in?" At the building they lived in back in Boston, they had that security feature. "Contact the manufacturer. See how we can make that happen."

"On it."

Fox tried to put the conversation out of his mind as he left Dean's place and walked into his dark apartment, a soft glow coming from the bedroom. He set the alarm and headed straight for the woman who turned him inside out in the best way.

He didn't want to bring this kind of turmoil into Melody's life. But she needed to know what it would be like living in his world.

He just thought he'd have more time for them to grow closer, so that when the bad stuff came up, it wouldn't matter. Because what really mattered most was that they were together, working through the issues as partners.

Not that Melody wasn't in it with him. She was. With his mom. With possibly changing her whole life to be with him. He couldn't get luckier than that.

And when he stood in the threshold to his room, there she was, propped up in the center of the bed, one leg stretched out, the other bent at the knee. Naked. One hand on her breast, teasing her pink, taut nipple. The other between her legs, two fingers stroking her pretty, pink flesh.

He was instantly, painfully hard. "Fuck. You're beautiful." He stroked his hard shaft over his jeans, trying to get the damn thing to settle down.

"That mouth," she said.

"Where do you want it?"

She spread her legs wider. "Where do you think?"

He practically dove onto the bed and buried his face in heaven, wet and delicious on his tongue. He feasted until she orgasmed. Twice. And while she lay replete, trying to catch her breath, he shucked off all his clothes, rolled a condom on, then rolled her over, pulled her up by the hips so she was on all fours, then thrust into her hard and fast. She came again and he rode it out with a locked jaw and clenched teeth. Just as her quaking center subsided, he moved in long, smooth strokes, building the sensations back up. He pulled out, she pushed back, taking him back in like she couldn't stand for him to be so far away.

Her moans drove him wild. The feel of her around him was the best caress he'd ever felt. And when she pleaded harder, he let loose the reins and slammed into her again and again until his balls pulled up and he came in spurts that wracked his whole body.

He fell forward with Melody as she collapsed into the mattress. He caught himself on his hands, not wanting to crush her. He kissed her shoulder and followed it all the way up her neck to just behind her ear, where he planted one last kiss and whispered, "So fucking fantastic."

She giggled, though it was muffled by the pillow where her face was practically buried in it.

Reluctantly he sat back, disengaging from her body. She moaned out her displeasure that he'd left her. He felt the same way. He'd love to stay buried in that sweet paradise every second of the day. He put his hand on her hip and rolled her over, concerned that she wasn't getting enough air, and because he really wanted to kiss her.

He leaned over her, pressed his lips to hers, and savored the feel and taste of her.

She hooked her hand at the back of his neck, held him to her, and kissed him back with such tenderness, his heart went soft and warm and he fell even more in love with her than he already was.

And maybe he should tell her that.

But first he should tell her the rest.

Or maybe the *I love you* first and the rest after?

She brushed her lips to his one more time, then mumbled sleepily, "Grab the covers and snuggle with me."

Best idea she'd had since the last one, when he found her naked and wanting him.

"Back in a sec." He went to the bathroom, did the condom cleanup, and slid into bed beside her. She was already mostly asleep and only sighed and pressed back into him when he covered them and pulled her close as they spooned.

Content and happier than he'd ever been, he held her and let the rest go for now, so he could enjoy this perfect moment.

She was his. They were starting to plan a life together. A life where he had someone he loved and trusted. Someone who'd never hurt or leave him. Someone who cared enough to change her life to be with him.

It didn't seem quite real. Not after the way he'd grown up.

And he'd do anything to keep her.

CHAPTER EIGHTEEN

F ox stared over at Melody sleeping beside him, her head on the pillow,
face turned toward him. One of her hands lay on his arm, the other
tucked under the pillow. The sheet covered most of her, except for her bare
shoulder and a tantalizing peek at the swell of her breasts.

Last night had been a disaster of a date in his book. What could have been
romantic and fun had turned into an awkward threesome with enough
tension and drama to try his patience. But Melody had handled it well.
He'd held his tongue.

It wouldn't happen again.

He hoped Amy had gotten the message loud and clear last night that he
and Melody were a couple. He wasn't interested in her. Not now. Not ever.
Because Melody was his forever.

They just needed to figure out the logistics of that.

But Amy's words came back to him from last night about how the
people he mingled with and did business with in Boston wouldn't accept
Melody. She didn't come from money. She didn't attend an Ivy League
school. She was from some dinky little town no one had ever heard of.

But so was he. And he fit in those circles. They needed him. And who
cared about the snotty ones who thought they were better than everyone
else? That only proved they weren't better in his mind.

He believed Melody would find her place.

If nothing else, she'd always fit right by his side.

He brushed his fingers over her long hair. The swelling where her stitches
had been put in had lessened. The cut didn't look so angry and red anymore.

She was healing. And nothing had stopped her from making love last
night, though he should have been more careful about her using her hurt

hand to hold herself up. She hadn't complained or asked to change positions, so he guessed she was okay. The bandage on her hand was pristine white, no blood, so she hadn't torn anything.

Seeing her waiting for him in their bed...he got hard just thinking about it.

He needed to wake her so they could shower, dress, have some coffee and breakfast, and head to Tanya's place.

He traced his finger along the side of her face and watched as her blue eyes fluttered open. "God you're beautiful."

Her eyes closed and a grin spread on her full lips.

He kissed her softly. "Time to wake up, sweet Dee. People to see. Things to do." He trailed kisses down her neck as she shifted onto her back and he covered her warm, lush body. He got to her nipple, laved it with his tongue, then sucked it into his mouth as she moaned. He gave her other breast the same attention, then headed south, bringing the sheet down with him, baring her chest to his avid gaze. "Such a pretty view."

She spread her legs wide to accommodate him between her thighs. "What are you doing?"

He kissed her right beneath her belly button. "What I promised. Showing you how much I appreciate you." He kissed her mound, then licked her clit.

She rolled her hips up to meet his hungry mouth and he feasted on her. He put his hands on her thighs and spread her legs wider as he stared at her sex. "So pretty. So pink. So fucking delicious." He dove in for more, sliding in one finger, then two as he licked and sucked her clit, taking her up and up and up until she crashed over the edge and came against his mouth as he hummed his satisfaction.

But he wasn't done with her yet. As she lay pliant and blissed out on the bed, he pulled out a condom, sheathed himself, then nudged her entrance with the head of his dick. "You want me, sweet Dee?"

"Yes." To prove it, she pushed into him as he thrust deep.

For a second he just stopped and savored the feel of being one with her again.

Heaven.

And then she rocked her hips against him as he withdrew and thrust back into her. Nothing felt better than this, with her.

Her inner walls clamped around him. His eyes rolled back as pleasure surged. He pulled out, then pumped back into her. Long slow glides of his body in and out of hers. The sounds she made...they were hot and needy and breathless. Demands for more. Appreciation for how good he made her feel. She made him feel amazing. So good that he quickly reached a fever pitch. But he wanted her to come with him, so he rubbed his thumb over her slick nub and slammed back into her, hard and deep, and she came as he emptied himself inside her.

Fucking feeling like a god, he caught himself on his forearms as he crashed down on top of her, his face in her neck, their breaths sawing in and out.

He was probably crushing her.

The grip she kept on his back told him she didn't care.

He could stay here, in this bed, the two of them nestled close, all day.

Then he wouldn't have to see Tanya, or Amy, or anyone else today.

Her fingers sank into his hair and rubbed over his scalp. "Do you want to tell me where you just went?"

He managed to rise enough to stare down at her. Her hair spread out in glorious waves; her kiss-swollen lips were red and soft. He thought about distracting her, but instead told her how he really felt. "I dread going to see Tanya. Every time. I thought it would get easier. It doesn't. All it does is bring up all those old nightmares."

"I get that. She hurt you. She allowed you to be hurt. And she's not exactly warm and sweet to you now."

No, she wasn't. And somewhere deep inside him, he wished she were but knew she would never change. But that little kernel of hope still lived inside him, and he hated it, because when Tanya was Tanya, it disappointed him. And he kept coming back because he couldn't turn his back on someone who needed him. "I want to have a relationship with her, but I'm not sure I can forgive what she did. Not when it doesn't feel like she's sorry. Not in a way that I believe she truly means it."

"But you're still hoping she'll give you what you want and deserve."

He nodded. "But I also know I'm not going to get it. Because she's not like me. Or I'm not like her. And I guess that's a good thing. But it also sucks because I care and she doesn't. Not in a way that makes her want to know me. Not in the sense that it's about me being her son and that matters."

She cupped his face. "I'm sorry. I'm sure it hurts. But you matter to me. And I know it's not the same as having your mother love you the way you deserve to be loved, but you're not alone. I care. I'm here. I will always be here."

He brushed his nose against hers and kissed her softly. "You're everything I ever wanted."

She smiled softly. "Maybe instead of wishing her to be something she isn't, accept that you have this chance to help someone who needs it. Let that be enough to soothe your soul. You—despite her and your father—have a kinder, gentler, more loving heart." She kissed one cheek, then the other, then stared at him again. "They didn't make you into them. You survived. Even better, you reached even greater heights than you probably would have if you'd stayed with them. You're happy. She's not, because she's alone." She brushed her hand over his hair, soothing him even more. "Well, she has you. You're the best thing to ever happen to her. She's lucky you give her the time of day."

She floored him.

"How do you put everything into perspective like that?"

"Because I'm on the outside looking in. It's okay that the broken child in you wishes for that love and healing, so long as the grownup you realizes she's not capable of giving it to you." She put her hand over his heart. "Protect that little boy from being hurt again, Fox. Because if you let her, she'll do it again."

"Maybe I can't fix the past, but you and I can have a different kind of future. Right?"

She swept her hand from his chest up to his jaw. "We're making it right now. You aren't like them. I'm not her. We care about each other too much to hurt each other."

He leaned into her hand. "I know you'd never hurt me."

"I know the same about you. So why are you worried?"

Because I'm keeping something from you.

He should tell her.

But the moment passed.

She raised her head and kissed his lips with a smack. "Relax. Everything is good. I'll be there with you today."

He wanted her with him every day.

All he had to do was be patient and let it happen. But it was hard when he wanted something this much.

CHAPTER NINETEEN

Melody stirred the pot of pasta on the brand-new stove in Tanya's amazingly updated kitchen. Fox hadn't just sprung for a new freestanding stove-slash-oven combo. No, he'd replaced her refrigerator, toaster oven, and the washer and dryer. The salesperson at the local appliance center had to have been ecstatic to see Fox that day.

"The carpet will need to be replaced if you're going to sell the house after I'm gone and you want to get anything out of it." Tanya's offhand remark in the other room came with a heavy sigh from Fox at the end.

"I'll worry about the house later," Fox said. "Right now, you've got everything you need and that's all that's important." Fox meant those words. And he probably had no intention of keeping this place. It held too many bad memories for him.

"Hardwood floors would be nice."

Of course she wanted new floors. Why not? She deserved better for her remaining few months, so long as Fox was paying for it.

He made a noncommittal noise, then changed the subject. "How are you feeling?"

"Same. I've lost a little weight. The doctor wants me to eat more. She said to eat smaller meals more often to keep my strength up. Protein and carbs."

"Well, Melody's got you covered. She made sure we stopped at the store on the way here to stock you up. Plus, she's making a lasagna. That will last you a few days. If you can't eat it all, or just want something different, put the rest in the freezer for down the road."

"Not sure how much farther I'm going to get down the road. I've been stuck in this place a long time. Sad to think I'm just wasting days here now."

Melody knew what was coming and wondered if she should step into the other room and help Fox out of this sticky situation.

"Tanya." Fox sighed. "I know you want to travel."

"A trip together is just the thing to make some memories. 'Course I know you're busy running that company of yours. You're needed there. I could go it alone. Spread my wings. See something new. That's all I'm asking."

"And what if you get sick? What if you need a hospital?"

"They got doctors on those cruise ships. They'd take care of me, get me what I need. You could get me one of those medical planes to bring me back to the states."

"I don't think it's wise for you to travel alone."

"I ain't got no one but you to go with me. Unless..."

Oh, Melody couldn't wait to hear this.

"You could hire a nurse to go with me. Someone who can be there in case I need help."

Silence.

Melody imagined Fox tallying up what that would cost him, deciding if it was worth his mom's happiness, or if it would risk her health, and how that guilt would eat him alive if something happened and he let it.

"I'm not comfortable sending you off with a stranger."

"A professional. Someone who can make sure I take my meds, check my vitals, make sure I eat enough and am resting...while I see something of this world. You saw the brochures for the cruises I want to take. I don't have time to fuss with whether I'll still be healthy enough to go in a month or two when you can get some time free. *If you can...*"

"Is this how you really want to spend your last days? Cruising around the Mediterranean? The Bahamas? South America?"

"Anywhere. Everywhere." Tanya's excitement couldn't be denied. "Fancy meals. New experiences. Meeting interesting people." Since Tanya didn't seem particularly human-friendly, given her lack of friends, Melody thought that last bit was pouring it on a bit thick.

"You're exhausted all the time. You probably won't be able to even leave the ship."

"This will breathe new life into me. I just know it."

Fox didn't look convinced. "If I'm even going to consider this, I'll want to talk to your doctor. If she says you're not up to a trip like this, then the answer is no. If you are capable, then I'll look into getting a nurse to go with you."

"I'll want to meet them, make sure they're good company. I don't want to be stuck on a boat with someone who doesn't treat me like I know my own mind. I'm not an invalid. I can do what I want."

Fox had to know that Tanya heard yes and nothing else in his response to her. "One step at a time."

"You can call my doctor on Monday, get the all-clear, hire a nurse, and I can be on the ship in three weeks."

"I'm busy Monday and Tuesday. I won't be back until Wednesday."

Tanya gasped in surprised. "What do you mean, back? Where are you going?"

"I'm taking Melody with me to Boston for a couple of days," he announced.

Melody dumped the pasta into the colander in the sink and raised a brow. This was the first she was hearing about this Boston plan.

Fox popped into the kitchen. "You heard that, didn't you?"

She left the steaming noodles draining in the sink and walked to him. "Yes. Why are we going to Boston?"

"So that's a yes?"

"I haven't been asked anything." She gently punched her fist into his rock-hard abs.

"You've got a couple days off. We can leave early tomorrow morning. Then you can come with me to work. I'll show you my company. We can do some sightseeing. I'll take you out to dinner at my favorite place. You can get a feel for the city, our place, what I do."

"*Our* place?"

"It could be. I want it to be."

Tanya strode in just as Fox was about to kiss her and tempt her to say yes. "You're moving to Boston with him?"

"That's the plan." Fox brushed his thumb across her chin. "Right?"

"Maybe," she hedged, then changed it to, "Probably," when his smile fell.

Fox kissed her quick. "I know you're going to love it. Please come. I already made the arrangements."

"You did? When?"

"While you were shopping."

"Is that what you were typing out on your phone?"

"My assistant is awesome. She can't wait to meet you."

Her jaw dropped. "Oh my God, Fox. You can't just..."

"What? Take advantage of you having a couple days off from the bar? Want to show you my life and make you want to be there with me? Two days, sweet Dee. That's all I'm asking for right now."

Butterflies fluttered in her belly. This was really happening. The first step in them actually moving forward with their plan to go to Boston.

Fox gave her puppy dog eyes. "I know what I want. It's you. Always you. Come with me."

Tanya stared at them, dumbstruck. "You two are really together."

Fox glanced at her. "You knew that."

Tanya shook her head. "I thought maybe while you're here you'd...hook up. I didn't think... You're going to take her back with you?"

"If she'll have me."

Tanya's eyes went wide, and she sputtered for a second, then said, "If she'll have you! Seriously! You're—"

"Going to do anything to convince her to make a life with me." Fox turned away from Tanya and stared at Melody, his eyes filled with a plea. "Say yes."

She knew he meant to going to Boston, but she wondered if he was also asking her if she was ready to make a life with him, too. The answer was surprisingly easy and the same to both those questions. "Yes."

Fox obviously heard it in her voice, because his eyes lit with sheer joy. "Okay. Well, that means I have a lot to do. Plans to make. Things I have to say to you." He looked around at their surroundings. "Not here. Not now. But soon."

Tanya fell into the seat at the table near them. "Oh my God. This is not what I expected."

"You're everything I ever wanted." Fox cupped Melody's face and kissed her right there in the kitchen with the meat sauce she'd made simmering on the stove.

"You didn't come here to help me." Tanya's softly spoken words echoed in the room. "You came here for her."

Fox shook his head. "Both are true. I am here for you. But I also wanted to apologize to Melody for what I said to her all those years ago. I wanted my best friend back. And now I have her. And you and I get a chance to make some better memories than the ones I've carried all these years." Fox was really trying to connect with his mom.

Too bad she didn't feel the same. "How are we making memories when you're off to Boston and you won't go on a trip like I asked?"

"Because I can't right now." He looked from Tanya to Melody, then back again. "I just bought another company and am going to be in the middle of merging the two together over the next several months. That's partially why I want to go back to Boston for a couple of days, and why I can't go on a forty-five-day cruise on the Mediterranean."

Tanya looked thoughtful for a moment. "Then I'll go without you and be happy that my son gave me such a gift while he's conquering the tech world." She scrunched her lips. "That's the right saying, right? You're in tech?"

Fox laughed under his breath. "Yes. Programming, to be specific."

"Right. Computers. And congratulations. It must be really amazing to *buy* a whole company."

"It's a big deal." Fox glanced at Melody, pride in his eyes and something else. Something that looked a little sheepish, mixed with regret.

The first, Melody understood. "I'm sure the boy who grew up in foster care never dreamed he'd one day own his own company, let alone buy another one." But the regret upset her. He should be really happy and excited. What did he have to regret about expanding his business? "While we're on the plane tomorrow, I'd love to hear all the details, so I can better understand what you do."

Fox's smile leveled up. "I can do that."

"Okay, well, I better get the lasagna done. I have some work to do at the ranch before dinner. When we get home later tonight, I'll have to stop by my place and pack."

Fox closed the distance between them, took her hands, and squeezed them as he looked her in the eye. "Thank you."

"For what?"

"Being you."

"I only know how to be me."

"That's what I love about you."

It wasn't lost on her that he said *love*, not *like*.

Fox turned to his mom. "Come on. You said your doctor wants you to get more exercise. Let's go for a walk."

"It's too cold out." Tanya glanced at the trees blowing in the breeze outside the back windows.

"It's not that bad. I'll get your sweatshirt."

Tanya rose, looking slow and a bit frail. "Fine."

Fox walked out, leaving Melody alone with Tanya.

"I guess you get the trip and I don't," she grumbled.

Melody stirred the meat sauce, then pulled a long noodle from the colander and laid it out in the tin pan she'd bought at the store. "You could ask Fox about going to Boston with us."

"He didn't ask because he knows I have a treatment on Tuesday."

"Do you have a ride?"

"Yes. He set it up."

"Good. Then we'll be sure to check in, make sure you're doing well."

Tanya sneered. "You think you've got him eating out of the palm of your hand."

Melody finished the bottom layer of noodles and spooned on a layer of meat sauce. "It's interesting that you see my relationship with Fox as me trying to get something from him by making him like me. Is that what you think?"

"Yes. Because he's got *a lot* to give."

"Yes, he does. Your kitchen is looking good because of it." She sprinkled on a generous amount of mozzarella. Tanya had requested she leave off the ricotta earlier.

"You don't think I see what you're doing to him."

She started on the next layer of noodles. "What am I doing to him, besides making him happy? Because that's all I want to do. I want him to put the past behind him and look toward the future and what we can have together."

"Yeah. You living the high life in Boston."

"I'm giving up a lot to be with Fox."

"And you want something in return for that sacrifice."

"What I'll get is something you can't buy. I want what my sister has with her husband and what my brother found with his fiancée. I want someone who is mine as much as I'm theirs. I want to build a family and a life with him. The kind of family I had growing up and the kind he deserved but never got."

"Because you took him from me."

She stopped what she was doing. "I didn't take him from you. You hurt him and lost him to the system because you refused to do what was necessary to get him back. And now, when you have a chance to make amends, you don't seem to even want to try to be the kind of mother he deserves, because you're too busy spending his money and planning trips."

Tanya's brow wrinkled with anger. "I asked him to come with me."

"Knowing that he can't just drop everything and sail around the world for months on end."

"Yes. He can. Someone else can run the business while he does whatever he damn well pleases."

"That's not Fox. He doesn't abandon what's his to someone else. He takes care of it."

"She's right." Fox walked in carrying a red sweatshirt and a black knit beanie. "I'm doing the best I can to be here for you and take care of my business. But I can't leave for a month and a half and work from a ship that at best has spotty Wi-Fi and cell coverage and think that my company won't suffer for it. While you're one of my priorities, you're not the only one."

"No," Tanya agreed. "I'm also not the top priority either. She is."

"Yes," Fox confirmed.

Melody sucked in a breath. "Fox. That's—"

"The truth. It will always be the truth. You are my number one priority. You will never come second to anyone or anything. I promise you that."

"I...I." She didn't know what to say. "I feel the same about you." She meant it. Even as her heart jackhammered with what that meant. She'd thought she and Fox would slip into love eventually, but nope. She'd fallen, hard and fast and with the same kind of wild abandon she did everything. She put her whole heart into what mattered to her. It didn't always work out for her. But a lot of the time it did. And in this case, with Fox, it was even better than she ever expected. Nothing and no one mattered more to her than him.

Fox's gaze softened on her. "Not the time or place," he said. "Soon. We'll get to it all soon." Fox looked at his mom. "What is it that you really want? Because it seems to me that before Melody and I got together, you were happy with me visiting and us just hanging out and getting to know each other."

"I'm happy with all of that and that you're here."

"Do you want me to go to your doctor appointments? I can make time for that."

Tanya shook her head. "That's not necessary. They're mostly just follow-ups and my treatment. Boring stuff that takes too much time, but I can do on my own."

"Then what more do you want?"

"A chance to make things up to you, like I've been trying to do."

Melody wanted to know how she'd been trying to do that, because it seemed to her that Tanya had simply asked Fox to let it lie in the past, dead and forgotten.

Fox looked even more frustrated. "You can't undo the past. We agreed to start over. But let's face it. We don't have a lot in common besides blood."

"Blood is everything."

Fox shook his head. "No. It's not. You taught me that the hard way. Blood doesn't make us family, it makes us related. Family is something altogether different. Melody's family taught me that."

"You're my son, Fox. That matters. That's something that will never change, whether you like it or not. All I'm asking is that we take the time we have and do something with it. I've lived a hard life."

Melody stepped back, giving Fox some room to finish his conversation.

Fox took a step closer to Tanya. "I know your life wasn't easy. I know the choices you made were probably the ones you thought were your only option."

"Sometimes there was no choice, just to hold on and hope it worked out."

"That's a hard way to live," Fox acknowledged. "I had a lot of days like that growing up in foster care." He said it matter-of-factly, without any accusation in his words or eyes, though it was implied in every word. "I don't have to do that anymore. You don't have to do that anymore, because I will make sure your last months are comfortable."

"All I want is something special before I die."

Fox's shoulders went lax and he nodded. "We'll talk about it, and the possibility of you moving into a nursing home facility in Boston, when I get back." That would give him time to think it over and decide how far he was willing to go to make Tanya happy.

"You'd want me with you in Boston?"

"After your trip, we'll evaluate your needs and go from there, because I'm hoping by then, Melody and I will be settled in Boston." He held out the sweatshirt. "Put this on. Let's go for that walk." He turned to Melody and kissed her softly, then pressed his lips to her ear and whispered, "I know you have to get to the ranch. I'll see you soon. Thank you for being here with me."

She leaned back and gave him a smile, hoping it eased his heart. "Anytime."

"I'm ready." Tanya stood by the back door.

Fox kissed Melody one last time, this one sweet and soft as he looked into her eyes and she saw reflected back everything she felt for him in her heart.

"I'll put the lasagna in the oven and set the time for twenty minutes, so don't be too long."

Tanya opened the back door, but said, "Thank you for cooking," before she walked out.

Fox brushed his hand down her arm. "I'll see you soon."

She kept her gaze on him as he left with Tanya. They walked across the yard and away from the barn Fox couldn't even look at, let alone go in, and into the trees.

She knew they'd never be mother and son. Not like her mom was with Jax and all of her girls. But maybe Tanya could find a way to soften enough to focus on Fox. To see the man he'd become and offer him some kind of recognition for his accomplishments instead of focusing on the wealth that came with his success.

That's all Fox wanted: his mother to be proud of him.

And maybe to see in her eyes that she knew he'd done it despite her absence and the hurt she'd inflicted on him.

If she couldn't give him that, then Melody would make sure he knew how much she appreciated him and how proud she was of him for all he'd overcome and accomplished. He truly was a good man.

And he was all hers.

She couldn't wait to go to Boston and take this step toward their future together.

Now all she had to do was tell her family she was making plans that would take her away from them. They'd be sad to see her go, but they'd want only her happiness.

She was happiest when she was with Fox.

And no one, not Tanya nor Amy, was going to spoil it for them.

As she was slipping the lasagna into the oven, the house phone rang. She didn't pay it any mind as she set the timer on the oven and washed the colander in the sink until the answering machine clicked on.

"Tanya, it's Brian. What time do you want me to deliver your stuff? Things are moving forward on the other thing. We have someone who's got an in we can use. It won't be long now and you'll get what you want. We all will."

Melody stared into space, wondering what that all meant and what exactly Brian was handling for Tanya.

Drugs?

What was Tanya up to?

Why would she partner with Brian on anything when she only had months to live? She could barely leave the house without exhausting herself.

But something was obviously in the works. What exactly?

Whatever it was, Melody would make sure it didn't touch Fox.

She'd keep an eye on Brian, and most especially on Tanya. That woman had proven to be bad to the bone in the past. She wouldn't put it past Tanya to pull some stunt to get Fox's attention and sympathy. Which would probably cost him a pretty penny, too.

Not going to happen.

I see you coming.

CHAPTER TWENTY

After Fox and Melody parted ways at Tanya's place, he'd gone back to the apartment and worked on a project that was time sensitive.

He got lost in the coding until his phone alarm went off. He quickly grabbed his wallet, keys, and a bottle of wine to take to dinner at Melody's folks place, then rushed out the door, making sure to set the alarm as he left. He couldn't wait to see Melody and her mom and dad. He was really excited about taking her to Boston.

He texted Melody on the elevator ride down.

FOX: On my way. Miss you.

She texted him right back.

MELODY: Miss you more. Park at the house, but walk over to the green barn—back room on the right. I'll show you my work.

He couldn't wait to see what she created, and how, up close.

FOX: Be there soon.

He stepped off the elevator as he hit send and stuffed the phone back in his pocket, and nearly slammed into Amy in the lobby. "Hey. Sorry. Wasn't paying attention."

She smiled. "No worries. How are you?" She stood right in front of him, blocking the exit, a look of anticipation in her eyes.

"I'm good. You?" He didn't want to come off rude, so he kept his voice neutral, not letting her see or hear that he was in a hurry to leave.

She leaned in. "I hope you know that I didn't mean to upset Melody. I just thought, you know, that we all work together, and we could share a meal like friends. Because I like you, Fox."

He wasn't sure what to say. "Let's just put it behind us."

Her whole face lit up, then she put her hand on his forearm and squeezed. "You're the best. You get it. I don't know a lot of people here, just you and the ones I've met at the center. And I hate eating alone. I'm sure you do, too, so it was nice to share a meal, talk, you know, spend some time together."

He pulled his arm free. "Uh, I have to go."

"Hold up." She glanced around like she wanted to be sure they were alone. As if that wasn't obvious. Then she met his gaze again. "I'm glad I have this chance to talk to you privately."

That sounded like a bad idea. "I really need to go."

She stepped even closer and dropped her voice. "It's about Melody."

That kept him rooted in the lobby. "What about her?"

"The other day I was coming back from my early morning run when I ran into this guy desperate to get into the building to see his girlfriend."

Fox narrowed his gaze. Was she talking about Josh? "What exactly did he say to you?" Fox had seen the security footage. Without any audio, he couldn't say what Josh had said to Amy.

"That he was worried because she'd had an accident and was hurt." Amy bit her bottom lip, looking uncomfortable but also anxious to tell him more. "He said that she's been playing some game with him, saying you two are old friends."

"We are. And more."

"Yeah, well she told him she's just letting you think it's more because you've got money and she knows you'll...share it with her."

"Melody's not like that."

"Are you sure? Because it seems to me she's got a reputation for going from one guy to the next. She uses sex to hook the guy, then she bleeds him dry. At least until she met Josh. He said they had something real, until her old friend showed up"—she eyed him intently—"and she saw big, fat dollar signs."

"That's a lie. Melody *briefly* dated Josh *years* ago, and dumped him because he was a dick to her."

Amy shook her head and put her hand on the outside of his upper arm. "I'm sorry, Fox, but she's using you. I thought you should know before she really hurts you."

He stepped back, putting distance between them, and making her hand drop from his arm. "Melody would never hurt me."

"We all think that about the people we care about, but it's always the ones closest to us who hurt us the most. I'm sorry, Fox, but it sounded like this guy knows Melody really well. I mean, they were together before you showed up and she set her sights on you."

That wasn't how he and Melody got together. *He* reached out to her online. *He* pursued her.

She told him she hadn't been seeing anyone in a while. And as soon as she knew he was the guy she'd been talking to online, she'd wanted to take their relationship to the next level.

Being with Melody made him happier than he'd ever been.

Amy frowned, sympathy in her eyes. "I hate to see you upset like this. Let me make you dinner."

"I already have plans."

"With her?"

"Yes."

She studied him for a moment and stepped close, warmth in her eyes as she placed her hand on his chest. "You deserve better." The sultry way she looked at him said she wanted to take Melody's place.

Like he didn't already know that. So this was all her trying to drive a wedge between him and Melody. "As I said, I've got plans." He sidestepped her and headed for the door.

"Have a good night," she called after him.

At the moment, all he could think about was what she told him about Josh.

Fox jumped into his car and drove out of the parking lot a little faster than he should, but he wanted to get on the road and see Melody. She'd clear this all up.

As soon as he hit the road out of town, he pulled out his phone and called Dean.

"What's up?"

"I need you to look into something."

"What?"

"The relationship between Melody and Josh?"

"The guy from the bar, who hangs out with the drug dealer?"

"Yeah. Him."

"Why?"

"Because Amy had some interesting things to say about the two of them."

"Consider the source," Dean shot back.

He did. But something didn't add up. Why did Josh lie to Amy? "Can you just do some digging and find out what they really are to each other."

"Why don't you just ask her?"

"I'm going to."

Dean let out a heavy sigh. "You don't trust her?"

"It's not that."

"Then what is it? Because checking up on your girlfriend is not cool."

"I know." But something didn't seem right about all this. It niggled at the back of his mind and he needed more information to make it make sense. "Just do it." Fox hung up before Dean could protest more.

By the time Fox made it to the ranch, parked by the house, and found Melody in the green barn, he was wound tight. But the second she looked up from cutting a thin piece of leather with a rolling cutter, the tightness in his chest eased.

It still didn't stop him from asking, "What's your relationship with Josh?"

The smile on her lips died and her eyes narrowed. "Hi to you, too." She sat up straight on the stool and studied him.

"You made it seem like you weren't friends."

She raised a brow. "What is this about?"

"Just answer the question."

"We grew up in the same town and went to the same schools. We know each other, but we've never been close friends. We went on a few dates that ended with him being a possessive asshole. I never slept with him. The end."

"Are you sure?"

She set the tool down and stood, anger flashing in her eyes. "Are you calling me a liar?"

Fox folded his arms over his chest. "Why is he telling people you and he were together before you started seeing me?"

"Two years ago is before you," she quipped.

"Why is he saying that you used guys to get what you wanted?"

Her face flushed red with anger. "Because he's an asshole. And what exactly did *he* think I wanted from those guys? A connection? Love? A partner? No. Had to be something a guy like Josh wants but can't seem to get easily because of the way he goes about it. So sex and money?"

He must have had some reaction to the last.

Her eyes went wide, then narrowed with fury. "Your own mother is using you for your money, so I get that you're hypersensitive to others doing the same. And now, what? Because a guy I kicked to the curb for being a jerk says some shit about me, you think I'm after your money. Fuck you. I haven't asked you for anything. I have everything I need. Or at least I thought I did until you came in here accusing me of lying and being some gold-digger." Tears gathered in her eyes.

The anger didn't stir him. No, it was the pain in her eyes that overshadowed all the other emotions in her eyes. Betrayal.

"Melody..." He reached out for her.

She stepped back, shoving the stool and making it topple. She held up her hand, finger pointed at his chest. "Don't you fucking touch me."

He stopped and held up both hands, knowing he was so very wrong and needed to make this right. "Amy caught me in the lobby. She told me about her conversation with Josh that morning he came to our apartment to check on you."

"You mean *your* apartment."

"It's *our* place."

She shook her head.

He'd really fucked this up. Shit!

She swiped away another tear. "Sure. Right. Josh couldn't help but point out that it's way more upscale than I'm used to and that must be why I liked staying with you. Josh got in his dig, implying that I was only with you because of your wealth and success and nothing else. I guess you believed I'm that shallow."

"No. Not for a second."

"Then what happened? Did Tanya put his crap in your head? Or has Amy finally flirted her way into your heart."

"No. The only woman I want is you."

"Really? Because you lost me when you accused me of using you for your money." She raked her hair away from her face and over her shoulder. "I'm not stupid, Fox. You own your own company. You make a lot of money. Enough to start charitable foundations in two states, buy two apartment buildings here, and renovate them for yourself and those working and attending classes at the center you also own. You're also taking care of your mom and buying her all kinds of stuff for her place."

She swiped away another tear. "It's your business how you spend your money. I thought what you did to help those less fortunate and in need of support was damn admirable. It showed you had a heart and cared about others. I mean, after the way your own mother treated you, you're still willing to give her a chance.

"But not me. Someone says some shit to you and you forget everything we've shared. You think all I've been doing is manipulating you in some way so that I can...what? Take your money. I've never asked you for a damn thing. I liked you and wanted to be with you before I ever met you in person or knew you were successful.

"But I guess I don't measure up because I don't have the financial resources you have. I don't have the poise and polish Amy seems to think she has to run in your circles. So why don't you just go be with her or find someone rich, because that's what matters."

"The only thing that matters to me is *you*."

"Sounds to me like you came here to defend your bank account."

"Damnit, Dee, I fucked up, okay? I didn't think it all the way through."

"No. You just accused me and condemned me because you don't trust anyone to be what they show you to be."

Exactly. Because who could you trust when your own parents mistreated you, abandoned you, and the very people who took you into their homes after that were more interested in the government check than actually taking care of you? Even the other foster kids were only out for themselves. They'd throw you under that bus to stay out of trouble, get a treat, or just so they looked better than you, so they wouldn't be moved again.

Fuck, he had trust issues. Big ones. And he was letting past fears and experiences ruin things with Melody.

Shit.

"I just want the truth."

"I've given you nothing but the truth. And if you can't see that, then get out." The tears spilled over and down her cheeks and she quickly dashed them away with her fingertips. "We're done. Get out!"

Those words smashed into his chest like a sledgehammer, pummeling his heart. "No, Mel, no. I'm sorry. I know you're not lying to me."

She sucked in a shuddering breath. "I have been more myself with you than I am with anyone else. I've opened up to you about my past and what I want in the future. I have never lied to you by word or deed. So let me make this very clear. Fuck Amy. Maybe you should look at her motives for stirring up trouble between us. As for Josh...he's not a friend, or even really an ex. We haven't shared any meaningful conversations. We aren't drinking buddies or fuck buddies. In fact, I don't like him, especially because of the way he treated me, and the company he keeps, and the leering looks he gives me and other women. He's just a guy I know but never think about. Clear enough for you?"

"Yes."

She picked up a piece of leather and tossed it in the trash. "Now if you'll excuse me, my family is probably waiting for me for dinner."

He caught a glimpse of a silver latch on the end of the leather she'd tossed. He reached down and pulled it from the trash.

"Leave it." She tried to take it from him, but he held it out of her reach and looked at it himself.

The craftsmanship was amazing. "Did you make this?"

"Yes. Give it back." She held out her hand.

He stared at the intricate work stamped into the leather band. "This is my car with a fox curled up on the roof. The road the car is on is actually a D." He looked her dead in the eye. "Because I call you sweet Dee." The D was on its side beneath the car. On each side of the D she'd stamped in a heart. Behind the car, she'd stamped in rows of dashes so it looked like the car was speeding down the road. And above the hood, a sun with blazing rays. "No clouds in the sky. Nothing but sun."

"For a bright future," she whispered.

His throat clogged.

She'd made this for him, then tossed it in the trash because he'd been an asshole of epic proportions. He hated that she'd toss it instead of giving it to him after all the time, effort, and meaning she'd put into it.

Nothing less than he deserved. And his mistake to fix.

"This is amazing work and detail." The clasp holding it together was a miniature D bit.

"Keep it. I have to go." She tried to walk past him.

It couldn't end this way. He hooked his hand at her waist and stopped her. "We're not done talking."

"I've said all I have to say."

"Then it's my turn."

She raised one brow, anger rolling off her, but she didn't push his hand away. "Don't you think you've said enough?"

He'd said a bunch of stupid shit. Now he needed to make things right. "You deserve the truth and an apology." He waited for her to look at him, then he shifted so he was right in front of her with both hands on her hips. He bent his head, touched his forehead to hers, and looked her right in the eye. "I love you." He squeezed her hips. "It's like this living, breathing thing inside me. It's all I think about. That and wanting you. Nothing will ever change that. And the fact is, you're not just enough for me, you're amazing and out of my league and way more than I deserve."

She put her hands on his forearms and squeezed. "Fox, that's not true."

He knew it was. "I'm selfish. I want you all to myself. And thinking of you with someone else sends me into a tailspin. It wasn't what Amy said, so much as the thought that maybe you were keeping your options open about Boston or staying here."

She shook her head, her tempting lips scrunching into a pout. "I thought I made my choice clear in as many ways as I could. I even agreed to leave Wyoming, my family, my bar to move to Boston with you."

"I still kind of can't believe you agreed to do that to be with me."

"No, you thought maybe I wanted to stay in town with a guy like Josh." The disgusted and disgruntled face she made showed how unlikely that was to happen.

He cupped her face. "I'm sorry. I took this amazing thing we've had for months and screwed it all up in ten minutes. A little self-sabotage to go with my other issues. Please, forgive me. All I want to do is put this back together, so we can go back to being happy. And to do that you have to know that, yes, I sometimes feel like I can't trust anyone. Even the people closest to me. Even when they give me no reason to doubt them. And I never doubted you. In fact, I told Amy you'd never hurt me."

Uncertainty clouded her eyes. "Do you seriously think your money has anything to do with why I'm with you?"

"No. But I do get that bringing you into my life means you'll see that what I have is glaringly more than what you do. But it also means that what's mine is yours."

"That works both ways."

"Except I have a hell of a lot more. You have no idea the scope of what I'm talking about because you haven't seen it. That's why I want to take you to Boston. I thought there you'd see what my life is really like now."

She released him to hold her hands up. "How does that change anything between us?"

"It doesn't."

Her hands went back to his arms, easing him in a way only she could do.

Because he wasn't finished and worried this next part could get him into trouble again. "Except that living in Boston will be a huge change for you. But I can try to make it easier on you because I have the means to give you anything you want."

"Look at how I live here. I don't need much. What I want is to be a part of your life and have my own life, too."

"Okay. Then, there's something you need to know. Something I haven't told you. A secret I need you to keep."

"Are you sure you want to tell me? Five minutes ago, I told you to get out."

He hesitated. "Did you actually want me to leave?"

Her grip tightened. "No. I wanted you to see me, not some version someone put in your head."

"I do see you. I know what makes you smile and what makes you sad. I know what's important to you and who. That's why I'm going to tell you my secret, because I know you'll keep it no matter what happens."

Her forehead wrinkled. "Okay."

"But first, I really need to know. Are we good? We're still together, right? Because I'm seriously freaking out that I've screwed this up and you really will toss me out the door." His heart was thrashing in his chest. He could barely breathe or think straight.

Her lips firmed into a tight line. "This is the last time you come at me with accusations. Next time you're upset with me, or about something, make it a conversation, because I don't want to fight with you."

"I don't want that either. I hate this feeling that I've lost the closeness we share."

She went up on tiptoe, wrapped her arms around his neck, and hugged him close. "Better?"

"Getting there." He tightened his hold on her, then spilled his secret. "I won the lottery."

"I feel lucky to have you, too."

He chuckled. "No. I literally won the lottery."

She leaned back and stared at him. "That's awesome."

He waited for her to ask how much.

She didn't.

So he told her, because she was waiting for him to share it because he wanted to, not because she'd asked. "One point one *billion* dollars."

Her eyes went wide, her arms went loose, and she fell back onto flat feet. Her eyes went blank. Shock. Had to be.

"I gave a hundred million to both Dean and Max."

She finally blinked. "Wow. That was generous."

"I didn't want money to come between us. The rest I used to grow my company and invest. Max handles the investments for all of us."

Warmth came back into her gaze. "That's amazing." She smiled. "And you have your friends, people you can trust, helping you."

He pulled her back into a hug. "And I have you. Right?"

"Yes. Always." Her arms tightened. "This doesn't change anything."

He leaned back and grinned at her. "Are you sure? Because it's a lot of money. Being with me means you'll never have to work or live without something you want or need."

She shrugged. "I mean, that's nice, but I like having a purpose and feeling like I've accomplished something. I'm not asking you to pay my way, so I can just...what? Sit around and do nothing but spend money on things I probably don't need? That might be fun for like a minute, but then what?"

"That's been my dilemma. I don't want you to want the money, but I also can't think of anyone else I want to spend it with because I want you to have nice things and feel like you can say you hate everything in the apartment, so let's redecorate it so you're happy."

She grinned and shook her head. "And you'd let me do that."

"If it made you want to stay with me, yes."

She pressed her lips together. "Shouldn't we decide something like that together?"

"The only thing I care about is that you're in my life."

"And do you believe that's what matters most to me, too?"

"Yes. So say it."

She went up on tiptoe, her arms around his neck again, and smiled. "I love you."

He kissed her like he'd wanted to the second he'd walked into her little workshop. Not nice and sweet but demanding and possessive and scorching hot. His tongue swept along hers. She tasted like desire and the chocolate kisses he'd seen in a jar on the workbench. Sweet temptation. He wanted more and slid his hands down over her ass to pull her up and against his rock-hard cock.

This felt the same, even if he was still unsure they'd resolved everything between them and she'd let everything he'd said go. He hoped in time, this wouldn't even be a memory. They'd both forget it and move on.

He looked forward to their trip to Boston now because she knew everything. He had nothing to hide anymore.

Well, there were still some things they needed to talk about. Like security. Someone could use her against him.

Even the thought of it made him hold on to her tighter and kiss her deeper so she knew he cared and that she mattered more than anything.

Someone cleared their throat.

He didn't want to stop kissing the beautiful woman in his arms.

She broke the kiss and turned to their intruder. "What?" Her annoyance matched his.

"Dinner's ready," Jax said from the doorway, a grin on his face. "Or I could tell Dad you're too busy making out with your boyfriend to bring him up to the house."

Melody growled under her breath, then turned to him. "Hungry?"

"Desperately," he said, knowing she, as well as Jax, would get his meaning.

Jax's laugh faded as he walked away.

He and Melody took a moment to cool off and get their desire for each other under control.

Melody looked up at him. "So, I can't tell them what you told me?"

He shook his head. "I'd prefer it if you let them think my wealth comes from the business I own."

"I don't like keeping secrets from them, but okay."

He wanted to ease her mind. "It's a security issue."

She went still. "That's why Dean is here. Is there some kind of threat against you? Someone wants money?"

"I've tried to keep the secret using a trust to conceal my identity. When I won, I was warned that no matter how hard I tried, people would find out I was the big winner. Blackmail, kidnapping, threats, people just begging for handouts, it all comes with the territory for some lottery winners. I read up on some of their tragic and terrible stories. I don't want that to happen to me or anyone I care about. Especially you."

"Are you afraid someone will do something to me, to get money from you?"

"It could happen."

She shook her head. "That's ridiculous."

"Is it? Because I'd pay anything to get you back if someone took you."

Her eyes went wide with shock. "Okay, now you're freaking me out."

He brushed his hands up and down her arms. "There's no threat. Very few outside my tight circle know about the money. I just don't feel right not telling you the potential is there."

"So who knows besides Dean, Max, and me?"

"My attorney, tax accountant, and..."

Her eyes went wide. "Tanya."

He nodded. "A social worker at the hospital thought she needed family support."

"So the social worker looked for you on Tanya's behalf and somehow found out you won the lottery."

He nodded. "I'm not sure how, but I assume she dug deep into my background and resources because she wanted to be sure I would be someone good in Tanya's life."

Tanya sure thought he was, because of what he could do for her. He'd feared she'd use the information for her gain. And she had. He'd spent a lot of money updating her appliances and paying off her medical bills. That trip she wanted to take around the world, not cheap. Not something she could afford at all.

But he could without it really making a dent in his bank account. And yet, he didn't just book the trip for her. It had nothing to do with the money and everything to do with his relationship with Tanya. He didn't want to reward her for her continued bad behavior and her inability to have a real conversation about the past that included a heartfelt apology for what she'd done to him and what she'd allowed to happen to him. He didn't think he'd ever forgive her for letting him go and never even trying to do what she needed to do to get him back.

He didn't want to think about that right now. "Come on. Your family is waiting." He took her hand and walked with her out of the workshop and into the barn.

"We need to talk more about this."

"There's nothing for you to worry about. Dean is keeping watch while we're here. When we get to Boston tomorrow, you'll have security. You won't see it, but it will be there."

She stopped dead in her tracks, her hand slipping free of his, just as they made it across the yard toward the house. "You're putting a guard on me?"

"It won't be obvious. Just someone to keep an eye on you. Just in case."

"I don't think I like that."

"It's more for my peace of mind than anything." He took her hand again and started toward the house. They were late. He didn't want her parents to get the wrong impression of him. Not after all they'd done for him.

CHAPTER TWENTY-ONE

M elody dropped the whole business about a bodyguard following her around. She'd make it clear to Fox that wasn't necessary.
No one cared about what she did, or where she went.

Except the part where Fox worried someone would take her to get
money from him did sound plausible. And ridiculous at the same time.

She was still trying to wrap her head around him winning the lottery.
She wanted to ask how it all happened. It must be a really great story.
Were Dean and Max with him when he discovered he'd won? Did they
celebrate? How?

She had so many questions, her mind reeled with them all.

But the second they walked into the house, she set that all aside as
she watched her mom rush Fox and wrap him in a hug.

For a second, it seemed Fox wasn't sure what to do, then he released
her hand and hugged Robin back as he said, "Thank you for everything
you did to keep me safe and fed and heading in the right direction."

Her mom stepped back and looked up at him. "I am so proud of
you." That pride shone in her eyes.

Fox swallowed hard, his throat working. "Thank you. I couldn't have
done it without you and Wade. Every time I thought things seemed
hopeless, you and Wade stepped in to help."

"You did the work. Even when things were hard, you persevered.
Things could have gone bad in a lot of different ways, but you stuck to
it and you made it out of the system with your head up, outstanding
grades, and a bright future that you didn't squander."

"I didn't want to let either of you down."

Her father joined them. "Never, son." Her dad looked from him, to Melody, and back to him. "And you make her happy, which makes us even happier to have you home."

Fox took Melody's hand.

"About home," Melody began. "Fox invited me to go with him to Boston tomorrow for a couple of days."

"That sounds like fun," her mom said.

"I'm thinking about moving there. With him."

Aria, Lyric, Jax, Mason, and Layla were seated at the island across the room and behind her parents. They all stopped talking and turned around to stare at her.

Lyric asked what they all wanted to know. "What about the bar?"

Melody owned a fourth of it. And she loved working there and being with her siblings, but she couldn't pass up this opportunity to spread her wings and be with Fox. "Fox and I don't have a specific date that we'll be going to Boston to live, but when that time comes, and I'm no longer working there, I'll relinquish my rights to the profits."

Jax shook his head. "We own it equally."

"But I won't be contributing to running it. It's only fair that my share goes back to you three."

Aria added, "She'll still own her quarter of the bar. If we sell, then she'll get her cut."

Melody nodded her agreement. "Fox will be here for a while yet, but I wanted you all to know that we've talked about the future and what we want and that means I'll be headed to Boston with him. This short trip we're taking is so that I can check out Fox's place, his company, and the city."

Fox put his hands on her shoulders, his chest to her back. "Melody loves it here. But I'm hoping she'll find her place in the city, too, with me. I've promised her she can come back to visit you as often as she likes. And we want you to visit us there."

"And what if she isn't happy there?" Wade asked.

"Then I'm going to have one hell of a commute from Wyoming to Boston every week."

"You'd do that?" Robin gaped. "You'd commute just so she could be here with us?"

"If that's what she wants, then that's the way it will have to be."

"But the expense of that..." Aria was always the practical one.

"My company is doing well, and I earn more than I'm worth. It's not a matter of money."

Melody couldn't let the comment about his worth go. "Your company's success is because of you and all the hours you put into each project. No doubt your employees and customers believe you're worth every penny."

He kissed her on the head. "That's just one of the many reasons I love her. She always reminds me what I do and who I am matters."

"It's no small thing you've accomplished, Fox." Wade grabbed two beers out of the fridge and handed one to Fox.

They popped the tops, clinked the long necks together, then drank.

Lyric poured her a glass of wine. "I'd love to come visit you, maybe catch a concert."

"Anytime," Fox said. "I've got two guest rooms at the moment."

Melody raised a brow. "How big is your place?"

His cheeks turned a little red. "Thirty-five hundred square feet. Three bedrooms, four baths in a high rise with a gorgeous view."

"Damn." Mason looked impressed.

Fox kept his gaze on her. "Like I said, if you want a house, we'll find one you like."

She shook her head and took a big sip of wine. "I'm just trying to take it all in."

"You'll see everything tomorrow. Then we can talk about what you like, what you want to change, or what you want to get that fits us better."

"I like that *us*." Robin opened the oven and pulled out a huge roasting pan with not one or two, but three roasted chickens.

While her sisters helped Mom get the food to the table, Melody introduced Fox to Mason and Layla.

When they all sat at the table and finished filling their plates with the succulent chicken, mashed potatoes with gravy, and broccoli, cauliflower, and zucchini medley, Jax made the next big announcement. "Layla and I are moving up the wedding to next month. We'll have it here at the ranch, like Mason and Lyric did, with just family and close friends."

"I thought you wanted to wait until early spring." Robin stared at Jax, confused.

Since Jax and Layla wanted a simple, fast wedding, it didn't take much planning. In fact, Layla had found her dress just last week. The rest—flowers, food, the small guest list, the honeymoon—was easy.

Jax and Layla shared a knowing look and smiles so big, their happiness couldn't be denied. "We need to do it soon, so that Layla's dress will still fit." A gleam brightened Jax's blue eyes.

Melody leaned into the table, her smile as big as theirs. "You're pregnant," she guessed, hoping it was true, because she knew how much they wanted to have a baby together. Especially after what they'd both gone through with their exes.

Layla kissed Jax, then turned to her. "Yes. We're having a baby. It's early yet, but the doctor said everything looks great so far. We truly didn't think it would happen this fast."

"You guys are going to be the best parents," Aria said, her words joyful, though a bit of sadness crept into her eyes. As the oldest, Aria had probably thought she'd be first to marry and start a family. Now, Lyric and Jax were both making plans and living them out with their partners.

Lyric and Mason shared a look, he nodded, and Lyric announced, "Looks like we're getting a couple of new Wildes."

Robin's head turned so fast, Melody wondered if she'd hurt herself. Mom gasped, "What?"

Lyric's joyful smile made Melody's heart light up. "We're pregnant, too. Though I suspect I'm further along than Layla."

Robin burst into happy tears, jumped up, and hugged Lyric.

Wade smacked Mason on the back.

Mom made her way to Jax and Layla and hugged them both.

Dad gave Jax a look filled with pride and a firm nod.

Fox squeezed Melody's shoulder. "You're going to be an aunt."

"The best one ever," she proclaimed, delighted for her brother and sister and their family.

From that point on, everyone ate, drank, and talked about everything from wedding plans to baby shower ideas to updates on the ranch and bar.

The night felt like a celebration of family and life and the promise of the future. And Melody looked around the table at all the faces that made up her family, then looked at Fox, in deep with the conversation about the latest HBO series blowing up.

It was nice to see them bonding and Fox jumping right in with all of them.

He fit.

And that meant everything because her family was so important to her.

Melody and Fox were the first to leave. They had a long drive back to town and needed to be up early to catch their very early flight. They stood on the porch after her mom and dad hugged her goodbye. The others were still inside.

Mom hugged Fox, then stepped back, still holding his arms. "Take care of my girl in that big city. Don't let her get lost."

Fox held her mom's gaze. "I want to take care of her for the rest of my life. And Melody will never be lost. She knows exactly who she is and where she's meant to be. I just hope it's always with me." Fox held out his hand to her dad. "Thank you for everything, most especially making me feel like part of the family tonight."

Her dad took Fox's hand and used his free one to grasp Fox's shoulder. "Not just tonight, Fox. You are family. Never forget that. Anytime you're lost, you find your way home. We'll be here waiting."

Fox bear-hugged her dad, then took her hand and led her to their cars. He stood beside hers, holding her hand, quiet and contemplative. "Do you know how lucky you are?"

"Yes. And I often take it for granted. But tonight...I feel very blessed to be a part of that group of amazing people, to know I'm loved, and welcome, and that they're all as excited for me to be with you and looking toward our future as they are about the two new Wildes coming into this world soon."

"I don't think your family is excited about you moving away. And maybe now that you're going to be an aunt, you're not as willing to leave." He took a step back, his body going rigid, like he was bracing for a blow.

She tried to ease his mind. "I haven't changed my mind about us."

"Are you sure? Because I feel like I really fucked up." Fear stamped his face with worry lines.

She put her hand on his chest, his heart racing against her palm. "You apologized. I've let it go. We're even taking a trip together tomorrow."

He let out a breath and his whole body seemed to ease. "I don't want to lose you."

"You need to stop looking for ways this could fall apart and instead enjoy being with me, because I'm committed to you, because I believe you're committed to me."

"I am. I want this to work. I want all those things I imagined in my head to be real."

"Like kids? Because I want at least two."

Surprise, joy, maybe a little shock lit his eyes. "Yes. Absolutely. Whenever you're ready."

"Great. Now can we please go home so I can show you how committed I am to us being happy together?"

Fox's eyes heated with lust as his gaze swept over her. "What did you have in mind?"

"You. And me. Naked. Your hands on me as I ride you to oblivion."

He hooked his arm around her shoulders, pulled her close, and crushed his mouth to hers in a searing kiss that left both of them panting and desperate for more.

Chapter Twenty-Two

F ox woke Melody before the crack of dawn the same way he'd put her to bed last night, by showing her how much he loved and wanted her. He couldn't stop wanting her. He took his time, though they had a plane to catch. But he couldn't help touching, tasting, kissing every inch of her. And when he was inside her...heaven. Every pant and moan and gasp let him know she was right there with him, burning in ecstasy. After the high, when they both settled into bliss, their arms around each other, he knew he was right where he wanted to be. Always.

The bright, open, honest smile she gave him when he stared down at her...it made his heart swell.

He loved her more than anything in this world. And he wanted to make her a part of his.

As they dressed, then headed for the airport, her sitting next to him in the car he'd ordered to take them to the private airstrip, Dean up front, he held her hand and thanked his lucky stars to have her by his side, taking this step toward their future.

He wanted her to love Boston. He wanted her to feel at home there. He wanted her to be happy in the life they'd make together.

Though they hadn't talked about his wealth and what it meant in their lives again, he knew she had to be thinking about it. The money changed everything. He knew it. Melody had to, too. And yet, she hadn't brought it up.

So he watched her as they pulled up to the hangar and she spotted the private jet waiting for them.

Her eyes went wide before she turned them on him. "This isn't the airport I'm used to."

"Me either," he admitted. "But we only have a couple of days and I need to make the time count. This is the fastest way to get there and back without the hassle of being on some airline's schedule and going through all the security and stuff."

"Is this how you normally travel now?"

"Most of the time." He gave her a sheepish grin.

Dean asked the driver to wait outside a moment, then turned in the front seat. "A lot has changed since Fox won the lottery. People know he's rich. They assume because of the business. It's a good cover. But it also puts a target on his back."

"And yours and Max's, too?"

Dean shook his head. "We've managed to stay under the radar. It's hard for the CEO and founder of the company to do that. He's too public now."

Melody glanced at him, then back to Dean. "What are you trying to tell me?"

"You're going to see people treat him a certain way when we get there. He's going to be in corporate mogul mode. Just remember, you know who he really is at the core."

Melody glanced at Fox, then Dean again, and shook her head. "You know, I'm really getting tired of being underestimated. I get that the money means you can have all the nice things, but it doesn't buy the things that matter. True friends," she said to Dean. Her blue gaze shifted to Fox. "Love."

"Melody..."

"What? You think I don't get it. You want me to love you because you're you, not because you have a shit-ton of money. Done. I do love you. But the quickest way to ruin it is for you to keep thinking that I'm here for the money and not the amazing sex." With that, she got out of the car, then turned back, a huge grin on her face.

Fox gaped at her, then everything inside him eased because of that smile and the woman who owned his heart. "So you're just using me for my body." He slid across the seat and followed her out. Who wouldn't follow the sway of those hips and the woman who knew just how to make him want to beg?

"Those are some good memories, but I'm after a lot more. A lifetime more." With that, she greeted the pilot with a "Hello" and disappeared into the plane.

Dean caught up to him. "Now, will you stop worrying?"

"Not until my ring is on her finger and she says, 'I do.'"

"When is that happening?"

"Soon." Fox shook the pilot's hand at the bottom of the steps. "Everything ready?"

"As per your instructions."

"Great. Let's go." Fox walked up the steps, ducked under the doorway, and found his beautiful girlfriend sitting in one of the front-row seats, her bag on the seat across the aisle. He sat next to her, put his hand on her knee, and squeezed. "Thank you."

"For what?"

"Being you. And doing this...taking a chance on us and Boston and a new life."

"I'm still nervous and unsure about what this life is going to look like, but I'm excited to be with you."

Dean walked onto the plane and past them to take a seat at the back, giving him and Melody a little privacy.

The pilot came in after Dean and closed the door. "We'll be leaving in a few minutes."

Fox nodded and fastened his seat belt.

Melody already had hers on. "What's the plan when we get there?"

"We'll go to the apartment. I want to show you it first. Then we'll head to the office. I'll show you around there." He winced. "I have some work I need to do."

"No worries. I thought I'd scope out the city a bit. I'll do a little walking tour around your company, see what's there to see."

"It's a business district."

"Yes. Probably with lots of restaurants and bars. Places I could work."

"Is that what you really want to do? Because you could do anything, even something new, something you never thought to do but could now because money isn't a factor."

She raised a brow and studied him. "You mean that."

"Yes. I'd rather spend it on making you happy than anything else." And this was where he felt things could get complicated between them again.

She put her hand over his. "I am happy."

"I know. I just want you to know, you have no limits now. So really think about it. What would you be happy doing if you had the money to do it?"

"I love doing what I'm doing already. But maybe it will be different in Boston and I'll want a change. We'll see."

"Okay. Just…"

"What?"

"Don't hesitate to ask me for what you want. If it means you'll be happy in Boston, I'll give it to you."

"We'll figure it out," she assured him.

Dean walked up to them with three champagne glasses. "Peach Bellini."

Melody took her glass, then eyed Fox. "How did you know this is my favorite brunch drink?"

"I may have asked your sisters a few questions last night while you were gushing over Layla's new painting."

"I'll heat up the cinnamon rolls and spinach artichoke frittatas once we're in the air." With that, Dean went to his seat in the back.

Fox held out his glass. "To the most beautiful woman in the world and new adventures."

Melody tapped her glass to his. "To making memories."

Fox drank to that, because it's everything he wanted. Now all he had to do was show her that life in Boston with him would be a good one. One filled with love and happy memories if Melody could find her place there and the thing that made her happy.

Chapter Twenty-Three

Melody squeezed Fox's hand as they sat in yet another chauffeured car driving down the busy streets of Boston. Dean sat up front. She gaped at all the sights out the window. Tall buildings, busy streets, tons of people walking on the sidewalks. They passed a pretty park. It was the only open space she'd seen in blocks. Still, the city fascinated her.

So many people.

She'd never traveled outside Wyoming, so this was all new and overwhelming to her. There was so much packed together in the city. Buildings, people, noise. Traffic like she'd never seen.

Where was everyone going?

They stopped outside one of the many tall buildings. A doorman came forward and opened the door. "Welcome home, Mr. Bridges, Mr. Reynolds."

She had no idea that was Dean's last name.

"It's good to be home." Fox turned on the sidewalk and held his hand out to her. "Come on, sweet Dee."

She slid across the seat, took his hand, and stepped out into the noisy city.

Fox tugged her close to his side and put his arm around her. "Mike, this is Melody Wilde. She'll be staying with me. Anything she wants or needs, make it happen."

Melody held her hand out. "Nice to meet you, Mike."

"Miss Wilde."

"Melody will do just fine."

"As you wish. May I take your bag?"

"I've got it." Fox took it by the strap and hoisted it onto his shoulder.

Mike opened the door for them.

Dean led the way, passing one bank of elevators on both sides of the hallway and heading to the one at the end.

"Why this one, and not one of those?"

Dean pulled out a key card and held it to the scanner. "And here's where things get weird."

"Why?" She glanced up at Fox.

"Because this elevator goes only to the penthouse floor."

She stepped into the elevator with him. "I see."

"You will," Dean said, leaning back against the mirrored wall.

Fox turned to her. "There are four penthouses on the top floor. Dean, Max, and I have three of them."

"And the fourth?"

"We haven't met him yet. He's an older gentleman. Been living here a long time."

The elevator dinged and the doors slid open, revealing a rich gray carpet and wood-paneled walls with a console table holding two large bouquets of freshly cut flowers. Their sweet scent filled the wide hallway. Their colors matched the beautiful painting of a garden pond, lily pads and water lilies floating on the surface, bright koi fish swimming beneath the surface.

Dean headed to the left.

Fox followed, bringing her along with him since they held hands.

Dean stopped at PH2. "Meeting's at eleven. Meet you at ten-thirty." With that, he used his key card to open his door. Before he closed it, he turned back. "I'll give you the tour later. Fox is anxious for you to see your place. I'm glad you came." He held his door wide, giving her a glimpse of a massive living room and floor-to-ceiling windows that looked out over the city. "This can be overwhelming at times. But then I remember it's just stuff. A big empty place. Except when Fox and Max are over. Then it feels like home."

She understood what he was telling her. "I'll see what I can do about making our place home."

Dean nodded.

"For all of us," she added. "Because family is always welcome." She wanted him to know that she considered him a brother, too. Just like Fox did.

"I wasn't sure about you at first. I thought you'd be dazzled by all this."

"I am a little bit."

"I get that. But on the plane, I heard you and Fox talking. You appreciated that he got you breakfast more than you gushed over the private plane and gourmet food."

"I appreciated both, especially that Fox took the time to think about getting me breakfast and finding out what I'd like...you can't put a price on that."

"That's what we all keep trying to remember. It's the little things that matter the most sometimes."

"They aren't little if they mean something."

Dean looked past her at Fox. "If you don't marry her, I will." With that, he closed the door.

Fox just stood there staring at her.

"What?"

"If I hadn't fallen in love with you already, I would have just now based on that conversation."

"All I did was say the truth."

He tugged her hand to get her to follow him down to PH1. "Dean and Max think things will change because we're together."

"I'm sure each of you at one time or another have had girlfriends and paid more attention to them instead of each other. For a while, anyway."

"Yes. But you're different. You're not just some woman. You're the one. And I am going to marry you. We're going to build a life. And that means things will change between me and Max and Dean."

"It doesn't have to. I like them. I don't mind that you guys are so close. In fact, I'm used to being around family all the time, so them coming and going from our place...not a big deal."

Fox tapped his key card to the scanner, then opened the door and pushed it wide. "Welcome to *our* place."

Melody stepped into the apartment and took in the massive expanse of the place. "My whole apartment would fit in your kitchen." That was past the office on her left. Natural wood cabinets, white countertops, stainless steel appliances, and black accents in the pendent lights over the breakfast bar and chairs. While the office looked well used with a massive desk holding three monitors and tons of folders and papers, the living space looked only partially furnished with two facing leather sofas, a massive wood coffee table between them, and three mismatched chairs that complemented each other with their green, blue, and purple fabrics that matched the light blue throw pillows on the couches. The massive gas fireplace on the right wall boasted a thick natural-wood mantle that had nothing on it. Two black lights were mounted on either side of the huge black, white, and dark blue abstract painting.

Though the seating area took up the center of the space—fireplace on one side, a floating wall on the left that held a giant flat-screen and media cabinet beneath—it left a huge expanse of empty space along the wall of windows and the back of the apartment. On the left side of the fireplace, massive double doors stood open. On the right, a dark hallway led to other rooms, she guessed.

Hardwood floors throughout made everything flow and seem even more expansive.

"What do you think?"

"I like it. It just feels so big."

"It is. I've got the basics, but the place needs more to make it feel warm and welcoming and like people live here."

She chuckled under her breath. "The only spot that looks lived-in is your office."

"I spend most of my time in there." He looked around the space. "What would you add?"

"A dining room table by the windows with lights overhead. A place where our whole family can sit and eat and talk."

Fox's eyes went wide. "I actually didn't think of that. We fit at the bar. Not all the places where I grew up had a place for me at the table."

"This is your home. You made a place for Dean and Max. Let's expand that."

"Okay." He grinned. "We'll pick something out together. It will be our first thing we do together here."

"Can the second be getting rid of that painting?"

"You don't like it?"

"It's okay. I'd just rather have something outdoorsy. Something that feels like you could get lost. A forest. A lake. A garden. Something that brings the outdoors in. Especially with all this city around us."

"Done. What else?"

"I don't know yet. I just got here. I need to be in the space and figure out what feels right."

"I love that the first thing you thought about was a place where everyone can gather."

"If I'm here, I want my family to be able to come and stay with us."

Fox pointed down the hall. "There are two bedrooms and baths back that way." He turned back to the office. "The door between the office and kitchen is a half bath. Next to the front door is a big closet." He turned again. "Master suite is just past the fireplace."

"I want to see." She headed that way.

"It's also kind of bare," Fox called after her.

She stepped into the room and gaped at the wall of windows on two sides of the room. Heavy black drapes hung to her left, at the corner of the room, and on the far side of the windows. In the center of the wall on her right was a king-size bed with a white fluffy cover over ocean-blue sheets. The base and headboard were more natural wood, making a simple, clean design. The nightstands matched the wood bed and each had two drawers with a cubby charging station. Cut crystal lamps with white shades sat atop them.

"We need some plants. There's nothing green in here or out there. With all the windows, we could have some really cool foliage. You could put a whole frickin' tree out there."

"Sounds awesome. Let's do it."

She turned to him. "This place feels so sterile. There's nothing on the walls. Aside from your change, a watch, and a few receipts on the dresser over there, you've added nothing personal here."

He turned to her, cupped her face. "I added you. That's all I need." He followed up that amazingly sweet, heart-melting, emotional declaration with a kiss to match, and she was lost. In him. The moment. The idea that this was the start of something bigger for them. This was the moment they intertwined their lives in a real and meaningful way by simply planning how to make this space *their* home.

He gave her two more tender kisses, then stared down at her. "As much as I want you in our bed, up against a wall, in the amazing bathtub in the other room, I have limited time here to get some stuff done at the office. I need to get ready for work." He took her hand and tugged her toward a set of double doors. He pulled one open, revealing a huge walk-in closet. On the left, his clothes took up about a quarter of the space. "Never let it be said that I didn't give you the majority of the closet."

"I don't need this much space."

"You might. I have a lot of dinner meetings. I don't expect you to come to all of them, but I'd love it if you came sometimes. You'll need dressy clothes for that. I'll set up an account for you, so you can buy whatever you need."

"You don't have to do that."

He squeezed her hand. "I want to do that. My world comes with some expectations and necessary flair. Hence the suits, the watches, the car service. If you look successful, people believe you're good at what you do. And while I love you in whatever you're wearing, and especially when you're wearing nothing at all, sweet Dee, I would love to see you in a dress and heels, knocking the socks off whoever wants to hire me and my company."

She had no problem dressing up for him. It was a simple request and she wanted to fit in. But... "What if I'm working at night, like I do now?"

He squeezed her hand again. "I'll understand and I won't complain. Much," he added with a grin. Then he pulled off his thermal and tossed it into the laundry hamper. He chose a plain white dress shirt from the bar and pulled it on.

She glanced down at her simple black jeans and bright blue blouse. "Do I need to change to come with you?"

"No. A lot of people at the company dress casually. As the head honcho I tend to dress up to meet with clients. I'm just wearing a dress shirt and slacks, no suit today because I'll mostly be meeting with my employees." To prove that point, he ditched his jeans and pulled on a pair of dark gray slacks and tucked the shirt into it. He looked classy and sophisticated.

"I brought a dress and heels. Just in case." She'd chosen her most conservative dress and basic black heels. She wanted to be prepared for anything.

"You don't need to wear that to hang out with me today. I know it doesn't sound fun to tag along with me, but I want you to see the place and what I do. I want you to feel comfortable coming to the office to see me." He sighed. "Because I spend a lot of time there."

"Looks like you spend a lot of time in your home office, too."

"I do. And if you're here with me, I'll do my best to put work aside and spend time with you. But truthfully, and I want to be upfront, so you're not surprised or upset, if there's a deadline looming...I will spend a lot of hours working. Dean and Max often get on my case about being about all work and no play."

"I get it. It's your company. You're in charge. You want to do your best."

He shook his head. "The real reason is that I didn't have anything else worth putting work aside for until you. I know I'm needed in the office, but all I want to do is spend the day with you. I want to take you around Boston and show you my favorite places. I want to find a local nursery and buy some plants. I want to take you to dinner and make love to you all night. I want to convince you that you can be happy here. With me."

"I am happy with you, Fox. Here. There. Wherever. Am I nervous about moving here? Yes. But I'll find my way. I always do. It will just take some time. So stop worrying."

"I can't help it. I've never wanted anything else this much."

"Me either," she confessed, letting him see her vulnerability the way he showed her his. "Now, how much space did you leave me in the bathroom?"

"Ninety percent of it. I'm a dude. I've got a bar of soap, a razor, toothbrush, a brush and comb."

She bet he had a few more things than that, because he always smelled amazing, like lime and the forest after it rained. She bet he had some product for that gorgeous, thick hair, too.

But the change in topic seemed to ease him as he pulled on a nice pair of black shoes with a belt to match.

"You look really handsome."

The boyish grin and blush surprised her. "Yeah? You like?"

She nodded. "All I want to do is mess you up."

He held his arms out wide. "Come and get it."

She went into his arms, up on tiptoe, and kissed him with all the passion he ignited in her every time his lips touched hers. She limited the messing up to sliding her fingers into that wild mass of hair. The silky strands glided through her fingers and he moaned against her mouth and pressed his thick erection to her belly.

"I'm going to be late," he grumbled against her mouth, then tightened his arms around her and said, "But I don't care." And then he picked her up, set her on the island of drawers, knocked off her shoes, undid her jeans, pulled them down her legs, along with her panties, and slid his hand between her legs.

She went for his belt, button, and zipper, then slid her hand over his length, squeezing as she stroked him over his boxer briefs.

Fox slid one finger then two into her.

She moaned.

His cock jerked in her hand. "Fuck, that sound you make drives me mad."

Just to drive her crazy, he thrust those two fingers deep and brushed his thumb over her clit. Her inner muscles tightened as wild pleasure raced through her.

"Damn, sweet Dee, you're so fucking beautiful. And I want in."

She slid to the edge of the counter, shoving his pants and boxer briefs down to his knees as he fumbled for a condom in his wallet. His shirt was in the way, so she undid the buttons and pushed it aside as he stroked his thick shaft. He rolled on the condom, positioned himself at her entrance, and thrust deep, taking her mouth in a searing kiss. Then it was all hands grabbing onto each other, hips pumping, soft moans, and passion flaring to all-out fireworks.

Fox leaned against her, his face in her neck, breath panting out against her damp skin. "I could have done that better."

"I'll let you try again later if you really think you can outdo that," she teased.

He somehow managed to raise his head and brush a kiss on her cheek, while she still had her head pressed to his shoulder. "I love you." The words were quietly spoken with a depth of emotion that made her heart swell. Then he wrapped her up close and held her so tight she could feel his heart beat against hers and every breath he took. "You have no idea what it means to me that you're willing to change your whole life to be with me."

His parents hadn't done a damn thing to love and care for him. His mother had left him in the system.

She knew exactly what it meant to him that she'd upend her whole life to be with him. Even more, she knew what he wanted most. Someone to hold on. Forever.

So she held him tighter and gave him the vow that would mean the most to him. "I'll never let you go."

They stayed like that, arms locked around each other, bodies still one. She let him decide when to pull back. But he barely let any space between them when he looked her in the eye, saw what he needed to see—all her love—and kissed her softly, then stepped back.

"We should get cleaned up. Dean is probably waiting for us."

"Fox?"

"Yeah."

"I love you, too."

CHAPTER TWENTY-FOUR

Fox impressed Melody from the moment they got out of the car in front of the building with the Fox Solutions name on it. She loved that the O in Fox was an image of a fox, looking like it was chasing its tail. So cute.

He gave her the grand tour. The first-floor entrance boasted a security desk, banks of elevators, a coffee shop, deli, and bookstore on one side, with a closed restaurant on the other. The second to fifth floors of the building belonged to a legal firm. The sixth to nineteenth floors were a collection of other businesses. And the twentieth to twenty-fifth floors housed Fox Solutions.

They stopped on each of Fox Solutions' floors, which all boasted the same glass doors that led into a reception area with a wide desk and the Fox Solutions logo on the wall. Fox walked her around each department, introducing her to people as he checked in with various managers, staff, and coders. He knew so many people by name.

By the time they reached the twenty-fifth floor, she could barely remember even a handful of the people's names they'd met. But it was sweet that Fox wanted her to feel comfortable here. He couldn't wait to introduce her as his girlfriend and talk about how she owned a bar and two other small businesses that she ran online. Several of the graphic guys had offered to help with anything she needed for her websites. They scored some points with Fox for that, but he shot them all down and said if she needed help, he'd be the one doing it.

She'd never thought to ask him for help with that sort of thing. But now, she had some ideas of things she'd like to do but didn't quite have the skill to pull off.

The twenty-fifth floor had a distinctly more polished and upscale vibe to the reception area.

Fresh flowers adorned both sides of the long reception desk. The wall behind the desk was backlit with a cool white light behind the company name and logo.

The receptionist wasn't as young as the others downstairs. She greeted Fox with a smile and efficiency. "Mr. Bridges, welcome back. Dara stepped away from her desk to attend to a matter and should be back in a few minutes. Until then, I've taken several messages for you." She handed them over. "I see you have a guest. May I get you both some coffee?"

"I'm fine. Melody?"

"No, thank you."

Fox took the lead on introductions, as he'd done downstairs. "Melody, this is Morgan. Morgan, my girlfriend, Melody."

"Pleased to meet you," Morgan said, extending her hand.

Melody shook it. "Nice to meet you."

Fox took her hand, like he did so often now. "Melody will be around today and tomorrow, then we'll be heading back to Wyoming for a time before we return for good. There is no meeting, phone call, anything more important than Melody, so if she calls or comes in, you send her right to me no matter what."

"Understood." Morgan smiled, giving her and Fox a once-over. "And if it's not too bold...you two look great together." She held Melody's gaze. "I hope you get him to stop working more than living."

"I aim to do just that." She leaned into Fox, loving his strength and that his employees cared about him.

"Please let me know if you need anything while you're here."

"Thank you."

Fox led her to the right and past a group of central cubicles with offices along the outside walls. She spotted an office each for Dean and Max, plus a handful of other people, until they reached the back and stood before a cubicle to the side of a set of impressive wood double doors.

"Your domain."

"Why are you whispering?"

"Because this place seems so...important." That really didn't describe what it felt like. "You are such a grownup. You're the head of a company. You have floors and floors of employees."

He chuckled. "Sometimes it doesn't feel real to me either."

"I bet little Fox never imagined this." She glanced around the spacious office, where most of the employees in the cubicles were trying not to stare at them.

"You always made me feel like I could do anything, like what was happening in my life wasn't always going to be that way. When I thought life wasn't worth living, you reminded me it was and why."

Tears gathered in her eyes. "Fox."

He brushed the back of his knuckles over her cheek.

"Melody," Dean called out as he stepped out of his office. "I've got something for you."

She waited for him to come to her and held out her hand to receive the card he held out to her. "That gets you into the building and onto every floor of Fox Solutions. There is no door it doesn't open for you."

"Why do I need access to every door?"

"Because if Fox is in the secure server room and you want to get to him, you can."

"Oh. Okay. Awesome."

"In other words," Dean went on, "if you come, find out he's somewhere else, and don't have the ability to see him, he'll have my head."

She glanced up at Fox, knowing he was the one who insisted on this. "Aw, that's super sweet."

Dean rolled his eyes. "You two are really starting to get on my nerves."

"There was a really pretty blonde down on the twenty-first floor, who asked if you were back, too."

Dean went still, then said, "We don't date employees."

Melody nudged his arm with her elbow. "When I move here, I'm going to be your wingwoman. I'll find you the perfect someone."

"Promise," he said, walking away.

Fox gazed down at her. "You said *when*, not *if* you move here."

"Definitely when. Now show me your inner sanctum."

Instead of doing that, he kissed her right there in front of everyone in the cubicles.

CHAPTER TWENTY-FIVE

Fox's office was massive and boasted two desks. One dead center where he could hold a meeting. The desk was clean and organized with a single screen, a high-tech phone system with multiple lines and an intercom, a white marble pen holder, and a beautiful wood file holder, stacked with color coded folders. Very minimal and organized.

The desk on the left was a tech geek's paradise. A comfortable place he could spend hours coding. Three monitors, a light-up keyboard, a mouse and keypad that looked like it did a hell of a lot more than point and click, and of course a bunch of toys. The cars and trinkets Melody had given him when they were kids, plus a bunch of other stuff from games she didn't really know, but the characters looked fun or ruthless depending on which game they came from, were scattered across the front of the desk.

Maybe she should ask Fox to teach her how to play, so they could do something he liked together.

On the opposite side of the office was a large seating area with a black leather sofa, four additional leather chairs that looked decently comfortable, and a coffee table, all atop a rug that was black and white and looked like a starry night. She loved it.

The second his assistant, Dara, got back to her desk, the phone calls started rolling in. One after another. Then people started lining up outside the office. They filled the small seating area out there, others standing around chatting with each other. And while the doors remained open, no one got past his assistant.

But the longer Melody lingered, watching Fox do his thing, the more she realized she was distracting him. He kept looking at her like he hoped she wasn't bored. Then he'd end one call or meeting and ask if she wanted something to drink or eat. Could he get her anything?

She assured him she was fine. She loved seeing him in action. Talking about one project then another, two very different things the clients wanted, but he could define the parameters, come up with potential solutions and problems, and assure the client they had everything covered.

She didn't understand all the technical jargon or why something couldn't be done the way the client wanted, but it sure did come through that Fox was brilliant at what he did.

The person in front of him was working on a project and had gotten stuck. Something wasn't working. He handed over his laptop to Fox after he'd had two other people look over the code.

As Fox studied it, Jeremy kept sneaking glances at her, seemingly intrigued by her presence in the office and what she meant to Fox.

He'd introduced her to everyone who came in. She tried to stay out of the way by hanging out on the sofa, where Fox could look up and see her but she wasn't intruding on his business.

After two hours, she'd had enough and wanted to get out into the city and explore. Fox didn't need her here. He wanted her here. And for her to find her place, she needed to get comfortable with her surroundings and check out what the city had to offer.

She rose and went to Fox, coming up at his side, taking a quick peek at the screen and all those lines of code that meant nothing to her, but apparently made some system run.

Fox turned from the code to look at her. "What's up?"

"I'm heading out for a little while, so you can concentrate and focus."

"I like having you here."

"I know, but you've got stuff to do and I'm going bar crawling."

He frowned up at her. "I wanted to take you to lunch."

"If lunch is at noon, you're an hour late. I'm going to ask your assistant to get something sent up to you, while I scope out what's around here."

"I'll go with you."

She shook her head, just as Jeremy groaned under his breath. His project was due in three days and without figuring out the issue he was having in his code, he'd miss his deadline. "I'll be fine on my own. I just want to see what's out there. Maybe I'll find someplace I'd like to work."

He held out his hand. "Give me your phone."

"I know how to use the map thing."

He rolled his eyes. "The map thing will help, but if you need a ride, you'll need a rideshare app." Fox took her phone, then briefly looked at Jeremy. "Give me a few minutes to get my girl set up."

"Not a problem." Jeremy glanced at her again. "You should check out O'Leary's and the Bend. Lunchtime is okay, but those places are really hopping at happy hour and late into the night."

"Do they have live music?"

"On weekends."

"Thanks."

Fox pulled out his wallet and a credit card.

"What are you doing?"

"Rideshare needs a card. You pay for the ride through the app."

"I have my own card."

"My city. My invite to bring you here. You want to go out and do stuff, it's on me."

"Fox, you don't have to do that."

"I want to. I need to know you're safe and have a way home."

"So you're asking me to get into a car with a stranger?"

He glared at her. "Be careful. Verify the license plate and face match the app." He held up the phone and showed her how to order a car and pay. The instructions seemed simple enough.

"I plan on sticking close to here for now, so I'll probably just walk."

"That's fine, but if you need a ride, you're all set. So please, I know it's new and not what you're used to, but use it." Worry lines creased his forehead.

"Okay. I'll see you in a few hours. Please eat whatever your assistant gets you."

"Will you meet me back here by six?"

She eyed him. "Will you be done by six?"

"I want to take you to dinner."

She brushed her hand over his head. "I'll be here then."

Fox stood, took her in his arms, and kissed her softly, sweetly. They had an audience. "Have fun."

"I have your number if I get lost."

"That's what the map app is for."

She rolled her eyes. "Just because it shows my location on the map doesn't mean I know where I am."

Worry lines creased his forehead. "I can have Dean go with you."

She headed for the door. "That's not necessary. I don't need or want a babysitter. I'll be fine. And if not, I'll order a stranger to drive me back here."

"You're not inspiring a ton of confidence," he called after her.

She turned at the door and looked back at him. "If you can figure out that code, I can find my way back to you."

"You better," he called after her as she headed to his assistant's desk. "Dara, can you please order some food for Fox. I'll be back later."

Dara nodded. "Absolutely."

It took a few minutes to catch the elevator down and walk out of the huge lobby, but by the time she hit the street, she had scoped out a few places she wanted to check out on the map on her phone.

She headed left and thought she'd start at the closest place to Fox's building. It would be nice to be able to dash over to see him during the day, or for him to come by and see her at night. That's if she decided to work in a bar or restaurant. It seemed the logical choice to get started here, so that she could find her bearings while she did something familiar.

Plus, it would be a great way to meet people.

The first place she found was a total dive. She kind of liked it. She hadn't picked any place that had high ratings. She wanted that diamond in the rough that she could help elevate. But the first place had watered-down liquor, no vibe, and customers who looked like they were barely holding on to their last five bucks.

The second place she checked out had a decent menu but a cranky bartender and no TVs for customers to watch a game or the news. There was only one waitress, who did double duty with serving drinks and food. She did an adequate job at both, but customer service and engaging with the customers was not on anyone's agenda. The place felt like it had no soul.

The third bar was a gem in the making. A husband and wife ran the place with smiles and small talk for customers as well as questions for the regulars they knew. She sat at the bar, ordered a club soda with lime, and watched everyone and everything going on around her.

When she moved here, she'd come back to this place. It felt familiar, even though it was much smaller than the Dark Horse Dive Bar. But they did a good business and the people seemed happy and at ease.

After ten minutes, she dropped some cash on the bar to cover the drink and tip and headed for the door. She liked the place, but it was too small, had no room for entertainment, and was just the kind of place you came with a friend to have a drink and talk.

Melody was used to a rowdier crowd, more going on.

Though, on second thought, she wouldn't mind a more upscale place where you had the bar vibe, plus a place where you could hang with friends, do business, or meet someone new.

She wanted that place where everyone felt like they belonged. She could see it so clearly in her mind. She just needed to find it here.

Two more bars. Both were nice, doing a brisk business even in that in-between time of lunch and happy hour.

As she left the next bar, she noticed someone who seemed familiar now, though he'd taken off his coat and wore sunglasses in the bright sunshine. He was about twenty paces away when he saw her looking at him. He immediately turned his back to her.

She went up behind him and tapped him on the shoulder. "Hi. Why are you following me?"

He turned and tried to look surprised. "Um...I'm not."

"I've spotted you off and on over the last three hours. You can't possibly say that's a coincidence given the number of bars I've been in and out of and the unpredictable route I've taken." She'd bypassed a couple of places, only to turn around and go back.

"I..." He stared at her with a busted look on his face.

"You work for Fox."

He didn't say anything again.

"Dean. He's head of security. You're one of his guys."

He sighed. "Fox wanted someone to keep an eye on you."

She pulled out her phone and called him.

"Hey, sweetheart, having fun?"

She gave her shadow a big shit-eating grin. "I'm about to since you sent me a drinking buddy."

"What?" Concern filled his voice.

She dropped the smile. "You didn't want me to be out here all alone, doing my thing, so you had me followed."

"Melody, I..."

She shook her head, even though he couldn't see her. "You two both lose your ability to speak when you get caught."

He sighed. "I just need to know you're safe."

"You should have simply told me you wanted to send someone with me for security."

"You said you didn't need a babysitter."

"But if you really wanted me to have one and it put you at ease, then yes, I would have allowed it. Not that I think it's necessary. No one knows who the hell I am."

"That's not going to last long. Once people find out you're my girlfriend, things will get...complicated."

"Tell me about my new friend."

"His name is Otis. Ex-marine. He's very good at his job."

"Which is?"

"Protection. Assessing threats. Keeping you safe."

"And what has he reported to you?"

Otis's eyes went wide for a second before he schooled his features and continued to scan the street around them.

"You've been to six bars. You didn't like any of them. A couple you simply walked through and left. One you ordered lunch, but didn't finish it. A couple others you ordered drinks but didn't finish them. You've been hit on by no less than five guys. One waitress was really chatty with you because she loved your hair. So do I, by the way."

Her jaw dropped as she gaped at Otis. "Seriously. You told him all of that."

Otis shifted on his feet uncomfortably. "It's my job."

"If this is going to work," she told both of them, "I get to tell Fox about my day. You can report any incidents or threats."

Otis nodded. "Yes, ma'am."

Fox agreed with, "I can live with that. So are you coming back to the office now?"

"Not yet. I haven't found the place."

"The last bar you went into will probably be out of business in the next week, since no one goes in because the place looks condemned on the outside."

"Yeah, but the hand-carved wood bar inside is amazing."

"Yet you didn't stay."

"It's not the right place."

"What are you looking for?"

"A place for everyone. Booths. Tables. A dance floor. Games. A vibe that says everyone is there for a good time. I'll know it when I find it."

"You're looking for a place where you belong in a city that feels unfamiliar." He got her.

"Every bar has a vibe and the people who love it. The Dark Horse Dive Bar is home. It's me. But I need to be a different me, here with you."

"I don't want you to be anything but what you are."

"I want to be me that's comfortable here."

"You're perfect, sweet Dee. You know that."

"I do. But I wish I could explain to you what I'm looking for and what I want, so that Wyoming Melody fits in Boston."

He hesitated for a moment. "Come back. There's something I want to show you."

"What?"

"Something I think you'll like. A place where you can be everything you are and more."

That sounded perfect to her. "I'm on my way."

Chapter Twenty-Six

F ox stepped out of the lobby just as Melody and Otis arrived in their rideshare car. Otis nodded to him, then ducked into the building. Fox took Melody's hand and stood in the waning sunshine with her.

"How was your day, dear?" She grinned at him and his heart kicked with the shot of joy it brought him.

"I missed you."

She eyed him. "You were too busy to miss me."

He shook his head. "I was distracted by your absence."

"You mean by all the texts Otis sent you, updating you on every little thing I did."

"He sent me pictures, too. I'll send them to you. They're really good."

"I want to see."

He pulled them up.

She scrolled through the five photos.

He loved the one of her standing in the middle of a bakery holding a pink frosted vanilla cupcake. The top was decorated like a rose in bloom. She had this huge smile on her face, right before he imagined she took a bite. Then there was the one of her handing a homeless man a cup of coffee from the bar she'd just come out of. The man's dog was giving her cheek a lick. And again, that smile.

Otis told him she spent ten minutes petting the dog and talking to the man.

That was his Melody. Sweet. Kind. Always smiling.

"Send these to me. I'll send them to my parents. They'll get a little glimpse of what I've been up to here. Mom will love those amazing wood doors at O'Leary's."

"Did you like that place?"

She'd eaten lunch there. "One of my favorites. The place is perfect. Well run. Good food. Drinks specials that fit their theme. Decent prices, too."

"But still not right."

"An Irish pub is nice and all, but I'm a country girl at heart, who's going to be living in the city. I want a little of both worlds."

He took a step backward and tugged her to follow him toward the door about ten feet down the block.

"Where are you taking me?"

"Someplace that could be the right place."

"Wait up," Max called from the lobby doors.

Dean walked out behind him.

"What are you guys doing out here?" Fox asked both his friends, wondering what they were up to.

Max did the talking for both of them. "We heard what you were doing and we figured out why, and we want in on it."

Melody eyed all of them. "Someone want to fill me in?"

Fox didn't answer her, but looked at Dean. "Do you know everything?"

"Nothing goes on in this building that I don't know about. And I for one think this is a genius idea."

"Maybe," Fox admitted. "If it feels right to her."

Melody looked at each of them, then narrowed her eyes. "I don't like being the odd man out here. What is this about?"

Fox pulled a set of keys out of his pocket and turned to the locked double doors behind him. "What do you think of the front?"

"Of what? I can't even see through the windows."

They'd been sprayed with something white so no one could see inside. It was temporary.

Above the doors was a discolored space where the sign for the restaurant used to be.

"It needs to be painted to differentiate it from the office building it's attached to," Melody suggested. "Bright white to offset the gray next door. I'd change out the windows and doors to black-trimmed ones. More contemporary and clean. It would make this place stand out from the neighboring buildings."

"That's easy enough," Max said.

"I like that idea," Dean added.

Fox unlocked the doors.

"Are we allowed in here?" Melody refused to move when he tried to get her to come inside.

"I got the keys from management next door. Come in."

Melody, Max, and Dean walked in. They all stood in the area that used to be the hostess station and seating for waiting customers.

"What do you think?" Fox asked.

She didn't say anything, just zeroed in on the massive bar and headed straight for it. Mirrors at the back with shelves for booze, lights to highlight the selection. That light would glow off the mirrors like a beacon for customers to come on up, sit a spell, and order a drink. The bar itself was polished wood. Not just squared-off boards, but thick slabs cut from a tree with the edges rounded like the curve of the trunk. The thick slabs were interlaced with dark green see-through acrylic. She smoothed her hand over the surface. Rustic but classy. She loved it. The front of the bar was black to match the barstools and the banquet seating breaking up the bar area from the front eating space. Black tables with additional black bar stools filled the area between the half wall that divided the kitchen on the left side of the building and the additional tables at the back. She turned from the bar and walked across the room to the kitchen. A full grill, huge ovens, gas stove, a massive walk-in refrigerator, lots of prep space. Perfect.

She turned to the tables up front and started counting them. Eight window tables. An additional eight tables down the center, then the banquette tables that could easily seat six, possibly eight if you wanted to get cozy. Along the wall right next to the kitchen, there were cozy booths that sat up to four. At the back, she counted eight more booths and sets of tables.

"What're you going to name this place?" Fox stood behind her as she stared across the huge expanse of the building.

"The Dark Horse. Not a dive bar, but a classy place with down-home roots."

"Where's the band playing?"

"At the back. Dining up front until ten p.m. Dessert served until midnight during the week and two a.m. on Friday and Saturday. We're closed on Sunday. That day is all about me and you."

"What's this place look like to you?"

"The bar is perfect. It's the inspiration for the rest. Freshly painted white walls, offset by all the black chairs and banquettes and the wood tables. They got that right. I'd replace the limited seating by the hostess check-in with deep green upholstered benches to match the color in the bar. Replace the multicolored pendent lights with green glass to tie things together even more. On the blank walls, massive black-and-white photos of horses in the wild. I'll ask Layla to take some on the ranch. A green neon sign out front. And the menu...comfort food. Steak and potatoes, mac and cheese, chicken and gravy, fried chicken, upscale for the city, but still with that nostalgic feel and taste." She turned to him. "Do you see it?"

"Yes. And you're right, it's perfect. You'd be right next door. I could come down and see you whenever I wanted. You could come up and see me."

She looked around the place. "It would take a lot of money to open this place."

"Good thing we have a lot of money." Fox grinned at her, like he was just as excited as her.

"I want in," Dean said from the bar.

"Me, too," added Max.

"What?" She couldn't believe they were talking about this.

"We'll stake you," Fox said. "Partners. All of us."

"But..."

"Dean and I want a fifteen percent stake each. Fox can take twenty, and we'll give you fifty. It's your place, after all."

"But I don't have that kind of money to put into this."

All of them shrugged at once.

Fox was the one who answered for all of them. "We want to do this. It will be up to you to do the work and make this place a success. We believe in you."

"I've never opened a place like this on my own."

Fox brushed his hand up and down her arm. "But you know how to run a place like this. You've been doing it with your family for years."

"I know but...it's a lot of money. What if it fails?"

"What if it's a huge success?" Fox countered.

She bit her bottom lip. "We would do this together?"

"If you mean I'd put up the money and you'd do all the work? Yes." He grinned at her. "You want this. This is what you were looking for today. Not someone else's place you could make great, but *your* place."

"I just...I can see it. Right here. Filled with people and music and the smell of amazing food. I see us, all of us, here in the place we made together."

"Then Max will handle the financing, Dean will handle security, I'll set up all the electronic ordering and reservations and whatever else you need, and you will take care of the rest."

There was already a list starting in her head. She'd need a food and liquor distributor, menus, a contractor to do the renovation. She needed to hire a manager, bar staff, waitstaff, a chef, and kitchen staff.

"I'll get started on securing the space," Fox announced like it was a done deal.

She grabbed his forearm and stopped him from turning to go back to the management office where he'd gotten the keys to let them in earlier. "You don't have to do this. I can find a job somewhere else."

"This is what you want. This will make you happy. That's all that matters to me."

She bit her bottom lip. "But what if you guys give me all that money and I fail."

"You don't fail, Melody. You bust your ass to get things done. If this place fails, it won't be because you didn't work your hardest to make it a success."

Tears gathered in her eyes. "You believe in me that much."

"Hundred percent."

"I second that," Dean called out.

"Third," Max added. "This is a good investment for all of us. The money you'll make on the bar will compensate for the restaurant, as they are notoriously known for small margins." Max's assessment actually made her feel better, because he was right, the bar profits would be considerable compared to the restaurant side of things.

"And I like the dessert idea," Dean added. "We need a dessert chef. Someone who can make those fancy cupcakes and cookies and pie."

"Are you hungry?" Fox asked.

"Now I'm starving." Dean shrugged. "This place could be known for its down-home baked goods. Cobbler and shit. That's a thing, right? You put ice cream on it."

"Oh," Max shouted. "You should make homemade ice cream."

Melody laughed under her breath. "For you two, definitely cobbler and homemade ice cream."

They both beamed at her, their smiles like hopeful, excited boys.

She turned to Fox. "So, we're doing this? Together?"

He wrapped her in his arms and grinned down at her. "Another family business."

And that was the perfect thing to say.

Because they were family. And even though she was leaving hers to start a new life, she'd gained a new one.

Chapter Twenty-Seven

Fox walked up the porch steps and knocked on the door. The TV was on, though the sound was muffled through the door. After a half minute with no answer, he pounded the side of his fist on the wood again.

Nothing.

He pounded again and called out, "Tanya. Open up. It's Fox."

She had to be here. Her car was in the driveway. She hadn't driven it in weeks.

Nervous butterflies fluttered in his tense belly.

He tried the knob and found it unlocked. Of course. Out here, neighbors were too far away to hear anything, let alone come knocking unannounced. Tanya didn't have any close friends, so...

The second he stepped inside, he scanned the living room on the right, then past the dining room to the left and back to the kitchen.

Tanya was on the phone, her back to him. "It needs to be soon. We're running out of time." She held the phone in front of her and stabbed her finger into it to end the call, then turned to him. "Fox. What a surprise."

Really? "You knew I was coming."

"I only meant you're early."

"Like five minutes." He raised a brow, noting the flush in her cheeks and the way she couldn't quite look at him. "What was that all about?"

"What?" she asked, like she didn't know he'd overheard the end of her conversation.

"You said on the phone that you're running out of time. For what? Did the doctor say something about your condition?"

She shook her head, then caught herself. "Yes, actually." The contradiction of her gesture with her words didn't slide past him. "As you know, my health has been holding steady with the meds, and of course, the better nutrition, since you've been bringing such healthy foods to eat."

He held up the bag of groceries he'd picked up for her. "I brought you more of the minestrone soup you like, plus some oranges, blackberries, strawberries, and blueberries. You can use the new blender I got you to make a smoothie if you'd rather drink them than eat them."

"I like that little thing."

"You can hide the raw spinach I got you the other day in the smoothie, too. The more vitamins and minerals you get, the easier it is for your body to stay strong and fight."

Her face softened. "You're always taking such good care of me."

"Well, you look and seem fine, so what's with the thing about you running out of time?"

She waved it off. "I'm just worried that I won't have enough time to do the things I want to do before...you know...the end."

"I think we all feel that way sometimes. But I get that for you it's hard to face the fact that you know the end is near."

"It makes you think about what's most important." She glanced past him. "You're actually here alone today."

Since he and Melody arrived home from their trip to Boston two weeks ago, they'd made it a point to spend as much time together as possible. But this week she was teaching her class. "Melody is working at the center this week. I told you that on Monday and yesterday and now today." He cocked his head. "Are you sure you're okay? You seem a bit off."

She took a seat at the kitchen table.

He stood with his back to the counter. "Talk to me," he pleaded, worried.

"You're planning on going back to Boston."

He folded his arms over his chest. "For me, that's home."

She pressed her lips tight. "She's going with you."

"That's the plan."

"And you're opening a bar together."

"She's opening the bar. I'm financing it." They'd told her all of this already.

Her gaze narrowed. "She's using you."

He shook his head. "She wanted to cancel the whole damn thing when she found out how much the liquor license was going to cost." Half a million dollars. What a fucking rip-off. But Boston only had so many licenses and a waiting list that could take years before your name came up for one. On the secondary market, owners of licenses could ask for whatever price they wanted. And people still bought them. He would be one of those people, because not only did the space he wanted for Melody come with the best location so they could see each other, as well as all the amenities Melody wanted for the restaurant and bar, but it came with a liquor license.

All he had to do was buy the whole damn place.

Melody balked at the idea. It was too much money. She'd never be able to pay it back. He got her point. Most restaurateurs backed out of opening in Boston for that very reason. A lot of places shut down because they couldn't make the place profitable.

Fox didn't care. He'd give her what she wanted, no matter the cost.

But he did give Dean and Max an out, letting them know that maybe it wasn't such a good investment.

They both stared at each other, then him, and said, "Fuck it. It's family."

They'd own the property outright. That alone would be a sound investment. So all Melody had to do was make the business profitable and they'd all be happy.

It took all three of them to convince her they meant it.

And then she cried, overwhelmed by their generosity and faith in her.

He wasn't about to tell Tanya all that. She didn't need to know.

"Melody is good at what she does. She has a vision for the space we found. She knows how to sell a good time to her customers. She's got an idea for a place that's different than other bars in Boston. People will love it." And if not, Melody would find something else that made her happy.

Tanya didn't relent with her disapproving glare. "She's good at using you."

"How is she using me? She was looking for a job. I offered her a place of her own."

"She put the idea into your head."

He sighed. "No. She didn't. In fact, she was adamant about not wanting to take our money until my friends and I convinced her to let us partner with her."

Tanya gave him a *See? She got what she wanted and you think you gave it to her* look.

He rolled his eyes. "Do you want to know why I'm here?"

She folded her arms over her chest, matching his pose. "Why?"

"To tell you that I thought about what you asked for."

Her arms fell down to her sides as she sat up straight. "The cruise?"

"Yes. If you want to go, I'll buy you the ticket and get you a nurse to go with you, so long as you agree to continue your treatment plan. I'll even throw in some spending money." A couple grand should hold her over for the forty-five-day trip.

She raised a brow, suspicion in her eyes. "What changed your mind?"

"If this is what you truly want and it will make you happy..." He shrugged. He was never going to have the kind of talk he hoped they'd have. He'd given up on that. He was tired of waiting for something that was never going to happen.

Tanya didn't have it in her. So he was letting her go on her trip to live out her last days in the sunshine, seeing new places and experiencing new things.

But Melody...she loved with her whole heart. She'd stepped into their relationship with every bit of her being, with the intention of making a life with him.

This thing he was doing with Tanya...it was a waste of time. He felt bad about thinking of it that way, but that's what it was. His desire to do something good felt more like an obligation he had taken on but wasn't his responsibility.

Blood didn't make them family.

She'd broken their bond when she hurt and abandoned him.

So this was his way of severing it this time, but in a kinder, gentler, distancing sort of way. *Bon voyage! I'm going home to be with the woman I love where we'll be happy.*

"So that's it. You send me away, so you can be with her and go back to your fancy life in the big city where you're the big shot at work."

Now she's complaining that she got her way. "What did you expect?"

"That you wouldn't be like me."

"I'm nothing like you. I'm certainly not him. I'm a better man because of her." In so many ways. *Because she saved me. Because she loves me. Because I want to be everything she needs and more.*

Because the only people who truly mattered were the ones who had your back.

He didn't need Tanya's apology or approval or admiration. Not even her consideration.

He was better off letting this go.

Tanya pouted. "She's taking you away from me again."

"No. It wasn't true then, and it's not now. You want to see something of the world before you die, I'm making that happen."

"So you can be with her."

"I made the trip here to try to forge some kind of relationship with you. There's too much history and not enough intention on either of our parts to turn this into something more than what it is. I hoped for more." He'd set his expectations too high.

"I deserve more than you're giving her," she snapped, fury in her eyes. "I'm your mother."

He scoffed at that, unfolded his arms, and stood tall, his own anger building. "You're the one who wants to leave the past buried. But if you want to dig it up and talk about what you deserve, I'm happy to grab a shovel and expose all the shit you put me through, so we can talk about how *I* deserved better."

"You did. I agree. But maybe consider what a shit life we would have had if I'd taken you and tried to raise you on my own."

"At least *that* I could have respected, even if we'd been poor."

"Poor! We'd have ended up in a shelter or worse, living on the street."

"And yet, you've somehow managed to keep this roof over your head. Why haven't you sold this place and moved on to greener pastures?"

"Because that good-for-nothing asshole of a father of yours owned it before we got married and left it to you!" She practically screamed at him now.

It brought back so many memories of the past of her shouting like that at his father.

He stood there, staring at her, completely at a loss for words. He had no idea his father had left him this place. "Why wasn't I told when he passed?"

She put her hand over her mouth and glared, though he caught a hint of regret that she'd let those words slip.

He glared at her. "You made sure I didn't find out. Didn't you?"

"I thought you'd kick me out, sell this place for what it was worth. Then where would I be? I paid off the lawyer fees and taxes on this place, the upkeep. It's mine. I earned it. What the hell did you ever do, except piss him off and make him come after me?"

Those words slammed into him like a blow. "You blame me for that? Take a look in the mirror. Better yet, maybe you'll find the answer in the bottom of a bottle. That's how so many of those fights started. You and him drinking yourself into a stupor only to come up fighting and looking for a target. Me."

"Boo hoo. You think you had a bad childhood? Who didn't? My father was just as bad as yours."

"So instead of picking a better partner, you fell for a man just like Daddy, then instead of protecting your child like you probably wished someone would have protected you, you take out all your anger toward them on me, perpetuating the cycle. Way to go! You became the monster you hated."

She leaned in with a nasty look in her eyes. "Let's see how well you do when you have kids."

"I will never...ever...lay a hand on them in anger. There will be hugs and kisses and affection and laughter. My kids will be happy." Like Melody was with her family. He'd wanted her family to be his when they were kids. Now they could have that together. "My kids will never know what it's like to cower and fear me. They will never feel indifference from me. They will know that I would do anything for them. Same goes for Melody."

"She gets that freely, but not me."

"She didn't break my trust."

"She got you taken away from the only home you'd ever known."

"And thank god for that because otherwise I'd be dead." He took a step toward her. "Don't tell me you don't know that, because I know you do. You beat me, then you kicked me out into the cold. You kicked me so hard that I was bleeding internally. Another hour in the cold and I'd have been dead. Dead! So fuck you! You're damn right you don't get my love and respect and admiration and loyalty the way she does."

Tanya stood and raised her hands, seeming to catch herself and what the consequences of his fury could mean for her. Because he was ready to walk out the door and never come back.

"Okay, Fox. Calm down."

That just made him angrier. "I'll calm down when you finally get it."

"Oh, I get it. I know just how you feel."

"If you do, that only makes what you did and this argument worse. It means you wanted me to feel this way to punish me for what happened to you."

"Maybe that is why I did it. I wasn't in the right frame of mind to see it. But I do see it now. And I'm sorry. I know that doesn't take away the pain. It's just some words. At least that's how I always felt when my father came at me, begging me to forgive as he blamed the booze, a bad day at work, some slight he thought I'd made. And I hope you are better than me, than him, than your father. But none of that changes the fact that I'm your mother. And all I want is a chance to have something good in my life before it's over."

"Always looking out for yourself."

"No one else ever looked out for me," she snapped, then her eyes softened again. "If she does that for you, well then…"

Yeah. No kind words for Melody. Just a partial acknowledgement that she did something good for him.

Probably the best he'd ever get. *Crumbs when I want a whole fucking apology sandwich with a side of remorse and understanding.*

How about a little support from her? What about…*If she makes you happy, then I'm happy for you?* Nope.

Everything was about Tanya. So he'd give her what she wanted and be done with it. "I'll put the house up for sale while you're on your trip. When you get back, you can use the money to stay in an assisted living place or hospice depending on your needs."

"Don't you want the house?"

"Why the fuck would I want this nightmare when I have a whole other life in Boston?"

"I just always thought…this is where I'd die."

"Why? You certainly didn't *live* here."

Her head tilted. "Why are you being like this?"

"Because I don't want to be here anymore, doing this. I want to be in Boston, taking care of my business and moving Melody into our home. I want to wake up happy and kissing her, and go to bed each night the same way. I want the past to be the past and the future to be the dream we share."

Tanya frowned. "And I'm not part of that."

"You've made it clear how you feel about her. And me. I'm just a means to an end."

She shook her head. "That's not true."

"Whether it is or not, that's how you make me feel. So take your trip. Have fun. Send pictures. I'd like to know you're okay and the time away is doing you good." She only had a few months left. He hoped she found some happiness and joy while away. "Other than that, I really have nothing else to say, except take care of yourself."

"I will, so long as you make sure I have the money to do so."

"Like I said, I'll sell the house and the money is yours."

Time spun out for a long minute.

"Thank you, Fox."

And on that note, he turned and left the house, wishing it was the last time he had to return, but knowing it wasn't. He'd get her on that ship first, then make sure she had a place to go when she returned. That would satisfy his conscience.

As for his heart...it belonged to one dark-haired, blue-eyed beauty who should be about done with her class and ready for their lunch date before she headed to the bar tonight.

CHAPTER TWENTY-EIGHT

Fox walked into Melody's classroom and grinned at how many students were still in their seats, asking questions and working on their ideas for their online shop.

"This looks great," Melody praised Danny, who was working on a logo. "The company name stands out. It's unique. The color scheme highlights what you're doing with your art. Fantastic."

Danny beamed with pride. And maybe a little love for the woman who'd taken the time to help him sell the art he loved to create.

"Now, you'll need to add a description and details for each piece you put up. Make sure to include the dimensions. If you can display the piece with something that can also show the size in proportion to something else, that will help people to see the scale."

Melody moved on to the next person in the row.

Amy turned her laptop to show Melody her new logo.

"Hmm." Melody studied it. "Amy's Cookies. It's simple. Based on the founder and baker. What do you think about putting a chef hat on the A? And maybe instead of the logo being a rectangle, you make it round. Like a cookie. It could even be a cookie. Like your signature cookie. Then the Os in "cookies" could also be cookies."

Amy frowned as she studied the simple name on a mint-green background. It had a pretty font, but wasn't really anything special.

Fox waited to see what she'd say to Melody's suggestions.

Melody didn't wait. She made another suggestion. "I think it would be cute if you had a cartoon version of you in a chef's hat. Perhaps you could commission Danny to draw something for you."

Pride made Fox's heart swell. What a fantastic idea.

Danny leaned over. "I could totally do that. You in an apron with a spatula that's like a magic wand that looks like cookie sprinkles or chocolate chips or something coming out of it, raining down on the Amy's Cookies words."

Amy's smile took up her whole face. "That would be amazing."

Melody left Amy and Danny to haggle over the cost and timeframe for Danny to complete the piece.

Melody made her way to him by the door. The second she was close enough, she reached out and put her hand on his chest, then rose up on tiptoe and kissed him softly. Chastely.

He wanted more. "You were supposed to end class thirty-five minutes ago. Don't you have work tonight?"

"I do, but so many of them wanted a little extra help."

He brushed his fingers over her soft cheek. "You're so generous and kind and supportive."

"Not sure Amy appreciated my suggestions."

"They were spot on and now with Danny's help, she'll have a logo that stands out in a very competitive market."

Melody studied his face. "Now tell me what's wrong?" She read him so easily. "What happened with Tanya?"

"I gave her what she wanted. She'll be leaving on that trip soon."

"Okay. Then we should talk about when I'm moving to Boston."

"Whenever you're ready. It can't be soon enough for me." He turned back to the class.

She put her hand on his cheek and made him look back at her. "Fox, honey, talk to me."

That sweet endearment meant so much to him and settled in that soft spot with her name written all over it. "She's..." He shook his head, unsure what to say that wasn't already obvious. "She isn't like you. To her, I'm just a means to an end. For you, I'm..."

"Home," she finished when he couldn't come up with the right word to describe all she was to him.

He cupped her face and brought her close, touching his forehead to hers. "Yes. Exactly." He choked up. Couldn't help it. Not with her.

Her blue eyes softened. "You're my air, my gravity, my center, my everything. I hope I'm that for you."

"Why do you think I need you so desperately? Without you...nothing is worth doing, or being."

"Then nothing can come between us. Nothing and no one can make you feel less than when you know I love you, your brothers love you. We're your family. Plus a whole bunch of Wildes. So this thing with your mom...let it go. You showed up. You helped her. If she's not willing to meet you halfway, then accept that you did your part. You got to say what you wanted to say. Rehashing it won't accomplish anything except to make you more frustrated."

"I know that's what I need to do."

"Doing it is harder. Hope springs eternal."

He rolled his eyes. "I guess so."

She grinned. "You took a chance and put yourself out there. You're sending her on an amazing vacation, which I'm sure made her very happy."

"Did it? Because it didn't feel that way."

That raised a brow. "But she's been asking for this since you got here."

He shrugged. "She always brings things back to you."

"She hates me."

"She thinks you're out for my money, but she's the one who wants me to shower her with gifts and trips."

She soothed him with soft strokes of her hands up and down his arms. "You do what makes you feel comfortable. You don't owe her anything, but if it makes you happy to do it for her..." Melody shrugged. "I just want you to know going in that it won't make a difference. She'll take it because she thinks you owe her because she's your mother."

"She was never that to me. Not in a kind and loving way. Hell, she can't even be supportive now about you, the one thing that makes me happier than anything."

"For what it's worth, my mom sent me a text this morning after I sent her a few pictures of us in Boston. The text said, *Marry him!*"

"You should. I'm a total catch," he teased, knowing full well he intended to ask her. Soon. When they were settled in Boston. He didn't want to overwhelm her with too much all at once.

"I'll think about it," she teased back, trying not to smile. "I mean, you are really fantastic in bed."

Fuck. He went hard just thinking about how she'd woken him up this morning with her sweet mouth on his hard cock. "Are you going to meet me there tonight?"

"No place I'd rather be."

"Good." He pulled her in for a kiss that was all too short and chaste as the students started packing up their stuff.

Danny stopped next to them. "Thanks for all your help today."

"My pleasure." The softness in Melody's voice said she meant it. "I can't wait to see how it all turns out."

Danny's cheeks went ruddy. "See you tomorrow."

"I'll be here."

Danny lingered. "You've got really great suggestions."

"Your talent will sell itself. Don't forget to look into shipping costs for some of your larger pieces, so you can price accordingly."

"I will." Danny ducked his head and left with some of the others, leaving Fox and Melody with Amy in the room.

Fox nearly groaned, but held it back as Amy approached, holding Melody's bag.

"Here you go." Amy's smile seemed too bright and cheerful to be genuine.

Melody took her purse. "Thanks. Off to get ready for your evening class?"

Amy turned to him. "Will you be joining us for dinner? The class is making steamed salmon, wild rice with button mushrooms, and steamed broccoli with a butter garlic sauce."

"Sounds amazing, but Dean and I have plans."

Amy glanced at Melody. "I take it you'll be working the bar."

"As always. Though Wednesdays aren't as packed as the weekend, so it should be an easy night." She pressed a kiss to Fox's lips. "I'm sorry I don't have time for lunch. And I might be a little late because I need to make the schedule for next week."

He brushed a lock of hair behind her ear, just so he could touch her. "You know where to find me."

Melody grinned, then nodded to Amy. "I hope you found the classes helpful."

"I did. When I get back to Boston, I'm going to set up shop. Maybe soon I'll even be able to do it full-time, instead of working for someone else."

"I love being my own boss," Melody said, pulling her car keys out of her bag. She gave him a quick kiss. "See you tonight." Melody walked out of the classroom, leaving him with Amy.

He immediately headed for the door, too.

"Hey, hold up a sec."

Fox reluctantly stopped. He had work to do, but didn't want to be rude. Not to someone who worked for him, even if she had made things weird. "What's up?"

"I heard you're opening a new restaurant in Boston."

How the hell did she hear that? He'd told Tanya. Melody had told her family. She probably talked to them at the bar, which meant others overheard them.

Small towns. Everyone knew everything.

"I would love to open my own bakery, but that dream is going to take some time. You know my skills and that I've worked in catering. I love baking and cooking. I'd love a job as a chef at your place. Or better yet, to be your dessert and pastry chef."

Not a good idea. But he didn't say so. "We're a ways from opening. And besides, the restaurant and bar is Melody's place. You'll have to talk to her."

She sidled up closer to him. "You could put in a good word for me." She was damn good at what she did; that's why he'd hired her so often and put her on at the center. "Come on, Fox." She pouted a bit with a gleam in her eyes. "You know I'd be an asset. And Melody and I already know each other. You can make this happen. I know you can."

"I'll tell Melody you're interested, but that's all I'll do. She's in charge."

"Well, if anything happens, like she decides to stay with her family here, I'd be happy to step in and open the place for you. I've got a ton of ideas for a really chic place that could cater to the Boston elite as well as wining and dining your clients. It'd be a match made in heaven."

Fox wanted out of this conversation and pointedly checked his phone when it buzzed with an incoming email. "I've got a meeting." He headed toward the door.

"Come to the dinner class. I'll make it worth your while. You know you can't resist my food."

Up until he started spending time with Melody, he'd often found himself in the kitchen with the students at dinner time, learning to cook and enjoying a meal with Amy.

She'd often brought him breakfast from the morning class, too.

He could see where she thought they were closer than they were. Fuck. "Sorry. I can't make it. I have a work thing."

He'd tell Melody Amy wanted to work at the new restaurant and make it clear it was up to her, but he didn't like the idea.

There. He'd fulfill his promise to Amy and let Melody know it wasn't what he wanted. She probably wouldn't either. Not when she'd pegged Amy's flirty intentions already.

But something nagged at him about the way Amy so casually mentioned that maybe Melody wasn't ready to leave her home and family behind.

No. She was baiting him again, trying to make him think something about Melody that simply wasn't true.

Melody had talked about buying a dining table for their whole family to fill and getting houseplants. And the way she had looked when she stood in the restaurant space and described what she envisioned for it... She wanted to come to Boston with him.

All he had to do was make sure she never regretted it.

CHAPTER TWENTY-NINE

Melody finished the schedule for the next two weeks, printed out a copy for Jax, then posted the schedule online so all the waitstaff could see which days they were on. That done, her feet sore from a long night, she headed out of the office to check the bar one last time to be sure all the cleanup had been done before she headed home to Fox.

She couldn't wait to see him. It had been a long day. Yes, she'd seen him for those ten minutes at the center after her class, but that wasn't nearly enough.

Things would be different in Boston. He'd be in the same building. She could go up and see him whenever she wanted. They could have dinner together every night. Then she'd stay to close or have a manager do it for her. They'd find a better balance in their lives together.

She stepped into the bar and found it clean and ready for the next day, with her two sisters and brother at the bar waiting for her. "What are all you guys still doing here?"

Lyric usually went home to Mason after the kitchen closed at nine. Jax didn't stay past ten when he worked late because he hated leaving Layla home alone. And though Aria closed with Melody most nights, she usually left while Melody finished the scheduling.

Jax put four shot glasses on the bar. He poured some really good eighteen-year Macallan into three of the glasses and cranberry juice in Lyric's because she was pregnant.

A baby.

Melody checked the urge to press her hand to her own belly as she thought about what it would be like to start a family with Fox.

He'd be such a good father.

They'd create the family he'd desperately wanted as a kid.

"What are we celebrating?"

Jax slid her a shot. Her sisters took theirs. They all held them up. "Mom told us about you opening a place of your own in Boston. We just want you to know, we love you, we wish you success and happiness and all the love you show us. To new beginnings. To your very own Dark Horse. To you, Melody."

Choked up, her heart three sizes too big for her chest, she clinked her glass to theirs and knocked back the shot, though it wasn't easy to get it down past the lump in her throat. "You guys are the best. And I'm sorry I haven't had the time to fill you all in on my plans, limited as they are at the moment on exact details."

Aria put her hand over Melody's. "It's okay. We've all been busy. We just wanted to take this time to let you know we stand with you, we are behind you, and we're so proud of you for going after what you want."

Lyric bumped shoulders with Melody. "We'll miss you like crazy. No one tames a rowdy crowd the way you do. No one runs the staff and tables the way you do."

Jax came around the bar and hugged her. "No one loves us the way you do."

She stepped back and wiped her eyes. "You guys...I'm not leaving yet."

Jax squeezed her shoulder. "We just wanted to take some of the stress off and let you know that we want you to be happy. This is a huge opportunity and we'd never hold you back."

"Especially from Fox," Aria added. "We see how much you love him. How much he loves you. That's special. And it's really brave to leave everything you've ever known behind to be with him and start something new."

"You know why I can do it so easily? Because I know all of you are here for me. I know Fox will never let me fall. So why not try to fly?"

Lyric hugged her. "You are going to soar."

She leaned into her sister. "You're going to help me find bands to play at my bar."

Lyric gave her a firm nod. "Damn straight."

She looked at all her siblings. "And you're all going to come and visit me. I'll be back as often as I can." She pointedly looked at Lyric's barely there bump. "And I'll be here when that one arrives. You can count on it." She turned to Jax. "That goes for your little one, too. I'm determined to be their favorite aunt."

"Hey, you've got some competition there," Aria challenged.

Melody looked at all of them, then around the bar. "I love this place. I love all of you. But I know this is the right thing for me."

"We know." Jax hooked his arm around her shoulders. "Come on. I'll walk you out."

"Do you think Layla would take some black-and-white pictures of the horses and ranch for me? I want to blow them up and put them up on the walls at the new place."

"I'll tell her to call you for all the details."

She leaned her head against her brother's shoulder. "Thank you."

"Of all of us, I thought it would be Lyric who flew the coop and landed in Nashville. Never saw you in a big city."

"It's where he is. And wherever he is feels like home to me." She smiled for her brother. "And I plan on bringing some of Blackrock Falls, the ranch, and this bar with me."

"This will always be home no matter how far you roam," he promised.

"I know." They stopped next to her car.

"Drive safely."

"I will. Be safe. You're going to be a dad now."

Jax grinned. "I can't wait."

"That's one lucky wife and baby."

"You're going to be here for the wedding, right?"

"Of course. I wouldn't miss it for anything."

Jax waved goodbye as he headed for his truck. She pulled out of the parking lot in front of him and headed in the opposite direction as him, back to town and Fox's apartment.

Their apartment, he liked to remind her.

She couldn't wait to wake him up and show him how much she loved him and couldn't wait to start their life in Boston. Together. That's all she wanted. Her and him, tangled up together in business, each other, and in love.

CHAPTER THIRTY

Fox's eyes crossed and the screen in front of him went blurry. He'd been working on some intricate coding, trying to get the system setup just right for a new client while he'd been waiting for Melody to come home.

He missed her.

He'd never felt this way about anyone.

Other women came and went without really leaving a mark on him. She was in his head and heart, as indelible as a tattoo.

She wasn't a memory that would fade. She was the past he couldn't forget and the future he wanted.

Her love was the warmth in his heart and the breath in his lungs.

He checked the clock. Just past midnight. She'd be home soon.

Anticipation rode him hard.

He scrubbed his hands over his face and dug two fingers into his scratchy eyes, then rose and turned off all the lights as he headed from his office to the bedroom. He'd take a quick shower while he waited for her.

He turned on the water, dropped his clothes in a pile on the floor, and stepped into the wide stall. The steamy spray hit his sore shoulders and tight neck. He stood there for a good five minutes, letting the heat and pelting spray relax him. After a quick soap and rinse, he stepped out, toweled off, turned off the lights, and crawled into bed, noting that Melody was running late tonight.

No worries. He'd just rest a little after a long day. She'd wake him with a sweet kiss. He'd tumble her to her back, kiss her senseless, then have his wicked way with her, his cock buried deep in her heat. The two of them connected. One. He'd love on her for as long as she wanted. He'd let her set the pace. If she wanted it quick and dirty, or slow and sweet, didn't matter to him as long as he had her in his arms.

He didn't know how much time had passed when he felt the bed dip and the sheet covering him slide down his skin. The soft cotton brushed over his cock in a delicious tease as sleep faded and he became more aware of his surroundings. His cock thickened with anticipation, especially when Melody planted soft kisses over his chest, making him moan. Anticipation built.

"Fuck, baby, don't stop."

Her soft hair brushed his skin, heightening the pleasure as she planted another open-mouthed kiss on his pec. He didn't want to move. He just wanted to feel.

And it only got better as she pressed one kiss, two, three down his happy trail, her mouth so achingly close to his cock. He wanted her lips around his shaft, her tongue licking up and down his length.

"Fuck, you drive me crazy." He wanted her mouth on him. Her hands, too. But instead she teased him with kisses up his stomach and sternum as she headed for his mouth, he hoped.

He got a whiff of her hair. The scent subtle and clean, not the usual raspberries he'd become used to in her hair and skin and lingering in the bathroom after her shower.

He paused for a second. Something felt off.

The bed shifted as she straddled him, her warm skin sliding against his as her thighs bracketed his hips. And just as she settled over him, her soft, wet folds sliding against his hard length, he smoothed his hands up her thighs and froze for half a heartbeat, then bucked *whoever* the fuck was on him off.

His heart jackhammered in his chest as he tried to catch a breath past his shock, fury, and yes, fear.

A startled shriek sounded seconds before he tapped on the bedside lamp and turned to face the fucking intruder.

"Fox! Seriously, it's just me."

He stared at Amy's flushed cheeks as she stood next to the bed naked and brushed her hair out of her face.

This could not be happening.

He spotted her clothes at the end of the bed, grabbed them, and tossed them straight at her, hitting her in the chest. "Get dressed. Get out. Hurry up." He bent his legs, not even a little self-conscious about being naked, planted his elbows on his knees, held his head, and rocked back and forth, trying to think through the rage and not look at the naked woman he wanted to physically remove from his apartment. Now.

Out of the corner of his eye, he saw Amy press her hands and one knee on the bed like she was about to crawl back to him.

Before he could say or do anything—

"What the fuck!" Melody stood in the open door, her face a mask of pain and fury. A tear slipped down her cheek one second before she fisted her hands at her side and repeated, "What the fuck!"

He leaped from the bed and took three steps toward her before he stopped in his tracks at her death glare. "Melody." Her name came out as a plea and apology all at the same time even though... "It's not what it looks like."

Her gaze bounced from him to Amy, who kept smirking while she pulled on her panties, and back again.

"Please," he begged. "Listen to me."

"This is a fucking nightmare, right?"

"More like a dream come true." Amy licked her lips, her gaze raking over him in one lascivious glance down his body.

"You fucking bitch!" Melody launched toward Amy.

He wrapped his arms around her middle and pulled her back.

Amy chuckled, standing there in her panties and now her bra.

His front door flew open and Dean's eyes went wide when he spotted Fox holding on to his wildcat. "Let her go," Dean ordered, coming toward them.

Fox released Melody to show Dean he wasn't trying to hurt her. Then he herded her out into the living room area toward Dean and away from Amy. "Baby, please listen to me."

"Damn, that is a nice view." Amy stood in his bedroom doorway, her hair all tousled, her blouse now on, though mostly open, showing off a red lace bra, her feet bare, jeans zipped but not buttoned.

Melody caught sight of her and rushed Amy again.

Fox hooked his arm around her middle and pulled her back, just as Melody swung her fist and missed Amy's smug face by half an inch, her hair flying out from the breeze. He pulled Melody back several feet.

Dean got between them and Amy, his head swinging back and forth as he took in the scene. "Dude. Fox, put some clothes on."

He wasn't doing anything until he explained to Melody exactly what happened.

"What the fuck is going on here?" Dean asked.

Melody shoved Fox away, then stood with her hands fisted at her sides. "You want to know why you had to let me in tonight? Because they were too busy fucking in his bed to hear me at the door."

"That is not what happened," Fox snarled, hurt she'd even think he'd touch another woman and hurt her that way.

Probably exactly what Amy intended.

Amy's leering gaze swept up him. "Do you blame me? Look at what he's packing."

Dean glared at Amy. "Bullshit. Fox would never cheat on any woman, but most especially *you*." He pinned Melody in his gaze. "You know that. Let him explain."

Melody turned to him, her gaze a tempest of emotions. "Put some damn clothes on, and then you can explain to me why that bitch was in *our* bed. Naked."

Fox felt like his heart was being ripped out of his chest watching yet another tear slide down her cheek. "I didn't do anything wrong. I swear it." He took two steps toward the bedroom and came up short when Amy stood there, grinning at him. "Get out of my fucking way," he snarled.

"Don't be like that. You know you loved it. You were so hard and desperate for me. Remember? 'Baby, don't stop. You drive me crazy,'" she mimicked him.

He took a menacing step closer to her. "You are going to regret fucking with me."

"Only that we don't get to do even more with each other."

"Move!" he raged at her.

The second she was out of his way, he rushed to the dresser, pulled out a pair of sweats and dragged them on. In the short time since he'd left the living space, Dean had taken up position by the front door, Melody stood with her hip against the back of the couch, and Amy sat at the breakfast bar looking smug.

He walked to Melody, his hands up to cup her gorgeous face.

She stepped back and put up a hand. "Don't touch me."

His hands fell to his sides and his stomach clenched, gutted by not being able to touch her. "I thought she was you."

Wrong thing to say.

Melody's eyes filled with renewed rage. "Really? Because we look so alike."

He tried again. "I fell asleep waiting for you. The second I felt the sheet sliding off me, I thought you were home and waking me up just like most nights when we haven't seen each other most of the day and we're desperate for each other."

"You sure did want it," Amy chimed in.

He pointed at her. "Shut your fucking mouth." He turned back to Melody. "She didn't say anything. I didn't open my eyes. I just wanted to feel you slide into bed and against me. She didn't touch me with her hands. She kissed my chest and stomach. I thought it was you." His heart clenched. This was so fucking awful. He felt violated and used. "When she came back up and I smelled her hair, I thought it was strange that you smelled different. I thought you'd changed your shampoo or something and dismissed it. Then she straddled my lap and rocked against me." He ran his fingers over the top of his head, pulling his hair in anger. "When I reached out to touch you for the first time...the second my hands slid against her thighs, I knew it wasn't you." He held her gaze. "I dumped her off me and turned on the light. The second I saw her, I told her to get dressed and get the fuck out."

"You told her to hurry up. You didn't want me to find her with you," Melody accused, like she didn't believe his story.

"Oops. Secret's out." Amy grinned like the Cheshire cat.

He ignored her and kept his gaze on the only woman who mattered. "Yes, I wanted her fucking out before you got here and saw that despicable shit. Not because I did something wrong but because it's just one more way she disrespects you, our relationship, and me."

He took a tentative step toward her. "Please. I know you're furious and hurt right now. But...just take a breath. Look at me. I would never do this to you, not after all I did to get you back. I love you. More than anything. You know that. I didn't want this. She somehow got in here and snuck into *our* bed. She knew that you'd be back late and planned this whole fucking thing. The second I knew it wasn't you, I put a stop to it. And I feel dirty as fuck after having her trick me and touch me like that."

"It's called sexual assault," Dean interjected.

He and Melody both glanced over at Dean, then pinned Amy with a look as she gasped.

"Oh come on," she groused. "That isn't even remotely true."

"Did he give consent?" Dean asked. "Because that shit goes both ways."

Amy's mouth hung open. "It's not the same."

Fox went with Dean's very real and true assessment of the situation. "I thought my girlfriend had come home and was putting the moves on me. Not you. Why would I think it was anyone but her?"

He wanted to wipe the smile off her face.

"Because you want me."

Fox and Dean rolled their eyes at her absurd response.

Melody glared daggers at her.

Dean stepped closer to Amy. "How did you even get in here?" He turned to Fox. "You didn't leave the door open. I had to let Melody in."

"Why?" Fox looked to Melody for the answer.

"Because my key card and keys to your place weren't in my bag." She pinned Amy in her gaze. "But I bet I know who stole them during class today. So convenient that you were the one to hand me my purse before I left."

Amy paled at the accusation.

"My cousin's a cop," Melody blurted out. "Maybe I should call him, so you can file charges," she suggested to Fox.

Amy stood, her hands up. "Wait a second. Look, this is getting out of hand. It was just..."

"Desperate," Melody supplied. "Wrong," she added with venom.

"How about illegal?" Fox folded his arms over his chest, seriously contemplating filing charges. "You stole from Melody, broke into my place, and sexually assaulted me. Not to mention the pain and suffering you've caused me and Melody."

Amy's eyes filled with panic. "It was stupid. I thought you would see that I'm your better match."

Fox fisted his hands at his side. "You thought stealing, breaking the law, tricking me, and hurting someone I love would make me choose you over Melody, who is honest, kind, smart, helpful, affectionate, unabashedly sexy, outgoing, and just fucking amazing? She didn't have to trick me into being with her. I want her desperately because of who she is and how open and honest and loving she is to me. All you are is fired and pathetic."

Amy gasped. "You can't fire me. I have a contract."

"Then you should have read it. I can fire you without cause. But sexual assault works, too. And I wouldn't use me as a reference either. Now get out." The last he practically snarled at her with his hands fisted at his sides, because he couldn't stand the sight of her a second longer.

Amy headed for the door and came up short when Dean didn't move out of her way. "What?"

Dean held out his hand. "Melody's key card and keys."

She pulled them out of her back pocket and slapped them into Dean's hand.

Dean took a step toward her. "You have twelve hours to vacate your apartment."

Amy glared. "That's hardly enough time."

"I could have you packed in ten minutes. I'm giving you time to get some sleep, book a flight, pack, and never come near any of us again."

Amy gave one last fleeting glance at Fox.

He only had eyes for the woman standing three feet away from him, her arms wrapped around her middle. Everything about her posture and vibe said Do Not Touch and it killed him.

Amy opened the door to leave.

Dean handed off the keys and key card to Melody, who opened her bag and dropped them in, right before she swore. "Damnit, I left my phone in my car."

"I'll get it," Dean offered.

She shook her head. "I'll do it. I could use a moment and some air." She glanced at him.

"Are we okay?" he asked, because it didn't feel like it.

She let out a long breath. "Yes." She closed the distance and, without touching him with her hands or body, brushed a soft kiss against his lips. "I need a minute."

"Take as many as you need. I need a scalding hot shower to get her off me anyway. And to maybe burn our bed."

Melody winced. "I'm sorry that happened to you. No one deserves to be treated like their feelings don't matter."

"What you're feeling right now matters a hell of a lot to me."

"It just shook me. The thought of you hurting me that way. The thought of losing you." Her eyes glassed over. "It cracked my heart wide open."

He wanted to wrap her in his arms, but he gave her the space she needed. "Never going to happen, sweetheart. I'd rather tear out my own heart with my bare hands than ever see you hurt." He laid his soul bare to her.

She had to believe him.

"I'll be back in a few minutes."

"Leave your phone. Stay with me."

"I have some notes on it for my class tomorrow. I want to go over them while we have breakfast."

He liked the sound of that. It meant she planned to stay the night.

She walked out the door, leaving him with Dean.

Fox didn't waste any time. "I want that bitch out of here as soon as possible."

"Done."

"And why isn't the elevator fixed, so only we can access this floor?"

Dean winced. "The guy is coming tomorrow."

"Too fucking late." He ran his fingers through his hair in frustration. "I want all the video footage of Amy stealing from Melody's purse in the classroom and breaking into my place."

"Are you going to press charges?"

He wasn't sure. "I want evidence and leverage. Hire someone to keep a fucking eye on her. I want to know she's gone and staying gone." Because he didn't think getting rid of her would be that easy. He made that clear to Dean. "If she's willing to do this, what else is she capable of?"

CHAPTER THIRTY-ONE

Amy was waiting by the elevator, looking smug with an infuriating grin.

Melody had a bad feeling about it, but didn't show an ounce of hesitation, just her disdain for the woman who thought she could steal another woman's boyfriend.

Amy touched her fingertip to her bottom lip. "Those things he said while I was in his bed..."

"Were meant for me, not you," she snapped. She wasn't going to let the bitch think she was jealous when she was royally pissed.

The elevator arrived with a swoosh as the doors opened. They both got in. Melody jabbed the 1 button with her thumb and tried to ignore Amy.

Amy turned and stared at the side of Melody's face. "He seemed really happy you were home. Damn was he ready to fuck you. And that cock..." Amy fanned her face.

Melody turned her head and locked eyes with Amy. "You should shut up now."

The elevator doors opened.

Melody realized Amy never pushed the 2 button for her floor. She dismissed it in favor of getting the hell out of there and away from temptation. Because she really wanted to punch Amy in her self-satisfied face. She seemed proud of herself for disrupting things between Melody and Fox.

Amy followed her toward the lobby doors. "You don't deserve him."

She spun around just outside the doors. "Fuck you. I treat him with respect. You think you can just force yourself on him and take what you want."

"I thought I wanted him," she confessed. "Now all I want is the money."

That set off an inner alarm. "What are you talking about?"

"You were supposed to run out of the apartment and building. But this works, too." Her gaze shot past Melody. "I think he's going to miss you."

Melody turned just enough to catch sight of the van and the guy wearing a black ski mask jumping out of it.

Amy grabbed her arm in a death grip, trying to keep Melody from running.

Melody let loose her rage and swung at Amy's face, hitting her in the jaw and mouth. Amy stumbled but didn't let go, so Melody swung again, landing another blow to her eye.

Free, Melody tried to run, but the other attacker slammed into her back, sending her to the ground. She scraped up her knees and palms as she tried to catch herself, but the weight of the guy sent her sprawling onto the pavement and losing her breath.

He took advantage, threw a hood over her head, grabbed her arms behind her back, zip-tied her wrists, then wrapped his arms around her middle and pulled her up and into the van.

The vehicle engine roared as they took off, Melody falling back against the metal side as they made a right turn out of the apartment's parking lot. She tried to suck in a breath, but it took several attempts to get any air.

The person who grabbed her off the sidewalk sat close beside her, his knees pressed to Melody's thigh. She tried to inch away from him, but ended up knocking into someone else.

"You fucking bitch. You busted my lip and I'll probably have a black eye."

Melody kicked out at her, hitting her in the thigh. "You deserve worse, you bitch."

But it was futile because the guy behind her grabbed her by the shoulders and shook her. "Be still before you hurt yourself, or get hurt," the guy mumbled, trying to disguise his voice.

Amy knew him, which meant he could easily be linked to her. And when Melody got free, she was going to make Amy and her accomplices pay for kidnapping her.

Until then, she tried to tamp down her fear, lower her racing heart, and think of a way out of this. "What do you want?" She had a feeling she already knew.

Amy's breath heaved in and out against the hood's fabric a second before she grabbed Melody's chin and held it tight. With the hood over her face, she couldn't see Amy, but she could feel the menace coming off her. "It's simple, bitch. Fox won the lottery. Now it's my turn to cash in. I wonder how much he'll pay to get you back."

Melody knew Fox would pay the ransom. She also knew he'd never let Amy and her coconspirators get away with this. "You had the perfect setup working for Fox. No doubt, you could have expanded that working relationship into catering gigs, even a full-time personal chef if you'd played your cards right. Maybe he'd have even asked me to hire you on at the new place we're opening."

"You would never hire me."

"Not for you. But for him, I'd do anything. But after what you pulled in his apartment and when he finds out you kidnapped me and why, he's going to ruin you. Not to mention make sure you're locked behind bars as long as possible. You can kiss the rest of your twenties and thirties goodbye. You'll be lucky if you aren't a haggard, hardened mess when you get out, with no job prospects, an arrest record for kidnapping and sexual assault following you around, and forty-year-old eggs getting older by the second. While all your friends are getting married and having babies, you'll be watching your back in the shower and hoping some beast of a woman doesn't make you her bitch."

Amy's fingers tightened on her jaw. "Fuck you!"

Melody headbutted the bitch right in the face and heard the satisfying crack.

Amy wrapped her hands around Melody's throat, shoved her onto her back, and tried to choke the life out of her. "I fucking hate you."

Melody only had her legs free and used them. She kneed Amy in the side. Once. Twice.

Then suddenly the guy's hand pushed down on Melody's chest and Amy's grip on her released as she fell away. "You kill her, we don't get paid," the guy snapped. "Now knock it off," he shouted, his tone gruff and almost familiar.

"They're going to let you take the fall," she announced to Amy. "You're the only one I can identify."

Amy's harsh pants and moaning ceased for a split second. Yeah, she understood now.

"You were just the means to get me outside and away from Fox. You thought after I found you in bed, I'd run out the door. They'd snatch me.

But it didn't work out quite that way, did it. You were supposed to be up in the apartment. Me and Fox, none the wiser you were the distraction."

"You walked right out and into our trap anyway." Amy didn't sound so confident now.

"And you walked out with me because you just had to see it go down, didn't you? Now Fox has it all on video, which includes your face, you holding me against my will, and you getting into the van."

"Fuck you!" The expletive lost its punch when delivered with a heaping dose of pain and garbled pronunciation thanks to the broken nose and what Melody hoped was a fountain of blood dripping down her face. Leaving evidence in the van and on her.

Let her try to explain her injuries.

Though Amy could probably tell a convincing kidnap story, making herself out to be the victim. She liked to use whatever worked to get her what she wanted. So far, none of her plans had worked out so well.

Fox wouldn't believe her anyway. Not now. Not ever again after what she did.

"Shut up and put this on your face," the guy said to Amy.

"She started it."

"Yeah, well, you'll get what you want soon enough when Fox coughs up all that money. Until then, we need her alive and well to carry out our plan."

Melody wondered what exactly they planned to do with her until they contacted Fox and set up the exchange.

What would they do to her after they got the money?

So far she'd held her own.

But what if Fox didn't want to play their game by their rules?

He'd never endanger her life. But things could go wrong.

She hated that they hadn't resolved things after that scene in his place with Amy.

What if I never get the chance to see him again and have the life we dreamed about?

CHAPTER THIRTY-TWO

Fox stepped out of the shower for the second time that night still quaking with rage. He snagged his already damp towel off the bar and patted down his raw skin. He'd had to scrub that bitch off him before he could touch Melody again.

How dare she!

If he'd done that to a woman...

He'd never do something so vile.

And how was he going to make this up to Melody?

He'd brought Amy into their lives. It was his fault he didn't see how far she'd go to get his attention. He should have fired her after she insinuated herself into his and Melody's dinner date.

He should have listened to Melody the first time she warned him that Amy had designs on him.

He tossed the sopping towel on the tile floor and went into his bedroom to drag on a clean pair of jeans and a thermal. He'd make Melody a cup of hot chocolate, maybe something to eat, then they'd sit and talk this out.

Barefoot and surly, he walked out into the living room expecting to find her on the couch, or in the kitchen. Instead, he stared at his haggard best friend. "Where is she?"

Dean looked up from his phone. "She's not back yet."

He stopped midstride to the refrigerator. "What?" It should have only taken her a few minutes to get her phone and come back up.

Dean shrugged a shoulder, then pointed toward the window. "Her car is still parked outside. Maybe she needed to take a walk around the block to clear her head."

Fox ran back into the bedroom for his phone and checked for messages. Nothing. He texted her.

FOX: Where are you? We need to finish our talk.

FOX: Please

He walked back out into the main living space, practically holding his breath while he waited for a response. Nothing.

He hit the speed dial for her and got voicemail. "Hey, it's me. I'm worried about you. Call me back."

Dean looked up, his eyebrows raised, suspicion in his eyes. "She's not answering?"

"She didn't respond to my text either." He held the back of his hand to his forehead, hoping his phone went off any second.

Dean stared at him. "I thought she understood this wasn't your fault."

"Me, too. She kissed me before she left. Not like she used to, but..." *I won't lose her. I'll get her back.*

"Pull up the security footage." Dean motioned with his head for them to go into the office.

Fox, heart pounding, senses blaring a warning, took a seat at his desk and pulled up the surveillance feeds, then rewound the lobby camera footage so he could see when Melody left and if she'd come back.

"Stop." Dean pointed to the right of the screen, time-stamped 2:22 a.m. "There she is."

Which meant he'd last seen her at like 2:18.

He looked at the clock on his monitor. 2:34. *Sixteen minutes since I last saw her.* "Fuck."

Amy stepped out of the elevator behind her.

And then his heart stopped when he saw the van, Amy holding on to Melody's arm, the ensuing struggle. He watched Melody deck Amy, not once, but twice, and his heart pounded with dread. She shouldn't have to defend herself like that. She shouldn't have to deal with someone he brought into their lives. She tried to run, only to be tackled by the guy from the van, then bound, and abducted. The van sped away with the woman who was his whole life.

"Fuck!" He stood to run after her on instinct, but Dean clamped his hand on his shoulder and pushed him back down into the chair.

"Wait. Think. We don't know who's helping Amy. We have no idea where they took her. We need to call the cops."

Fox shook his head. He didn't want to wait around for the local cops to try to figure things out. He needed someone who had both the means and incentive to get Melody back. He tapped the name on his phone and waited for the call to be answered.

"It's two-forty-two in the fucking morning."

Twenty-four minutes without her.

"Who is this?"

"Lyric, it's Fox. Melody's been kidnapped. I need to speak to Mason." He needed an FBI agent who'd do anything to keep his wife happy. One who would move heaven and earth to make sure her sister came home alive.

"Start talking," the gruff voice said immediately.

"Long story short, one of my employees broke into my place tonight, trying to break up me and Melody. It didn't work. Melody went down to her car to get her phone and take a minute after what happened. Amy must have followed her down, there were words exchanged in the lobby, then a van pulled up; one guy wearing a ski mask jumped out. Amy tried to subdue Melody, but she got in a couple of punches, which are on the surveillance video, she tried to run, got tackled and subdued by the van guy, who bound her wrists, put a hood over her head, then dragged her inside, right before Amy jumped in with them. They sped off. Now fucking help me find her."

"So at least two assailants in the van, plus Amy, and Melody as the hostage."

"Yes."

"Van details?"

"White, nondescript panel van with a side sliding door. No window in the back. Probably a delivery vehicle or rental."

"Did you get a plate?"

Dean was playing with the video footage and shook his head.

"No. The angle's bad. Not enough light this time of night to see more than the outline."

Mason remained all business. "Why would they take her?"

He exchanged a look with Dean. "If it was just Amy, I'd say revenge and to get Melody out of the way so she could have me. But with others involved and after Amy made some pointed remarks to me, I'm guessing I'll get a very high ransom demand."

Mason didn't mince words. "Several hundred million sure does put a target on your back, doesn't it?"

Fuck. Mason knew.

"What are you talking about?" Lyric asked. Obviously Fox was on speaker with both of them.

"I might have done some digging on Melody's boyfriend," Mason confessed.

"You background checked Fox." Lyric didn't sound annoyed, she sounded grateful and appreciative.

"Just to be sure he didn't have any skeletons in his closet we didn't know about, Angel."

"Great. So you know my not-so-secret secret."

"Yeah, but I've got resources. How did Amy know about it? Did you tell her?"

"No. I don't share that with anyone."

"Does Melody know?" Lyric asked.

"Yes. But I only told her right before our trip to Boston."

"Why would you keep it from her?" Mason asked.

"Because I wanted her to want me, not my net worth."

"Melody is not like that," Lyric, snapped, defending her sister.

"I know that. When you only have less than a handful of people you can really trust, it's hard to open yourself up to others. Not when you've been disappointed, abandoned, mistreated, and used the way I have since I was a kid. But I don't have to worry about that with Melody. She's amazing. Now help me get her back."

"We need to call the cops and get them looking for the van," Mason said.

"Fine. But I want you in charge. When the ransom demand comes, I will deliver it."

"First, we need to figure out who has her," he pointed out. "Who else knows about the lottery win?"

"Dean and Max, my two best friends. Our attorney, tax accountant, and financial advisor. My mom, because her social worker discovered it," he reluctantly admitted. "And a woman Dean was seeing seriously a while back that none of us have had contact with for over two years."

"That's a tight circle." Mason sounded impressed Fox hadn't blabbed to the whole world about his windfall.

"We were warned about letting word get out. The money is held in trust accounts, insulating us."

"Because you shared with your buddies." Mason had some skills at digging. Exactly what Fox needed now. His skill. His resources.

"Yes. They're my only real family. Except now I have Melody and the Wildes. And you," he added, hoping Mason would be another brother he could count on.

"I'm with you on this," Mason assured him immediately. "So of the people who know about the money, who could have told Amy?"

No one in his circle would tell Amy. Dean barely tolerated her. So... "It could have come from a competitor of mine who dug up the secret and shared it."

"How would Amy hear about it from someone like that?" Mason asked.

"Amy is a chef. She does a lot of catering in Boston. I hired her to come here to teach for a few months on contract. She could have been working a party, one I was at, which is how I met her, and overheard the rumors."

"Or she simply knows you own your own successful business and are rich in your own right," Lyric suggested.

Fox was shaking his head. "No. The way she insinuated knowing but also not saying it out loud made it seem like someone told her to keep it quiet."

"Why?"

"Because I don't share my personal business with anyone besides Dean and Max and now Melody. Part of the reason I was reluctant to get so close to Melody was because I knew my wealth made her a target."

"She's not going to care about that," Lyric interjected. "She loves you. You don't put boundaries on that. You take the risks because you know the rewards far outweigh anything bad that comes your way."

"And will she forgive me for being terrorized and kidnapped after finding another woman in our bed tonight? Because that might be one too many bad things to overcome. Especially if they hurt her. Or worse." He choked out those last words.

Dean squeezed his shoulder. "They won't hurt her. Not if they want to get paid."

Fox picked up a pen and threw it against the wall. "Where the fuck is she?"

"We'll get her back," Mason assured him.

But it felt empty. *He* felt empty without her.

2:54. *Thirty-six minutes without her.*

CHAPTER THIRTY-THREE

Melody leaned forward in the chair she'd been tied to after her captors had pulled her, struggling and kicking, out of the van and into the barn or shed—whatever the musty, earthy smelling place was—a while ago. She'd kind of lost track of time. She'd been through a lot tonight. A long shift at the bar. Finding Amy naked in her boyfriend's bedroom. The anger and hurt she'd felt when she thought Fox had cheated on her. The utter relief when he'd told her what really happened, that turned into rage because Amy had done something so vile to him.

Yeah, that rage was still simmering.

That bitch better not come near her again.

And now, here she was with a hood over her head after trying to escape being kidnapped and getting in a few good licks at Amy's smug face, her wrists and ankles bound to a hard wood chair, her captors outside having a muffled argument. She couldn't hear exactly what they were saying, but if she had to guess, the two guys weren't happy about how Amy handled things.

Fox had to know she was missing. Which meant he'd be looking for her.

She didn't have her phone. That was still in her car. Which meant neither Fox nor her family could track her.

But maybe her kidnappers would be stupid enough to call Fox for the ransom. He was a super genius when it came to computers. She bet he could hack his way into finding out where the phone was calling from. If not him, then Mason and the FBI could do it. Because Fox wouldn't leave anything to chance. Not when it came to her. He'd call Mason the second he suspected something was wrong.

The two of them had hit it off at the family dinner. They'd talked a lot about tech.

She didn't understand most of it, but she knew Fox would use any means necessary to get her back. Including his vast financial resources. He'd pay any amount.

And she hated that for him. He shouldn't have to squander it on three assholes who thought they could take her and his money and get away with it.

The door squeaked on its hinges, alerting her that someone was coming in. With the hood still over her face, she could only see shadows through the fabric in the dimly lit space.

Her heart raced as she waited to see what happened next.

"I bet you're scared shitless right now." Amy. Gloating.

"Not really." Though the rough ropes were digging into her wrists, making them raw and bloody.

"You should be."

"Why? What are you going to do to me? Hurt me? Kill me? Do you really think Fox will pay if you do either of those things?"

"Oh, he'll pay. He's so fucking desperately in love with you, he'll pay anything to get you back." If she couldn't have Fox, she'd take the consolation prize. His money.

"I bet that really pisses you off. I saw the utter disgust and rage that you'd tricked him written all over his face. He hated that you'd touched him. You know why? Because I'm the only one he wants touching him. The second he touched you, he threw you out of his bed."

"You fucking bitch!" Amy's hands slammed into Melody's shoulders, sending her and the chair back.

Melody hit the hard-packed dirt with a thud, slamming her head into the ground. She lost her breath for a second, but then she laughed. "You want a go at me again? Untie me and I'll mess up your face even more than I already have."

Amy screamed, the door squealed again, then just as Amy grabbed Melody's thigh, she was pulled away.

"Don't touch her again." This time the gruff voice was different from the guy who'd pulled her into the van. Had to be the driver. "I told you to leave her alone. We'll make the call, get our money, and we'll be out of here. No harm. No foul."

Except Melody had been harmed. She'd been scared, tied up, and left wondering if she was going to die tonight. This morning? The bar had closed at midnight on Wednesday. She'd left around one-thirty and got to Fox's maybe twenty minutes later. It had to be like three in the morning now. Maybe later.

Amy sure had been hurt, too. She bet Amy sported a black eye and bruised jaw to go with her busted lip and broken nose.

And kidnapping was very foul. Not to mention taking money away from a good man.

"How did you even know about the money?" She didn't think Fox would share that with Amy.

"None of your business," the guy whispered, still trying to conceal his voice.

"Since I'm the one you kidnapped, and we're talking about my boyfriend's money, I think it very much is my business, asshole."

"That smart mouth could get you hurt."

"What are you going to do about it? Set Amy on me? The woman who has fucked whatever plan you had to take me and not get caught. If I were Amy, and smart, I'd be wondering what you two guys were going to do about the fact that Amy will be tied to the kidnapping. How are you going to keep her from giving you up? I mean, she's proven already to be a liability."

"Shut up, you bitch!"

Melody couldn't do anything except stare straight at the black hood and wonder if these three idiots had ever really had a good plan in place. "You do realize my brother-in-law is an FBI agent, right? So the second he finds out I'm missing, what do you think he's going to do? I think he'll check the traffic cams downtown from where you took me from. Then he'll pull surveillance from not only Fox's building, but the businesses along the street. They'll find the van, which direction it went, maybe even see who was driving."

Suddenly the chair tipped back up and she got a little dizzy from the sudden jarring movement that had her sitting upright in the chair once again. "Shut the fuck up." The low, growled warning didn't deter her.

No. She was beyond angry. Fear didn't even play a factor. These stupid chumps didn't know who they were messing with. "Who's scared now?"

"Fox will pay the ransom." Amy sounded so sure and confident.

"Or he and my FBI brother-in-law will find you and have you locked up behind bars. Forever."

Some sort of scuffle between the guy and Amy occurred in front of her, but neither of them touched her again. Instead, she heard them walking to the door, the squeak of the hinges, and then silence once again.

She took a calming breath to slow her racing heart and prayed that what she hoped was happening was actually what Fox and Mason were doing right now. Or soon.

Come get me, Fox. I need you.

CHAPTER THIRTY-FOUR

Fox and Dean had met Mason at the police station nearly an hour ago.

4:08 a.m. *One hour, fifty minutes without her.*

With Mason working with Officer Bowers from the Blackrock Falls PD, they had officers checking the three traffic cams downtown by Fox's apartment building and leading out of town. They knew which way the kidnappers went. Just not where they'd ended up with Melody.

His heart clenched just thinking about her and what she must be going through right now.

Fox checked his phone again. No calls. No texts. No ransom demand. Nothing.

What are they waiting for?

Dean eyed the phone in Fox's hand. "They're settling in with her somewhere. They'll call soon."

Mason broke away from the group of officers he'd been conferring with and held up his phone. We have a very bad image of the driver."

Fox squinted at the photo, trying to make out the guy's features. "I don't recognize him."

Dean shook his head, too. "Could be any of a dozen light-haired white guys."

Mason's phone dinged with a text. He typed something back. "Sorry. That's Lyric wanting an update. She's agreed not to tell the rest of the family until morning. Hopefully, we'll have Melody back by then."

"Why haven't they fucking called?" Fox raked his fingers through his hair, pulling on the strands, desperate for word. Desperate for *her*.

Something in Mason's eyes made him freeze.

"What?"

"Are you sure this is a ransom and not Amy seeking revenge or something from Melody? You said she tried to seduce you away from Melody. Could she be trying to get rid of a rival?"

Which meant Melody could be dead right now.

Panic choked him.

No. He refused to think the worst. She was alive. She wouldn't go down without a fight.

Mason frowned. "Except, she'd do it alone. She wouldn't want anyone to know about it. But we know she was working with the two men. They'll be expecting something for their trouble. Which brings us back to a ransom."

Fox caught on to Mason's line of thinking. "Maybe Amy's plan is to ransom her, then something goes wrong and Melody gets killed in the crossfire, and Amy thinks she'll get me all to herself, and her accomplices get paid."

Dean put his hands on his hips. "That doesn't feel right. That's complicated and leaves too many chances for failure. Amy's attempts to win you were direct and focused on you, never the money."

Fox played out different scenarios in his head, trying to find the logic in all of this. "It doesn't make sense. Amy hardly knows anyone here. Definitely not someone who'd be willing to commit a felony for her, let alone two someones. So…"

"You think someone else is using Amy's hatred of Melody to get her away from you, so Amy can then have you all to herself. Or at least that's what they made her think, when really it is about the money." Mason waited for him to explain.

Fox swore under his breath, not wanting to think it, or even believe it, but this was happening here. In Blackrock Falls. And the only person in town who knew his secret, knew people capable of pulling this off, would use anyone to get what she wanted, and wanted his money more than she cared about him was… "My mom. Tanya has to be involved." He didn't know how, but he knew she didn't like Melody, which meant she wouldn't bat an eye at using her to get what she wanted. The life she'd always dreamed of having.

Mason's eyes filled with sympathy. "If it's her, I'm sorry, man. What she and your father did to you… I hope there's a special place in hell for child abusers."

"If she had anything to do with this, there's a cell on earth waiting for her." Fox headed for the police station door.

Mason and Dean followed.

Fox spun back around. "I'm going alone. I'll take care of this."

Mason shook his head. "You need law enforcement to take her down."

Fuck. "I go in alone. I'll get a confession out of her."

"And if you can't?" Dean asked.

"Then we'll wait for the ransom demand and I'll pay it."

4:17 a.m. *One hour, fifty-nine minutes without her.*

He'd do anything to get her back, including facing Tanya, her denial, her warped sense of what she thought she deserved, and the reality that his selfish mother was never on his side. She'd never wanted his happiness. She only wanted what he could give her.

The only people who cared about him were the family he'd made.

And the person who loved him the most—Melody.

He wouldn't stop until he got her back and everyone involved paid.

CHAPTER THIRTY-FIVE

4:46 a.m. *Two hours, twenty-eight minutes without her.*

Fox wasn't particularly surprised to pull into his mother's driveway and find the lights on in the house at nearly five in the morning. He parked the car, took a deep breath, then rushed up to the door, knowing exactly how he wanted to play this out.

Dean and Mason were in a separate car. They'd have his back.

But he didn't need help getting Tanya to talk. He had a feeling he'd get exactly what he expected from her.

He didn't bother knocking on the door. He didn't have to.

She opened it for him. "Fox, what are you doing here so late?"

"Actually, I think it's early."

Her gaze darted past him as she scanned the yard. "What's wrong?"

"Melody's been kidnapped. I'm expecting a ransom demand any second."

No surprise or concern showed on her face. "Then what are you doing here?"

He took a step closer to her, then another, backing her up and into the house. "I need to know who you told about the lottery win."

"No one." She held her hands out, then let them drop. "You asked me not to tell anyone."

Fox shrugged. "Your social worker knows. What about your doctor. A nurse. The grocery store clerk. The travel agent in town you've been talking to about all the trips you want me to pay for." He tried to hold back his temper, but those last words came out with a bite to them.

She shook her head. "I didn't tell anyone. You asked me to keep it a secret."

"But you didn't. Because someone knows. Someone took the woman I love, the woman I plan to marry and have a *real* family with. The woman who makes me happy. The woman who would do anything for me, including saving me from you."

Her shoulders squared. "You don't need to be saved from me. I'm your mother."

"That's biology. You've never been a real mother to me. Not when I was young. Not now. I'm just a means to an end. And if you used the woman I love to get money out of me, I will make sure your pathetic life ends even more miserably. But if you tell me what I need to know right now—you put me out of my misery—I'll give you a million dollars." He held up his phone. "I can transfer the funds to you right now."

The surprise and greed in Tanya's eyes turned to calculation. "I don't know anything. I didn't do anything."

The house phone rang.

Fox walked to the kitchen where the phone sat on the counter. "Who's calling you at this hour?"

4:49 a.m. *Two hours, thirty-one minutes without her.*

"It's probably just a telemarketer."

He raised a brow. "At five in the morning?" He stared at the caller ID. Local number. No name. Probably a burner phone. Her coconspirator?

Tanya tugged his shoulder, pulling him around to look at her. "I'm sorry about the trouble with Melody, but I know nothing about it." Her gaze darted away, then came back to him.

She's lying.

"I really wish, for once, you meant that. But you don't. Because you only care about yourself. And I'm betting that you're involved in Melody's kidnapping. It wouldn't surprise me if you planned it. So here's what I'm going to do. I'm going to call that number. How much do you want to bet they'll ask for a ransom for her?"

He started to punch the number into his phone.

Tanya grabbed him by both arms, her nails digging into his skin through his thermal, and shook him, panic in her eyes. "Just pay me the money and I'll tell them to release her."

He sighed, even as a sense of inevitability and utter hatred and rage swept through him. "Where is she?" He growled out the words, hating her, wanting her to pay for what she'd done.

4:51 a.m. *Two hours, thirty-three minutes without her.*

Tanya stepped back and shook her head. "Forty million."

He nodded. "Right. One million wasn't enough. Not for you and your"—he narrowed his gaze as he considered—"three accomplices." Three in the van. One bitch of a mother pulling the strings.

Her eyes went wide.

"I'm not stupid," he spat at her. "Where is she?"

Tanya stood stubbornly quiet and defiant in front of him.

"Fine. Have it your way. The FBI can deal with you."

Her eyes went wide, then even bigger as the back door opened and Mason walked in with his gun trained on her and his badge attached to his belt.

Fox stared down his mom. "Everyone in town knows Lyric married an FBI agent, and you thought it was a great idea to kidnap her sister." He shook his head. "Forty million," he spat out. "You won't see a dime. Enjoy prison." He headed for the front door to get his laptop out of the car, so he could track the phone number.

"Fox! Wait!" Tanya shrieked. "I need a lawyer."

"I'm sure one will be provided to you, since you don't have any money to pay for one. Mason will tell you as he arrests you."

"There's no proof. It's my word against yours."

Fox held up his phone. "They heard everything we said to each other. And I recorded it." He'd left an open line to Mason when he walked into the house.

Before Fox made it into the entryway, Mason stopped him with more news. "Dean did some snooping outside. He found a white panel van hidden in the barn out back. Cops are going over it now."

Which hopefully meant the kidnappers were close.

Fox glared at Tanya. "Explain that to a judge." He shook his head and left that house for the last time. Nothing good ever happened in that house. Maybe he'd burn it to the ground.

5:04 a.m. *Two hours, forty-six minutes without her.*

It took Fox all of two minutes to hack the phone number and determine exactly where it was, not even three miles away. Then he looked up the property records for the place and found it had been foreclosed on some time ago. Perfect place to hide some nefarious shit like a kidnapping. He sent all the details to Mason as evidence.

5:11 a.m. *Two hours, fifty-three minutes without her.*

Dean stood next to him with his arms folded over his chest as Mason led Tanya out the door.

Mason held up a plastic bag filled with Tanya's medication. "She refused to leave without these. Said one of them is an experimental drug that's put her in remission."

Fox glared at Tanya. "No wonder you didn't want me at your doctor visits. You didn't want me to know you were getting better."

"I wanted you to let me see the world."

Fox shook his head. "And I agreed to your trip, but you still went through with this. Why?"

"Because I wanted more than just *one* trip. I wanted a better life."

"Now, you'll have a good long life behind bars. Enjoy your stay. The accommodation and amenities are shit and the view sucks. And the food...good luck scarfing that down."

She tried to rush him, but Mason held her back by the arm, her wrists shackled behind her. "Please. Don't do this. I'll tell you where she is if you make them let me go."

"I already know where she is. Now I'm going to go get her."

5:14 a.m. *Two hours, fifty-six minutes without her.*

Mason handed Tanya off to Officer Bowers. "Put her in a cell." Once Tanya was secure in the back of the patrol car, Mason turned to him. "Let's go get your girl."

"Yes, let's go get Melody," an unfamiliar man said, walking up on them from the driveway.

"Uh, who are you?" Fox asked.

The new guy grinned at Mason. "Assistant Special Agent in Charge Nick Gunn."

"Brothers," Dean said.

"Brothers," Mason acknowledged. "About time you got here."

"It took a helicopter and a car. You can update me on the way. If I don't help get Melody back to her family, safe and sound, Aria will have my ass."

"We don't want that," Mason admitted. "Lyric is asking for updates every ten minutes."

"Yeah, and I'm going to catch hell for keeping this from Aria."

Fox was already sliding behind the wheel of his car. "I texted you the address," he said to Mason. "Now let's go. You're wasting time."

5:18 a.m. *Three agonizing, terrified hours without her.*

Fox drove away from Tanya's place, vowing to leave it and her in his rearview forever. He might own the place, but he didn't have to keep it.

"We'll get her back," Dean assured him from the passenger seat. "So slow the fuck down before we get in an accident. These roads are dark as fuck."

Because they were out in the middle of nowhere.

"One deer and we're toast."

But it wasn't a deer that appeared in Fox's headlights but a woman, walking along the road, coming toward them, away from their final destination. And he'd recognize her anywhere.

He hit the brakes and swerved to the side of the road, stopping right behind her as Mason also skidded to a stop in front of her.

Mason's car's headlights spotlighted her and Fox as he leapt out of his car and ran to Amy. "Where is she?"

Amy held her arms wrapped around her middle, her head down, as she shook. "The-they dumped me on the shoulder and told me to follow the road back to town." She glanced around her, eyes wide and filled with fear. "I don't know where I am, or how far it is to a house or town. There's nothing out here." She shivered again as her eyes darted from him and Dean to the two men behind her wearing badges and guns, their hands hovering over their weapons.

"Where. Is. She?"

"The-they have her. It happened so fast. They took her, then ordered me into the van."

"After she kicked your ass," Dean pointed out. "We saw it on the video."

"She attacked me."

"After you held her so the guys you're working with could take her," Fox snarled.

Amy shook her head. "No, that's not what happened. She was furious with me for going to your place."

"You mean sneaking into my bed and sexually assaulting me?" Fox asked, letting Mason and his FBI brother know Amy had some serious charges coming her way in addition to kidnapping.

"That's not what ha-happened."

Fox had enough. "Looks like someone broke your nose after you got into that van."

She gingerly touched her fingertip to the swollen flesh. "It hurts. I need to go to the hospital."

"Tell us where Melody is and we'll take you there," Mason offered.

5:22 a.m. *Three hours, four minutes without her.*

"We don't have time for this shit. Tell me where she is."

"I-I'm not sure." She turned pleading eyes on the two agents.

He wasn't having it. "Cut the crap and this fake performance. You're not scared. You're out here for a reason."

"Yes. To get back to town to tell you they want twenty million or they'll kill her." She pulled a slip of paper out of her pocket. "Look. Here. It's the account and routing number. Send the money and they'll give her back. That's why they took me and let me go." She held out the slip of paper. "So I could give you this."

"Huh." Fox snatched the slip of paper from her hands but didn't even look at it, then dropped a bomb on her. "Tanya asked for forty million."

Amy's eyes went wide.

Fox sneered. "Guess she planned to screw you and the two goons you're working with out of the majority of the money."

"No. No. I don't know anything about what's going on. Tanya?" She acted like she didn't know who set this all in motion.

Maybe she didn't. Maybe it was one or both of the guys who took Melody and brought Amy into this.

Just as the pieces started to fall into place, Mason stepped closer to Amy. "They could have given you the ransom message at the apartment and left without you when they took Melody. Why take you all the way out here, just to make you walk back? Fox was right there, upstairs."

Amy didn't look so certain anymore.

Fox closed the distance and put a bunch of pretend sympathy into his eyes and expression. "Amy, I know it's been a long night for you."

Amy smiled up at him. "Yes. Yes, it has. I was terrified they'd hurt me. And look at my face." She pressed her hand to her jaw. "It hurts, Fox. Please. I just want to go back to your place where I'll be safe."

"This is as close as you'll ever be to me again. This fucking ruse you've got going is shit. Those dumb fucks realized calling me for the ransom would only allow me to find them faster. Right?"

Amy's whole face fell into shock, then acceptance that she'd been caught. And just like that, the calculation came back into her eyes. "I want immunity. Then I'll tell you who took her and where they are."

Fox swore. "I know where she is and who has her. The only one who connects to Tanya and you is that dickhead drug dealer Brian, whose best friend is Josh, who you met outside my apartment building. Coincidentally. But you know what's funny? Josh used *you* to get to Melody, a woman he's been obsessed with for years." He took a menacing step closer to her. "If he touches her, if he hurts her, that's all on you, too. And I will make sure you never see the light of day again."

Nick stepped forward and pulled Amy's hands behind her back.

"What are you doing?" she screeched, trying to get away, but she was no match for Nick.

"You're under arrest for kidnapping." As Nick led Amy back to Mason's car, he read her her rights, and put her in the back seat.

Mason put his hand on Fox's shoulder. "Good job figuring this out. Now, what do we need to know about these two guys who have Melody? Are they armed?"

"I would presume so." Fox turned for his car. "I'm done wasting time."

Mason caught up to him. "We'll park away from wherever they're holding her. We'll go in quiet and check things out. We will not go in half-cocked. The last thing we want is for them to hurt the hostage."

"I need her back," he choked out. "Now."

Mason squeezed his shoulder. "I know. But we have to do this the right way."

5:28 a.m. *Three hours, ten minutes without her.*

"Fine. All that matters is that we get her back safe and unharmed."

5:29 a.m. Three hours, eleven minutes without her.

CHAPTER THIRTY-SIX

Voices rose outside whatever building her captors had stashed her in.

"Stay away from her," one of the men shouted just as the outside door squeaked again, then shut with a heavy bang. "We get the ransom and leave her here for them to find."

"I just want to make sure she's secure."

"She's not getting out of that fucking chair. Now stay out here and keep a lookout. I need to make a call."

"She's still not answering."

She? She who?

"Fucking probably passed out in front of the TV, stoned out of her mind."

Silence returned and Melody tried again to loosen the ropes around her wrists, resulting in more rope burns and blood. Lot of good that did her.

She was so tired and desperate to get out of here. She hated having the hood over her head. She couldn't see anything. Not that she needed to see to know that she was in a dark space. A single lightbulb across the room provided a drab sense of light and shadows in the distance through the black fabric cover over her head and face.

Every once in a while she heard the scurry of tiny feet. No barn cat here to chase the mice away. Though she thought she heard the hoot of a barn owl above her, so maybe the mice did have something to run from.

The door screeched open again and the heavy footfalls drew closer. Whoever had come in didn't speak, just stopped right in front of her, an ominous presence that made her heart race and her mouth go dry.

Anticipation and dread soured her gut. "What do you want?"

"You. It's always been fucking you." The words were dark with fury and desperation.

Inevitability. Like this had been coming for a long time.

There was something familiar in his voice, though she still couldn't quite place it.

His hands clamped onto her arms above her wrists. "Look what you've done to yourself." He started tugging on the ropes.

She thought he was freeing her hands; instead, he twisted the ropes so her hands were bound together in front of her. She was still tied to the chair by her feet. "Did you call Fox for the ransom? How long until he pays it?"

"Our dear friend Amy is off getting the money. No phone required. Just a simple transfer of funds from your *boyfriend*." He snarled the word, but slipped out of his low whisper, and that's when she knew exactly who was in front of her.

"Josh." His name was barely a whisper on her breath.

"You're fucking mine." He grabbed her shirt and lifted it up her body.

She locked her arms at her sides, so he couldn't pull it over her head, but he grabbed the ropes at her wrist and yanked her arms up with one hand and pulled the shirt up with the other. The second the shirt cleared her head, pushing the hood off with it, she stared her attacker in the eyes as he hooked the shirt behind her head, essentially keeping her arms raised for him. "You fucking asshole."

The jerk grinned at her as he pulled a gun from his waistband and pointed it in her face. "Keep your fucking mouth shut or I'll put a bullet in you."

"And then you won't get your money."

"I want something else right now." He pressed the tip of the barrel of the gun to her throat, then dragged it down her sternum, between her breasts, down her belly, and shoved it between her spread thighs and right into her crotch. "You're mine."

She let him see the defiance in her eyes. "I'm his."

"Because he's rich." He practically spat out the words.

"His money doesn't even make the top one hundred on my list of why I love him."

"Bullshit."

"Says the guy who kidnapped me and is now threatening to rape me to get what he wants."

He got right in her face. "You never gave me a chance."

She glared daggers at him. "You proved why I shouldn't have tonight."

"Maybe. But I'm still going to have what I want and that rich asshole is going to get you back knowing I was all over you."

She leaned in close. "He will kill you for this."

"Baby, I'll be long gone, spending his money on a beach with a babe, and no one will ever fucking find me." He tucked the gun in his waistband, hauled her up, and shoved her back into the pole beside her, hooking the ropes around her wrists on a large nail. The height took her feet off the ground and tilted the chair back. Her body was contorted to the side because of the chair. He got to work on her ankles. The second one of her feet was free, she tried to kick him, but he twisted the end of the rope around her other leg and secured her feet together, then released her other foot, leaving her dangling from her wrists, standing on her tippy toes. It hurt like hell to have most of her weight suspended by her bruised, bloody wrists, but she still tried to raise her feet and kick him.

He swatted her feet away and laughed in her face. "Perfect. I set this up when I scoped this place out. I got the height just about right." He set the gun on the chair, leaned in close, and put his hands over her breasts, his body pressed to hers as he licked her cheek.

She tried to turn her head, but he just grabbed her chin with one hand and pinched her nipple hard with the other. He made her look at him as he thrust his cock into the V of her thighs and groaned. "I'm going to fucking enjoy this."

"Bite me."

He did. Right on top of her breast above her bra. He didn't break the skin, but it hurt like hell and she cursed, then headbutted him the second he raised his head to taunt her again. He stumbled back, then rushed her again. She picked up her feet, wrenching and hurting her wrists even more, and kicked him in the chest, sending him to his ass on the packed dirt floor.

And then it felt like the room erupted with chaos. The door squeaked open and thudded against the wall as Mason rushed in, gun drawn. Behind her, another crash sounded as someone rushed up behind her.

"Give me a reason to shoot your ass," Fox said as he stepped up next to her, a gun held in his hands and pointed right at Josh's head. "Please. Just one reason."

Josh glanced at the gun he'd set on the chair she'd been tied to earlier after he'd shoved the barrel between her legs.

Mason and Fox kept their guns on Josh as Dean closed in from the side, pulled Josh's arms behind his back, and cuffed him.

"Get me down," she begged, her voice hoarse from the tears she tried to choke down.

Fox tucked his gun at his back as he turned to her, glanced at his watch, then said, "Five forty-three. Three hours, twenty-five minutes without you."

"Too long," she agreed with the sentiment.

He reached out to touch her, but his gaze dropped to the bite mark on her chest. He spun around and clocked Josh right in the face, breaking his nose, then punched him in the mouth with his other hand, sending his head snapping back again.

Josh fell to the floor on his ass again and spit out two teeth along with a gush of blood. "You broke my nose and knocked out my teeth, fucker."

"You're lucky I don't kill you for touching her." His shoulders heaved up and down with his heavy, angry breaths.

"Fox," she called to him softly. "I need you." She needed him away from Josh before he really did attack again and kill him.

Fox turned to her immediately and gently wrapped one arm around her waist to lift her up, then carefully pulled her wrists from the nail. He set her on her feet, then pulled her shirt over her head and ever so slowly lowered it along with her arms.

She held her hands out toward him. "Take them off."

Instead, he cupped her face. "I'm sorry."

She shook her head. "Not your fault. None of it." The first tear slipped over her lashes and down her cheek.

He gently brushed it away with his thumb. Then the next. And the next. Until he pulled her into his chest and she cried all over his shirt as he held her in a loose embrace and she tried to burrow her way into him.

"Ambulance will be here in a few minutes," Mason said.

She gasped and turned to look at him beside her. "There's another man. Probably Brian. Those two are always together."

Mason nodded. "Nick got him before we came in. He's in cuffs right outside. We have Amy in custody, too, along with Tanya. They're all going down for this."

She looked up at Fox. "Tanya?"

"Pretty sure she masterminded this whole thing."

"Fucking bitch." She caught herself, realizing that it had to be devastating for Fox to have his mom do this to him. "Sorry. You must be—"

"Enraged. Out for blood. Ready to make sure none of them ever leaves a cell for the rest of their lives. Yeah, sweetheart, I'm all that and more. But more than anything, I'm relieved you're alive."

"Me, too. So I can tell you again how much I love you. I knew you'd come for me."

He brushed his hand down her tangled hair. "You're not mad that this happened because of me."

She shook her head as Mason dropped down beside her and undid the ropes around her ankles. "Not your fault. All you ever did was love me."

"I plan to do that forever if you'll let me. Even if you won't," he confessed.

"We're building a life together, remember? You promised."

He hugged her close. "I promise I'll always keep you safe."

She knew what that meant. "I don't need guards. I just need you."

"Yeah, well, you're getting security as well." He looked down at her. "Please. For my sanity."

"We'll talk about it when we move to Boston."

His eyes went wide. "You still want to come with me?"

"No one is going to take away our dream, or split us up. Not Amy. Not Josh. Not your mother."

"Tanya is not my mother. She's nothing to me. *You* are everything." He brought her hands up and kissed her knuckles on both hands, then gently undid the ropes. She winced and cried some more as the abrasive cord left her tender skin.

"Ambulance is here," Dean announced, stepping close. "You okay?"

She put her hands flat against Fox's chest, right over his heart. "I am now."

Fox kissed her on the head, then lightly brushed his thumb over the goose egg knot on her forehead. "What happened here?"

"Headbutted Amy and broke her nose, then that fuckface when he tried to rape me."

"That's my girl. So fucking fierce." He brushed her hair back and stared down at her. "I love you so much."

"I love you, too. Now can we get out of here? I hate this place."

"Can you walk?" Dean asked.

She leaned into Fox's side as he wrapped his arm around her. "Don't let go."

"Never." He helped her out of the building.

She stopped short and stared at the two cop cars, Mason and Fox's cars, and the ambulance all clustered in the driveway between an old house and—she turned and looked at the building behind her—yep, a shed.

The paramedics rushed forward and helped her onto a gurney. Fox stayed right beside her, never leaving her side, or letting go, whether he had a hand on her arm or her thigh as the paramedics checked her out and loaded her into the ambulance.

Exhausted, she let sleep carry her away, knowing Fox would take care of everything. He'd watch over her. She would never be alone. Not for the rest of their lives.

CHAPTER THIRTY-SEVEN

Melody woke with a gasp, her hands flying up to protect herself against...nothing. She stared up at the ceiling in her apartment because Fox thought she'd be more comfortable at her place. And just like at the hospital each time she'd drifted off, then woken up, when she endured all the questions from the doctors and police, when she'd been hugged and coddled by her family, Fox was there. Right beside her.

He took her hands and leaned over her from his side of the bed so she could see him clearly. "It's all right, sweetheart. I'm here. You're safe." He kissed one palm and then the other. "You're safe," he assured her again.

She breathed in, then let out a long exhale to calm her racing heart. One more time. Okay, two. Then three. Finally, she felt settled in reality and calm and the soft glow of the egg-shaped nightlight Fox made Dean run out and get because she didn't want to be in the dark. "How long did I sleep?"

"A couple of hours." He'd brought her home from the hospital late this morning. They'd kept her all day yesterday and overnight for observation. She was exhausted, dehydrated, and had a nasty headache from headbutting Amy and Josh, but no serious injuries. Well, except the psychological trauma. And let's not forget the sore knuckles from punching Amy, and the severely bruised and abraded wrists that Fox rewrapped after he helped her shower because her hands were sore and she was so fatigued.

"What time is it?"

"Closing in on three o'clock. You missed lunch. Hungry?" He set her hands on her stomach, then leaned on his right hand as he stared down at her but didn't touch her again.

They hadn't had a lot of time alone to talk. And she'd kind of been out of it at the hospital even when she was awake. There'd been a few minutes here and there where they were alone together, but most of the time, there'd been someone from her family, law enforcement, or the medical staff with them.

Her mom and dad wanted her to go home with them to the ranch to recover. All she'd wanted was to be alone with Fox.

She didn't want anyone to see her break down. She didn't want to plaster on a fake smile and pretend everything was all right to ease their minds.

With him, she never had to do that.

And he had been there. He'd seen what that asshole did to her. She didn't have to explain.

She glanced past him at the laptop he'd set on the bedside table. "Working?"

Distraction, more like it. He'd been silently fuming since he found her.

She didn't blame him. His mother had betrayed him again. For money this time.

So selfish. So horribly unkind.

That was as nicely as she could put it. Because that fucking bitch deserved everything coming to her.

Tanya had even lied about the severity of her illness. No wonder she never wanted Fox at her appointments.

He'd have been so happy to hear that she was getting better. He'd have hoped for more time to build some kind of relationship with her.

But Tanya killed that hope inside him once and for all.

She'd begged to see him.

He refused every time one of the officers relayed the message.

She'd turned her back on him. Now he had to do the same to save himself any more heartache.

Melody would never forgive her for what she did, how she treated him, and not seeing that she'd be so lucky to have Fox as a friend and ally.

They could have at least been friendly with each other. And Fox would have taken care of her.

Now... His eyes filled with hate and rage and his fists clenched tight any time someone said her name.

He shook his head. "I was checking in with Mason and the DA. Making sure the four responsible for scaring and hurting you get what they deserve."

She didn't think he'd let them get away with scaring *him*. He'd spent his whole life wanting to get back to her. And they'd taken her away from him.

He'd suffered so many tragedies and losses. She couldn't imagine what he'd do, what he'd be like if something terrible had happened to her.

Well, it had. And he was angry.

But she was still here. They were together.

But things felt off. Strained. Fragile, even.

It shouldn't be this way. Not between them.

She blamed Amy. And Tanya. All of them.

But more than anything, she wanted to get back the closeness she shared with Fox.

"It's infuriating that Tanya only cared about the money and tried to steal it from you, especially after you were so generous with her."

"She hurt you to hurt me because she knew I'd fucking give everything I have, my fucking life for you."

She rose up onto her elbow and faced him. "But you won't touch me, except to hold my hand, then let it go moments later, like you can't stand not to touch me, then you don't want to again."

He reached over and brushed her hair away from her forehead and looked her right in the eye. "You're right. I want to touch you so badly, I ache with it. But after what you've been through, the way you distanced yourself from everyone and everything at the hospital, holding yourself and curling up the way you did... After the way that asshole touched you, I thought maybe you didn't want anyone, me, touching you."

"I just...needed some time to let the nightmare fade enough, to not feel like I was still in it."

The shower he'd helped her take had been very...clinical. Soap her up, rinse her down. Get the job done, nothing else. She'd tried to wash away the memories, the feel of Josh's hands on her. Then they both climbed into bed and she'd crashed, knowing Fox was right beside her. That he wouldn't leave her alone.

Then she thought about Fox asleep in their bed at the apartment, waiting for her to come home to him and waking up to someone other than her touching him. "I think we both could use a reminder of what it's like when we're together." She pushed the blankets to the bottom of the bed, rolled over, and straddled Fox's hips as he fell back onto the pillow he'd been using to prop himself up while he toiled away on his laptop.

He wasn't wearing a shirt, because she'd come out of the bathroom and pulled it off him and put it on herself, needing his scent and heat to surround her while she slept. Now... "I need you." She pulled the shirt off over her head and sent it sailing through the air. Then she took him by the wrists and put his hands on her bare breasts. She covered his hands with hers and squeezed the firm mounds.

His eyes blazed with desire. "Are you sure?"

She rocked against his hard length, wishing he wasn't wearing sweatpants. She didn't want anything between them. "Don't hold back, Fox. Love me."

He rose up, cupped her face in his big, warm hands, and kissed her, his mouth open, tongue thrusting along hers. The kiss was a possession. A claiming. "I love you more than anything. If I lost you..." He shook his head, kissed her hard and fast. "Can't happen. Never happening." Then he rolled them back to her side of the bed and she landed on her back with him between her thighs. His mouth crashed down on hers again. Raw. Wild. His tongue slid against hers as his cock rocked against her core. "You're so fucking beautiful and strong. Fierce. And mine."

He kissed a trail down her neck to her chest. He hesitated for the barest of seconds before he planted a kiss right over the bruising bite mark, then took her nipple into his mouth and sucked and laved at it, making her moan his name.

"Fox."

"That's right. It's me, making you feel this way."

"So good. Don't stop."

"Anything for you." He took her other nipple into his mouth and slid his hand down her side, over her belly, then between her legs. His fingers softly brushed over her folds, stroking up, then down as he thrust one finger, then two into her. His lips left her nipple with a tug, then pop. "You're so fucking wet for me." He thrust those two fingers again.

"I need you."

"You have me. Always." He slid down the bed, spread her thighs wide, then licked her pussy from bottom to top. Those two fingers returned, sliding in and out as he licked her clit, circling the bud with his tongue, driving her insane. "Let go. I've got you." That deep, rumbly voice rolled through her along with her orgasm as he continued to stroke her with his tongue and fingers, drawing it out. Wave after wave of pleasure.

Just as she sank back into the bed, the head of his thick cock brushed her entrance, nudging in just an inch. "I love you." He thrust in to the hilt, then went still, savoring the moment they were joined. One. Connected in bliss.

She grabbed his ass and pulled him in deeper.

He swore, then groaned in ecstasy. "Nothing feels better than being inside you." And then he moved, pulling out slowly, thrusting back in, building the need inside her once more as she clung to him, gave herself over to him and the insane pleasure until he let go, too, and slammed into her.

Lost in the wild abandon of it all, they came together with hearts racing and pleasure overwhelming them.

He collapsed on top of her, then rolled to his side, taking her with him, so they were face-to-face as they clung to each other, still joined. "Marry me. I'll get you a ring, I'll do the whole proposal thing right, I promise, but I need to know you'll be my wife."

"There's nothing I want more. Yes."

He crushed her to him, his lips pressed to hers in a kiss that was filled with love and need and excitement. His half-hard cock swelled inside her again and she rocked against him.

He rolled her to her back. This time their lovemaking was slow and sweet, with kisses that lingered and tempted, their bodies moving together, hands brushing and sweeping over sensitive skin until their need rose like a wave, building before crashing into the soft caress of the warm sand.

In his arms, lying heart to heart, she felt what their future would always be. Them. Connected. Loving each other through the good and the bad. Together.

Chapter Thirty-Eight

Melody wiped a tear from her cheek and hugged her brother Jax so hard he groaned. She leaned back and stared up at him, so handsome in his tux. "I am so happy for you and Layla." The wedding ceremony had ended a few minutes ago. It had been short and sweet and filled with meaning, because they weren't just starting a life together, they were starting a family, too.

Layla was a beautiful bride in a white gown with a fitted long-sleeve top that had a wide V-neck, with floral appliqués and a barely there back. The chiffon skirt draped from her waist to the floor in a church-length train that puddled at the back of her feet, but wasn't long enough to hinder her during the reception. If you didn't know she was pregnant, you'd never tell in that dress. It was sexy and beautiful. Just like Melody's brother's bride.

Inspiration for Melody's upcoming wedding. She and Fox hadn't set a date. She was still waiting for her proposal and ring. She suspected Fox was waiting for them to officially move in together in Boston next week.

With everyone involved in the kidnapping locked up behind bars for the last two weeks awaiting their trials, they had no reason to stay here.

Aria had already hired two new waitresses to replace her. Melody had been training them the last few days while Fox worked from the apartment or center, getting ready to hand it over to the director he'd hired to run it for him.

They'd be coming back often, but she couldn't wait to start her life with him in Boston.

"You look happy, too." Jax's love for her shone in his eyes. "It does my heart good to see you smiling again."

She pulled her hands from around his neck and stared up into his sparkling blue eyes, so like hers. She'd miss him. All of them. But she needed to go, to stretch her wings, and be with the man who made her this deliriously happy. "I'm letting go of the past and moving on to my future with Fox."

"You're up next. Right?"

She couldn't wait to marry Fox. "Soon. I want to be his wife as much as he wants me to be his wife."

"And you'll open your restaurant. You'll build something of your own."

"The Dark Horse will be a piece of home. Who knows, maybe I'll become a restaurant mogul."

"I have no doubt if you put your mind to it, you could rule the world."

"I want what you have with Layla. Love. A family. A life we make together, filled with happy memories."

"Well, I know I won't have to worry about you. Not when you have Fox and his buddies."

Yes. Dean and Max came with Fox and she couldn't be happier about it. "I gained two new brothers along with my very loving and protective fiancé."

"Are you talking about me?" Fox asked, joining her and Jax, along with Layla. Fox had whisked the bride onto the dance floor so Melody could have a moment with Jax.

Jax hooked his arm around his bride's waist and pulled her close. "We were talking about you and Melody getting married next."

"We have to set a date." Fox smiled at her, not a single nerve or hesitation about getting married.

She snuggled into his side. "I don't want to wait. I want to get married as soon as possible."

Fox grinned. "Your wish is my command. Here? Or in Boston?"

"Doesn't matter as long as everyone we love is there."

He nodded. "So, small and intimate."

"Unless you have a bunch of business associates you want to invite."

He shook his head. "I want the people who matter to be with us."

"Then I want to get married under the stars with a ton of flowers, have a lovely dinner with our family, and slow dance with you all night."

Fox pulled her close and kissed her. "If that's what you want, that's what we'll do."

"And Dean can go back to doing his normal job instead of being my shadow." She glanced over her shoulder. He held up his drink and saluted her.

"You wouldn't let me hire anyone else to look after you."

She rolled her eyes, knowing she wasn't going to win this battle. "Instead you demoted him from head of your security to babysitter."

"When we get to Boston, you're getting a proper bodyguard."

She huffed dramatically, even though she was bluffing. "Fine. Otis is my new best friend."

Fox relaxed. "Dean will go back to work for the company. And we'll also have a personal assistant to take care of the house and errands and stuff."

"What?" She gaped at him. "We don't need that."

"We do if we want to have any time together once you start working on opening the restaurant and I'm back in the office."

Layla beamed. "I'd love a personal assistant. I get so lost in work, I forget to eat sometimes."

"That's why you have me, sweetheart. I won't let you ever get too lost." Jax kissed Layla like no one was watching. They got lost in each other.

Fox took Melody's hand and led her to the dance floor and right into a slow dance. She pressed her cheek to his shoulder and held him close, loving having his arms around her. "I just want you safe."

"I know you do. That's why I grumble but never say no when it comes to my protection and your peace of mind."

"My life comes with certain drawbacks."

"*Our* life has far more joy and fun and purpose than annoyances or distractions or truly bad things. You and me, we'll focus on the good, the love, the laughter and memories we'll make together."

He kissed her. "Always."

She kissed him back. Forever."

Epilogue

The week after Jax's wedding, Fox and Melody finally arrived at their Boston home.

"Did your car arrive?"

Fox had his beloved Mustang transported back from Wyoming to Boston because they'd wanted to fly home.

"It's in the garage downstairs."

"Do you think the movers delivered everything yesterday?"

"I know they did. Mandy checked all the boxes and unpacked for you." He'd hired Mandy through the Boston New Adult Education Center to be their part-time personal assistant. As soon as Dean and Max found out about her role, they wanted her help, too, so from one day to the next, she now worked full-time for the three of them.

"It feels weird to have someone who does stuff for us."

"You'll get used to it. I bet you'll even love it when you're neck-deep in opening the restaurant and you have no time to even think about making a meal, let alone going grocery shopping." He kept his arm around her shoulders, then surprised her by dipping low, putting his other arm behind her legs, and lifting her up into his arms. "Now. Today's our first day living together here, so I'm doing this right and carrying you over the threshold."

She giggled. "I think you're supposed to do that after we get married."

"That's next month. Right now, I just want to do this thing right." He pushed open the door and carried her inside as she gasped and everyone waiting for them shouted, "Welcome home!"

Melody stared at their entire family seated around the huge, long table by the windows across the room. Enough seating for everyone they loved. Her whole immediate family, including Jax's wife, Layla, and Lyric's husband,

Mason. Dean and Max were there, representing Fox's family, with enough empty space that they could add a few more to the crowd.

Down the center of the table were three flower arrangements filled with colorful blooms in dark pinks, reds, and white. And all over the apartment were dozens of plants. Exactly what Melody had described when he showed her the apartment the first time they came there together.

"Fox. I can't believe you did this. How? Why? What?" She hugged him close, tears in her eyes, because she'd thought she'd said goodbye to everyone yesterday, but he'd flown them all here last night to surprise her.

He walked toward the table and their family and set her on her feet as everyone watched them.

And then he took her hand and went down on one knee.

"How?" he repeated what she'd asked. "I just asked them to be with us on this special day and they all said yes. Why? Because I wanted you to see from day one that this is our home, that there's a place here for everyone we love. As for what? The proposal I promised."

She gasped when he pulled out the ring and touched her fingers to his lips. A tear slipped down her cheek, but she was smiling.

"You've been my best friend since we were kids. You looked out for me. You protected me. You loved me even then. And I needed you. Your light. Your love. Your compassion. Your understanding. You made me laugh and smile and see the good in a world that seemed so brutal and dark. You gave me hope." He kissed her knuckles, then looked up at her. "You saved my life. And now you are my life. I love you. More than words can say. I am so lucky to have a friend and lover, a partner I trust and want to do everything with, by my side. There is nothing in this world that I want more than for you to be my wife. Will you marry me?"

She was already nodding about halfway through his speech. "Yes."

He slid the ring on her finger, kissed her knuckle below the stunning rock, then scooped her into his arms, lifted her off her feet, and kissed her with all the love and passion he felt for her.

The cheers were loud and filled with joy, punctuated by a champagne cork popping.

And a month later when they were all together again on a rooftop garden decked out in twinkling lights and more flowers than he'd ever seen in one place thanks to their amazing florist, it seemed like yesterday they'd celebrated the proposal with their loved ones when his bride walked down the aisle, took his hand, and they promised to love each other forever.

He gave her the stars. She gave him everything he'd ever wished for and thought was beyond the moon.

Acknowledgements

I hope you enjoyed Melody and Fox's story. For more information about upcoming releases and sales, please sign up for my newsletter.

I never thought I'd have to publish this book myself. But after my publisher dropped the series, I didn't want to disappoint readers, who wanted Melody and Aria's stories. It was a huge learning curve to do this *not* so on my own. Because there were a lot of people who helped me self publish this book.

Thank you to Sophie Jordan for answsering so many of my basic questions and encouraging me to do this.

Thank you to my amazing editor Susan Barnes (www.susanbarnesediting.com) for your amazing insights, comments, and suggestions. Your reaction comments were the best! And, yes, I will add more to the beginning of the story. It always makes it better.

Melissa Frain (www.melissafrain.com), thank you for doing the copyedit during an exceptionally difficult time. I appreciate your hard work and dedication to getting it done when your family needed you most. Your reaction comments were much appreciated. I was happy to surprise you in the book.

Angela Haddon (www.angelahaddon.com), you are an amazing cover artist. You took the picture I sent you and turned it into a beautiful cover that seemlessly complements the other two books in the series. I appreciate how easy you made the process and how you saw what the pictures I sent could be with your magic.

To my amazing agent, Suzie Townsend, thank you for always having my back, guiding me through this crazy business, sharing your insights and expertise, and always cheering me on. I couldn't, and wouldn't, want to do this without you.

Steve, I love you. What else is there to say after 33 years of support and encouragement, kids, laughter, fun, and everything else that goes into a life together. I can't imagine doing any of this without you by my side.

About the Author

New York Times and *USA Today* bestselling author Jennifer Ryan writes suspenseful contemporary romances about everyday people who do extraordinary things. Her deeply emotional love stories are filled with high stakes and higher drama, family, friendship, and the happy-ever-after we all hope to find.

Jennifer lives in the San Francisco Bay Area with her husband and three children. When she isn't writing a book, she's reading one. Her obsession with both is often revealed in the state of her home and how late dinner is to the table. When she finally leaves those fictional worlds, you'll find her in the garden, playing in the dirt and daydreaming about people who live only in her head – until she puts them on paper.

Please visit her website at www.jennifer-ryan.com for information about upcoming releases.

Printed in Great Britain
by Amazon

47757282R00165